Yard Sale

Everything Must Go

By

Marlene Mitchell

BEARHEAD PUBLISHING LLC

- BhP -

Louisville, Kentucky
www.bearheadpublishing.com/marlene.html

Yard Sale

By Marlene Mitchell

Copyright (c) 2007 Bearhead Publishing LLC
ALL RIGHTS RESERVED

Cover Concept by: Marlene Mitchell
Cover Design: Bearhead Publishing LLC
Cover Photography by: William Strode
Pulitzer Prize Winning Photographer

First Printing - June 2007
ISBN: 0-9776260-9-1

Previously Published by:
Harmony House Publishers

NO PART OF THIS BOOK MAY BE REPRODUCED IN ANY FORM, BY PHOTOCOPYING OR BY ANY ELECTRONIC OR MECHANICAL MEANS, INCLUDING INFORMATION STORAGE OR RETRIEVAL SYSTEMS, WITHOUT PERMISSION IN WRITING FROM THE COPYRIGHT OWNER

Disclaimer

This book is a work of fiction. The characters, names, places, and incidents are used fictitiously and are a product of the author's imagination. Any resemblance of actual persons, living or dead is entirely coincidental.

Proudly printed in the United States of America

Yard Sale

Other Novels by Marlene Mitchell:

Return to Ternberry
The Chester County Boys

To order: www.bearheadpublishing.com/marlene.html

Dedication

To my family - Gene, Terry, Sandy, Scott, Sarah and Sydney.
Without their support and confidence in me,
this book would never have become a reality.

To Norma
Celebrate Life
One day at a time
Marlene Mitchell

Chapter One

Henry Franklin raced his car through the gate of the estate. He could see the gardener busily pruning the bushes. Turning off the motor, Henry coasted within inches of the old man's legs. Laying on the horn, he watched as the gardener jumped head first into the privet hedge. Standing up, his face scratched, the gardener angrily shook his fist and cursed in Spanish. Henry roared with laughter as he guided the car to a stop in a newly planted bed of geraniums.

Once inside the house, Henry's mood became somber. He wasn't in any hurry to see his parents. Shoving his hands into his pockets, he made his way across the foyer and through the open French doors.

"We are on the terrace, dear." Henry knew where his parents were, but it seemed his mother always needed to make that same announcement. His father was reading the paper, as he did every Sunday morning after breakfast. Henry ambled across the white marble terrace and flopped down on the settee. His father peered over the top of his glasses with the same condescending look Henry had come to recognize as reserved especially for him. The look that meant, where have you been? Stand up straight. Don't put your feet on the settee.

"What was all that honking about?" his father asked. "Have you been harassing the gardener again?"

Henry did not answer. He watched as his mother poured a cup of coffee, her hand shaking from the weight of the silver pot. The hot liquid spilled into the saucer as she pushed the cup toward Henry. He waved it away as if he were dismissing her along with the half-cup of coffee.

"Your father has decided to let you catch the train here in Newbury rather than driving you to Camberton. He has an appointment later this morning that he cannot miss. Is that all right with you, dear?" she asked.

Henry grunted and closed his eyes. It really didn't matter to him if he left from Newbury or Camberton. The destination would still be the same. He didn't care if he ever got to the Chicago School of Medicine.

Joseph Franklin rose from his chair and tossed the newspaper on the glass-top table in disgust. "I can't believe it took until nineteen-twenty-eight to get a direct telephone line to London." He muttered something else to himself as he left the terrace. He turned back to Henry, pointing his finger. "You be ready on time. Do not make us wait for you." Henry rolled off the settee and sauntered over to the railing. Drumming his fingers on the stone ledge, he turned his back on his mother. Conversations with his parents were always so boring. He watched as his mother's prized pair of black swans, a gift from his father, glided silently across the lake.

"Henry dear, I hope you are listening to me," his mother said as she rambled on. "Martin has packed all of your things. I took the liberty of buying you a set of luggage and also a new grooming kit. I know how you hate your clothes to be messy. Please remember to say goodbye to Martin and the rest of the staff before you leave. I know Martin is going to miss you. My goodness, he has been with you for almost seventeen years." Agnes continued to sip her coffee.

"You tell them goodbye. I'm going to take a nap. Don't wake me until it's almost time to leave," Henry responded sullenly.

Henry lay across his bed and stared at the ceiling. He wasn't really tired. He just needed time to think and time to devise a plan to get him through this mess his father had created for him. He turned his face into the soft down pillow. The first thing he needed to do was talk to his mother alone before he left for the station. He had to make it perfectly clear to her that there would be expenses at school that his father did not intend to pay. Henry had already decided that he was not going to live in abject poverty like his father had when he attended medical school. Poverty, Joseph said, had made him study harder and keep a clear mind on what he wanted to accomplish. Henry would make a secret pact with his mother. That shouldn't be too hard. After all, just a simple tear or sniffle could convince Agnes that her only son was suffering. The second plan would not be as easy. He had to contrive a way to make his stay at the university as short as possible. This would take more effort to accomplish.

The afternoon light began to filter through Henry's window, casting diagonal shapes on his wall. When he was a child, he would pretend that these shapes were a maze from which he had to escape before the shadows grew long and disappeared behind the green velvet curtains. Those were the days that he loved his room the most. On those long cool afternoons when he was sent upstairs to nap, he would line his metal cars and trucks in perfect order across the floor, winding them around the highboy and under his bed. He would build pyramids from his blocks and arrange his entire army of toy soldiers on the window seat, each one facing the lake as if it were poised for battle against the black swans. Other times he would pretend to be sick and stay in bed all day. His mother would read to him and put her cool hand on his forehead to check for a fever. Martin would bring him warm soup and crackers on a tray. Sometimes his father would look in on him, bringing him chocolate ice cream. Yes, he was going to miss this room.

As he grew older, he had considered this part of the house to be his private domain. Henry insisted that all that entered must knock first. The rest of the house belonged to his parents, but this room was his alone. With the door closed, he could pick at his nose or even burp without the stilted looks from his father. He did not have to listen to the persistent rambling of his mother as she tugged at his clothes or ran her fingers through his hair. There were days when the house was quiet, his mother off to one of her many charity events and his father away at his office or the hospital doing some bit of miracle work for which he was so famous. Henry would sneak down the winding staircase, past the prying eyes of Martin, slide past the kitchen door and into his father's library. Dragging the desk chair to the tall shelves, he would retrieve one of the large anatomy books from the top shelf, the books his father had told him never to touch without permission. Shoving it under his robe he would return to his private domain. Henry would pull the covers up over his head and while looking at the pictures of naked bodies he would groan in delight. Learning to pleasure himself became one of his favorite pastimes.

Now once again he was being dislodged from this room. He felt the same anxious foreboding feelings as when he was sent away to the Lincoln Preparatory School for young men and later to Manard College. Both times, his father had insisted it would be for his own good. He looked around the room at all of his possessions and a vague feeling of sadness came over him. Perhaps this would be the last time he would ever see them again.

Each time he returned home in the past, his mother would have a surprise waiting for him. She would buy him a complete new wardrobe or more toys and games, sometimes even books, which she knew he would just toss aside. What would he get for going to medical school? Maybe he would get a new car or another trip to Europe if he finished out the year.

Henry rose from the bed and stretched. He needed to have a talk with his mother about money matters before he left for school. Henry needed her full attention. He wanted to make sure she understood that he would need more money than the paltry sum his father had proposed as an allowance. Joseph gave Agnes a generous allowance to take care of the household affairs and all social events. Joseph liked to surround himself with people of notoriety and influence so Agnes often hosted parties. Henry felt like he was just an extension of his father's inflated ego; a mass of human clay that his father had created and molded into a likeness of himself. As time passed, the sculptured clay was beginning to harden into a much different form.

Henry could hear his mother's voice coming from outside. As he glanced out the window, he could see her standing in the driveway. Her arms flailing about, using her grating, high-pitched voice, like the sound of fingernails dragging across a chalkboard, she directed Martin as he placed the new luggage into the trunk of the car. Henry lounged against the wall and smiled to himself as his mother had Martin remove the luggage from the trunk and start over.

He remembered a similar scene on his thirteenth birthday. On that day, his mother had been running around the car, pulling out presents she had bought for him and calling out orders to Martin to be careful with the boxes. She had decided it was time to give her son a "grown-up" birthday party before he went away to Switzerland for the summer. After all, she had said, grownups would bring nice presents to Henry and fill her summer social obligation at the same time. She had arranged for a large white tent to be erected on the lawn next to the lake. There were blue balloons and yellow streamers lining the driveway as hired valets stood waiting to park the limousines and luxury cars that pulled into the gate. A three-tiered yellow birthday cake decorated with thirteen candles took its place of honor on the center table under the tent. Servers in black dresses and white aprons circulated among the guests with trays of wine and cheese. Henry had stood between his parents at the entrance to the tent. He was dressed in new white knickers and a blue blazer. As each new arrival placed a brightly wrapped present on the long table, he had been anxious to open it, but his father had told him that all of the guests must be greeted first. Most of them looked unfamiliar to Henry; they were friends from the country club and his father's business associates. Some had come to the party merely to be seen at the Franklin house as the reporter from the newspaper flashed pictures for the Sunday Society page.

Henry had been tired of standing. His feet had hurt from his new patent shoes. He'd danced from one foot to the other, as the line seemed to go on forever. Men in linen jackets and white shoes grabbed his hand and tousled his hair. Women in their finest day dresses and summer hats pinched his cheeks and kissed his forehead with their painted mouths. Their pearls smacked against his face. He had wanted to grab the beads and pull them from their necks. He hated every moment of being on display. He just wanted to escape to the table filled with presents. As the crowd finally began to thin, an elderly gentleman carrying a small present came toward him. Henry could tell it was just another silly book. His father had placed his hand on his shoulder, pressing down like a brass weight, as if to let him know that this man was important. He whispered to Henry, "Be polite and don't fidget." As he extended his hand to the older man, he said, "Dr. Francis, how nice to see you. This is the birthday boy, my son, Henry."

"Hello young man. I'm finally glad to have the opportunity to meet you. Your father and I have been friends for years and I want to wish you a special happy birthday."

Henry forced a limp smile as Dr. Francis knelt down on one knee, his face just inches away from his. Henry could smell the tobacco on his breath.

"Your father talks about you quite often. Have you decided yet what you want to be when you grow up?"

Suddenly as if he had become a ventriloquist's wooden puppet manipulated by strings attached to his mouth, the words just tumbled out. "I want to be a doctor, like my father."

Joseph grinned and patted his shoulder. Henry had said it, those terrible words. It was as if his father had just been handed the tablets on Mount Sinai. Henry regretted even mentioning the word "doctor." It was that one short sentence he had said to a total stranger that continued to haunt him all of his young life. Martin, summoning him to the dining room, interrupted Henry's thoughts. "I see you had a fun time packing the car," Henry said laughing.

"Very funny Master Henry. I hope you don't choke on your last meal at home."

After lunch, Joseph became impatient to leave for the railroad station. "You know how I hate being late. I suggest we get going," he said looking at his pocket watch. Henry sighed and took his mother's arm and escorted her to the car.

The depot at Newbury was small and dingy. It smelled of stale cigarette smoke and day old milk. The trains were always late and today was no exception. His mother had insisted they come early and now they sat shoulder to shoulder in the cramped, hot room, surrounded by the new luggage. There were crying babies and small children tugging at their mothers' dress hems. Weeping wives stood holding hands with their young husbands in military uniforms and old men carrying bundles tied with twine sat on the floor against the wall. Henry's mother looked peculiarly out of place in her sable coat.

Joseph pulled his gold watch from his pocket and checked the time. He walked briskly to the door of the depot and stared down the track. Henry smiled to himself. He wondered if his father really thought that by his sheer presence at the doorway, the train would magically appear. Joseph looked at his watch again. Shaking it, he placed it to his ear to make sure it was keeping time.

Agnes could tell that his patience was growing thin. She wished she had just asked Martin to bring Henry to the station. "Why don't you sit down, dear? I'm sure the train will be coming soon."

"Is it ever possible for a train to be on time?" he growled. "Why have a schedule if you're not going to keep it?" Henry wanted to tell his father to leave, to go home and tend to his business, but he was enjoying watching him become more and more irritated by the minute.

The train pulled into the station minutes later and the room began to clear. Everyone gathered up their belongings and trudged toward the open door. As Henry moved toward the train steps, Agnes threw her arms around her son. "I am going to miss you so much."

Pressing her hand in his, he could feel a round cylinder of money slip from beneath her glove. Henry smiled and simply said, "Goodbye, Mother."

Joseph was already pacing the wooden planks of the depot. He shook Henry's hand. "I am counting on you to make your mother and me

YARD SALE

proud. Don't disappoint us." His arms reached out to Henry, but it was too late. Henry had turned away and was boarding the train for Chicago.

Finding a window seat, Henry tossed his bags beside him. There was no way he was going to share his meager space with a stranger for the duration of the trip. He lowered his head and pretended to be asleep. As the train pulled away from the station, he reached into his pocket and retrieved the roll of bills his mother had given him. He rolled it between his fingers like a fine Cuban cigar. He wanted to savor the feel of crisp new bills. She had come through for him, just like she always did. Agnes loved him unconditionally, and over the years he had learned to use that love to his advantage. Henry knew exactly when to thrust out his lip or squeeze a tear from his eye. There were times when he was in prep school that he needed money to hire bullies to keep the other bullies away from him. In college, she sent money for a fictional car that helped to buy term papers and test results. She was his only ally and now he needed her more than ever.

Chapter Two

  The Student Registry Hall was filled to capacity by the time Henry arrived. Students were sitting in the hallway, leaning against the walls and standing in an unending line. There were canvas bags and suitcases covering the floor, waiting to be claimed by their owners. Henry sat his luggage in the first empty space he could find and made his way through the door. Two hours later it was his turn.

  The registrar sat behind the counter in front of large stacks of papers, flipping through them as he spoke. With his red pen in hand, he asked, "Name?"

  Henry replied, "Franklin."

  The clerk sighed, "Franklin what?"

  "It's Henry Franklin."

  Running his finger down several sheets of paper, the clerk began barking orders at Henry. "Okay, Mr. Franklin, you are in building C, room three-twenty-eight. That's around the corner, second building on your right. Take your bags with you. There are no bellhops here. You will be expected to be in the student-meeting hall at seven a.m. sharp." Handing Henry a blue folder, he continued, "Here are the maps of the campus and your class assignments. Read them carefully. All changes must be made by the end of the week." With that, he dismissed Henry with a nod of his head and said "Next."

  Henry took the map and stuffed it into his pocket. He didn't need it. He had been to this campus many times before with his parents. Each year the medical school would host an alumni dinner. Henry's father made sure that he took the time off to attend. Their family would stay at the dean's house and the dean would take them on the same boring tour of the campus. As they passed each moldering building, he would assure them that the school was still producing the most competent doctors in the country. At times he seemed embarrassed by the austere conditions of the school, but always assured them that changes would be made soon to improve the buildings.

That evening, dressed in their finest clothes, Henry and his parents would attend the alumni dinner and awards ceremony. Long boring speeches were a test of endurance for Henry. His mother would try to make sure he did not become restless; she would hold his hand and give him butterscotch candies and whisper in his ear that if he were patient, she would buy him a present when they returned home. After the dean's droning speech, extolling the school's accomplishments for the year, he would introduce Dr. Joseph Franklin. Joseph would stand, beaming as his fellow alumni gave him a round of applause. He would walk to the podium and make his speech. It was almost always a carbon copy of the previous year. The evening would end with his father presenting an endowment check to the school. The audience would murmur as the dean read the amount and once again there would be a standing ovation for his father. It was Joseph's finest hour and each year he made the check larger than the one given the year before.

The dormitories on the campus looked all the same to Henry. Rectangular buildings, three stories high, made of chipped and decaying brown bricks. The windows were covered with faded yellow shades and torn screens. Two students shared each tiny room, much to Henry's dismay. He had planned on a private room and the idea of a community shower room repulsed him.

Someone had already put his coat on one of the beds by the time Henry arrived and luggage very similar to his sat next to the closet. Henry's arms were tired from the long walk across campus carrying his heavy bags. He tossed them into the corner and looked around at the meager surroundings. There were two small beds and two desks, but only one chair. Opening the closet, he pushed the clothes already hanging there to the side. If he were in prison, he imagined that it would be quite similar, except there were no bars on these dirty windows.

Henry's roommate was John Keel, a Harvard graduate from New York. Although he seemed nice enough, Henry found him to be too nosy. He immediately began asking Henry questions about his family and schooling. Henry had other things on his mind. He didn't need to make friends with someone who could be of no value to him. John rattled on about how excited he was to be at the Chicago Medical School. Like Henry, his family had enough money to send him elsewhere, but this was his choice. He could not believe his luck to have Dr. Joseph Franklin's son for a roommate. He rambled on and on until Henry lay down on the bed and pretended to be asleep. By the end of the first week Henry's lack of interest in making conversation with John was quite apparent. He usually answered John's questions with grunts or nods. John finally gave up and stopped talking to Henry altogether.

Packages arrived daily for the students, but none to rival those delivered to Henry's room. Left in front of his door were wooden crates and boxes filled with presents from his mother. There were new linens and tins of chocolates and teacakes. She sent a brass desk lamp and the latest model radio, which he played constantly to the dismay of John Keel. His mother arranged for a local woman to pick up Henry's laundry each week. His clothes were returned pressed and lint free as he requested.

John complained bitterly as Henry's swelling possessions began to filter their way to his side of the room. They argued each day and Henry decided he wanted this ridiculous twit out of his life. A few days after one of their disputes, John developed a rash, which engulfed his entire body. It threw him into fits of itching until his skin turned bright red and bled from his constant scratching. The infirmary doctors could not seem to determine what was causing the rash, but prescribed ointments and pills for him to take. The rash persisted until John would rise from his bed in the middle of the night sobbing and scratching he would run to the shower room. Most days he could not eat, and with the constant lack of sleep his parents decided he should leave school until he was well.

After John left the dorm and all of his possessions had finally been removed from the room, Henry stuffed John's sheets and pillow into a laundry bag. Waiting until the hallway was quiet and dark, he placed the half-empty can of itching powder between the folds of the linens and carried them to the incinerator in the basement to be burned.

Henry began his study of the other new students from the day he arrived on campus. He watched how they dressed, checking their shoes to see if they were worn or unpolished. He observed them in the cafeteria and in class. Henry wanted to see which students were paying attention and taking notes. He had been through this same routine many times. He was proficient in spotting those he thought might be able to help him. At prep school and again at college he found that there were always students who would be willing to help him with his studies if he paid them enough money. It had made his life simple until now. This may be his biggest challenge ever. Slowly he began to narrow his list of candidates. One in particular held his interest. He was small in stature, with a swarthy complexion and spoke with a thick accent. Henry had seen him in the library several times and also around his dormitory. He needed more information before he could make his move. The student's name was Alejandro Barrios. Henry checked the register on the first floor lobby to see who shared a room with Alejandro. It was a student named Robert Cumming. Henry wandered the second floor hallway until he found their room. The door was open and Robert was sitting at his desk. Henry knocked lightly. "Hello, I'm looking for Robert Cumming."

"You're looking at him. What can I do for you?" Robert said as he looked up from his book.

Henry moved inside the door. "Well, someone told me you were from Bangor, Maine. I have some close relatives there and I just wanted to know if you would like to share a ride sometime? That is, if we ever get a break from this place."

Robert laughed. "Thanks, I'll think about it. I wouldn't mind getting out of here for a while myself. Better still maybe I could just get my roommate to leave. Come on in and have a seat."

Henry knew he had an opening. "Well I'm lucky, I don't have a roommate anymore. What's going on with yours?"

Robert leaned back in the chair. "Man, where do you want me to start? He stinks for one thing. He eats sardines and hot peppers in his bed. He reads his text aloud in Spanish and he washes his same clothes every night and hangs them over a chair. Every time I get up, I step in a damn puddle of water. I've complained about him, but it hasn't done any good."

Henry began to think that he had made a mistake. Surely someone like Robert just described couldn't be of any use to him. "Sorry about your luck, Robert. Maybe he won't stay long," Henry said.

"You know what?" Robert continued, "That guy is real smart. He is here on some kind of grant from his government. You better believe he'll stay." They talked for a while longer before Henry went back to his room to start working on his plan.

There were only two telephones in the dormitory hallway and it was almost impossible to find them free. Most of the time there was a line of students waiting to make calls. The operators were slow to connect your party and many times the lines would go dead in mid-sentence. Henry waited till after curfew. Checking the dark hallway, he dialed his home number. "Martin, it's Henry. Can you hear me?" Henry cupped his hand around the phone to muffle the sound.

"Yes, Henry, I can hear you, but why are you whispering? Do you have any idea what time it is?" Martin replied in a languid voice.

Henry looked up and down the hallway. "Listen, Martin I don't have much time. I want you to do me a favor. Call the school registry office tomorrow and see what you can find out about a student named Alejandro Barrios. I'll spell it for you."

"And why do you need this information, Henry?" Martin asked.

"It's really none of your business, but if you must know I think he needs some help and I want to see what I can do for him."

Martin began to laugh. "Oh, come now, Master Henry, I know you better than that. You're trying to tell me you are actually concerned about someone else when you have so many problems of your own?"

Henry knew the conversation was going nowhere. He was irritated with Martin. "I promise to tell you all about it later. I just thought maybe I could count on you just this one time."

Martin softened. "I still think you're up to something, but I'll see what I can find out for you."

Chapter Three

A summons from the dean surely alarmed most first year students. It usually meant they should start packing as their days were numbered. When Henry received the call to come to the dean's house he wondered what had taken him so long. Certainly by now his father must have talked to the dean several times about Henry's progress at the school.

The dean's house was situated at the very end of the campus. It was large and old, but unlike the rest of the buildings, its shutters and porches had been recently painted. There were neatly trimmed hedges and the front porch held an array of pots filled with fall flowers. Henry had overheard some of the students talking about the volunteer work they did for Dean Parson. They would trade book fees and lodging for a day of painting and cleaning at the dean's house. Although it was never talked about in front of the faculty, it was certainly frowned upon by the College Board. Yet there was still a long list of students willing to give up their Saturdays to ease their school financial burden.

Henry decided to take Mrs. Parson one of the many boxes of sweets his mother had sent to him. He made a special effort to arrive on time. A young woman opened the door. She smiled pleasantly at him and escorted him into the parlor. She was slender and small with auburn hair pulled away from her face into a starched bun. Henry knew that the dean had no children of his own and assumed she must be just a domestic.

"Henry, it's good to see you again. My, you have grown taller," Mrs. Parson said as he handed her the box of chocolates. "Thank you, dear, this is very sweet of you."

Dean Parson stood behind her, looking even heavier than the last time Henry was at the house. He was a copious little man with thin strands of hair combed over the top of his balding head.

The same young woman who had answered the door served dinner. She moved quietly around the table, putting bowls and compote dishes in place. Backing away from the table, she waited for Mrs. Parson to dismiss her. Dean Parson made small talk over roasted lamb and browned potatoes. He talked about the weather and how much he respected Henry's parents and also mentioned the fate of poor John Keel. After recovering from his rash, John developed a case of shigellosis due to the stress of leaving school. Henry remarked that it was such a shame and he really missed having John as a roommate. He pushed his plate aside, tired of the conversation and wondering what was the real purpose of his visit. He would find out soon enough, but not in the presence of the dean's wife. She excused herself from the table and thanked Henry for coming. Taking her box of chocolates, she left the room. Dean Parson ushered Henry into his library. Opening a carved wooden box, the dean offered Henry a cigar, which he refused. The dean handed him a glass of brandy. Henry wanted this evening to be over as soon as possible; maybe the brandy would help.

As they stood by the fireplace, Dean Parson began to speak in his usual repetitious voice. It sounded to Henry as if he had prepared the speech and rehearsed it to make sure he had left nothing out.

"You know, Henry, in less than two years I am due to retire from this institution. I have had a fine and satisfying career here, but now I am ready to take my leave. My wife and I would like to travel abroad." Dean Parson began to pace around the room, puffing on his cigar, as if he were an expectant father. "I think you are a fine young man, but I'm sure you know that this school usually does not accept students who have not achieved the highest marks in college. It was only due to the urgent request of your father that you were even considered. He assured me that this was your life long dream and that you would do everything in your power to produce good grades. Of course, now that you are here, you are on your own merit and no special dispensations will be made for you." He cleared his throat and sat down. He seemed unable to make eye contact with Henry. "I do believe it would be better for both of us if we kept our visits to a minimum as a courtesy to the other students. We will not talk of this matter further unless of course you have questions." He sighed as he finished his oration.

Henry rose from his chair. "No sir, I think you covered everything and I agree with you wholeheartedly. I promise I will not embarrass you or my family. Please thank your wife for the lovely dinner." He could see the look of relief on the dean's face. The evening was more benign than Henry had thought it would be.

YARD SALE

As Henry walked across the porch, he pulled a large clump of flowers out of one of the pots and threw them into the bushes. Henry smiled to himself. The poor, little, fat bastard must have his back against the wall since Henry was the son of one of his largest benefactors. He wondered how much money his father had paid the dean to let him stay in school. It should be interesting for all of them. He needed to get started on a plan right away.

The letter from Martin came just in time. The first grade posting was already on the bulletin board in the student organizational hall. Henry scanned the board, looking further and further down the list until he found his name with a two-point grade average next to it. It was a low enough mark to be forced to leave the school at the end of the next grading period if he did not improve. He took Martin's letter from his mail slot and headed to his room.

Dear Master Henry,
It took me quite a while to get this information for you. I met with many obstacles and some very uncooperative gentlemen at your school.
The student you inquired about, Alejandro Barrios, is from a small village near Santiago, Chile. He was admitted to the medical school due to his outstanding performance at the university in Chile. He participated in several scholastic competitions and always emerged the winner. Although he was given one year of free tuition and living expenses, his financial outlook is bleak. After this year he will have to look elsewhere for financial aid. I hope this information will be of benefit in whatever devious scheme you are plotting. Perhaps this once you could help someone other than yourself.
Sincerely, Martin

Henry hated the cafeteria. The chipped black and white tile floor and the blended smell of food coming from the kitchen annoyed him. It was always noisy with the constant clanking of trays and utensils. Most of all, he hated waiting in line to be served food that he considered barely edible. First year students were not allowed to leave the campus, which left him little choice but to suffer through lunch everyday.

Henry glanced around the crowded room. With his tray in hand, he almost passed by the table occupied by Barrios. Barrios sat with his head bent and his right arm surrounding the bowl in front of him. He spooned the soup into his mouth as if at any moment someone was going to snatch it away. Henry backed up and stood in front of the table. "Is it all right if I sit here?" he asked. Barrios barely looked up. He nodded and Henry sat down across from him. Henry had bought a cup of coffee and a roll. Barrios continued to eat and Henry heard the clink of the spoon against the bottom of the bowl. As he pushed his roll across the table, Henry asked, "Do you want this? I'm not very hungry." Barrios eyed the roll for only a moment before he plucked it from the table. Breaking it into small chunks, he began to sop up the last few drops of watery soup, wiping the sides and the bottom of the bowl until it was almost clean enough to put back into the cupboard.

Henry watched in disgust. Without saying a word, Barrios rose from the table and left the cafeteria. As he walked past a stack of trays waiting to be retrieved by the kitchen workers, he picked up a half-eaten sandwich and stuffed it into his pocket.

On Tuesday, Henry bought an extra sandwich and once again joined Barrios at the same table. Barrios was reading a textbook and drinking a cup of coffee. Henry sat down and placed the sandwich in front of him.

"Why do you buy food if you are not going to eat it? It is very wasteful," Barrios grunted.

Henry shrugged. "I bought this for you. I noticed that you were not eating, so I thought that maybe you might like a sandwich."

Barrios' eyes narrowed. "How do you know I have not already eaten my lunch?"

"Never mind then, I'll just throw it away," Henry said as he reached for the sandwich.

Before he could touch it, Barrios opened the wax paper and began to eat. With his mouth full of food, he asked, "What is your name?"

"It's Henry Franklin. I'm a first year student."

Barrios suddenly seemed anxious to talk to someone and before the lunch hour was over, he had told Henry more than he actually cared to know.

Barrios was one of eleven children born to indigent parents in a small village in Chile. The death rate was very high and only five of his siblings lived past the age of twelve. There was much disease and little food in his village. His parents loaded their few possessions into their truck and became migrant workers. Along with his siblings, Barrios worked in the sugar beet fields, traveling from one plantation to the next during the growing season. The plantation owners provided the migrants with small huts or windowless tents to live in while they worked. They were charged high prices for their lodgings and food, leaving them very little to live on. At times when the work became scarce, due to the droughts or flooding, his family had been forced to live in the back of their rusted pickup truck.

One of the plantation owners had a compassionate wife who insisted that her husband build a one-room schoolhouse on the property for the children. After finishing his work, Barrios would go to the school. The teacher came to his father after a few weeks and told him that Barrios was very bright. She wanted him to continue going to school. His parents decided they would sacrifice this one child and let him stay on the plantation. He worked weekends and nights to help his family, sending them the few dollars he made. At night he would study by the small lantern in his tent. When the growing season was over he worked as a handy man in the manor house. He did well and was given grants and scholarships from the government. Once he finished college, he was finally allowed to leave Chile and come to the United States.

His goal was to become a doctor and go back to his home to help the poverty stricken people of his village. He finished the story by telling Henry that this was truly his life's dream.

Henry listened intently, trying to find out exactly how much money Barrios had, but he said nothing about his finances until he rose to leave.

"I must get to class now, Henry. Maybe I will see you tomorrow. You do not have to buy me food, but I greatly appreciate it, since I have only enough money to eat one meal a day." Henry had found his mark. Every day they would sit together and Henry would pay for Barrios' lunch. He began to thank Henry and told him the extra food helped him keep up his strength for his studies.

On Friday, Barrios was not in the cafeteria. Henry bought a couple of sandwiches and an apple and headed back to the dormitory. He found Barrios sitting in his room. "I missed you at lunch today, are you sick?" he asked.

Barrios sat at his desk holding a letter in his hand. His eyes were red and swollen.

"I am sorry Henry, but I am going to have to leave and return home. My brother has died and my parents need me."

"Need you for what?" Henry questioned.

"To work. I have to take my brother's place in the fields. My family has no money for the winter."

The time had come for Henry to make his move. He wasn't really sure Barrios could be trusted, but he had no choice. He could not let this opportunity get away from him. Henry reached into his pocket and unrolled one of his few remaining bills. "Here, I want you to take this. You can send it to your parents and maybe they will allow you to stay in school a while longer."

Barrios eyes widened. He touched the corner of the twenty-dollar bill, pulling his fingers back, as if he had just touched hot coals. "I have never touched a bill that large in my life. Are you very rich, Henry?" he asked.

Henry smiled. "Well, I will be very soon. That is, if I can make it through this year. I want you to take this." He held out the bill, half expecting Barrios to refuse. Barrios took the bill and folded it gently in half and placed it in his shirt pocket.

"I will go to the bank exchange first thing in the morning and send the money to my family. I will pay you back, Henry; I will pay you back every cent. Thank you," Barrios said in a humble voice.

Henry was nervous. He began to pace around the small room. It was time to divulge his plan to Barrios. "My father is a doctor. He has a large practice in Massachusetts and travels around the world teaching and lecturing. Unfortunately I am an only child and it is my father's wish that I become a doctor also." Henry watched Barrios out of the corner of his eye. "I have no desire to pursue the medical profession or any other profession as a matter of fact. I never did well in school. Fortunately I was always able to get enough help to muddle through it, but now my father had made me accept an impossible agreement. I have to finish one year of medical school. I cannot flunk out or quit. Once I complete this one year, I can leave this miserable place and take my inheritance and go on with my life. It's a shitty deal but I have no choice. I am willing to do whatever it takes to get through this year, even if it means paying someone to help me." He stopped, looking to see if there was any reaction from Barrios.

"So you want me to help you. Is that it Henry, you will pay me to tutor you?"

"No, Barrios, I don't want you to tutor me. I want you to do the work for me. Don't you see we can both win? I'll get my money and you will have enough finances to stay in school and become a great doctor. All I need is a lousy passing grade."

Barrios looked shocked. "I cannot believe what I am hearing. You want me to cheat for you? I am an honest man, Henry. I do not cheat."

"Okay, if that's your decision. You can think about it when you're at home in the beet fields working your ass off for pennies," Henry snapped as he turned to leave, "You can keep the twenty."

Before he had taken just a few steps, he heard Barrios barely whisper. "I will do it, Henry, I will do your work for you."

Henry smiled to himself. It had all been too easy.

They agreed on a place to meet each day so that Henry could give Barrios his assignments. The location was changed often to keep anyone from getting suspicious. No mention had been made of the amount of money he would give Barrios, but after checking his finances, Henry decided to call his mother and have her send him more money. It was a simple request. He needed some additional books and he had inadvertently left his wallet somewhere. She of course agreed to wire him the money.

Henry was never sure where his mother got the money she gave him. He knew she had a household account and a generous allowance, which she spent freely. Surely she didn't ask Joseph for money; there would be far too many questions. Henry's father was a generous man. He gave to many charities and was not shy when it came to his personal comforts. Although he had made an ample amount of money in his practice, initially it was Henry's mother who had brought most of the wealth into the family when they married. It was his mother's dowry that had financed his father's schooling and helped to set him up in practice. Yet his father now controlled all the money, which he said was something a woman should not have to worry with. Henry liked that idea. He decided when he married that he too would be in control.

    Life at school began to form a rhythm. After the second grade postings, there was a procession of students leaving the dorm. "The lucky ones," Henry called them. They were the students that did not do well in their studies or were disillusioned with the school. The dormitory took on a more somber demeanor. There was much less laughter and rowdiness. The telephones in the corridors rang fewer times in the evenings and there were many empty rooms. Barrios transferred to the third floor, just two doors away from Henry. The exchange of assignments was much simpler. They were careful only to nod to each other in the halls at school and they no longer ate together in the cafeteria.
    Henry spent his evenings transcribing the notes Barrios had given him that day. He swore to himself as he tried to decipher the chicken scratch writing. His test notes were copied onto thin tissue paper, easily hidden in his pen lid or in the cuff of his shirt. Money began to change hands on a weekly basis. Henry hoped that Barrios would at least take part of the money and buy some new clothing, but he still wore the same tattered jacket and faded shirt every day.

Chapter Four

With the burden of studies lifted from him, Henry wandered around the campus or slept in the library after class. On Saturdays, he dressed meticulously, brushing all the lint from his clothing. Walking a few blocks away from school, he hailed a taxicab and went into downtown Chicago. The city was always bustling with activity on the weekends. As he walked along Lake Shore Drive, Henry scrutinized the tall hotels towering above the tree-lined streets. He longed to stay in one of these hotels, take a luxury bath and have his food brought to him by room service.

First-year students were on a ten o'clock curfew seven days a week and forbidden to leave the campus without permission. Henry didn't care. He needed the time away. He would eat lunch in one of the finer hotels, and for a few extra dollars have the waiter fill his silver flask with brandy. Then, making his way along the lake, he would sit on one of the wooden benches on the pier and sip his brandy. He watched the white sailing ships glide into port with men and women in white yachting clothes, laughing and talking on the upper deck. That is where he should be instead of this damnable quandary in which he was mired.

On occasional Saturdays, Henry would leave the main streets and follow the narrow, shadowed corridors to the flickering lights of the back alleys. There he could gain entrance to one of the clubs or speak-easys by slipping a dollar through the small window in the door. It was inside this smoke filled chamber, Henry would select one of the faceless females who would lead him up the sagging stairway and down the darkened hallway to her room. His father had called these prostitutes disease-ridden parasites. They were the same type of women his father had frequented years before. For five dollars and one hour Henry could forget everything except his own bodily pleasure.

The frozen Chicago sky released a coating of sleet onto the campus and the barren trees groaned under the weight of the crystal ice. Henry ran across the quadrangle toward the library. He cursed as he slipped on the icy steps. Barrios had urged him to start on his outline for his anatomy class, but Henry was tired. He had been to the city. His stomach ached from the raw whiskey he had consumed at one of the clubs, causing him to spend most of the night in the bathroom.

The dormitory overseer, a tall, portly woman, frowned on students sleeping past eight o'clock, even on the weekends. She rattled their door handles and banged on the metal rails with heavy pots to wake them up. Henry failed to see her purpose, except to add further aggravation to his life. Today she had been especially noisy. Perhaps she knew he had come in late.

The library was crowded as he maneuvered between the aisles. Three of the books he juggled landed on the floor with a thud. Eyes turned to see who was causing the disturbance.

"Here, let me get those for you." Henry heard a female voice, with a clear melodic accent, but he could not see her face as she knelt to the floor to retrieve his fallen books. When she arose Henry recognized her as the same young woman he had seen working at Dean Parson's house weeks before.

"You have quite a stack there. I'll help you to a table," she whispered as she placed his books on the corner of an already occupied table.

Henry mouthed the words "thank you," and she smiled. She wore the same gray dress and her hair was swept on top of her head in loose curls; held in place with tortoise shell combs. He watched her as she walked away. She stopped to place several books on a shelf and talk to a few students.

Henry had not been in the company of a proper woman in a long time. He fancied himself to be a solitary person and found most of the women he knew boring. His mother insisted that he escort some of the girls from the country clubs to social functions, but he found them to be twittering females who were too virginal for him. He was not content to sit in their parent's parlor for weeks holding hands and making idle conversation. He remembered the girls from Manard College who hung around the fringes of the campus and were willing to climb into the back seat of his Mercedes for a few dinner dates and a promise that he really cared about them. They were foolish. Yet he liked the way women smelled, their soft skin and the curvatures of their bodies, but to be in a relationship meant one more person to share with, one more person to question him about his whereabouts and pry into his personal business. Henry decided that when he was ready to choose a wife it would be on his own terms. He would select someone who could make a comfortable home for him. She would be a quiet woman of poise and good breeding. They would travel to Paris and London and he would drape her on his arm like a bejeweled walking stick. For now, he was content with the prostitutes in Chicago.

  The young woman walked by his table again. This time she laid a heavy medical volume next to him. "I thought you might want to look through this one. It is very good."

  Henry said "thank you" again and wondered why she had taken the time to bring him another book. Was that just part of her job? She returned to her desk and he to his studies. He was curious about her and occasionally looked up to observe her while she read. He wondered if she had a gentleman friend. He would come back to the library when he had more time.

  Barrios had begun to leave notes along with the papers that he delivered. In his scrawled handwriting, he began requesting a few extra dollars each week. He wrote that he was unable to take a job with the custodial service because of all the extra work he had to do. Henry would just have to pay him the salary he would have received: an additional four dollars a week. He no longer seemed embarrassed taking the money and at times his look of contempt for Henry was obvious. Henry decided to keep the notes.

  The third grading period moved Henry to a three-point grade average. He must talk to Barrios. He had told him all he needed was a passing grade, yet seeing his name on the honor roll and being congratulated by his fellow students gave Henry a lift he sorely needed. He decided to celebrate by going into the city for lunch and perhaps taking in a show. Having someone with him would be nice. He walked briskly to the library, pulling his collar up to shield the biting wind. Rubbing his hands together, he looked around the half empty room, but he did not see the girl. An older woman sat at the same desk she usually occupied. "Excuse me, could you tell me if the young lady with the accent is working today?"

The woman put on her glasses and looked up at Henry. "Are you a friend of hers?"

"Yes," he replied.

"Well then, you should know that she had a family emergency. Didn't she tell you? Her mother passed away. She has taken a leave of absence. You can leave a note for her, but I have no idea when she'll be back."

"No, that's not necessary," Henry said as he turned to leave. He went back to the dormitory and slept the rest of the day.

The end of the school year was just one week away. Students were gearing up for finals, and the mood of the dormitory was intense and somber, but not for Henry. He was joyous. One more week and he would be free of this place forever. He lay across his bed, humming to himself, pondering over what he would buy first when he got his money.

Finals were to be given in the lecture hall on three consecutive days. He made plans with Barrios to sit in the back row next to each other so that the answers could be passed to him. It was a simple plan and Henry was sure it would work. He knew that his professors trusted him. After all, the son of Dr. Joseph Franklin would never think of cheating.

The day before the first exam, Barrios wrote Henry a note requesting one hundred dollars to help him with the test. The slimy little bastard was bleeding him dry. Henry had only sixty dollars left to get him home. He promised to pay Barrios the other forty dollars by the end of the week. Barrios grudgingly agreed.

There was a party in almost every room in the dorm the night after the last exam. The bathtubs in the washrooms overflowed with beer and bootleg whiskey. Students in only their underwear ran through the halls smacking each other with bath towels. Loud ragtime music blared from phonographs and the smell of cigar smoke was thick. The house overseer had retired early. Having been through this many times before, her only warning was that anyone who vomited must clean it up, or all of the students would have to deal with her in the morning. It was a festive mood and for the first time Henry joined in. Some of the students wandered into his room, having heard stories about the fellow with the silk sheets on his bed and the latest model radio. Robert Cumming joined the other students crowded into the tiny room. Henry lounged on his bed smoking a cigar.

"I really like this radio, Henry, there aren't too many available yet," Robert said.

"Ten bucks and it's yours," Henry replied jokingly.

Robert pulled a ten-dollar bill out of his pocket. "Sold! You've got a deal."

A bidding war began for the brass desk lamp, followed by someone offering Henry three dollars for his bed sheets. Henry began pulling linens and clothing from his closet. Jumping up on his desk chair, he began to take bids for his leather coat and luggage. Before the room cleared, he had sold all but a few pieces of clothing and two textbooks, which he pitched into the wastebasket. He lay on his bed, covered with dollar bills and laughed aloud at the success of his sale. He counted out forty dollars and put it in an envelope for Barrios. The rest would buy him a ticket home.

The test results placed Henry fourth in his class, putting him on the dean's list and a special mention in the campus newspaper. Henry was disheartened by the grade. When he chastised Barrios for not getting him a lower grade, Barrios laughed and told him he should be thankful that he was now considered brilliant. Henry threw the forty dollars on the desk. "Here's your damn money. I hope you choke on it." He slammed the door hoping that it would be the last time in his life he ever saw Barrios.

Henry packed his few remaining belongings into a small satchel and headed to the train station. He called his mother, distraught, telling her that while he was inside the station buying a ticket, someone stole his luggage off of the depot platform. He had already contacted the authorities, but his lovely suitcases and all his clothing were gone. She promised that Martin would meet him at the station, and not to worry, she would take care of everything.

Chapter Five

"Oh darling, I'm so glad to see you! I've missed you so much," his mother exclaimed as she ran down the stairs to greet him. "How was school? You must tell me everything."

"Please Mother, not now, we have plenty of time to talk." He looked around, wondering why his father was not there to meet him.

"Your father is in New York, dear, but he will be home by dinner. He is so anxious to see you."

Henry sighed. Too bad the feeling wasn't mutual. For once he wished his father were home. It was his time to gloat. He had finished the year and now he wanted his money.

Henry's room looked wonderful. The richness of the colors and the plush carpet under his feet made him feel euphoric. His mother had managed to fill his closet with new textures and smells. Tweeds and leathers hung neatly side by side. Henry dressed for dinner, taking time to admire himself in front of the full-length mirror. He felt the softness of the silk shirt against his body and the scent of new cologne on his face. It was good to be home.

Joseph opened the door to the parlor and greeted Henry with a robust handshake. "I just wanted to tell you how proud I am of you and I owe you an apology. You have far exceeded my expectations." He draped his arm around Henry's shoulder as they walked to the dining room. The cook had made a sumptuous meal for Henry's homecoming, preparing all of his favorite food. His mother talked incessantly through dinner. Henry hoped she would not bring up the matter of his stolen luggage. He was afraid his father would have too many questions. The tension between him and his father had subsided and for that he was grateful. For once they spent the evening together without arguing.

"After breakfast tomorrow I want to take you to Boston," his father said. "I have something to show you."

Henry could only imagine it to be a trip to purchase a new automobile for him, or, perhaps even better, a trip to the family attorney to settle the matter of his financial future.

Arriving in Boston around noon, the surprise turned rancid very quickly when Henry realized that the destination was the third floor of an upscale medical building in the heart of downtown Boston. Joseph escorted him through the suite of offices, pointing out where the newest x-ray equipment would be placed. He opened the door to the laboratory and to his library, which was filled from floor to ceiling with medical books. The tour was boring. Henry had been to these offices many times before. It was only when they reached the end of the hallway that he began to understand his father's excitement. On the seamless glass door, printed in gold letters, was the name, Henry J. Franklin, M.D.

"Why is my name on this door?" Henry asked, tapping his finger on the glass. "Is this your idea of a joke?"

Joseph did not answer him. He opened the door and stepped inside. "Isn't this one of the finest desks you've ever seen?" He rubbed his hand along the smooth mahogany finish.

Henry said sharply, "You haven't answered my question."

"In just a few short years this will be your office. Dean Parson has agreed that you can complete your internship here in Boston, so you can use this office right after graduation," his father replied.

Henry recoiled at the thought. "Wait just a damn minute. We had a deal, remember? One year of medical school for my financial freedom. Well, I did it. I went to your damn school and now I'm finished. Over with! Out of that place forever!"

Joseph began to laugh. "With the grades you made, do you think I would be foolish enough to let you quit? I'm afraid I always thought of you as less than adequate but I am elated that you proved me wrong. Trust me, son. The next years will not be quite as hard as the first one."

Henry clenched his fists. He wanted to kill his father at this moment. He wanted to grab his throat and choke him to death. "You can't mean this. You know I have no intention of becoming a doctor."

Joseph walked to the desk and sat down. The smile was gone from his face. He pulled his pipe and tobacco pouch from his pocket and slowly began to fill the bowl. "I guess we have to play hardball. I am recanting my former offer. This is the new one. Three more years of medical school or leave now with the clothes on your back."

Henry could feel the rage engulfing his body. He began to shake and choked back the sobs that were obstructing his throat. "I can't do this. I won't go back. Please tell me this is all some kind of a mindless joke. You know I hated every minute I was at school."

Joseph continued filling his pipe. He seemed calm. "It's not a joke, Henry. I have never been more serious in my life. I will not let you fail yourself. Someday you will thank me for what I am doing for you." He rose from the chair and pushed it under the desk.

Henry slowly slid down the wall of the hallway. He put his head in hands and began to cry. "How do I know I can trust you to keep your promise this time? You lied to me before."

"I had a contract drawn by my attorney. I'll get a copy for you," Joseph said in a disgusted voice. He turned off the light in the office and closed the door. "What did you think I was going to let you do, piss away all your money and start on mine? And don't ask your mother for money. She has coddled you long enough. You need to grow up." He stepped over Henry. "You're pitiful. You know that Henry? Just pitiful."

As he walked down the hall, Henry shouted after him. "You're a bastard. Just go home. I'll take the train when I'm good and ready. I might never come back to your damn house."

Henry spent the night in a barroom playing pool and drinking until he fell sound asleep in the corner. One of the cleaning ladies woke him in the morning. He staggered into the street, squinting from the bright morning light and caught the first train home. The depression he felt was overwhelming. He had no idea if Barrios was returning to school or if he would even be interested in helping him again. All he knew is that he had never felt so alone and betrayed.

Joseph left a copy of the contract on Henry's dresser. It stated that funds would be provided to him for his tuition, books, housing and a small allowance to live on and nothing more. Any request for additional money would have to be authorized by Joseph. Upon receiving his diploma, he would receive an amount of money equal to one-half of his father's estate.

YARD SALE

Henry followed his mother around the house, begging her to persuade his father to change his mind. He cried pitiful tears and pleaded, but Agnes just wrung her hands and cried too. She said Joseph had already told her what he had done and warned her not to go against his wishes. There was nothing she could do except continue to provide Henry with a few dollars as she had done the previous year. He hated her also. He wanted to kill her and throw her into the lake and watch her body sink beneath her precious swans.

Henry had no choice but to finish his sentence: three more years of torture. The hatred he felt for his father became the driving force in his life. School would resume in just three weeks. He needed that time to squeeze every dime out of his mother. The task became easy. She carried her guilt quite well. He left for school with his wallet thickly padded.

Chapter Six

Barrios could not afford to make the trip home to Chile at the end of the semester break. The medical school allowed foreign students to stay in the dormitory, but the cafeteria was closed and the furnace in the dormitory was turned down at night to save fuel. He shivered under his thin blankets. Barrios found a job as a busboy in an off campus restaurant and ate whatever leftovers he could salvage from the kitchen. Each night he would empty his pockets to count the change left him on the tables. It was a meager amount compared to what he had taken from Henry. That money made a profound difference in his family life, but now he had nothing to send to Chile and even less to live on. With luck, he would be able to find work on the campus when school resumed and perhaps it would be enough to let him stay at least a few more months.

At the beginning of the new semester, Barrios spotted Henry unloading his second round of possessions into his old room. He could not believe that Henry had come back to school. Henry had made a promise to him that he would not return, but Barrios felt all along that Henry could not be trusted. For this he should be grateful. He wondered how long it would take Henry to come to see him.

After the dormitory lights were turned out for the night, Henry glanced up and down the empty hallway. He quickly made his way to the third door and knocked lightly.

"Come in, it's open," Barrios said stiffly. "I am surprised to see you here. What happened? Did you decide you were smart enough to become a doctor after all?"

Henry wanted to slap the smirk from his face. "It's because of you, you stupid bastard, that I'm back. I told you all I needed was a passing grade."

Barrios folded his arms over his chest and leaned back in the chair. "Oh really, Henry, I'm stupid. I don't think so. It is your greed that put you back into this school and unfortunately it's my greed that's keeping you here. You lied. You said you weren't coming back so it is going to cost you twice as much this year for my help."

There was nothing left to say. Henry slammed the door, sending a small picture crashing to the floor. He hated Barrios. His list was growing longer. Before he left home, he had also added Martin to the list of those he wanted dead. Martin had laughed in Henry's face when he found out that he had to return to school. "Poor Henry, we are certainly going to miss you," Martin had said in a mocking voice.

He heard someone calling his name. "Good to see you back," Robert said. "I've got some new things I'd like to show you."

Henry was in no mood for Robert. He had enough problems of his own. "Maybe later, I need to get settled in."

"I saw you talking to the Chile bean. What was that all about? I was surprised to see him this semester," Robert said.

"I was just answering some of his stupid questions about the curfew. He's a slime," Henry replied.

Henry had never had a true friend. No one could tolerate his arrogance for very long, although it didn't seem to bother Robert. Robert was very much like Henry. He delighted in making sport of the other students with his constant banter of ethnic slurs and name-calling. Barrios was one of his favorite targets. Henry wanted to make sure that he had not raised any suspicion. Robert had a keen eye. He began to join Robert, laughing loudly when some innocent student became the butt of one of his jokes. They ate lunch together in the cafeteria and played handball after class. Robert was an ass and Henry had decided to stop the friendship when the suggestion was made to go into Chicago to have some fun, at Robert's expense, of course. Slipping away from school almost every night, Chicago became their playground. Henry enjoyed helping Robert spend his money on bootleg liquor and the women who walked along Front Street.

Barrios stood at the window and watched as Robert and Henry escaped across the darkened campus. He felt as if he was once again under Henry's thumb. This year he would make sure that Henry paid him in advance for each assignment he completed since Henry seemed to have so much money to throw away on nonsensical things.

Chapter Seven

On October twenty-ninth, nineteen hundred and twenty nine, the news came of the Stock Market crash. The airwaves were flooded with news of the disaster and the front page of the newspapers turned into one bold headline. Classes were canceled for the week and many panicked students tried to call their parents. The telephone lines were tied up for hours, finally going silent from the overloaded circuits. Three days later Henry was able to reach his home. It was his father who took the call. In a less than friendly tone, he told Henry not to worry. He should not be concerned about the stock market, but to concentrate on his studies. Henry was relieved that the crash had not affected his family's wealth. A steady procession of students began to leave the dormitory, including Robert, whose father had lost everything. He sobbed as he packed his suitcases to leave school. Henry avoided leaving his own room until after Robert was gone. To save money, the university decided to merge the remaining students into one dormitory building. Henry dreaded the idea of having a roommate again. He paced the floor of his room, trying to compose a speech that would convince his father he would be better off living alone in the residence hall.

Henry sucked in his breath as the telephone rang for the third time. He knew he had to get past his anger and hold his tongue if he wanted his father to concede.

"What is it Henry?" his father asked in an agitated voice. "We just talked a few days ago." In the most sincere voice he could muster, Henry begged his father to let him move into the residence hall. "I'm warning you Henry, you better not be up to something. You know you will have a lot more freedom living there, so you need to keep your mind on what you're doing."

He knew his father was beginning to soften. It just took a few more references to the difficulty he had studying in the noisy dormitory. "You know, Father, you were right. I'm glad I'm back at school," he lied in his most convincing voice.

"I still think this is a white wash job, but I'm going to give you the benefit of the doubt but not without a stern warning to watch your step. I'll talk to the dean tomorrow and see if there are any openings in Franklin Hall."

Franklin Hall consisted of two structures connected by a covered walkway. The married students and their spouses occupied the front building, while the other building was rented to anyone lucky enough to secure a room from the long waiting list. By the end of the week, Henry had moved into his new living quarters.

Agnes was thrilled that Henry had moved into Franklin Hall and managed to make several trips to Chicago during the school year to visit him. Each time she pleaded with Henry to forgive her for not standing up to Joseph when he insisted Henry return to school. She was so very sorry. She convinced Henry she only sided with his father to keep him from completely losing his entire inheritance. She was once again his ally. He knew it was useless to stay mad at his mother and crossed her off his list of people he wanted dead.

As she walked around his room on her first visit, Agnes began to reminisce about the time she spent living here while Joseph completed his last year of internship after they were married. At that time, the buildings were already old and decomposing. Plaster hung from the sagging ceilings and the furnaces belched black smoke and cold air from the vents. Rust water dripped from the sinks and the shared bathrooms housed overflowing toilets. Agnes had been appalled at the thought of living in such conditions and convinced her father to make a large donation for repairs to the building in Joseph's name. When Joseph received his medical degree, the building was renamed Franklin Hall.

Henry was running low on money and convinced his mother it was time to visit him again. He leaned against the depot railing and watched as the train pulled slowly into the station. Taking his mother's hand as she stepped onto the platform, he lightly kissed her cheek.

"Oh, I just had the nicest chat with a young lady on the train," Agnes said. "We had tea together. She is just returning from Wales. Poor thing, her mother just passed away recently. She told me she works in the school library."

Henry tried not to appear too interested. "Did she say what her name is?"

"Why, yes, she did. Her name is Grace, Grace Cardiff."

After a day of shopping for clothes and eating in one of Chicago's finest restaurants, Henry was relieved to see his mother leave. Her constant babbling annoyed him, but not enough to keep Henry from spending her money. When he returned to his room, he found the envelope she had put in one of the packages with the twenty-dollar bills neatly folded inside a sheet of her monogrammed stationery. Henry decided it was time he made another trip to the library.

Grace recognized him the moment he entered. He was dressed casually, yet he had a demeanor of quiet confidence as he strode across the wooden plank floor. He stood before her desk and waited until she looked up again.

"Hello, I'm Henry Franklin. My mother, Agnes Franklin, said she met you on the train. She told me about the death of your mother and I just wanted to come by and give you my condolences. I hope she did not intrude on your privacy. Mother forgets herself sometimes."

"I'm glad to meet you, Henry. This is so very kind of you. Please don't apologize, it wasn't an imposition," she said. "Your mother is a lovely woman. She made me laugh for the first time in quite a while."

Henry smiled. "I hope it wasn't at my expense." Henry studied her face. She had pale, delicate skin and clear blue eyes that held his attention. "I know you have just suffered a great loss in your life, but it would please me very much if I could take you to dinner some evening to thank you for putting up with my mother." He really hadn't known what to say. His speech sounded wooden and stilted.

"I'd like that very much," she said. "Thank you for asking."

Grace was pleasant company and Henry found himself relaxed around her. She knew little about him. When he finally told her about his family she seemed unimpressed by the magnitude of his wealth. She was more interested in his studies and his decision to be a doctor. They had dinner twice in the next month, but school had become grueling. Barrios was always lurking in the shadows with his hand out. He used his studies as an excuse not to see Grace and she understood. Sometimes when his money was extremely low, they would sit in the foyer of the residence hall and talk. She told him the story of how she came to live in Chicago. He had never associated himself with a woman of such poor beginnings other than those whose services he paid for. Henry said she could have told him anything she wanted about her past and he would have believed her. Grace seemed surprised when he said those things to her. "What would I gain by not telling you the truth? Lies always have a way of catching up with you."

"Yes, I know," he replied. "I was really only teasing you."

Grace hadn't thought much about her past life in quite a while. Her conversations with Henry began to bring back the fond childhood memories of her life in Wales.

✧✧✧

Unlike the rest of the Catholics in Monmouth, Wales, Grace was an only child. Her parents had tried for many years to have children; after many miscarriages, they were overjoyed when she was born. They had lived in a small two-room cottage a mile from the town. Her father worked in the coalmines in Brecon. Arriving home at night with his clothes blackened from soot, he would kiss her cheeks, leaving black smudges on her face. They lived a simple life, unencumbered by the changes that were going on around them. Her father's love of books filtered into her life. He read to her every night until the candle burned too low to see the pages of the books that he had borrowed from the library.

In the summer, when the rains had passed, her mother would pack a basket of apples, cheese and cold spring water. They would make their way across the tall grassy fields, through the lush green forest and onto the banks of the Usk River. Sitting beneath a shade tree, her mother would crochet spools of silken thread into webs of filmy lace. The lace she would sell in the Town Square to buy sugar and other spices. On a good day of sales there would be peppermint candies for Grace. Grace and her father would walk to the bank of the river watching the paddleboats make their way to the ports along the English Channel. They would fish with long cane poles. Her father would lie on his back reading to her as the summer sun warmed their faces. Sometimes they would just sit in the soft grass, smelling the delicate scents of life. As the afternoon light began to stream through the trees, her father would carry his sleeping daughter home to her bed. In the winter, he would stay up very late to keep the fires in the hearth burning, touching her hair with his callused hand as she slept beneath the eider quilts. Her father was a kind and gentle man and she loved him very much.

  Those were the good memories, but life in Monmouth was beginning to change. When Grace was ten, the factories and mines began to close. Most of the young men in the village left for London or America. With each exodus, the town took on a new tone, and soon entire families began to leave. With the closing of the coalmines, Grace's father made the decision to seek a new life in America. He wanted his only child to have an education and he needed to feed his family. It was a grueling trip across the ocean and life was not easy for them in the new country. Somehow her father's optimism made her believe that just around the corner was always something new and exciting. He found work in a steel mill for a few dollars a week. It was arduous work that left his skin pocked with burn marks. Her mother missed her homeland. Her depression began to surface as she stared out of the tenement house window at the concrete world below her. The new sights and sounds made her feel uneasy. Fingering her rosary beads each night, she prayed that they would be able to go home some day. She feared for Grace's safety and held her hand tightly each day as they made their way across the busy streets to the public school. Grace missed her life in Wales. The freedom she once had was now restricted, but Chicago was a wondrous place for her. She loved the decorated store windows, all of the new foods, but most of all, she loved school with real paper instead of a slate to write on. There were friends to giggle with and rows of books to read.

  As the years passed her father's promises of a better life diminished and he developed an unshakeable illness. He spent weeks coughing and was unable to eat, which ultimately left him too weak to get out of bed. His body would sweat profusely and the coughing never ceased. At times, he tried to struggle out of bed and go to work, but his employer had finally suggested he go to the University Hospital for free medical care where he was immediately admitted into a ward. In desperation, Grace's mother took a job as a domestic in Dean Parson's house to be near her husband. Grace and her mother moved their meager belongings into a small attic room provided for them by Mrs. Parson. Grace was forced to quit school and found a job in the hospital laundry. Working through the night, her hands red and blistered, she would spend her days at her father's bedside as his condition worsened. Grace held his head and spooned clear broth into his mouth until finally his wasted body, racked with pain, gave out. Before he died, he told Grace that he was sorry that he had not given her a better life.

Grace and her mother grieved for months. Her mother blamed their decision to come to America for her father's death. She became a hollow shadow of herself, spending her days working in the Parson house and her afternoons in the church praying. She hardly spoke to anyone except Grace. At times she would sit for hours, listening to the haunting Celtic lullabies on the used phonograph that Mrs. Parson let her use. Grace knew her mother was torn between returning to Wales and staying in Chicago with her. Grace went to Mrs. Parson and explained the situation to her. Mrs. Parson agreed to let Grace stay on in the house if she would take her mother's position. She was sixteen now and capable of taking care of herself. Her mother could return to Wales and live in the convent in Newport. Grace's decision to stay in America was heart wrenching. As they stood on the pier, they hugged and cried, holding on to each other as long as possible. Her mother asked Grace for her forgiveness for leaving. Grace wiped away her mother's tears and told her everything would be all right and they would write often to each other. Somehow they knew that they would never see each other again even though Grace told her mother that she would visit her some time in the future. As her mother boarded the ship, she handed Grace a package wrapped in white paper and tied with a silver string. She had planned on giving it to Grace on her wedding day, but she knew she may never see that happen. Grace opened the package when she got home. It was a white lace tablecloth, each delicate stitch crocheted by her mother's loving hands. She wrapped the cloth around her shoulders and lay down on the bed. She cried herself to sleep. Except for her father's death, it was one of the worst days of her short life.

Grace stayed on at the Parson's house for two more years. Her days were filled with scrubbing, cleaning and serving at the frequent dinners given by the dean and his wife. Two nights a week she would take the bus to the public school where she had enrolled in evening classes. She wrote long letters to her mother telling her how much she missed her. Her mother's replies were usually just short notes, written in the precise script of one of the nuns at the convent. She sent Grace prayer cards and novenas and told her she prayed for her happiness every day.

Henry listened to the stories of her childhood with little interest. He could not relate to most of the things that she told him. He could not comprehend their lack of money or the simple life they lived, but most of all, the love she had for her father. That, he imagined, may have been exaggerated.

Chapter Eight

Grace was putting books on the shelf as Henry sat watching her. "It's so stuffy in here and it's such a nice day, I thought I might pack a few sandwiches and a thermos of lemonade. We could have a picnic lunch on the lawn outside the residence hall," she said without turning around.

Henry made a face. He did not like to sit on the ground or bother with insects flying about his head. "Yes," he said, "that sounds like a good idea. I'll meet you in front of the library at noon." They found an open spot on the already crowded lawn and Henry spread the blanket. He tried to find a comfortable position, finally leaning back on one elbow, his hand propped under his chin. Grace spread the food on a cloth, brushing away the ants that already had begun to invade their space. As usual, Henry tried to avoid any mention of his schoolwork. He shifted his weight and tried to enjoy the dry cheese sandwich Grace had given him.

"So tell me, Grace, how did you get here?" He motioned toward the library.

"After a couple of years working and living at the Parson's house, I began to feel a little uncomfortable."

"Why, was the work too hard for you?" Henry asked.

She hesitated; he could tell she was getting nervous. "Well it really doesn't matter. It all worked out for the best. It was Mrs. Parson who thought I should leave. Mrs. Parson was able to get me the position in the library and a furnished room in a pleasant house just a few blocks from the school."

Henry began to get the picture. "There must have been a reason she wanted you out of her house. It was because of the dean, wasn't it?"

Grace tore her sandwiches into small bites, not looking up at Henry. She could feel the flush on her neck and face. "Dean Parson had become very irritating. There were times when I could feel him watching me as I worked. He would make remarks that were embarrassing to me. There was no lock on my door, so at night I would prop a chair under the latch. Once I saw the doorknob turning and I stayed awake all night. I could hear the Parsons arguing later that night. The next day Mrs. Parson made all of the arrangements for me to leave."

Henry sat up straight. "Why, that little bastard! Oh, Grace, forgive me for the profanity, but it upsets me to think of what he did to you and probably others, too. That is all he did, wasn't it?"

"Of course, Henry, there is nothing more. I trust you to keep what I have just told you to yourself. I don't wish to make trouble for anyone."

Henry nodded, "But the first time I saw you, it was at his house. Why would you ever go back there?"

"It wasn't anything I really wanted to do, but I had to depend on my small salary at the library for all my expenses. Sometimes I needed extra money. I liked Mrs. Parson and as long as I stayed away from the dean everything was fine."

"So you were paid when you worked for the Parsons?" he asked.

She really wanted to change the subject. Grace was afraid she had told him too much already. "He never paid me directly, but the compensation was deducted from my rent at the residence hall."

Henry stood with his hands behind his back as he began to pace back and forth. "So let me get this straight, you worked as a domestic for him, and he let the university pay for your lodgings? That is very interesting."

Grace had no idea where Henry was going with his train of thought. She folded the napkins and put the glasses back in the basket. "I really don't want to talk about this anymore. It's all over with. I haven't been in the Parson house for over a year."

Henry apologized for his interrogation, passing it off as concern for her.

Henry had a tough week. Barrios had been sick for three days and none of Henry's assignments had been touched. He threatened Barrios if they were not done by Monday, he would not pay him for any of the work he had already completed. Wrapped in a blanket, Barrios sat at his small desk and worked into the morning hours. His lack of sleep and unhealthy state cost Henry an extra twenty dollars. Henry was now very low on money once again and needed desperately to get in touch with his mother.

That evening, by some stroke of luck, he received a call from his father. His parents would be in Chicago for the alumni meeting on Saturday and they wanted Henry to join them for dinner on Friday. Since he was now a student, he was not allowed to attend the alumni dinner. If his father was soliciting a peace offering, it was much too late. Henry was still very upset with him, but dinner in a downtown restaurant would be nice.

"I was wondering if it would be all right if I brought someone with me?" he asked. Surely with Grace along, his father could not spend the entire evening trying to convince Henry that he had made the right decision for him.

"And just who do you wish to bring with you, one of your woman classmates?" his father said in a condescending tone. Joseph had never gotten used to the idea of women in the medical profession. He believed they were more of a hindrance than an asset and that medicine was not a proper calling for women.

Henry sighed, "No Father, it's a young lady I met here at school. She is not a student. She works in the library."

"Is there something your mother and I need to know? I have told you over and again not to allow yourself to get involved with anyone while you're still in school. There is plenty of time for that later."

Henry couldn't resist. "As I recall, Father, you married Mother while you were still in school. Don't worry yourself. She is just a friend. Mother has met her once already."

Henry was relieved to see that Grace had a new dress. He had no idea she had borrowed it from one of the ladies at the residence hall. Her friends on the floor had joined in her excitement. They mixed powders and rouge for her cheeks, laughing as they made red clown circles on her face. They pulled dresses from their closets for Grace to try on and draped necklaces and scarves around her neck. Her final choice was a rose colored silk with a white lace shawl covering her shoulders. She wore a single strand of pearls and wisps of curls escaped from the gold barrette holding her hair on top of her head. She looked lovely and Henry was pleased. He smiled as he helped her into the car his parents had sent for them.

Grace was nervous all week about meeting Henry's father. She had seen his picture on an announcement for the alumni dinner in the library. Once again he was the key speaker. Like Henry, he was a handsome man, yet he had a stern demeanor. Grace secretly hoped it was just the flash of the camera that made him frown.

The dining room sparkled like diamonds. Beaded chandeliers hung from the ornate ceiling and each table was dressed with blue china and crystal. It was the most elegant room Grace had ever seen. Her shoes sank into the plush carpet as they crossed the room to meet Henry's parents. She truly hoped she would not embarrass him. His father rose from the table as they approached. He extended his hand to Henry and pulled the chair out for Grace. Agnes was delighted to see her again. "Oh my dear, don't you look pretty. That is a lovely dress."

Grace thanked her. She could see Henry's father looking at her. She turned her head and smiled at him as Henry introduced her.

The night could not have been better. Henry let Grace carry the conversation. In her lilting Welsh accent, she charmed his father with her knowledge of medical books. He was impressed as she rattled off the names of the newest books available, since she knew he must be much too busy to research such things himself. She told him of her determination to finish her education and become a teacher. He agreed that it was important to follow your convictions, looking futilely at Henry. She laughed at his inane jokes and flushed when he complimented her. Agnes seemed relaxed and contented that the evening was such a pleasant one for a change.

They sat close together on the ride home. Grace felt giddy from the champagne. She rambled on about the restaurant and his parents. She looked beautiful in the dim light of the passing cars. Henry wanted to touch her, to kiss her soft lips. He pulled her close to him and turned her face toward his as he took her into his arms. She gently pushed him away. Henry sat back and crossed his arms over his chest. He was angry at her constant rejection of his advances. He was tired of her same excuse that they must not do anything foolish to cause a change in their plans. Maybe spending time without his company would make her change her mind. He was sullen for the rest of the ride home.

It had been several weeks since Grace had seen Henry. He hadn't telephoned her and he made a point to stay out of the library while she was working. Today he had no choice but to go the library to locate a book he needed for one of his classes.

She was sitting at her desk when he entered. She looked up and smiled as he came toward her. "Where have you been, Henry? I've missed you." She seemed very glad to see him. "I've waited for you in the foyer several times," Grace said.

Henry shrugged. "I've been busy. I need this book," he said, handing her a piece of paper.

"Oh. I was sure that it must have been your school work taking up all your time." She rose from her desk and looked at her watch. "Let me get the book and then I can leave. Would you like to walk with me?"

As they strolled along, she made idle conversation, never referring to their time apart. He was only partially listening until he heard her mention his mother's name.

"What about my mother?" he asked. "What did you say?"

"I said that when I talked to your mother the other day she said to tell you hello. I told her I hadn't seen you in a while."

Henry stopped on the path and snapped at her. "What do you mean, you talked to my mother? Did you call her?"

His voice frightened her. "I called her first to thank her and your father for the lovely evening and she has called me several times since then."

"And just what do you and my mother talk about? I can't understand why she would call you. Are you telling her things about me?" He was only inches away from her face, his eyes narrowed as he stared at her angrily.

"No! No! We don't talk about you. She just calls to chat and I enjoy talking with her."

She started to walk again. Henry grabbed her wrist and pulled her back. "So she didn't ask you any questions about me?"

"You're scaring me! Why are you so mad?" She pulled his hand away from her wrist.

He stepped back from her and gently touched her shoulder. "I'm sorry, Grace. I just get so mad at my parents sometimes. They are always interfering in my life. They twist things around, and I don't want you to get caught in one of their schemes. I care about you too much."

"Really, Henry, I can hardly believe your parents mean you any harm. They seem like very nice people to me. In fact, your mother has invited me to come for a visit when the semester is over." Grace was not sure what had really happened between them, but she was left with an unsettling feeling.

They parted ways at the end of the path, Henry telling Grace he would call her. He watched her walk away. How could his mother be so stupid as to invite her to their summer home without asking him first? He did not plan to spend his summer entertaining the virginal Grace.

It took several days for Grace to stop thinking about what Henry had done to her. Somehow she convinced herself that he was just under a lot of pressure with the end of the school year so near. She decided to pack a picnic lunch and ask him to join her. Henry agreed to meet her in the foyer of his dormitory. It was time for him to put an end to his relationship with Grace before she became too close to his mother. He was sitting in the foyer of the dormitory when she entered, his back to her and the telephone in his hand. Henry could see Grace's reflection in the glass doors as she came across the room. Grace sat down on the sofa behind him to wait for him. She had no intention of eavesdropping on his conversation, but he began talking in a loud irritated voice.

"Really, Mother," he said, "I can't believe you would even consider inviting her to the summer house with our family. She hasn't even finished school; she works in the library and sometimes as a servant for the Parsons. Whatever would she have in common with your friends?"

The stinging words echoed in her ears. It was if as her legs had turned to rubber. Grace tried to steady herself as she quietly got up from the sofa. The tears had already begun to flow down her cheeks as she picked up the basket and started toward the door. Henry watched her leave. He held the telephone, the dial tone still buzzing in his ear.

Chapter Nine

Henry needed a drink. He needed a lot of drinks. His arguments with Barrios had become an almost weekly event. Barrios was pressing him for more and more money. He decided to spend the day in Chicago. The Jacket Club was one of his favorite haunts. He liked the way the people knew his name and how the girls at the bar smiled at him when he arrived. They knew after a few drinks Henry became free with his money and time spent with him was usually short. It made him feel good when they walked past him, kissing him on the cheek, or when the bartender would have his drink order ready before he sat down.

Rita was one of his favorite women. She was big and brash with carrot colored hair. Rita was always laughing and telling bawdy jokes. She was patient with Henry and her room decorated all in pink, was cleaner than most. On the nights that he had too much to drink she would let him spend the night for five extra dollars. He needed Rita tonight. She answered her door in a flimsy pink nightgown. "Henry, damn it's good to see you. Come on in, honey, and have a seat." She put her ample arms around him and crushed his head to her bulging chest. "Honey is this a social call or business?" she said laughingly. Henry held a ten-dollar bill between his two fingers, waving it by her face. Rita grabbed for the bill. "Looks like business to me, darlin'. What's your pleasure, top or bottom?"

Henry grinned. It was going to be a good night. A few minutes later Henry groaned as Rita rolled over to the other side of the bed. The weight of her body exhausted him. He reached for a cigarette as he sat up in bed.

"I'm gonna call downstairs for a beer: you want one?" Rita said as she rolled out of bed.

"Sounds good to me," Henry replied pulling the covers up over his naked body.

She walked to the window and lit a cigarette. Her face changed colors with each blink of the neon sign below. "Did I ever tell you about the time I went to your school?" she said.

Henry laughed. "Yeah right, you went to medical school. What course did you take, male anatomy or venereal diseases?"

Rita stuck her tongue out at him. "Very funny. Don't interrupt me, it's a good story." She plopped down upon the bed sending Henry bouncing up and down. "I get this call one night from some squeaky voiced man saying he heard I made house calls and wondering if he sent a taxi, would I join him for the evening? I said sure, if the price was right. The taxi takes me up to the school and I'm thinking that maybe some of those shithead medical students are playing a joke on me." Rita stopped talking to answer the door, returning to the bed with two bottles of beer. "Well anyway, it's this big house on the edge of the campus. I go to the door and this fat little guy is peeking out the curtains."

Henry sat up. "Did the house have green shutters and hedges going up the path?"

"Yeah, that kind of sounds likes the house. Didn't I tell you not to interrupt me?" Rita took a drink of her beer and lay back against the pillow. "I go upstairs to the bedroom and before I even get all my clothes off, this guy begins to get real nervous and says I have to leave. He starts picking up my clothes telling me he's afraid his wife might be coming home soon. I go all that way and he wants me out of his house. I tell him to just pay up and call me a cab. He starts telling me he ain't going to pay me because we didn't do anything, so I start hollering and he runs out of the room. When he comes back, he tells me that he has called security and told them I broke into his house. I say sure, I always take my clothes off when I rob houses. I knew he was bullshittin' me, but I don't need any trouble. I damn near killed myself walking home in high-heeled shoes."

Henry began to laugh, and Rita playfully threw a pillow at him. "Don't you laugh at me, school boy. It wasn't a total loss." Rita reached into the nightstand drawer and opened a small satin box. She pitched something across the bed at Henry. "That is a genuine mother of pearl cameo. I took it off the fat guy's dresser before I left. I wonder what he told his wife when she found it missing?" Rita yawned. "I got to get some sleep. You spending the night?" She began to snore before he answered her.

Henry dressed and laid another five-dollar bill on the night table. He picked up the cameo and put it in his pocket. In his dormitory room that night, Henry placed the brooch in a brown leather pouch under his mattress, the same pouch that held the notes written by Barrios.

It was payday for Barrios. They met in the anatomy lab after class. Henry shoved the folded envelope under the microscope on the table. Without looking up, Barrios picked it up and put it into his frayed jacket pocket. "What grade do you want this semester, Henry?"

Henry sat on a tall stool, swinging his legs. "Very funny. I expect a perfect four-point grade average. I did more than my share this year."

Barrios snickered. "You are pathetic. Let me see the calluses on your fingers from writing."

Henry jumped from the stool and began walking around the lab. He hated the smell of formaldehyde and the sight of jars containing decomposing body parts. How anyone could find this interesting was beyond him. He pointed his finger in Barrios' face. "Don't be calling me names, you little shit. Look into the mirror if you want to see a pathetic person. Don't do anything stupid. All I need is a passing grade. Nothing more." Henry slammed the door on his way out.

Chapter Ten

When Henry returned to school in the fall, Grace had already moved from her rented room and resigned from her job at the library. She had moved into one of the women's hotels in the city and took a teacher's assistant position in a Catholic grade school. In the evening she attended classes at Miss Borden's Preparatory School for Young Women. Grace thought of Henry often, but she was still too upset over what he had said about her to his mother. Even more puzzling was why he never once tried to see her after that day. Whatever the reason, Grace was too embarrassed to try to contact him. Agnes had called several times, leaving messages for her, but Grace did not return her calls. Henry had hurt her deeply. She couldn't understand why she still cared for him. He had rejected her and she needed to move on with her life, but no matter how she tried, thoughts of Henry continually returned to her mind.

Henry spent the summer in Paris. His parents paid for the trip as a reward for another successful year of medical school. To save money, he rented two rooms in a boarding house on the Left Bank, rather than the upscale hotel his mother had chosen. He spent most of his time in the bistros and cafes to avoid going back to the small and dingy apartment. He drank away the nights, falling into bed as the sun began to rise each morning. The Depression had continued to drag on and before he left to go to Paris he heard his father say things like "tightening up our belts" or "holding off on purchases." These words made Henry nervous, since he was not accustomed to hearing them in the Franklin house. His father still insisted everything was all right with their finances, but told Henry this might be his last trip abroad for quite a while.

The third year of medical school passed quickly. The class work on cadavers completely disgusted Henry. He paired himself with Barrios and let him do most of the cutting and dissecting while he stood nearby with his hand over his mouth to keep from vomiting. Barrios would laugh at Henry, making gagging noises as he cut into the flesh of the cadaver. Barrios became Henry's shadow. He helped Henry with his lab work and prepared him for his clinicals. "You cannot fudge when we do our hospital rounds, Henry," Barrios said. "The doctors will catch you if you do not know the answers to their questions."

"I'm not completely inept, Barrios," Henry sneered. "I have learned a few things since I've been at this damn school."

"Oh, really, Henry. That's news to me."

Barrios continued to press Henry for money. He complained that his workload was too much for him and he needed to send more money home to his family. Henry didn't care. To him, they sounded like a bunch of freeloaders. Perhaps if Barrios sent them nothing at all, they would learn their lesson.

Henry finished his third year with barely a passing grade. He knew the next year would be even harder and he begrudgingly took Barrios' suggestion to stay at school and take extra classes. He was too close now to take a chance on failing. Henry wanted his money and cursed his father each summer morning he arose early for class.

Without taking a break, Henry entered into his fourth and final year of school. It was the most grueling year of all since most of the class time was spent at the University Hospital. He had to rely on his wits to avoid the staff doctors and stay out of the way of anyone who could connect him to Barrios, even though their dislike for each other was obvious. It was crucial that they do their rounds together and at times it was Barrios who made jokes about Henry to the other medical students. Henry seethed as they poked fun at him, calling him the "young Doctor Franklin-stein."

The doctors employed by the university hospital were tired and irritable. They were now required not only to teach classes, but also take shifts in the wards, since the Depression had forced the administration to reduce the hospital staff. The shortage of doctors worked to Henry's advantage. Many times the rounds were cut short or conducted by a resident doctor who did not take time to ask questions of the students.

Each time Henry entered the hospital his back stiffened. He went quickly to the ward he was assigned without making conversation with any of the doctors or interns. He hated the smell and sounds in these wards. The first time he was asked to check a patient's wound, he could feel the nausea swirling around in the pit of his stomach. He could not understand why anyone in his right mind would choose medicine as a career. It certainly was not something that he would ever dream of doing.

Chapter Eleven

It was March 18, 1931; Henry's twenty-fifth birthday and only four months before graduation. His father sent him a gold pocket watch inscribed, of course, with "Henry Franklin, M.D." inside the cover and his wonderful mother sent him money. He had just finished his rounds at the hospital and was heading across campus when he saw Grace coming towards him. She looked beautiful. She was wearing a pink dress and black boots. Henry didn't know what to do; should he say hello or just turn and go the other way? Before his decision was made, she turned toward him and he could not avoid her.

"Hello, Henry, how are you?"

"Good, Grace, and yourself?"

He seemed heavier to her and had grown a mustache. "You're looking well, Henry. I like your mustache."

"Thanks," he stammered, for a moment not knowing what to say. He wanted to choose the right words. "Are you working in the library again?"

"No. I have to use the library for reference work. I have a part-time position doing research for some of the professors. I gather information for them, grade papers, that sort of thing." She seemed nervous and anxious to leave.

"Oh really," he said. "That sounds interesting. I suppose helping them prepare test material is grueling."

"Yes, it is. I'm sorry, Henry, but I really have to run. It's nice seeing you again." She moved quickly around him, lowering her head down as she walked into the library. She could feel her heart pounding in her chest. Grace often thought that someday she may run into him, but she had never really prepared herself for this day.

It didn't take long to find out where she was living. There were only three women's hotels in Chicago. On the second telephone call, he located her. He chose a florist near the hotel and ordered a dozen yellow roses to be delivered to Grace along with a note.

> *My Dearest Grace,*
>
> *How good it was to see you again. I have missed you and have wanted for so long to express to you my deepest sorrow for any misunderstanding or hurt I have caused you. I saw you leaving the foyer of the residence hall that day so long ago. When I tried to reach you, you had already left the campus. Sadly, just hours later, I received a telephone call informing me that I had to return home immediately for a family emergency. When I returned to school, you had moved away and left your position at the library. I assumed that you no longer wished to keep company with me, since you did not leave a note or forwarding address. So with a broken heart, I respected your wishes. I will be at the Warwick Hotel Restaurant on Saturday evening at seven o'clock celebrating my birthday alone. I would be ever so grateful if you would join me for dinner. I am anxiously awaiting our meeting.*
>
> *Respectfully yours,*
> *Henry*

Henry rose from his chair as Grace approached the table. She had a yellow rose tucked in her hair. Henry smiled and held out his hand to her.

"Happy Birthday, Henry. Thank you for the beautiful roses," she said shyly. "I have a small present for you. It's just a box of handkerchiefs. I'm sorry I didn't have time to get you something nicer."

"It's of no matter, Grace. You being here is my best birthday present," he said.

"In your note you said you returned home because of a family emergency. Please tell me your parents are doing well," Grace said in a concerned voice.

"They are fine. I didn't mean to alarm you. It was Martin who was ill. He is my valet and also a dear friend. He had taken ill, but he has recovered fully now."

Their conversation during the meal was stilted. Grace talked about her job and he about his schooling. They both seemed preoccupied with their food, avoiding any talk about what had happened to their relationship.

As the waiter removed the last of the dishes from the table, Grace finally gathered enough nerve to tell Henry she overheard the remarks he made to his mother. It had upset her terribly and she assumed that Henry did not care for her at all.

Henry reached across the table and took her hand. "I don't know where to begin, Grace," he said with a pleading look in his eyes. He worked very hard to convince her that what she heard that day was as an attempt to save her the embarrassment of spending time with his mother's friends who would also be at the summerhouse. His mother refused to take no for an answer, insisting that Henry bring Grace home with him. Aware of how nosy and insensitive those women were, he didn't want Grace to suffer through their condemnation. He wanted to protect her from their prying. Only by saying these cruel things to his mother was he able to convince her not to press the issue. He sighed and rubbed his head, as if he were in great pain.

"I must tell you, Henry, when I received your flowers and note, I decided I would not meet you here tonight. You hurt me deeply, and I didn't want to give myself any false hope that this was anything more than dinner. I re-read your note several times and you seemed so sincere. I'm glad I came, Henry."

He looked at her with sorrowful eyes. "You know I never meant to hurt you, Grace. I have missed you and thought about you often."

She had so many questions. How was his family, his grades, and was he seeing anyone? With each answer and apology, Henry became more and more convincing. She wasn't sure if it was just that she wanted so much to believe him and relieve the ache in the back of her mind, or if she had truly been wrong about him. She was beginning to fall for his pathetic lies. The feeling that she was not good enough for him had caused her to doubt herself. By the end of the evening, it was Grace who was apologizing for not giving him a chance to explain. Holding her arm, he walked her back to the hotel. When they reached the steps, he kissed her cheek and said goodnight, making sure she agreed to see him again. As he turned to leave, he began to whistle. Perfect, he said to himself, just perfect.

When Henry returned to the residence hall, Barrios was waiting for him. He sat on the steps, reading as usual. "Where have you been? I've been here for over an hour." He was agitated. "Do you think I have nothing better to do with my time than to wait for you?" Henry kept on walking, passing by the building as if he did not see Barrios. Barrios jumped up and began to follow him. "Don't walk away from me, Henry. We need to talk," he snapped.

Henry wheeled around. In the dark shadows of the building, he grabbed Barrios by the front of his shirt. "You listen to me you little shit, you know better than to come here, and what gives you the right to threaten me?"

Barrios didn't back down; he slapped Henry's hand away and smoothed his shirt. "Okay, smart boy, you want to know why I'm here. I'll tell you. Finals will cost you one thousand dollars. The money will be payable in advance."

Henry threw his head back and laughed loudly. "You can't be serious. There is no way I can pay you that kind of money even if I had it, which I don't."

"I suggest you find some way to get it, if you want to get a passing grade. This is the last of the finals and I will never have to look at your worthless face again." Barrios crossed the street, dodging cars as he disappeared into the darkness.

Henry cursed him out loud. He would have to find a reason to get the money from his mother. That could wait till tomorrow. He was too tired to worry about it now.

There was a message waiting for him that his father had called several times while he was out of the dormitory. That was unusual. Henry wondered what was so urgent. Calling home, it was his mother who answered the telephone. Joseph would be in Chicago Friday on a business trip and he wanted to make sure Henry was available to see him. Henry tried to coax the information from his mother, but she said she had no idea what was going on. "By the way, Mother, I really could use some extra cash. I have been seeing Grace again, and I would really like to buy her something nice."

"I'm so glad you two are back together again, darling. You know I have always been fond of her, but unfortunately I don't have any extra money at this time," his mother replied.

"You're joking aren't you? You have nothing at all that you could send me?"

"I'm sorry, Henry, but I have no extra cash. Perhaps your father can give you a few dollars when he sees you on Friday. Good bye, dear."

His mother hung up before he could ask again. What is going on? Maybe his father discovered that his mother had been sending him money. That is probably why he was coming to Chicago. Henry had to prepare himself for the wrath of Joseph Franklin.

On Friday, Henry met his father in the lobby of the residence hall. Joseph looked tired, his clothes rumpled from the train ride. In his dormitory room, Henry motioned to his father to sit down. Joseph sat quietly for a moment, his head bowed.

Henry grew impatient. "What is it, Father? Is something wrong with Mother?"

Joseph put his head in his hands and began to sway back and forth. "I wish I knew a kinder way to tell you this, Henry, but there isn't. I thought I was holding my own with this damn depression, but I was wrong." He walked across the room and sat down on the bed next to Henry. "My accountant kept warning me, but I was so busy with my practice, I just didn't pay enough attention to what he kept telling me. I thought I was being frugal. He called me earlier this week with some very disturbing news. It seems after he reviewed all of my accounts, I have very little money left."

"What about my inheritance? The money you promised me is surely in a safe place." Henry could hear his heart beating in his chest, his breath coming in short gasps.

His father continued talking as if Henry was not even in the room. "No, I'm afraid it is all gone. Except for your mother's jewels and a few dollars in the safe deposit box, we have very little cash at our disposal. We have decided to sell our estate in Camberton and move to the summer home in Ternberry. It's much smaller and the cost to maintain it will be considerably less. Unfortunately, I had to let most of the staff go, except for Martin, of course, and a few others. I have hired a company to liquidate our assets. We are still waiting to hear the final outcome. Hopefully with a little diligence and hard work we can turn this money situation around quickly."

Henry began to sob. "Surely you have some money coming in from your practice and lecture tours?"

Joseph's face was ashen. "Most of my patients haven't been paying me for quite a while. Everyone is strapped. I had no idea my money had dwindled away. I thought we would have enough to live on for a while out of your mother's account, but strangely, she has been making large withdrawals for quite some time." Joseph shook his head. "Poor thing, she is so distraught, I didn't have the heart to ask her what she had done with all of the money. I have suffered with the decision to tell you this before graduation, but I felt you had the right to know. You know how I feel about keeping secrets in the family. Thank God you almost have your degree." Joseph suddenly seemed animated. "Son, we can do this." He had never in his life called Henry 'son.' "After graduation, you can do your residency in Massachusetts. I still have my offices in Boston." He paused for a moment. "At least I think I still do. Well, anyway, no matter. We can set up a practice together and in no time we will be just fine."

Henry was not listening. He just wanted to bolt from the room and run as far as his legs would carry him. All these years of planning and doing without his own personal comforts to support Barrios. Four years of his life gone. For what? He looked at his father, this tired old man, walking back and forth, still rambling on and he made a promise to himself that he would never be like him. He would have more money than his father ever had and more possessions. No one would ever take them away from him. "Just get out of here and leave me alone," Henry sneered.

It took Joseph several moments to realize that Henry actually meant it. "I know you are upset. I'll give you time alone to think about your options. I will see you at graduation." He left Henry sitting alone in the dim light of late afternoon wishing his father were dead. He probably had a pretty good life insurance policy.

Henry spent the next two days in bed with a bottle of acrid whiskey as his only companion. He staggered to the bathroom and back again, falling across the bed in fits of anger and disbelief. Someone had knocked on his door several times, but he never bothered to answer. The following day, they knocked again, this time with more urgency. Hollow eyed, his clothes stained with his own vomit, he stumbled to the door. "Who is it? What the hell do you want?"

A nervous voice filtered through the door. "Uh, I'm sorry to bother you, Mr. Franklin, but a Miss Grace Cardiff is trying to get in touch with you. She told me to let you know that she is worried about you." He could hear the footsteps moving hurriedly down the hall. Henry fell back into bed, waking in the morning with his head pounding. Dry mouthed and hungry, he made his decision. He had to find some way to graduate from school. He had little chance of coming up with a thousand dollars. What he needed was a new plan. Henry dressed and went to the telephone in the foyer. "Grace, could you please meet me in the campus park? I have something very important to ask you."

Grace shivered under the gray sky. It had been threatening rain all day and she hoped it would hold off until Henry got to the park. He had taken his time to bathe and shave after he called her. Brushing his clothes free of lint, he dabbed after-shave on his face. Smiling at his own reflection in the mirror, he put on his sunglasses to conceal his bloodshot eyes. It was time to put on the performance of his life. He walked briskly up the pathway and took her into his arms before she had time to protest. Henry kissed her tenderly.

Grace pulled away, laughing. "Henry, what on earth is the matter with you? Where have you been? I haven't seen you in almost a week and now..." before she could finish her sentence, he kissed her again.

"Sit down, Grace. We need to talk."

Henry told Grace about his father's visit and the loss of the family's wealth. "I had to take a few days to console my father. He was very distraught. I had to convince him that the money did not mean that much to me. It is now more important than ever to finish school and help my parents get back on their feet."

"I am so proud of you, Henry. Helping them would be a noble thing to do."

Without notice, Henry dropped to one knee in front of the park bench. Grace's eyes widened as he took her hand. "Grace Cardiff, I love you. I can't bear to live the rest of my life without you. I know I have very little to offer you right now, but I need you by my side. Will you do me the honor of becoming my wife?"

Grace gasped as he pulled her toward him. "I love you, too, Henry, but I need some time to think. This is all so sudden."

"Take all the time you want, Grace, but my love for you will always remain the same."

Grace wavered for only a moment. Tears began to roll down her face. "I'll marry you, Henry. I will be proud to be your wife."

Henry smiled to himself. Another part of his plan completed.

They talked about when and where to get married. Grace wanted to get married by a priest. Henry said he didn't care who married them as long as it was as soon as possible. He could look into lodgings for them in the residence hall. It would be comforting to have her with him as he studied for his finals and she could continue her position with the professors, to help out with the finances, of course. Grace wanted to call his parents, but he said no. It would be better to tell them when they came for graduation. After all, his father had a lot on his mind right now.

Henry and Grace were married the following Saturday in the campus chapel. Grace looked radiant in her white suit. He bought her a plain gold wedding band, which he placed on her finger, pledging his eternal love. The priest gave them his blessing and wished them a long and happy life together.

With the few dollars he had left, they spent their first night together in the Warwich Hotel honeymoon suite. Room service sent flowers and a bottle of champagne along with their dinner. Grace was nervous and was unprepared for the lust Henry possessed. Long after he had turned on his side and fallen asleep, Grace lay in the darkness wondering if perhaps she had rushed into the marriage. She never knew this side of Henry. She was unaware that this was the first of many nightly raids on her body.

When they returned to their new room in the residence hall, Henry had classes to make up and Grace returned to work. With the help of some of her friends, they managed to move her things into the cramped room she would share with her new husband. She put a white coverlet over the sagging bed and a small vase of flowers on the nightstand. Folding the lace tablecloth her mother had given her, she placed it over the chipped wooden table. Their lodgings were only temporary; it would have to do for now. The semester would be over in just a few weeks. Grace knelt next to the bed, her head bowed. She prayed to the Virgin Mary to give her strength to be a kind and loving wife for Henry.

Henry looked up from his reading as Grace came through the door. "You're home early. I thought you had to go to the library for a few hours?"

YARD SALE

She removed her hat and put on her apron. "I have some bad news, Henry. I can no longer work for the professors since I am now married to a student. They said they knew I would never provide you with information about their test questions, but it is school policy. I told them I understood."

Henry slammed the book down on the desk. "That's just great. I was counting on you staying at that position. I mean for the money. We barely have enough to live on now, and without the extra, it's going to be tough," Henry groaned. This was just his luck. Without those test answers he was still going to have to depend on Barrios. Henry had no idea where he would find the money to pay him. Why hadn't he thought to check the school regulations before he jumped into marriage?

"I can put my schooling on hold till the fall semester and take on more hours at my other job. That would help, I'm sure," Grace said. She wanted Henry to say that it wouldn't be fair to her, and they would make out somehow, but he didn't.

"I think that's a good idea. You can quit tomorrow," he said as he returned to his book. That was the end of the discussion.

When Henry met with Barrios he explained that he had just married and had used all of his money to set up housekeeping, but not to worry; his parents were sending him a large check for a wedding present. Henry was in a generous mood and wanted to share his good fortune so he was adding an additional five hundred dollars to the price they had already agreed on.

Barrios showed no emotion. He knew Henry too well. "So you are telling me I should continue to do your papers without getting paid. For how long?" Henry assured him it would only be for a couple of weeks. Barrios was not convinced, but the idea of getting five hundred extra dollars appealed to him. Grudgingly he agreed to Henry's terms.

"Who is this poor girl who has fallen for your lies, Henry? I feel sorry for her," Barrios said as he turned to leave.

"It's none of your damn business. Just keep your nose out of my personal life."

The papers were excellent. Barrios had studied well and now he wanted his money. He knew the finals were going to be grueling and he worried about getting caught cheating. They had been very lucky up to this point. All he needed was just a few more weeks to finish his schooling, and then he could go home. He was so close to his goal. With the fifteen hundred dollars, he could continue his studies at one of the city hospitals in Chile.

When Henry asked for another extension, Barrios was livid. Henry said his parents were out of town and he had not received their check. They argued and Barrios screamed angrily at Henry that he wanted his money and he wanted it now. Barrios told Henry to meet him in the laboratory after class. They could not take a chance continuing their conversation in the hallway.

Barrios looked at his watch. Henry was late as usual. He had spent the time waiting writing down his expenses and the final amount he wanted from Henry. He decided that fifteen hundred dollars was not enough. The door opened and Henry entered, looking back into the hallway to make sure no one had seen him. He crossed the floor and sat on the stool next to Barrios. Henry reached into his pocket and pulled out a stack of tattered papers and placed them on the counter in front of him.

"What is this?" Barrios asked, pulling the papers closer to him.

Henry smacked his hand and picked them up. "This is your fifteen hundred dollars. Seventeen notes that you have foolishly written to me over the past four years. I was smart enough to keep them."

Barrios still did not understand. "What are you talking about, Henry?"

"Well, amigo, you were stupid enough to put your demands of payment in writing. Dumb enough to tell me what papers you wrote for me. Face it my little friend, your butt is cooked. Do you understand that?" Henry shoved the notes into his pocket. "Technically mine is too, but you see, I really don't give a rat's ass. I have had it with this place. Of course I will understand if you want to go to the dean, who incidentally is a friend of my father's, so you just go right ahead."

Barrios sat there for a moment still trying to comprehend what Henry was saying. With his hands trembling, he jumped off the stool. "I know everything I have done for the past four years has been wrong, but at least I was doing it so that I might be able to do some good in this world. But you, you don't have a conscience at all do you, Henry? Your soul is as black as the devil's. What do you want out of this life?"

"Just two things, Barrios, money and more money." He patted the pocket where he had placed the papers. "So what's it going to be, a passing grade for me or a boot in the ass for you?"

Barrios put his head in his hands as tears began to well up in his eyes. "I could have been a good doctor, Henry. I could have saved more lives in one day than you could have in a life time."

"Oh please, spare me your sad little story. I'm sure your parents would love to know how you got your degree. See you in class." Henry flipped off the light as he left, leaving Barrios standing in the darkened laboratory.

It had begun to rain when Barrios left the building. He pulled his frayed collar up around his neck, and clutching the front of his jacket, he made his way across campus, not really sure where he was going. He was crying; the tears mixed with the rain blurred his vision. He had shamed his family and himself. He would go to the dean right away and tell him what he had done. Hopefully the dean would be merciful and not tell his parents why he was being expelled. He had to do this; he had to clear his conscience of all the terrible things he had done. This time he would not give into Henry's demands. The overwhelming guilt he felt was just too great to live with the rest of his life. His feet were numb from the frozen rain as he began to run. Barrios stepped into the darkened street with his head down. He didn't see the car coming. For a split second there was a flash of light before him.

On the second page of the morning paper there was a small article about a student who was hit by a car on the Chicago School of Medicine campus. He was pronounced dead at the University Hospital. His name was Alejandro Barrios.

Chapter Twelve

"What are you doing?"

"I'm dusting."

"Well go somewhere else and dust. Can't you see I'm trying to study?"

"I'm sorry, Henry, I didn't mean to disturb you," Grace said as she folded the cloth and put it under the sink. She sat down and laid her head against the faded chair, trying to hold back the waves of nausea that swept through her body. She closed her eyes, but it only made it worse. It was too soon to go to the doctor. She already knew what he was going to say. How would she ever break the news to Henry? He seemed unusually stressed since the death of one of his classmates. When she asked Henry if he knew him, he became angry and left the room.

It was difficult for Grace to understand what had happened to her. She never knew being married was going to be such a struggle. Her parents always seemed so happy. That is what she wanted. After all, she and Henry loved each other. She couldn't understand why he was always in such a foul mood. She wondered if he was sorry he married her. Perhaps she wasn't being a good wife to him. He was hardly ever at home and when he was there, he very seldom talked to her. He complained about the cheap cuts of meat she bought to save money, shoving his plate across the table. At times, he would pull his clothes from the closet, throwing them on the bed in a heap. He was upset with the way she had ironed his shirts. Henry wanted them all hung in the same direction, with only the two top buttons closed. At night in bed, he would reach for her, even sometimes over her protest, throwing his body on top of her. In her own mind, she knew this wasn't right. Her mother had told her once that when two people love each other, the tenderness would show itself in the darkness of night. Where was that tenderness? Surely not in her bed. Grace rose from the chair and put the kettle on the burner.

"Would you like a cup of tea, Henry?"

He stood up, stretching his arms over his head. "No, what I really want is a beer." He grabbed his jacket from the coat tree and left without saying goodbye.

Henry shoved his hands into his pockets and headed toward the bar. He stayed out until after midnight, knowing that tomorrow would begin the first day of finals.

The news that he had failed all of his finals came as no surprise to Henry. Staring down at the paper returned by his chemistry professor, he read the words, "failed" in large red letters. Tearing off the top page, he put the test in the stack with the others, and tossed them in the wastebasket as he left the building.

Grace had made a special dinner to celebrate the end of the school year. She knew Henry would be jubilant. She waited for hours, sitting by the window, watching the sun set behind the line of trees across from the campus. Her potatoes were now a pale shade of gray and the meat had shriveled and stuck to the pan. She cleared the table and went to bed, falling asleep long before he came home. Henry had been drinking again; he smelled of cigarettes and stale beer. He staggered as he tried to remove his pants, shaking the flimsy bedstead.

Grace sat up. "Where in the world have you been?" she said, startled by his appearance. Henry looked at her with bleary eyes. "Celebrating, yes sir. I've been celebrating."

"I made dinner," she stated.

"Well, good for you," he said as he let his shoes drop to the floor before falling back across the bed. Grace rose and turned on the light.

"Jesus, what are you trying to do, blind me?" Henry covered his face with the pillow.

Grace was shaking. "Listen to me, Henry Franklin. I worked today and I rushed home to make a decent meal for you that is now in the trash. I sat and waited until I was too tired to wait any more, and besides that I'm pregnant." The words just tumbled out. That is not how she intended to tell him. Henry peeked out from under the pillow.

"You're what? Jesus Christ, is there anything else that can happen to me today?" He sat up in bed, feeling as though he was going to be sick at any moment. Grace fell into his arms sobbing, and for the first time in weeks, he held her close. He assured her everything was going to be okay. After all, he was almost a doctor; he could take care of her. He waited until he was sure she was asleep. His head was aching and he wanted to sleep, but he had no other choice. It was time to call in his final option. Quietly putting on his clothes, Henry made his way across the bedroom without turning on the light.

The campus was dark and quiet and a low fog had settled over the walkways. The massive oak trees with their twisted branches threw shadows on the path. Henry shivered as an almost eerie feeling came over him. He needed courage, lots of courage, to get through the next hour. Sipping on his flask of brandy, he made his way to the house at the end of the campus. Henry turned the flask up and emptied the last few drops into his mouth as he staggered past the hedgerow and onto the porch. Leaning his shoulder against the wall to steady himself, he banged on the door with his fists until he saw the hall light go on. Moments later Dean Parson answered the door, a striped robe covering his plaid pajamas. "Henry, it's the middle of the night. What is wrong?"

Henry pushed the door open and stepped into the entry hall. "I need to talk to you. It's urgent."

Dean Parson waved to his wife, who was standing at the top of the stairs. "Go back to bed, dear, I can handle this." He pointed toward the library and Henry pushed passed him, positioning himself in the large chair in front of the desk.

Dean Parson turned on the lamp. "Now, what in God's name is so important it can't wait until morning? Has something happened to your parents?" Henry pulled the test sheets from his pocket and threw them on the desk. Dean Parson picked them up, putting on his glasses. He sat down and began to study the papers. Shaking his head he said, "Well, this is unbelievable. You've done so well up till now. I suppose I could try to get you a few make-up tests, but I'm not certain it is even possible." Dean Parson was clearly irritated.

"Keep your damn make-up test. You can do better than that."

"Look, Henry, it's late and I am in no mood for your silly games. Get to the point," Dean Parson said as he threw his glasses down on the desk.

"Oh, I'm sure you wish this was a game." Henry tapped his finger on the papers. "I want a passing grade on all of these tests. Get out your pen and start changing these numbers."

Dean Parson stood up and leaned over the desk. He glared at Henry. "I think you had better leave right now. I know you have been drinking so I will pretend we never had this conversation."

Henry didn't move. He stretched his legs in front of him and leaned back. "Oh, but we are having this conversation. Let's talk about personal servants who work in your house and get paid by the school, including my wife."

Dean Parson's eyes narrowed. "I see, a little blackmail. Sorry, Henry, but it won't work. The school is well aware of what I do, and even if they didn't know, whom would they believe, me, or a failing student and his wife? I have a mind to call your father."

Henry reached across the desk and picked up the phone. "Here, go ahead and while you're talking let him know how much of his donations actually went to the school and what portion ended up in your back pocket."

Dean Parson slammed his hands on the desk. "You little son of a bitch. What gives you the right to accuse me of stealing? You have no proof that I took one dime of your father's money. Get out of my office and off this campus before I call security."

Henry still didn't move. He began laughing. "You're going to call security to come and remove me just like the night you were going to call them to get Rita out of your house."

"Rita! I don't know anyone named Rita!" Dean Parson said in an angry voice.

"Oh, that's right, you probably never knew her name. Who takes the time to find out a hooker's name? Well, the cab driver who brought her up here knew who she was." Henry reached into his pocket and pulled out the cameo brooch. He held it up to the light, like a jeweler examining a fine diamond.

The Dean's eyes widened. "Where did you get that brooch? It was stolen from my wife."

"You'd like for your wife to believe that wouldn't you? Funny, this was the only piece missing. I'm sure Rita would be glad to explain to your wife where she got it," Henry snickered as he twirled the brooch on his finger.

Dean Parson was stunned. "In all my thirty years I have never dealt with the likes of you. I can't imagine the shame your father would feel if he knew what you were doing."

Henry leaned back in the chair and propped his feet on the desk. He knew he was winning. He could see the sweat beads forming on the dean's brow. Dean Parson's face was red and he was shaking. "Either call my father or cut the bullshit Parson. It's no skin off your nose if I graduate."

Dean Parson sat in the chair facing Henry feeling defeated. He couldn't take the chance that Henry would follow through with his threats. He had less than a year left before his retirement. Any hint of a scandal would ruin him, not to say what his wife would do to him. "Give me the damn cameo and I'll take care of it."

Henry grinned, "You take care of my grades and I'll send you the brooch." He rose to leave. "By the way, I'm not sticking around for your stupid graduation. Just send my diploma to my parents' home in Ternberry." This time, as he left the dean's house, Henry picked up a pot of flowers and smashed it, sending pieces of pottery and dirt flying across the porch.

He slept late the next morning. Grace had already left for work, leaving him a biscuit and some jam on the table. She had pulled the shade up as she did every day, telling Henry that the morning sunshine was like a glass of orange juice. He would have preferred vodka in his glass of orange juice. He dressed, ate two bites from the biscuit and headed across the campus.

Henry approached the counter at the student registry hall and took a deep breath. A pinched-faced lady was behind the counter talking on the telephone. Henry waited a few moments while she chatted. He began to drum his fingers on the counter. She covered the mouthpiece with her hand. "May I help you?" she said in an impatient voice.

Henry smiled, "You sure may. I'm sorry to interrupt your call. Unfortunately, I cannot be here for graduation and I want to make sure you have the correct address to send my diploma." She laid the phone down and pulled a large gray ledger from the file cabinet. Henry could feel his heart beating in his chest, fearing that at any moment the door would open and security would drag him screaming and kicking from the campus. He had to remain calm. When she looked up and asked his name, he smiled again.

It seemed to take forever as her finger traveled down the page. "Franklin, Franklin, yes, here it is. Oh my, aren't you a special one. The dean himself has signed off on your grades. The address I have is in Port Arthur, Massachusetts. Is that correct?"

"That's just fine, thank you." Henry gave a sigh of relief as he left the campus without looking back.

He stopped by the florist and the bakery on the way home. When Grace opened the door, Henry was sitting at the table. He had lit the candles on a small white cake and placed three yellow roses in a water glass. "Happy third month anniversary," he said. " I have a present for you," Henry said as he pinned the cameo brooch on her dress lapel.

"Henry it's beautiful. I am so surprised. Thank you so much."

"It's over Grace, it's finally over. I have passed all my finals and tomorrow we are leaving this place forever."

"But Henry, what about graduation? You have worked so hard for this moment. It's only a week away. Surely you want to stay to walk across the stage and receive your diploma."

"I wouldn't care if it was in two days. We are leaving this hellhole forever. I will not have my pregnant wife living in a place infested with germs and rats," Henry said as he took Grace into his arms. " I didn't want to tell you, but I have seen signs of rats around here for a while and last night I saw one run across the bedroom floor. This morning when I woke up, I found a half-eaten biscuit on the table. It makes me sick to think those animals are eating off of our table."

Grace gasped. "I am so very afraid of rats. I remember when I was young they would creep into our house at night. My father would kill them with a rake and I would cover my ears to keep from hearing them squeal. When we lived in the tenement we heard stories about rats that climbed into the cribs of babies at night." She shivered at the thought. "But how can we get ready so quickly?" she asked. "I have to resign my job. We have to pack our things." Grace was flustered.

Henry jumped onto the bed like a ringmaster in a three-ring circus. He directed her attention around the room. "Ladies and gentlemen, in this corner we have one rocking chair with a cushion covering the hole in the seat. Over here we have one beat up old table and two mismatched chairs, and let's not forget this bed, complete with a lumpy mattress and sagging springs. See anything we need? I don't. Let the next poor bastard who moves into this rat hole have this shit. All we need is our clothes."

"Henry, watch your language." Grace giggled as she watched Henry jump up and down until the bed slats gave way sending the mattress to the floor with a loud thud. She felt as if her life was finally coming together and all the mean things Henry had done and said to her were now over.

The next day, Henry wired his parents that he was on his way home, telling them that he had passed his finals and had a big surprise for them. Grace wrote a short letter to the headmistress of the school, begging forgiveness for not giving her more notice. On the way to the station Henry reminded her several times that there was no need to bring up the past to his mother.

Grace was worried his parents would be upset that they had married without telling them and now with the baby coming, the situation may be even more complicated. Henry assured her everything would be fine. He fell asleep on the train, while Grace tried to fight off the nausea in the swaying passenger car. She put her hand over her beautiful new pin and prayed to the Virgin Mary to keep her baby safe and for Henry's parents to accept her into their family.

Chapter Thirteen

Martin was waiting for them at the station. He stood by the car in his black chauffeur hat, looking much older to Henry. His back bent, he walked with smaller steps. Henry helped Grace off the train and walked toward the car.

Martin doffed his hat and bowed, "The prodigal son has returned, and whom may I ask is this lovely lady?"

"This is my wife, Grace," Henry replied.

Martin took her hand and kissed her fingers. "My dear, you must be a saint."

As they pulled away from the station Grace leaned forward in the seat of the car. She didn't want to miss anything. It wasn't long before the city yielded to tall aristocratic pines lining the road and thick underbrush dotted with yellow wildflowers that covered the ground. She rolled down the window, listening to the crunch of the pinecones under the wheels of the car. As they rounded the final turn, she could smell the crisp salty air as the ocean exploded before them. The ebullient surf crashed against the jagged crag of rocks onto the shores of Ternberry. The house was visible now, rising above the tall yellow grasses, which seemed to be waving to her. It was a large white clapboard with blue shutters. The afternoon sunlight turned the upstairs windows a brilliant shade of gold. "Oh my goodness," Grace said. "It's the most beautiful house I've ever seen."

"You have got to be kidding. I think you've been in the city too long," Henry said. She didn't care what he said at this moment; she loved it. She could picture herself sitting on the upstairs balcony rocking her baby as the summer sun sank beneath that invisible line that separated the ocean from the sky. She would hold her baby in her arms and amble along the catwalk at the very top of the house, watching the ships pass on their way to Boston. Ternberry reminded her of her beloved homeland, Wales.

Henry stepped from the car first and greeted his mother. She hugged him tightly. When she saw Grace, she let out a squeal. "Darling Grace, how are you? I am so glad you came to visit us."

His father stood on the porch watching and Henry knew it was time to break through the barrier. A lot depended on his relationship with his father. Joseph did not move. Henry slowly ascended the stairs toward him. He put his arms around his father. "I'm sorry I treated you so badly the last time we were together. You were right," he said in a hushed voice.

Joseph nodded and smiled. "We'll talk later." Henry was sure they would.

The news that Henry was not planning to attend his graduation was more of a shock to his parents than the fact that Grace and Henry were married and expecting a baby.

"I just can't believe you wouldn't want to be there," his father said, shaking his head. "Standing on that stage and receiving your diploma is the culmination of all your hard work. I do hope you change your mind."

Henry explained to his parents that he felt Grace was in no condition to continue working or living in the residence hall. He told them about the rats and the lack of sanitary conditions.

"Well, it really wasn't that bad," Grace said. "We had a fairly nice room." Henry glared at her and she hurriedly added, "but the rats, that was just too much for me to deal with."

Agnes insisted that Henry and Grace take the second floor for their private living quarters. There were two large rooms with an adjoining bath and a balcony on the ocean side of the house. Grace imagined that the white polished furniture reflected the coolness of the upstairs in the summertime when the breeze would waft through the sheer curtains. She put her arms around Agnes and kissed her cheek. "Thank you so much. This is more than generous of you. Of course we will only impose on you long enough for Henry to get established," Grace said as she leaned over the balcony and breathed in the fresh ocean air.

"Nonsense, you stay as long as you like. I have always loved this house. I hope you are comfortable here," Agnes said as she guided Grace on a tour of the remaining rooms.

The evening meal was a celebration. Joseph brought a special bottle of wine up from the cellar, kidding Grace that she was only allowed a tiny sip. Agnes was thrilled that at last she was going to have a grandchild. She also said that since they now entertained very little, it would be wonderful to finally have another woman in the house.

After dinner Henry and Joseph sat on the front porch smoking cigars and drinking brandy. Henry really wanted to bring up his financial situation, but before his glass was empty, Joseph handed him an envelope. "This is a small gift for your graduation and I suppose now for your wedding also. I wish it could be more, but that will come in time."

Henry peered inside the envelope, eyeing the five crisp one-hundred-dollar bills. "Thank you. This is most generous," he said wishing to himself that it had been more.

"I do have some good news, Henry. I have finally accepted the hospital's offer to become chief of staff. Now that I am no longer traveling, I can devote my time to the duties of running the hospital."

"That's wonderful, Father, just wonderful." Henry wondered what benefit his father's position would be to him. Surely as the chief of staff's son he would not have to work nearly as hard as the other interns.

Before going into the house, Henry took three bills out of the envelope. He handed the envelope with the remaining bills to Grace as she dressed for bed. Henry lay on the bed, his hands behind his head, watching her. Her waistline had now disappeared and a small rounded stomach protruded through her nightgown.

Grace sat at the dressing table, brushing her hair. She could see Henry's reflection in the mirror. "Why are you staring at me?" she asked.

"I was just wondering how long it would take you to lose all that weight after the baby is born."

She continued to brush her hair, the curls bouncing back around her face. "I have heard that some women are never the same size or weight after having a child."

"Well, that's a real comforting thought," he muttered to himself.

Grace pulled back the covers and climbed into bed. "I must remember to thank Joseph personally for the gift."

Henry shook his head. "There's no need to do that, Grace. I've already thanked both of my parents for the money."

"But Henry, two hundred dollars is a lot of money, especially the way our finances are right now. Besides, they were gracious enough to let us live in their house."

Henry answered in an angry tone. "Would you leave it alone for once? I told you I'd take care of it. My father would be embarrassed if you approached him about money." Once again the discussion was over.

Grace began to feel at home in Ternberry almost immediately thanks to the kindness of Agnes and Joseph. They seem to go out of their way to make her comfortable. As the weeks passed, Grace insisted that Martin include her in some of the lighter household duties and let her maintain the upstairs living quarters. This made her more comfortable and that she was not just a guest in the house.

Grace and Agnes were always talking. Henry wanted to know what was really going on between the two of them. He watched them walking on the beach or sitting on the balcony giggling like two schoolgirls. He wanted to know if they were talking about him. Whenever he asked Grace, she would say, "Oh, this and that, mostly woman things." He would just have to find out for himself. Waiting until he heard them in the kitchen together, he slipped behind the pantry door. Grace wore an apron over her ballooning stomach as she chopped the vegetables for dinner. Henry inched his way into position so he could hear what they were saying. Something about babies, or was it gravy? He wasn't sure.

"Looking for something, Henry?" Martin said as he silently crept up behind him.

Henry jumped. "Dammit, Martin, you scared the crap out of me."

Martin began to laugh as he removed the dinner plates from the pantry shelf. "I suggest if you would like to know what they are talking about, you just ask them instead of hiding in the pantry like a scared mouse. I don't think they would be amused to know you are spying on them."

Grace overheard them talking. "Henry, is that you? Whatever are you doing in the pantry?"

Henry stepped into the kitchen. "None of your business. I want you to stop cooking. You're not a servant anymore." He turned and stomped out of the kitchen.

Agnes patted Grace on the shoulder as she passed behind her. There was silence in the kitchen as Grace continued to slice the carrots with a vengeance. "I'm sure he is just upset about something that has nothing at all to do with you, dear, don't take it to heart. Let's go have a cup of tea on the terrace," Agnes said.

"Do you like living here?" Grace asked as she settled herself into the wicker chair.

Agnes drew her shawl around her shoulders. The afternoon sun was low on the horizon, sending a cool breeze across the terrace. "I do now and it's even better since you and Henry are here. It was very difficult for Joseph and me at first. After we lost most of our money, we had to sell off most of our possessions. The house had so many rooms and there were things I didn't even know I had. Selling them was not too disturbing, but I must say I suffered a good deal of stress when my furs and jewels left the house with strangers." Agnes stopped for a moment and sipped her tea. "I gave my precious swans to a dear friend of mine for safe keeping and I insisted that Joseph keep all of his books. Actually it was sort of a cleansing experience for both of us, but when I arrived here I suddenly realized that this was not my summer home any longer. I had no winter home to go back to." Agnes pulled the coverlet off of the back of her chair and laid it across Grace's legs. "I had to learn a new lifestyle. It was difficult learning how to be more self-sufficient and not depend on others to do everything. For some reason it has brought Joseph and me closer together. He still has a terrace to sit on and read his morning paper and he really seems to enjoy going to the hospital every day." She reached across and squeezed Grace's hand. "We now have you and a grandchild on the way and I couldn't be happier. I used to think that money was the answer to everything. How wrong I was."

Grace settled back into her chair. She looked over at Agnes and suddenly felt very close to her. Her respect for her mother-in-law had grown considerably. Grace yawned. "I'm not very hungry, I think I am going to go to bed. Tomorrow is Henry's first day at the hospital and I want to get up early to see him off." She bent and kissed Agnes on the head. "I love you," she said.

Grace backed into the bedroom carrying a tray. "Good morning, Henry. I brought you some coffee. My goodness, don't you look handsome?" Grace sat the tray on the dresser and watched as Henry put on his tie and jacket.

He cocked his head looking over his shoulder. "I don't have time for coffee. Is there any lint on the back of my suit?"

Grace brushed her hand across his shoulders. "No, you're fine. Are you nervous about going to the hospital?"

Henry pulled on his lapels and ran his hand over his hair. "Why should I be nervous? After all, my father is the Chief of Staff. What could go wrong?"

Henry received a warm welcome when he arrived at the hospital. Everyone wanted to meet the young Dr. Franklin. They shook his hand, patted his back and offered him coffee. He reveled in the limelight, thanking them and telling everyone how honored he was to be at the same hospital as his father. He was assigned to do rounds with three other interns and he listened carefully as they made their diagnosis on each case. Then writing on his own set of charts he would concur with them, hoping that the staff doctor would not ask him any questions. It seemed like a simple enough process.

Henry liked wearing his white coat with his stethoscope dangling around his neck. He would wink at the girls as he passed the nurses' station. He was tired of looking at his pregnant wife, who he had little desire to even be near. The nurses would greet him with a smile. The other young interns were eager to share information with the son of the chief of staff, hoping Henry might mention their names to his father. Most of the younger nurses were also agreeable in helping him to write prescriptions. He learned quickly which staff doctors to avoid and when to disappear. He also found that it was easier to work the night shift. The hospital was quiet, with not much going on in the early hours before dawn. He was able to get past his turn in the emergency room twice. Once his excuse was that he was not feeling well enough to work and blamed the other time on Grace's pregnancy. It wasn't as bad as he thought it would be. Not yet anyway.

Chapter Fourteen

Colin Joseph Franklin was born on a biting cold February afternoon. Martin had driven Grace to the hospital that morning. Henry was working the late shift and was asleep in the doctor's lounge when they arrived. One of the interns woke him, but he rolled over and said that he should be notified after the baby was born. After all, what could he do but get in the way. A few hours later, he wandered into Grace's room. She opened her eyes and smiled. "Have you seen him, Henry? He is so beautiful. I'm so happy it was a boy."

Henry nodded, "Yes, I just looked in on him. He's doing fine. You go back to sleep. I'll see you later." He ambled down the hallway to the nursery. Knocking on the glass, he mouthed the words, "Which one is he?" The nurse picked up a small bundle wrapped in a blue blanket. She peeled back the corner and held the baby up to the window. Henry stared at him for a moment, thinking to himself that he looked like a wrinkled old man. He returned to the lounge and fell back to sleep. This time he awoke to someone roughly shaking his shoulder.

"Get up Henry!" Joseph said. "You could at least stay awake long enough to go visit your wife and son. She has been asking for you for the last several hours."

Henry stretched and sat up. "Okay, I'm going. You needn't get so angry. It's only a baby." Joseph grumbled something and left the lounge, shaking his head.

The house seemed in constant chaos after Grace came home from the hospital with Colin. Colin was the center of Grace's world. She loved to just look at him, touch his soft skin, and rock him in her arms. There were times when the whole family, including Martin, would gather around the bassinette just to watch him sleep, except for Henry, who felt that they had formed a tight little circle, with him on the outside. How anyone could get that excited about a baby was beyond him. Grace could sense his antagonism. She tried to include him in the daily rituals surrounding the baby, but he always claimed to be too tired or too busy. At night he would become angry when Colin woke him with his wails of hunger. Grabbing his blanket and pillow he would retreat into the other bedroom.

Grace put Colin down for a nap and went to the kitchen to fold diapers. Henry was sitting at the table, with a napkin tucked into his collar, eating a sandwich. "I'm sorry, Henry, I was planning on making a nice lunch for you today. Do you want anything else to eat?" He shook his head and kept on eating. "Are you unhappy with me, Henry?" Grace sat down facing him. "I know it's been different since the baby came, but things will get back to normal soon, I promise."

"What is normal around here? I'm just unhappy with the whole situation. I'm tired of living here. Maybe it's time we move," he said throwing the sandwich in the sink.

Grace was stunned. He hadn't mentioned anything about being unhappy at Ternberry. "But I love it here! The fresh air is so good for Colin and your parents are always saying how much they enjoy our company."

"Don't be so naïve, Grace. Do you think they would honestly tell you the truth? You're the mother of their precious grandson. I'm so glad you're comfy here," he said in a whining voice.

Tears welled in her eyes. "Why are you being so mean? You know your parents love you and I have grown so fond of them. It would be sad to go now. I do believe you're jealous of my relationship with them and the baby." She knew she should not have said those words as soon as they left her mouth. She didn't want to rankle him again.

Henry leaned back on two legs of the chair, glaring at Grace across the table. His eyes narrowed as he banged his hand on the table, causing her to jump. "Don't you ever say that again, do you hear me? I am not jealous of my parents, you or that baby. You're just living in a dream world. I hate the long damn drive every day."

Grace backed up against the sink as Henry paced across the room. His arms flailing, he continued to rant. "Sometimes I'm so tired I can hardly stay awake. Maybe it's me who needs to get away from here. It would be nice to have some privacy once in a while. If I could rent a small place near the hospital I could stay there when I'm on night duty." He stopped for a moment, trying to gauge her reaction. "You know the baby keeps me awake, and dammit, I need my sleep. I'm trying to make a living for my family." His voice softened as he rubbed his eyes, trying even harder to convince her how tired he was. "You know, Grace, living here in my parents' house I feel like I am being smothered."

Grace was relieved that he had calmed down. He just needed sleep and everything would be okay. "If you think we can afford it, maybe it's a good idea."

"I'll make sure we can," Henry said as he left the room.

The following week Henry found a two-room efficiency a couple of blocks from the hospital. Martin packed towels and linens for him and even threw in a small pot, in case Henry was so inclined to heat up a can of soup, which Martin doubted. He couldn't believe that Grace had bought into another one of his schemes, but Martin knew the whole family would be better off if Henry stayed at his little apartment and never came back. Joseph found the whole idea idiotic. He tried to talk to him, but Henry insisted it was all Grace's idea and he just wanted to make her happy.

Summer in Ternberry was like living in a Winslow Homer painting. The bright blue of the sea and sky seemed to melt together on the horizon, interrupted only by pure white clouds. The glistening sand held a rainbow of untouched shells and other treasures from the ocean. Clumps of golden sea oats lined the bluffs and tiny green vines with pink flowers found their way down the dunes to the shore. Agnes and Grace would take Colin to the beach every day. He would sit on his blanket and Grace would hand him smooth cream-colored seashells, which he tossed in the air with delight. They would build fantasy castles and watch as the waves came in to reclaim them. His skin had taken on a healthy glow and the sun had turned his hair the color of golden wheat. Henry said Grace looked like a beachcomber and should cover her head when she went out. The bridge of her nose was now covered with small round freckles, but she didn't care. She loved to take off her shoes and walk in the shallow pools formed by the big brown rock that sat just below the bluff. In the evening after she read to Colin and tucked him into his crib, Martin would sit with him while she walked on the beach and climbed onto the big brown rock. Grace loved to sit and look out into the endless ocean as the sun claimed the horizon in those last few minutes of daylight.

Henry was gone most of the time and Grace felt guilty that it didn't bother her. When he was away there was peace in the house. There was music from the radio and the off-key voice of Joseph would ring out as he sang some foolish children's song to Colin. Agnes would shake her head and laugh. They had quiet conversations at dinner, interrupted occasionally when mashed potatoes or carrots were thrown on the table from Colin's high chair tray. When Henry was home, Grace had to feed the baby in the kitchen. Henry said he wanted quiet and a civilized dinner without someone else's food on his plate. Grace began to sense a growing tension between Henry and his father. They very seldom spoke to each other when they were both in the house. When she asked Henry what the problem was, he said it was just hospital business and for her not to worry.

It was early on a Saturday morning when Grace heard Joseph call up the stairs to Henry in an irritated voice. She knew Henry was still sleeping, but Joseph's insistence woke him. He came down the stairs still stretching and yawning and called to the kitchen to have someone bring him a cup of coffee. Grace laid the grocery list on the counter and walked into the hall with the coffee. She heard voices, loud, angry voices. She stopped outside the study door.

"Dammit, Henry, I don't expect to keep getting these reports about you from the staff doctors. What the hell is the matter with you? You know you never leave a patient alone in that condition." Joseph was almost shouting.

"I had to go to the bathroom, that's why I left," Henry replied in a whining voice.

"Well, the next time, just piss in your pants. When you're given an order, you are to follow it to the letter. You could have cost that man his life."

Now Henry's voice was getting louder. "Oh, you mean the illustrious Dr. Fields told you that I am not following his orders? Well, he's wrong. I've bent over backwards for him. The self-righteous bastard yelled at me right in the hallway in front of everybody. He tends to forget that I am your son."

"He has a right to yell at you wherever and whenever he wants. He is in charge of that floor and the interns that work for him, including you! And dammit, Henry, stay away from the nurses' station. It doesn't look good for you to be hanging around those young girls. They have work to do and so do you."

Grace could feel her face getting flushed. She was embarrassed to hear this. As he turned to leave, Henry slammed the door of the study sending two of the glass panels crashing to the floor.

"You're going to pay for those, too," Joseph said angrily.

Henry left the house and was gone for three days. Grace was worried about him. He had never been gone this long. She called the hospital, but they said he had left messages at the desk that he was sick and wouldn't be in to cover his shift. There was no answer at the apartment. She decided she would have Martin drive her into Boston.

Martin agreed to take her even though it was against his better judgment. Before leaving for the city, Martin called the apartment manager telling him it was imperative that he speak to Henry. He waited a few moments until a groggy voice answered the telephone. "Henry, this is Martin. I just wanted to tell you that Grace and I are coming to Boston this morning to see you. I suggest if you have anyone or anything in your apartment that shouldn't be there, you take care of it right now." Martin hung up without waiting for a reply. He cared too much about Grace to let Henry hurt her again. Even though he would love to tell Grace what a true bastard Henry was, he knew it was not his place. He wished that somehow she could come to that conclusion on her own and soon.

Grace knocked lightly on the door. It took a moment until he answered.

"Come in, it's open." His voice was raspy and low. He was lying in the bed, covered to his neck with blankets.

"Oh my goodness, Henry, you really are sick." She put her hand on his head. "Why didn't you call me? I would have come right away."

He sat up in bed, his clothes rumpled with the stubble of two days growth on his face. "I didn't want to bother you. I know you have your hands full with the baby."

"Please come home with me. You need someone to take care of you," she pleaded.

"I'm beginning to feel better today. In fact, I'm planning to take my shift at the hospital tonight. I feel bad that I've missed so much time at the hospital."

"Are you sure? Perhaps I should stay here with you. Let me get you a damp cloth," Grace said as she walked toward the bathroom. Her eyes traveled around the room. Nothing seemed out of place. In the bathroom, she opened the hamper and the medicine chest. What was she looking for? She felt so guilty. It was Joseph's remark about the nurses that she couldn't get out of her mind. Henry convinced Grace there was no reason to stay with him. She was reluctant to leave, but he assured her he would be home tomorrow. She kissed his cheek and left without ever mentioning the nurses.

Henry reached for the paper bag he had stuck under the covers. It was time to empty the trash. Inside the bag were a few empty whiskey bottles, sandwich wrappers from the deli and a pair of white nylons with a runner in the left heel.

Joseph sat in his office with his head resting on his hands. He was exhausted. It had been a long day with back-to-back surgeries that took every ounce of his concentration. He had checked on his patients and they both were doing well. Once he had looked through his mail and messages, he would be on this way home. He rifled through the stack of papers on his desk. One marked "confidential" caught his attention. He groaned. It was another complaint about the quality of Henry's work. He hoped after their last heated conversation that Henry would try to do better. The whole situation was becoming a source of embarrassment to him and the hospital. Joseph felt totally responsible. Why had he pushed so hard for Henry to become a doctor? How could he have done so well at school and his performance at the hospital be totally unsatisfactory? Maybe he needed to have a talk with Dean Parson and see if he could shed some light on the situation.

He lay down on the couch and rubbed his eyes. It was time to make a major decision. After all, Henry now had a family. He needed to choose another profession other than medicine to support them. When the stock market took its toll on his wealth, Joseph managed to save the donation he planned to give to the medical school. It was the largest sum ever and had been put aside in a trust to be delivered to the school in

YARD SALE

January. Joseph decided he would call his attorney and have the money redirected to his son. Henry could then make his own decision about his life. Joseph slept in peace for the first time in weeks.

Chapter Fifteen

The cold gray days of winter and the tension between Henry and Joseph made Agnes decide it would be nice to get away from the house for a few days. It would give everyone a chance to cool down and perhaps keep her from getting depressed about spending her first winter in Ternberry. She wanted to visit old friends in Pittsburgh and stop to do some shopping in New York on the way home. Joseph agreed with her. He needed a vacation too. He decided to make a truce with Henry, and asked the hospital to put Henry on light duty. As soon as he returned he would take his son to his attorney and have the money transferred into Henry's account at the bank.

Henry was in a good mood. His parents would be out of his life for a while and he had very little to do. He planned to spend most of his time in Boston. The idea of spending his free time at home with Grace and the baby did not seem very appealing.

Agnes hugged Grace and kissed Colin on his cheeks. "Oh, you little sweetheart, your grandmother is going to miss you."

Joseph patted Henry on the shoulder. "Take care of our family. We'll see you in a few days. I have a surprise for you when I return." Joseph waved and got into the car. He rolled down the window. "Think about what you want to do with your future while I'm gone."

Henry watched the car as it pulled away, wondering why his father always had to play these stupid mind games. His father knew damn well that Henry had very little choice when it came to his future.

Grace cuddled Colin, as he struggled to free himself from her arms. "This could be a nice vacation for us, too. I mean, we have the house all to ourselves. We can spend some time alone together, just the three of us." Henry smiled and walked inside. Tomorrow he would make up some excuse and go back to his apartment.

YARD SALE

The telephone ringing woke Grace from a sound sleep. She turned and pushed Henry gently in the back not wanting the shrill sound to wake Colin. Her eyes focused on the clock. It was five a.m. It was probably the hospital calling.

Henry fumbled for the phone, half asleep. "This is Doctor Franklin." He was silent for a moment. Throwing the covers back, he sat up on the edge of the bed. The silence continued and his questions began. "When?" More silence, "Where? Are you sure?" Henry turned to Grace. "It's my parents. There's been an accident."

Suddenly everything began to move in slow motion and her eyes fixed on Henry's mouth. He was saying words, Pennsylvania, mountains, fog. "Oh my God, are they hurt?" She was shaking as she grabbed Henry's arm. "How badly are they hurt?"

Henry waved her away. "Be quiet for a moment so I can hear what this man is trying to tell me." They spoke for a minute longer. Henry put the receiver back on the telephone and got out of bed. Reaching for his pants, he began to get dressed.

She couldn't wait any longer. "Henry please, are you going to tell me what happened?"

"They must have gotten lost in the fog last night. My father probably made a wrong turn somewhere. There was a sharp curve in the mountain road. The driver in the truck behind them saw it happen. He said the car just flew off the mountain, careening down the slope."

"How can he be sure it was them?"

"The driver ran to see what happened, but by the time he got to the edge of the embankment the car was already engulfed in flames. He hurried to the next town and got the police. They tried to climb down to the car, but the embankment was too steep. The officer I spoke to informed me that the search team found some of the luggage that had been thrown out of the car. It belonged to my parents."

Grace put her hands over her ears; she didn't want to hear this anymore. She didn't want that image in her mind. Her cherished Agnes and Joseph were gone. In an instant, while she slept, they were gone. She put on her robe, checked on the baby and went to Martin's room to wake him. It was as if she were walking in her sleep through a bad nightmare.

Martin and Grace sat in the parlor; their arms wrapped around each other, tears rolling down their faces while Henry paced the floor waiting for a call from the Pennsylvania coroner to confirm what he already knew to be true. The coroner finally called and said he would issue death certificates even though they could not recover the remains.

The next few days were chaotic. There were reporters at the house, each wanting an exclusive story about the death of Dr. Joseph Franklin and his wife. Martin intervened, answered their questions and sent them away. Telegrams and cards arrived daily from all parts of the world, along with baskets of fruit and flowers. The telephone rang nonstop until Henry took it off the hook. Grace stayed in her room. She felt as if she had a hole in her heart. She had loved them almost as much as her own parents. Her grieving kept her awake at night, and it was only Colin who kept her centered during the day. She had no idea what Henry was feeling. He hadn't cried at all and seemed to be quite calm.

The hospital wanted to hold the memorial service in the chapel, and Henry agreed. The sanctuary was filled to capacity, spilling over into the hall. It was only when Henry stood at the podium giving a heart wrenching eulogy to his parents that Grace fully understood the extent of what she thought was Henry's grief. She wanted to hold him in her arms. She never knew it was Martin that had written the eulogy the night before the service. Martin had found Henry asleep on the couch in the library, with the smell of whiskey on his breath. He sat down at the desk, tears rolling down his face as he wrote the poignant words he would like to say to dear Agnes and Joseph. He laid the paper on Henry's chest and went to his room to mourn.

The weather turned cold with chilling winds blowing across the dunes. The dark gray clouds hung over the bay most of the week. It rained almost every afternoon and Grace could not take Colin out of the house. He was cranky; teething on her fingers as she rocked him silently back and forth in the chair Joseph bought her the day Colin was born. Henry was tired of Grace moping around the house and told her to find something constructive to do, like clean out the closets in Agnes's bedroom. Grace couldn't bear to do it alone and asked Martin to help her. The closet smelled of Chantilly. It was Agnes' favorite and she wore it all of the time. Grace took the bottle of perfume off of the dresser. Holding it close to her, she crumpled to the bedroom floor and sobbed. Martin said it was too soon and they should leave it for another time. They drank tea in the kitchen and talked about their memories. Martin managed to bring a smile to Grace's face with stories of his life with the Franklin family. She was grateful for him.

Henry was slumped down on the sofa in the library, drinking a glass of brandy, when Grace entered. "Martin told me you resigned your position at the hospital. Why didn't you tell me?" she asked.

Henry sat up. "It is no business of Martin's what I do. I could not face going to the hospital every day without my father. It was too painful. Besides, we have this house now and I'm sure my father had a decent life insurance policy. I should just fire Martin for butting into my business."

"Oh my goodness, Henry, don't say that!" Grace gasped. "Martin is just like family. He loved your parents too."

"He is a servant, Grace. I can let him go anytime I please." Henry knew he had Grace's attention. "I am going to go to Boston tomorrow and start settling my father's business affairs. I also need time away to get over my grief. This house is a constant reminder to me."

Grace slowly nodded her head. "How long will you be gone, Henry?"

"As long as it takes, Grace. As long as it takes."

Grace stood beside the car with her shawl wrapped tightly around her shoulders. She shivered as she waited for Henry to start the car. "The weather will be getting bad soon. We may get some snow. Please be careful. I don't want anything to happen to you. I'll miss you."

Henry put the car in gear and headed down the driveway. He smiled to himself. He had found some cash in his father's desk and he still had the key to his apartment in Boston. Yes sir, he would be careful.

While he was in Boston, Henry called on Mr. Phillips, his father's attorney. Mr. Phillips said it would take at least a month for him to finalize his parents' assets and process Joseph's will. Henry was angry. He did not want to wait and wanted the information as soon as possible.

Passing the hospital, Henry decided to stop before going to the apartment. When he finally made it to his father's office, after being stopped every few feet by someone wanting to extend condolences, he locked the door behind him. His father's extra pair of glasses still lay on the desk; his white jacket hung on the back of his chair. Henry walked across the room and sat down in the brown leather chair. Joseph's secretary had already removed all of the medical files and put most of his personal effects into several cardboard boxes. All of his books had been stacked in the corner. Henry glanced up at the wall that still held his father's certificates, degrees, and diplomas. He took them off the wall one by one and put them into an empty carton. Balancing the box on his hip, he kicked the door shut and left the hospital.

When Henry returned from Boston, winter had finally settled into Ternberry with a vengeance. Sleet and freezing rain covered the roads, making the driving treacherous. The winds blowing off the ocean were biting, rattling the shutters and windows with each gust as the temperature dipped below zero.

Grace put Colin to bed, covering him with an extra blanket. She sat at the table reading her book while she waited for the water to boil for her tea. She could hear voices coming from the dining room and wondered if Martin and Henry were actually having a conversation. Pushing the door slightly open, she could see Henry standing on a chair, peering into the top of the buffet. He was counting out loud and making notations on a small pad of paper. "Whatever are you doing?" she asked.

"Hush! You made me lose count…three, four…oh, dammit, I'll just put down twenty. If you must know, I'm going to take inventory of everything in this house."

"Whatever for?" Grace asked in a puzzled voice.

"I'm trying to decide what to sell and what we should keep." Henry jumped down from the chair and opened the paneled doors to the sideboard.

Grace was startled. "What do you mean? Why would you want to sell your parents' things and so soon? It's just too soon."

Henry threw the pad on the table. "Face it, Grace, living here in the winter is a nightmare. It's a great summer home, but I can feel the wind blowing through the whole house and trust me, it's going to get worse. This house is not built to be lived in year round. By summer most of the shingles will be off the roof and the roads will be full of holes and ruts. We do not have enough money right now to sink into repairs for this place. It's time for us to move on," Henry stated.

Grace was too drained and she knew it was useless to argue with him. She loved this house, even though it was lonely without Agnes and Joseph. She couldn't imagine leaving it. It seemed as though she belonged here. It was her home. "Where will we go?"

He seemed animated that she was interested in his decision. "I'm thinking we should move someplace in the South. Somewhere where it is warm. I can open a practice in a nice little town. It would be good for you to finally have a home of your own. You could be around other people for a change. Maybe even make friends with women your own age." By now Henry was pacing back and forth. "I have to see Mr. Phillips next week, then I'll have a better idea of what we can do financially."

Colin began fussing and Grace rose to leave the room. "Maybe you ought to wait a while longer. You might change your mind about leaving," she said as she left the room, not really wanting to hear his answer.

The meeting with Mr. Phillips was scheduled for ten o'clock. Henry waited anxiously in the reception room, shifting his weight from side to side in the chair. He had a rough idea of the amount of money his father left him, but of course he hoped for more. If his calculations were right, there should be enough to make their life quite comfortable. He told Grace it would be better if he handled this matter on his own. He said all this talk of money and property might make her even sadder.

Mr. Phillips welcomed Henry into his office, motioned to a chair in front of him and offered him coffee. "Well, Henry, let's see what we have here. Unfortunately your father has not changed his will since he lost most of his estate in the stock market crash. He called me just before his death and wanted to set up a meeting, but sadly it never happened. I just can't tell you how devastated I was when I heard the news of their deaths."

Mr. Phillips cleared his throat and began to read the will. It stated that Henry was entitled to all of his assets and holdings, with the exception of the summerhouse and its contents. His father had willed Ternberry to his faithful friend and companion, Martin Chancery.

Henry grasped the arms of the chair, his knuckles turning white. For a moment he was speechless. "What the hell do you mean, he left my house to his servant? There has to be a mistake! And what the hell are his assets?"

"Easy now, Henry, there is no use to get upset. Please let me finish." Mr. Phillips scanned the paper quickly, trying to find something positive to tell Henry. "Your father had an insurance policy through the hospital. It is not huge, but ample enough to buy another house for you and your family. I'm sorry, but except for the money left in trust to the school, everything else has been depleted. Of course, Martin may want to give you some of your parents' personal things from Ternberry."

Before he could finish, Henry was on his feet, stomping around the room. "Jesus Christ, I can't believe this. What the hell did I do to deserve this? Dammit, does Martin know about the will? Surely my father didn't tell him he was leaving Ternberry to him. What about the meeting he had planned with you? I'm sure he was going to change his will!"

Mr. Phillips was beginning to feel uncomfortable. "Getting this upset is not going to change things. Your father was a fair man. He never told me what the meeting was about, and Martin has known for some time that your father was leaving him the property. If you feel you want to contest the will, it is your choice. I may remind you that this could be tied up in court for a long time and you would need the services of an attorney." Mr. Phillips stood up and folded the papers, as a signal to Henry to leave his office.

Henry drove home in the icy rain, cursing and beating on the steering wheel. The car tires squealed as he sped into the driveway. Leaving the car door open, he took the steps two at a time. Henry flung open the front door and yelled at the top of his lungs, "Martin, where are you? Dammit, get in here right now."

Martin sat the tray he was polishing on the kitchen table and dried his hands slowly on a towel. He folded the towel neatly in half and hung it on the rack. Evidently Master Henry must have been to see the attorney today, Martin thought to himself. He smiled and casually walked into the foyer. Through all of Henry's sputtering and cursing, Martin was able to determine that he was quite unhappy with the will. "I want you to go see my attorney and have the deed to Ternberry put back in my name."

Martin folded his hands over his chest. "I don't think so, Henry. You are now living in my house." He felt badly for Grace and Colin. He had thought about giving the house to Henry, but now he could not bring himself to grant Henry his request.

Henry decided he would not spend one minute more than necessary in the same house with Martin. He answered several ads in the medical journal news for towns that were looking for a general practitioner. He decided he would leave Grace and Colin behind and try to secure a position and suitable housing before he sent for them. Even though it was close to the holidays, Henry said the sooner they found a new location, the better it would be for everyone. After the check came from the insurance company, Henry packed his suitcases and left Ternberry. He vowed to himself that he would never step foot in the house again.

The Thanksgiving holiday passed with little fanfare. Martin was sick with the flu. Grace made chicken soup and served him in bed. He was embarrassed and said he should be making her a big turkey dinner, but she still was not in the mood to celebrate. Christmas came and Henry was still not home. He wrote to her saying that he had been to several interviews and found some to be promising, but he hadn't yet decided. She could not understand what was taking him so long. With his credentials, finding a medical practice should be quite easy. Grace and Martin put up a small Christmas tree for Colin. They hung garland on the front door and put candles in the upstairs windows. On Christmas Eve they exchanged presents and watched as Colin played with the boxes and ribbons. Henry's present remained under the tree unopened.

"You're lonely, aren't you Grace?" Martin asked as he set the two plates on the dinner table.

"Yes, I suppose I am," she sighed. "It's Christmas and my husband is not even here to celebrate with us. If it weren't for you and Colin I just don't know what I would do," she paused, looking out at the ocean's tranquil surface reflecting a golden hue from the setting sun. "I still miss Agnes and Joseph."

Martin patted her on the shoulder. "I do, too. Such a tragedy."

"What are your plans now, Martin? I'm so sorry that Henry blew up at you. He had no right to deny you what Joseph wanted you to have. I want you to know I am happy for you," Grace said in an apologetic voice.

Martin smiled. "I wouldn't have expected any less of a reaction from Henry. Unfortunately, he has never liked me very much. Please don't take this personally, but the feeling is mutual." Martin caught himself before he continued. What he really wanted to say was that Henry was a self-centered, disrespectful bastard and she deserved much better, but Henry was her husband and he had no right to say those things to her.

"I don't wish to disappoint you, Grace. If it will make you happy, I will give the house to Henry. You know, of course, you can live here forever. I'll even be willing to put up with Henry. This is such a large house. I really don't see the need for you to leave."

Grace put her arms around Martin. "Thank you. I want you to know that Colin and I love you. You deserve this house. I would never dream of you giving it to Henry."

"That is the nicest thing anyone has said to me in a long time," Martin said in an embarrassed tone.

Grace helped Martin clear the dishes from the table. "You know, Grace, I have saved my money over the years. I've had very little to spend it on. When Joseph told me he was leaving me this house, I was elated that he thought that much of me. Yet I fully expected to be dead long before either of them. Now I would like to do some traveling. I have a few relatives still living in England and a very dear friend in Maine. I think I will still enjoy coming back here in the summer months. I will miss you and Colin. It would make me feel much better if I knew you were safe." Martin put the last of the dishes into the cupboard. "When Henry finds a position and drags you off to some God forsaken place, I want you to take most of this furniture. I certainly don't need it. It is just more for me to dust."

Grace shook her head, "Oh, I couldn't take your furniture."

"Yes, you can and you will," Martin was adamant. "Trust me, you will need it. And I do have one more thing for you." Pulling an envelope from his vest pocket he handed it to her.

"But you already gave me a Christmas present. What is this?"

"It's not another Christmas present. It's what I call your survival present. Wherever you are, if you need me or want to come back to Ternberry, you can use this money. I have also enclosed a key to the house. Please do not give it to Henry. It is for you and you alone." Martin covered her hand with his as she held the envelope. "Now put it somewhere safe."

even managed to visit. She lay in the hospital bed and worried about Colin at home under the care of his father. Grace wondered where they would be this time next year. Her life was disconnected and she no longer even tried to make friends in the new towns. Henry said that it was probably a good idea not to get too close to anyone until his practice was established, which of course, never happened. She knew they would be moving soon. Henry was giving her very little money, telling her that his practice was slow and he had only a few patients. He began to spend more and more time away from home.

Henry was sitting at the end of the bar, smoking a cigarette, another one of his new habits. His finger circled the top of the beer glass, as he tried to forget about his family and failing medical practice.

"Mind if I sit here? I need to take a load off my feet," someone said as he sat down on the next stool. Henry shrugged. Before he could turn back around, the man stuck his hand out.

"My name is Jim Rowert. What's yours?"

Henry extended a limp hand. "Henry Franklin."

Jim Rowert was a tall, emaciated man. His clothes hung on his body like those on a scarecrow in a cornfield. His complexion was pasty and sallow, and as he lit a cigarette, he began to cough. "Damn cough, I can't seem to shake it. I got to give up these weeds. I've been on the road all week. My nerves are shot."

Henry picked up his cigarettes and put them in his pocket. Putting fifty cents on the bar he decided to leave rather than listen to someone cough and wheeze all night. "I think you should take care of that cough. Stop by my office tomorrow and I'll write you a prescription for something to clear it up." At least maybe he could collect an office visit from Jim for listening to him cough half the night.

Jim grabbed Henry's arm. "No shit, you're a doctor? Give me your card, Doc. I'll be by first thing tomorrow if you think you can fit me in."

Henry smiled, "Oh, I'm sure I can manage."

Jim was waiting for Henry in the parking lot when Henry arrived at his office. He ushered Jim into his exam room and after a brief check-up, Henry wrote out several prescriptions and handed them to him.

"Well, Doc, do you think I'm going to live? Nothing fatal I hope." Jim Rowert began to laugh loudly, causing him to cough and gag until his face turned scarlet red.

"Just take these medications and you'll be fine."

"Come on by the joint tonight and let me buy you a drink," Jim said, as he paid his bill in cash and left.

Jim Rowert traveled from state to state selling heavy equipment for a manufacturing company. He made good money and liked to spend most of it on alcohol. He also liked to talk. He would buy drinks all night for anyone who would sit next to him and listen to his endless stories about his life on the road and his three ex-wives. Every night at the bar, Henry listened to him talk until he was sick of the sound of Jim's voice. Even free drinks were not worth another night of listening to Jim's stupid jokes and bragging. Henry looked at his watch, he knew by now Grace would be in bed and already asleep. He wouldn't have to put up with the cold stares she gave to him when he came home late after a night of drinking.

"Well, Jim, it's been nice talking to you, but I probably won't be seeing you anymore. I'm trying to line up a new position somewhere. This town is just not the right place for me."

Jim tugged on his jacket. "Listen, I got this friend who lives over in Stockbridge, Kansas. He owns this big manufacturing plant and he's been looking for a company doctor. Probably a young guy like you wouldn't be interested, but it's a gravy job."

Henry sat back down on the stool. "Tell me more about this place. What's it called, Stockbridge?"

Jim was more than happy to keep on talking. He ordered another round of drinks. "Well, he's got this factory and a lot of people working for him. Every time they get a hangnail, they want to run to the doctor and file a claim so they can get out of working and still get paid. It's driving him crazy. He needs someone there to put on Band-Aids and look at these claims. I gotta go take a whiz. You think about it." Before he left the bar, Henry had the name and number of Tom Sutton, the man he was to see in Stockbridge. He had a good feeling that this might be just the job for him.

YARD SALE

Henry traveled to Stockbridge the following week and Grace once again knew they were moving. She began to pack up the dishes and linens even before she knew where or when they would be relocated.

The interview with Tom Sutton was perfect. Tom couldn't be more pleased that Henry was willing to work for him. They discussed salary and before Henry could make his demands, Tom offered him a sizeable wage.

Stockbridge was by far the nicest place they had lived since leaving Ternberry. It was a large town with wide streets and rows of white houses with neatly trimmed lawns. Using the last of the money from his inheritance, Henry put a down payment on a house in a quiet middle class neighborhood. Grace was excited at the thought of finally settling down and living in their own home. When she arrived in Stockbridge, Henry took her to see the house. She walked through the rooms, opening closet doors and looking out the back door into the green fields behind the fence. Sitting down in the middle of the empty living room floor, she burst into tears.

"For Christ's sake, now what's wrong? I thought you would like this house," Henry said in an irritated voice.

"Oh, I do. I love it. That's why I'm crying." He shook his head and walked away.

Tom Sutton ushered Henry around the plant, talking over the roar of the machinery, ending up in the office that Henry would occupy. It had little resemblance to a doctor's office. There was a leather exam table, a small desk and a few cabinets containing supplies.

Tom threw his hard hat on the floor, sat down in the office chair, and propped his feet upon the desk. "Okay let's get some things straight, Franklin. I call a spade a spade. I don't know what your game is or why you're here and I don't want to know. As long as you have them shingles to hang on that wall, everything will be fine." He pointed his finger at Henry. "Now you're going to hear all kinds of bullshit complaints from these farts; everything from pulled muscles to smashed fingers. Some on the up-and-up, some just a load of crap." He tapped his fingers on the desk. "I have a business to run here. I'm counting on you to know the difference between a real complaint and con job. I want you to let some of these claims go through. Just enough to keep the union off my ass and the rest of the time you just patch them up and send their lazy butts back to work. Do we see eye-to-eye on this, Henry?"

"Yes sir," Henry replied. "No problem, Mr. Sutton, no problem at all."

Tom rose to leave. "By the way, you get a bonus for every one of those claims that get denied." He winked as he left the office.

Henry was elated. He would work hard to keep this job. It was exactly what he had been looking for. On his second day, he put his diploma and license on the wall of his office, along with the other certificates that had belonged to his father. The one hundred dollars he had paid to have Joseph's name replaced with his own and the dates changed was going to be a good investment. Tom Sutton was impressed as he looked over the array of frames on the wall.

"I still can't figure out what you're doing here, Henry. Just as long as it's nothing illegal everything will be just fine."

Within weeks Henry had devised a bonus plan for employees who had worked a full year without filing a claim. He instituted a safety program that gave time off to employees who were accident free for a year. At first, Tom balked, but when Henry showed him how much money he would save, Tom slapped him on the back and bellowed. He praised Henry for the fine work, not realizing that fewer accidents would mean fewer people Henry had to deal with.

After only a few weeks at the plant, Tom Sutton's invitation to his home for dinner came as a surprise to Henry. He had heard from the other employees that Tom was not one to socialize with the people who worked for him. Tom said he wanted to meet Henry's wife, but wouldn't mind if they left the kids at home. Grace was unsettled about hiring a sitter, but after a few calls to neighbors she managed to find an elderly woman who could come to their house. She dressed nervously, trying to look her best. It had been a very long time since she had been out for a social evening. Henry handed her the lint brush and she brushed the back of his jacket. He complimented her on her dress, but told her to do something with her hair, which insisted on falling into curls around her face. She pulled it back with a barrette, but at the last minute changed her mind and let it fall on her shoulders.

The Sutton house was by far one of the largest in Stockbridge. Its long cobbled driveway reminded Henry of his parents' home, and he was immediately jealous. Mrs. Sutton was pleasant, asking Grace how she liked living in Kansas and inquiring about the children. Tom and Henry laughed about things going on at the plant. It was an enjoyable evening. On the way home, Henry began talking about moving again. Grace sat up, her back stiffened, when he mentioned the word moving.

"Don't get all upset, Grace, I'm not talking about leaving Stockbridge. I was thinking I wouldn't mind having a house in Tom's neighborhood."

"We can't afford that kind of house. My goodness, it probably costs ten times as much as our house," Grace remarked.

"I don't care," Henry said, slapping his hand on the steering wheel. "I want what he has, that kind of house, the kind of car he drives, and his income. I had it all once, and by God I'm going to have it again."

"I like our house," she said softly.

Chapter Seventeen

The winters in Kansas were harsh, almost as bad as those in Massachusetts. Snow covered the ground for over three months while temperatures stayed below freezing. The children were restless. They were tired of the cold and no longer interested in making snowmen. Anna was lonely when Colin was in school. She sat at the window each day and waited for the bus to bring him home. On the days when the snow was too deep to go to school, Colin would cause most of the turmoil in the house. He could only tolerate his sister for a short time and delighted in teasing her. Anna would then scream at the top of her lungs, while Colin laughed and locked her out of his room.

Grace spent hours playing simple card games and making cookies with Anna and Colin to keep them entertained. She would run through the house with the children playing hide and seek. Of course, they knew when their father came home, all running and loud voices had to stop immediately. He did not tolerate what he called their disrespectful disobedience. In the evening, Grace would read to them or play tickle games. When the children laughed hysterically, the sound would bring Henry to their bedroom door. Grace would push their heads under the blankets. They would cover their mouths and try not to laugh. Those were the good times that made life with Henry bearable. His mood swings came less often now that he had a steady income, but his drinking had increased. It bothered Grace, but to keep peace in the house, she said nothing.

When spring finally blossomed in late April, the trees seemed to burst into bloom overnight. The crocuses and daffodils popped their heads up from the warm earth and the cool breeze was filled with the aroma of lilacs.

YARD SALE

Grace opened the bedroom windows, the curtains blowing in the cool morning air.

"Close the window, dammit, I'm freezing." Henry pulled the covers over his head.

Grace smiled. Nothing was going to ruin her mood. Today was Henry's birthday and she planned a special evening. With a few dollars put back every week from her grocery money, she bought Henry a new pale blue jacket. She closed the window. "Please try to be home tonight on time, and happy birthday."

He grunted as he got out of bed and headed toward the bathroom.

After Henry left, Grace pulled the linen trunk out of the closet. Underneath the extra blankets, tucked in the corner, she found the box that held the tablecloth her mother had given her along with the envelope from Martin. She had never opened Martin's letter and wondered if she should give it to Henry. She held the envelope in her hand remembering Martin's words to her. She put it back in the trunk. Grace spread the lace tablecloth over the dining room table. Smoothing out the wrinkles, she admired her mother's handiwork. She picked irises and daisies from the yard and put them in a glass bowl. Her afternoon was spent preparing dinner and making sure everything was just perfect. At six o'clock she set the table and fed the children in the kitchen. They promised they would be good while she had a special dinner with their father. Grace handed them a new box of crayons and two new coloring books as the front door opened.

"What's for dinner, woman? I'm hungry," he said in a slurred voice. She knew he had been drinking. Henry walked straight to the dining room and began eating before Grace sat down. He seemed to enjoy his food and asked for seconds. Only the ticking of the mantel clock and the silverware clinking on the china broke the silence.

"How was your day?" she asked.

Henry put down his fork and leaned back in his chair. "I had a good day. Tom called me into his office and," he stopped. "Grace, are you listening to me?"

"Yes, I just thought I heard the children," she said as she turned her head toward the kitchen door.

"God dammit, can't I finish one sentence without you worrying about the kids?" Henry was agitated.

"Momma, Anna just stuck a crayon up her nose!" Colin yelled.

Grace stood up. Henry lunged across the table, grabbing her by the wrist. "Sit down and finish your dinner." He glared at her. "Sit down right now, I mean it!"

Grace pulled away, rubbing her arm. "I just want to see what they're doing. You hurt my arm."

Henry jumped up. The chair tipped over backward and his plate crashed to the floor. As he whirled around to leave, his cuff button caught on the tablecloth, toppling the gravy boat and the flowers. "Get that damn rag off my table and clean up this mess! And by the way I saw that blue jacket you bought me. Take it back. What do you think I am, some kind of queer?"

She jumped as she heard the door slam. She knew he would be gone for the evening.

Colin and Anna had disappeared up the back stairs to her bedroom. They were huddled together in her bed. She went to her children and held them close, trying to soothe away their fears once again. When they were asleep, Grace washed and ironed the tablecloth. She folded it neatly and placed the envelope from Martin in between the folds. That evening, Henry apologized to her. It really didn't matter to Grace. Each argument forged a deeper wedge between them.

Chapter Eighteen

The war had begun in Europe and suddenly the factory was filled with new faces. Many of the men had been drafted, leaving vacant positions. To his dismay, Tom Sutton was forced to hire women to fill the void in the plant. The women came to work in tight blue jeans and snug fitting sweaters. They operated the machinery and forklifts. These same women came to Henry's office with blisters on their hands and bruised elbows. He made a point to wear his crisp white coat to work every day. They smiled at him as he walked down the aisles, pretending that he was there to check on the safety regulations.

On one particular day Tom Sutton watched from his office high above the whirling machinery. He tapped on the glass as Henry passed his window and motioned him into his office.

"Listen, Franklin, I just want to give you a word of advice. In a nutshell, stay away from the women. I want you to keep it strictly business. They have husbands and boyfriends and you don't need to be dipping your noodle where it doesn't belong."

Henry laughed; he had never before heard that expression.

"I'm serious," Tom, said sharply. "You have a wife of your own at home and you wouldn't like it if she were taking extra milk deliveries. Grace is a good-looking woman, Henry. I bet she could do better than you. She has those emerald green eyes, and that accent, it's a killer."

Henry was not amused. "What do you mean by that?"

"I'm saying you better play in your own backyard. I don't want any trouble in my company. Is that clear? I like you, Henry; you've done a lot for me. Just cut out the crap." Tom put on his glasses and started to read the newspaper. He had nothing further to say.

Henry hated him at that moment. He wanted him dead. He had no right to talk to him like he was some idiot. Tom wasn't his father and who gave him the right to talk about his wife? He wasn't actually jealous; he just didn't like someone else making remarks about Grace.

"Yes, we're clear." Henry forced a smile, and went back to his office to pout. The telephone was ringing when he opened the door.

"Henry, you've got to come home. Colin is sick," Grace said in an anxious voice.

He hated Grace calling him at his office with every trivial thing. "What's wrong now?" he asked.

Colin had complained earlier in the week of a sore throat, but when Henry looked into his mouth, he said it was nothing and told him to gargle with some salt water. The sore throat persisted and by Wednesday Colin was too sick to go to school. He began coughing and refused to eat.

"He's burning up with fever. I've taken his temperature twice in the last hour and it has gone up two degrees. I'm very worried about him, Henry." She stood by the bed, placing cold compresses on Colin's head. "I really think you should come home and take a look at him."

"Just give him a couple of aspirins and I'll be home as soon as I can." He hung up before she could say anything else. Grace called back twice, each time more concerned. The telephone rang in Henry's office, but he did not bother to answer it.

Jim Rowert had an appointment with Tom Sutton that afternoon. He invited Henry to stop off with him after work to have a drink. Henry paid no attention to the time and when he arrived home it was after eight.

Grace was frantic. She met him at the door. "Where have you been? I think we should take Colin to the hospital. He is so limp. He can't even open his eyes." She ran back to the bedroom. Henry followed after her, putting his hand on Colin's head. He could feel the heat radiating on his fingers. "I'm sure this is nothing more than a childhood virus. I want to wait until morning to see if the fever breaks. I'll call the pharmacy and get something to help him sleep."

By midnight Grace was in a panic. Wrapping Colin in a blanket, she called to Henry. "I'm taking him to the hospital, with or without you. If you won't take us, I'll call a cab."

Henry yawned, "Don't be ridiculous." He left to pull the car out of the garage while Grace called a neighbor to come and stay with Anna.

The hospital was fifteen miles away. She held Colin on her lap, rocking him back and forth; telling him everything would be okay. The emergency room doctor took one look at Colin and ushered Grace and

Henry into a waiting area. Grace tried to follow the doctor, but he assured her they would take good care of him.

"Listen to me, Grace," Henry whispered. "I want to do the talking. You are too emotional right now. I'll give the doctor all the facts. Trust me, I can handle this better than you."

A nurse appeared at the doorway with a clipboard in her hand. She needed Colin's medical history and answers to a few questions about his condition. "When did you first notice that his fever was over one hundred and five degrees? How long has he been sick? Have you given him any medication?" Henry answered the questions without so much as flinching.

"He's just been sick today, and no, no other complaints. My wife only gave him aspirin once this morning."

Grace stood up and touched Henry's arm. Before she could say a word, the nurse turned and left the room. "Why did you tell her that? He's been sick almost a week. I've given him aspirin every day and what about the medication you gave him to help him sleep? Don't you think they need to know the truth?"

Henry brushed her arm away. "They don't need to know all of that petty stuff, Grace. It's not going to help them diagnose his case. I think it would be best if you did not mention that I am a doctor. Doctors are not supposed to treat members of their own family." She was stunned. Grace wanted to run after the nurse and tell them the truth, but instead she sat on the green couch and broke down into tears. Henry patted her head, as if she were a stray puppy. "Now, now, I'm sure everything is going to be just fine. You don't think I would have waited this long if I thought Colin really had something serious, do you?"

It seemed like hours before the doctor appeared. "Mr. and Mrs. Franklin, I'm Doctor Sellars. I'm afraid I have a bit of bad news. Colin has slipped into a coma. Now, don't be too alarmed at this point. High fevers can cause mild comas. I only wish I could have seen your son sooner. I think this could have been prevented."

Grace jumped to her feet. "Is he going to be all right? How long will he be in a coma?"

"We don't know yet. It seems he has some sort of infection. The blood test will let us know more. That is going to take a couple of hours. I suggest you try to get some rest. I'll come and get you as soon as I know something."

"Can I see him?" she asked.

"You can see him for a few moments and only through the window," he said, pointing down the hallway to a set of swinging doors.

Grace stood at the glass looking at her seven-year-old son. There were tubes coming from his nose and mouth while an IV dripped into his arm. He looked so small lying in the hospital bed. As Henry approached the window, Grace grabbed his arm. "Come here. I want to show you what you have done to your son. Look at his face. I will never forgive you for this, Henry," she said as tears began to flow down her cheek.

"Oh, I knew this was coming. Now it's my fault Colin is sick. When the doctor comes back and tells you all he has is a virus and that he'll be fine, you can tell me you're sorry for blaming me." Instead of going back to the waiting room, Henry left the hospital to find somewhere to have a drink, leaving Grace alone to pace the floor and cry.

Hours melted into days, days into weeks, and Colin remained in a coma. The test confirmed almost one hundred percent that he had encephalitis. The doctor explained to Grace that in most cases it was curable if it were caught early enough, but with the duration of Colin's fever, he was afraid there might be some brain damage. To what extent he would not know until Colin woke up. Grace refused to leave the hospital during the day. The neighbors rallied, keeping Anna and preparing meals for Henry. At night, when she was at home after the nurses made her leave the hospital, she would hold Anna in her arms and try to answer the questions of a four-year-old.

"Where is my brother? When is he coming home?"

Grace cried herself to sleep each night, praying for her son. Henry had returned to work, since he said it was just too painful for him to stay at the hospital and working would help him keep his mind off his beloved son. Tom Sutton told Henry not to worry. He had good insurance and everything should be covered. Henry failed to mention this when he accepted a donation from the plant employees to help him with the medical bills.

Three months and four days after that terrible night, Colin awoke from his coma. Grace was by his bedside when he finally opened his eyes. She screamed and the nurses came running. Although his eyes were open, he stared at Grace as if she were a total stranger. She held his hands and his face, saying over and over again, "Colin, it's me, it's mommy! Please tell me you know who I am, oh please, sweetheart."

After a few more days of tests and examinations, the staff doctor told Grace he needed to talk with her and Henry. They sat in the straight back chairs facing his desk, Grace wringing her hands. She had prepared herself for the worst.

"This is a very sad time for me. I wish I could give you better news. I have children of my own and I know how difficult this is for you. I'm afraid that because of the high fever and duration of the coma, there are parts of your son's brain that have suffered irreparable damage. To what extent, at this time, we do not know." He closed the file folder with Colin's name printed on the corner in bold letters. "We'll do everything we can for him until we determine the level on which he will be able to perform. Do you have any questions at this time?"

Grace stared at him with hollow eyes. Questions, of course there were questions, many questions. Could her little boy ever walk again or talk? Could he run and play with the other children? Could he give her hugs and kisses and laugh out aloud when she tickled him? Would he be able to go to school? She just wanted him to be Colin again.

"No, I don't think we have any questions," Henry answered, squeezing Grace's hand.

As the days passed, Grace began suffering from exhaustion. She rarely ate and slept only in small segments in a chair by Colin's hospital bed. She wanted to be awake in case he needed her. He just lay in the bed staring at the ceiling. At times his whole body would shake and saliva would run from his mouth. The doctors said he was having seizures and needed a feeding tube inserted to prevent him from choking and gagging. Grace wanted to help. She wanted to hold him and try to feed him, but the nurses would make her leave the room, sending her to the lounge to cry. At home, the house was in disarray. Henry began taking his clothes to the laundry and bringing home food for dinner. Anna spent most of her time with the neighbors. She missed her mother, but when Grace was at home, she really never seemed to have time for her. Her shattered nerves would get the best of her and Grace would snap at Anna, regretting it instantly. Late at night Grace would go to Colin's room and lay across his bunk bed, smelling his scent on the pillow. She looked around at his toys that he would never play with again and the ache in her heart was almost too much to bear. She decided to leave his room just as it was, in case by some miracle, the doctors were wrong and he fully recovered.

As Grace prepared for their weekly meeting with the doctor to discuss Colin's case, she could sense that this meeting was a little more intense. Colin's medical file, which now took up four folders, was placed in the center of the desk.

Doctor Sellars let out a sigh. "Well, I'm not going to beat around the bush or keep your hopes dangling any longer. Our findings are that Colin has suffered one of the severest forms of encephalitis. It is a miracle he is alive. His prognosis is not good. We have no idea how much of his brain is still functioning, but we do know that he will be unable to walk or control his bodily functions and his level of communication is limited to indistinguishable sounds. He will most likely have seizures and need around-the-clock assistance to keep him from choking. I am very sorry. I wish I could have done more for your son."

The words rang through Henry's head. He remembered the ward at the university hospital, the one the interns called the Vegetable Patch. The ward duty there was a nightmare of sounds and smells. He had hated every moment of his shift in that ward. There were more words in the report, but they did not matter. The doctor concluded by saying that it would be best if Colin were placed in a facility equipped to handle patients with extreme problems. Dr. Sellars stood and extended his sincerest sympathy to Grace and Henry, telling them the hospital would be prepared to move Colin whenever they reached a decision. Doctor Sellars left the room, leaving Grace and Henry staring at the empty desk.

Henry stood and reached for Grace's hand. She ignored him and walked slowly to the door. That night as they lay in bed, Grace stared into the darkness.

"Grace, I know you're awake. I just want you to know that I don't think you should blame me. I never really knew he was that sick, and I think the doctor is right. I've seen these cases before, and it will be best for you and Colin if we put him in an institution where he can be taken care of properly. Good night." He turned on his side and began to snore.

In her restless sleep, Grace could hear someone screaming. It was a child's voice, not a scream of pain, but of sheer terror.

"Why doesn't someone help me? Where are you, Mother?" the child cried. She could see the little boy lying in a huge white bed, but he was not moving.

"I can see you, but I don't know where you are! Please tell me where are you?" a woman asked. No one answered and the screaming began again. Grace covered her ears. "Stop it, stop it, both of you! Can't you see I'm trying to sleep?" The woman laughed. "Is that what you call it, sleep? Maybe you are in a coma. What about the child? He is all alone in that institution."

She woke with a jolt, her back wet with perspiration. Henry was shaking her. "Jesus, Grace, take it easy. You're having a bad dream. You were screaming," he said as he tried to calm her down.

Grace rose from the bed and walked into the bathroom. In the shadows of the room, she could see her outline in the mirror. She stared into the glass, taking a long private look at who she really was. She was Colin's mother and she would never send him to an institution while she had one breath of life left inside her. She washed her face with cool water and went back into the bedroom. Henry was sitting on the side of the bed, still shaken by Grace's screams.

"I have made my decision. I am going to bring Colin home. I am not putting him away somewhere to die. My life cannot go on pretending he doesn't exist. You need not bother with him. I am his mother and I will take care of him. I will not abandon him." She stood up to Henry with more conviction than she ever had in her life.

Grace spent weeks working with the nurses learning the proper way to care for Colin. They gave her instructions on how to insert the feeding tube so that he wouldn't choke. She learned to exercise his muscles and take care of his toilet needs. It was difficult, but little by little, she was able to correctly turn him, wash his hair in bed, and brush his teeth. He was like a rag doll, responding occasionally with grunts. The most important lesson Grace had to learn was what to do when he had a seizure. The doctors were amazed at her ability to handle him and finally concluded that she could take him home.

The furniture in the spare bedroom was replaced with a hospital bed and a cot. Grace wanted his bed placed in front of the window so he could see the morning sun and hear the birds singing. With everything in place, the ambulance brought Colin to his home, to a room filled with oxygen tanks and ventilators.

Each day became a replica of the previous one. Grace arose at five a.m. and checked on Colin. She made a pot of coffee, and spent her one solitary hour of the morning making out a list of supplies or trying to decide what to feed Henry and Anna for dinner. She then woke Henry, prepared his breakfast and got Anna ready for kindergarten.

At first Anna had been afraid of her brother and ran from the room when she saw him. "That's not my brother," she cried. "That's not Colin!" Slowly she began to venture into the room and soon made a point of throwing him a kiss every morning before she left for school.

Once Anna and Henry were out of the house, the long day was devoted to Colin. Each feeding took over an hour and just to bathe him and do his body exercises took the rest of the morning. While he slept in the afternoon, she tried to straighten the house and start the evening meal. After dinner she put Anna in the bathtub and she sat on the floor talking with her about her day at school. Grace checked on Colin around ten, and then completely exhausted, she would fall asleep on the cot next to his bed.

Henry was very little help. Sometimes he would call and tell her not to make dinner, that he would be out late. This was the only break she had in her busy day. He stayed out of the way, hoping that eventually Grace would make the decision to put Colin in an institution so that their life could become somewhat normal again. He was unhappy with the way his shirts were returned from the laundry.

Chapter Nineteen

The years seemed to melt away, one falling into the other, with little or no change in the Franklin house. Tom Sutton's business continued to flourish and Henry was given a sizable raise. He decided that it was time to find someone to help Grace. Since she refused to let anyone near Colin, she did agree to have a part-time housekeeper, which would take a lot of the burden off her. There was a procession of housekeepers over the next several years; they could not put up with Henry's grumbling and insults for very long. He complained about the way they laundered his clothes, and he disliked the food they prepared for him. Anna paid little attention to most of them, since they never bothered to talk with her. She was able to ready herself for school and many days she never saw her mother until late in the evening. On the difficult days, when Colin was having seizures, Grace would not come out of his room all evening. Anna missed her mother. She missed the fun times.

It wasn't until Renard came to live with them that some resemblance of Anna's life returned to the house. Renard was just seventeen years old. Her parents still lived in France and they had allowed her to come to America to attend school. After Grace interviewed her, Renard asked to see Colin, and without hesitation went into his room. "Oh, you poor baby," she said, smoothing back his hair. Grace hired her without talking to Henry as most of the previous housekeepers seemed to be afraid of Colin and stayed away from him.

Renard was full of life. She would dance around the kitchen with the broom, singing to the radio and making Anna laugh. She loved to cook and have picnics in the backyard. She would take dinner on a tray to Grace every evening before she left to go home. "You eat this, Mrs. Franklin, you need your strength." They would sit together by Colin's bed, and for the first time in years, Grace would laugh when Renard tried to tell her something in her broken English.

Renard paid special attention to Anna. She knew Anna was lonely and missed her mother's attention. Renard would brush Anna's long chestnut colored hair, tying it with red ribbons. She would tell her stories about life in France. On warm afternoons they would sit on the porch and drink cool glasses of lemonade. It was one of the best summers Anna could remember. Grace appreciated Renard's help, yet she knew she should be spending more time with her own daughter instead of leaving her care to someone else. Henry liked Renard immediately and there were times when Grace was annoyed at the laughter coming from the kitchen. She just knew Henry was making a fool of himself. Grace only hoped he would not offend Renard.

Colin had never been able to sit up without choking. Grace propped pillows on each side of his head and each day raised the hospital bed just an inch, until one day she called the whole family into his room to see him sitting up. Anna and Renard began to clap, which scared him. His body stiffened and he began to scream. Henry became irritated, chastising Grace for trying to pretend that Colin was getting better.

Renard began to spend most of her time at the Franklin house since she had taken over most of the household duties. Henry said it was silly for her to pay for a room when she could stay in Colin's old room. Grace was reluctant to remove Colin's things, but now the toys seemed juvenile, so she agreed to let Renard come live in the house. It was Renard who suggested a wheel chair for Colin so they could take him outside. "He looks so pale and thin. He needs sunshine and fresh air," she said. At first Colin was frightened of the chair. His body would become rigid and he would slide to the floor. After days of coaxing, he finally managed to stay in it long enough to be pushed out to the front porch. His head bobbed up and down and he screamed. He seemed glad to be outside.

Grace and Renard sat on the front porch as Colin slept next to them in his chair. They watched as Anna and her friends rode their bicycles up and down the sidewalk. Renard reached over and touched Colin's face with her handkerchief, wiping away the drool running down his chin. "I think what you are doing for Colin is very brave and wonderful," she said softly to Grace.

"It's not wonderful Renard. In fact there are times when I don't think I can stand it for another day," Grace said.

Renard hugged her knees as she sat on the step. "Dr. Franklin told me that you blame him and it makes him very sad."

Grace seemed surprised. "Well isn't that something. I never thought he ever talked to anyone about Colin. I guess I've always wanted to believe it was his fault, but I should have listened to my own heart instead of waiting for Henry to make a decision. If I would have taken Colin to the hospital earlier in the week, he may have gotten well, but I can't change what has already happened. I just hope Colin forgives me."

"I do not mean to pry, Mrs. Franklin, but sometimes I worry about you and Dr. Franklin. You do not seem close. There is no love for each other in your eyes," Renard said as she continued to wipe Colin's face.

"Oh, Renard, I wish I could explain it to you, but it's a very long story," Grace said with a sigh. "Right now it takes so much energy to deal with Colin and so many things have happened between Henry and me that we have just grown apart."

"When a family has a crisis it is better they stick together and rely on each other for support. Maybe you need to spend some time alone together. If you and Dr. Franklin would like to get away for a few days, I will be glad to stay here with Colin and Anna." Renard rose to take Colin back into the house. Grace looked into Renard's face and wondered how she had become so wise at such a young age.

It was a rainy Sunday afternoon. A slow steady rain dripped off the eaves and made puddles on the sidewalks. Henry was bored. The taverns were closed and there was nothing for him to do. He had been thinking all morning about his position at the factory and wondered if it was time to leave. He was tired of bandaging smashed fingers and having employees limp into his office holding their backs. Each week there was more paper work. Mounds of insurance forms and now a new program called workman's compensation were keeping him busy. There were employee records and folders piled high on the corner of his desk. It was all so menial. His salary was good, but he imagined that by the time his father was this age, he was making three times as much. He still wasn't making near enough money to move to Cherry Street. There were times when he would drive up and down the streets in Tom Sutton's neighborhood, looking at the houses and pretending that he was on his way home to his own house in this neighborhood. Leaving his job now meant going back into private practice. He had no idea how he could arrange that. He barely passed the Kansas State Medical Boards. Henry remembered the look on the county clerk's face as she handed him his license, a look that said, "Please don't practice in my neighborhood."

Henry wandered around the house, watching the rain streak down the windows. Grace was still asleep in the chair next to Colin's bed. Opening the buffet door, he found a bottle of brandy. He stuffed it into his jacket pocket and retreated to his study. Henry read for a while, sipping the brandy. He finally dozed off and awoke when the room was almost dark. There was the aroma of roasting meat wafting from the kitchen. He yawned, stretched, and headed down the hall. Renard was sitting on a kitchen chair, her foot propped on the step stool, polishing her toenails. She was humming to a song playing on the radio. Henry stood at the door watching her. She had seemed like such a young girl when she came to live with them. Now, three years later, she had blossomed into a striking woman. Renard had no idea that he had been watching her. There were times when Henry would see her running through the hall to her bedroom, fresh from a shower, with only a towel barely covering the curves of her body. Late at night, after he came home from the bars, he would quietly push open her bedroom door and watch her sleep, her long legs flung over the covers. Henry had tried to entice her several times, but whenever he made suggestive remarks, she would throw her head back and laugh as if he were joking. Clearly she had no interest in him.

Renard looked up to see him standing there. "Well, hello, I hope you are hungry. Dinner will be ready in about ten minutes." Henry walked to the kitchen sink and filled a glass with water. Leaning against the drain board, he continued to stare at her.

She smiled. "What are you looking at? Do I have flour on my face?"

"No. It's just that I never see you very much anymore. I suppose you have a boyfriend that is keeping you busy," Henry said.

Renard moved to the stove and began putting potatoes into the boiling water. "I have no time for boys right now. I must finish my studies so that I can return home, then there will be boys; French boys." She smiled again, rolling her eyes. She took the lid off of the pot again, stirring the potatoes with a large wooden spoon.

"You know, you have turned into quite a beautiful young woman. I guess you hear that all the time."

Renard giggled. "Please stop! You are embarrassing me."

Henry was silent for a moment. Sipping his water, he continued to stare at her.

Renard did not hear him as he quietly moved across the room and stood behind her, his face touching her hair. Henry placed his hands on her hips. "Maybe if you stayed here I could teach you what American men are like. I think I would be a good teacher." He reached down and kissed her neck.

Renard stiffened and cried out, "What are you doing? Stop it!" His arms tightened around her waist. She dug her nails into his hands until his grip loosened. Picking up the wooden spoon, she turned and hit Henry across the cheekbone. Renard began to cry and fled from the room.

Henry touched his stinging face. He could feel a welt beginning to form. He cursed to himself. He needed ice. As he turned to open the refrigerator, Henry caught a glimpse of Anna standing outside the back door. Anna turned to run, but Henry strode across the kitchen and swung open the screen door. Catching her by the arm he pulled her toward him. "How long have you been standing there? Answer me, dammit!"

Anna began to cry. "You're hurting me, daddy!"

He loosened his grip and she bolted down the steps. "God dammit, come back here, and I mean right now!" Henry yelled angrily. Anna stopped. She was afraid of what he would do if she ran any further. Pulling her out of the rain, Henry knelt down in front of her, his breath hot on her face. "Listen to me little girl, I don't know what you think you saw, but it is none of your business and you had better just keep it to yourself. If I even hear you breathe one word to your mother, you will have to answer to my belt. Now go to your room." He pushed her toward the door and Anna ran like a frightened rabbit.

Propping a chair against her bedroom door Anna sat down on the floor until Grace called her for dinner. Renard stayed in her room, telling Grace she had a headache and just wanted to rest. Anna sat at the table trying to choke down her food. Looking up from her plate, she would catch the ominous stare from her father. The mixture of fear and hate she felt for him at that moment nauseated her. Pushing back her chair, she asked to be excused.

"You don't want to eat, Missy, then you can just go to bed," Henry said throwing down his fork. "And don't bother Renard, she doesn't need you hanging around her all the time."

Anna lay on her bed, tears rolling down her cheeks. She wanted to run across the hall and tell Renard that she was sorry for what her father had done, but he might be lurking outside the door waiting to pounce on her. Anna knew that if Renard was now afraid of her father, she would not want to stay in their house any longer. The thought of her leaving made Anna feel sick again. Tomorrow she would beg Renard not to leave.

Once Grace had taken up her sentry duty in Colin's room, Henry crept up the stairs. He knocked lightly on Renard's door, but she would not answer. As the first light of morning seeped into the house, Henry heard a car pull into the driveway. He looked out the bedroom window and watched as Renard put her bags into the car. She walked around to the passenger side, looked up at the house and left. Henry went to her room. On the desk was an envelope with the words "Grace and Anna" written in her delicate handwriting. Henry took the envelope, tore it into pieces and flushed it down the toilet.

Grace was stunned when she found Renard had left without so much as a word to her or Anna. She wanted to call the school and talk to Renard, but Henry said it was just as well that she was gone. Lately she had been making undue advances on him and he was beginning to feel uncomfortable with her in the house. Grace and Anna missed her terribly, and Grace continued to wonder why Renard had really left. She did not believe Henry's story. Anna wanted to tell her mother what happened, but was too afraid of what her father might do to her. By the time Grace got up enough courage to call her, Renard had left school and returned to France.

It was Henry's decision that there would be no more housekeepers. If Grace needed help, he would hire a nurse to care for Colin.

"Really, Henry, a nurse? I don't think so. Colin would be so stressed with a stranger in his room. He would probably start having seizures again," Grace said.

"All right then. Anna is old enough to sit with Colin. She can watch him after school and on the weekends. He sleeps often; it shouldn't be hard for her to learn to tend to his needs. You can get back to running this house properly," Henry said.

Anna could not believe what she was hearing. Why should she have to take care of Colin? When would she be able to play with her friends? She knew the matter was not open for discussion. It was her father's final word and her mother agreed with him for once.

Anna hated Colin's room. No matter how much her mother scrubbed and cleaned, the smell of urine never seemed to go away. It was an acrid smell that made Anna's eyes water. When she sat too close to Colin's bed, his skeleton fingers would reach out and grab her clothing. Yet if she moved away, he would scream in his low guttural voice. Thrashing back and forth, he would begin to cough, bringing Grace rushing into his room. She would rub his face and murmur to him until he was calm again. "Don't you love your brother?" she would ask. Anna nodded her head, wanting to scream, "No, I don't, he is not like a real brother. He scares me and I don't want to be in this room." She was afraid her father would find out and punish her, so she said nothing. She discovered that he liked her to read to him, usually falling asleep after a few pages. Anna would then sit by the window watching her friends playing hopscotch in the street.

Chapter Twenty

Colin took two years of Anna's young life as he struggled to stay alive. Three days after his fourteenth birthday his seizures became so severe that Grace was forced to have him admitted into the hospital. Just as his illness had begun eight years earlier, Colin slipped into a coma, and died a week later with Grace at his bedside.

At the cemetery, Anna sat next to her mother. She wanted to cry. Squeezing her eyes tightly together, she tried to shed at least one tear for her brother. His death had granted her a pardon from her imprisonment and for that she was grateful. Grace grieved for her son. She grieved for his wasted life. She stood at the gravesite until the coffin of her baby boy was lowered into the ground. Grace slowly walked away. She looked over her shoulder to see the grave workers standing nearby leaning on their shovels. Henry waited impatiently by the car, smoking a cigarette. He opened his arms as she came toward him. Grace passed by him and got into the car.

Once at home, Grace took off her hat and gloves and laid them on the bed. Her black dress was rumpled. She wanted to take it off, but there was too much to do. Henry had invited everyone who came to the funeral back to the house. The neighbors brought food earlier and the kitchen overflowed with bowls and casserole dishes. Grace wondered if she would be missed if she slipped away to her bedroom. She just wanted to weep for her dead son.

Henry stood at the bottom of the stairs, yelling for her. "Grace, come on, get down here. People will be arriving at any moment to pay their respects. We need to set out the food. Dammit, Grace, I need your help."

She came slowly down the steps and began clearing the flowers from the dining room table. "Help me," Grace said, as she pulled the heavy

YARD SALE

linen trunk from the closet. "I need a table cloth. I want the one my mother made for me."

Henry raised his eyebrows as he pulled the trunk into the middle of the room. He decided now wasn't the time to argue with her over table linens. He flipped open the locks and retrieved the cloth. As he unfolded it, a crinkled yellow envelope fell to the floor. Henry picked it up. "What's this?" he asked, holding it up to the light.

Grace had forgotten she had put the envelope in the trunk. "That's mine," she said, reaching for it. "Give it to me."

Henry pulled his hand back, holding the envelope over his head. "Oh really, what is it, a secret love letter?"

She could not believe he was being so flippant on the day they buried their son. "No, it's from Martin. He gave it to me on the day I left Ternberry. He said I should use it if I ever wanted to leave you and come back to Ternberry."

"Why, that sneaky bastard. Let's see how much I'm worth." Henry ripped open the envelope. Inside there were five twenty-dollar bills, a key, and a thin sheet of paper. He dropped the money on to the table and began to read the paper. It simply stated that on upon Martin's death, Ternberry would be given to Colin. Martin said he knew Grace would want her son to have the property, and he was sure Colin would always take care of her. Henry was stunned. He had no idea if Martin was even still alive. Since Colin had died, Henry was sure the property should belong to him. Surely by now, Martin must have passed on. "Have you heard from Martin since we moved to Stockbridge?" Henry asked.

"No. I heard from him a few times after we left. I'm sure he has no idea where we live now. I wrote to him, but the post office said he was not picking up his mail. I assumed that he must be traveling and that he had closed up the house. What is that paper? What does it say?"

"Oh, nothing, just a note saying he hopes everything would work out for us. You can read it later. Here." He handed Grace the money and stuffed the letter into his pocket. Henry was amused. It turned out to be a good day after all.

"I would like to read the letter. Please leave it on my dresser," Grace said.

Henry nodded. "Sure, no problem." On the way to the kitchen he threw it into the trashcan.

Later that week, Henry hired an attorney to locate Martin, which was actually quite easy. Martin was living in a retirement home in Boston. He was bedridden and gravely ill. Henry wrote a sorrowful letter to him informing him of Colin's death and how poor Grace was grieving so badly that he feared for her health. All she wanted, he wrote, was to return to Ternberry with her daughter. If Martin could see it in his heart to deed the house to her, she would be ever so grateful. Grace wanted desperately to visit with him.

The reply came several weeks later; a letter addressed to Grace in Martin's shaky handwriting. He was sending her the signed deed, giving the house and property to her. Martin had written a short note, saying he would love to see Grace again and how sorry he was about Colin. He wrote that his own health was failing rapidly and he did not expect to live much longer. He begged her to come see him soon. Grace never saw the letter. Henry signed Grace's name to the deed and sent it to his attorney with the authorization to execute the sale of the property immediately. The tourism trade was booming on the east coast, and even though Ternberry was probably in dire need of repair, he expected to get a fair price.

Henry spent hours calculating each move. With the money from Colin's insurance and the sale of Ternberry, plus their own home, he was sure he could afford a house on Cherry Street. He was elated. For once things were looking up for him. Although Grace now spent most of her time in her room and Anna avoided him completely, he did not care. Whether they liked it or not, he was determined to turn them into a respectable, upper class family.

Finding a home in Tom Sutton's neighborhood was the most difficult task of all. Few houses were for sale and most were out of his price range. It wasn't until late summer that the house at 704 Cherry Street became available. The owners were anxious to sell and agreed to Henry's asking price. The house was a large red brick, with imposing columns on each side of the front porch. The circular driveway was hidden under an arch of giant oak trees and ended at the marble stairs. Henry fell in love with it immediately.

Grace was not in the mood for one of Henry's games, but he insisted that she and Anna go with him. When she asked where they were going, he just grinned and told her it was a surprise. They drove through the front gate of the house on Cherry Street and Henry parked the car under the canopy of trees. "Come on, I want to show you the inside," Henry said as he bounded up the steps.

Grace stared at the house in disbelief, wondering if Henry had completely lost his mind. He opened the door and ushered them inside. Their footsteps sounded hollow as they crossed the empty foyer. Grace stood for a moment looking up at the winding staircase before them. Henry began running through the rooms like a child in a fun house maze. He opened doors and showed them all the furniture and effects that the previous owner had left. Rushing back into the parlor, he beckoned for Grace and Anna to follow him. Henry stretched out his arms as he approached the bay window. Sitting in its own private alcove was a black grand piano. "Just look at this," he said, as he ran his hand across the keys. "Anna can take lessons on one of the finest pianos in this town. Isn't it amazing?"

Grace had hardly grasped what he was saying before he pulled her away from the parlor and into the library. The walls were covered with barren bookshelves that reached the carved walnut ceiling. "And this will be my room. For once I will have my own private room." He grinned as he walked around with his hands behind his back, as if he were counting off each step.

"There's a great kitchen and four or five bedrooms upstairs. This is the house I want, Grace. We could be happy here."

Grace leaned against the wall trying to overcome her shock at what Henry was saying. It was an insane idea. She just wanted to leave and go back to her own home. "Why in the world do we need such a big house? After all, there is just the three of us now. Besides, we could never afford all of this. Let's just go home," she said as she opened the front door.

Henry slammed the door shut. "I knew it! I knew that was what you were going to say. Dammit, Grace, just once can't you agree with my decision? I know we don't need it, but I want it. For your information, I've already bought this damn house, so you had better get used to it. This is where we are going to live," he growled as he turned off the lights and left Grace and Anna standing in the darkened foyer.

If Henry thought that life would suddenly be wonderful once they moved to Cherry Street, he was sadly mistaken. Anna hated the house and the neighborhood. She moped around the house during the day and at night the long dark hallways and unfamiliar sounds of the house frightened her. She hated the moaning sound of the wind in the oak trees and the crackling of the furnace as it released it blasts of heat into the air. She spent long hours reading in her room alone. It was her only escape away from the sterile existence of her new home. Grace also found no joy in the house. There were too many large rooms filled with cumbersome furniture. The enormous task of cleaning such a big house was endless leaving her exhausted each night. After dinner, which Henry insisted they eat in the dining room, she would fall into bed, too tired to even think about her daughter. Anna would sit alone with her blankets pulled over her head, shielding herself from the loneliness, which slowly invaded her world and became her constant companion.

Tom Sutton was surprised to hear that Henry had moved to Cherry Street. Henry explained to him that he had just received a large inheritance, and although he could have afforded much better, it was Grace who fell in love with the house. Tom agreed it was a fine place and gave Henry a list of gardeners and domestics that Henry would need to keep such a large house running properly. Tom volunteered his wife's assistance to help Grace find the right accessories and drapes he was sure she would want. Henry, grinning, said his study was first on the list. He made trips into Kansas City to buy a large mahogany desk and leather chair. Combing the bookstores for volumes to fill the shelves, he bought any book with a cover he found appealing. He was determined to make his study better than his father ever had.

Grace worried each time a delivery was made to the house. Could Henry possibly be spending more money than he actually had? He refused to discuss financial matters with her, and she was at a loss to figure out where the money was coming from. Surely his salary from Tom Sutton could not match their new lifestyle. Even though she cared little for the house, Grace did not want to move again.

Chapter Twenty-One

Anna wondered if there was anyone actually living on Cherry Street. The houses were shuttered and withdrawn behind the walls of stone and neatly trimmed shrubbery. She would amble down the sidewalk, passing each house. Were there children inside as miserable as she was? Was there another young girl in one of the upstairs windows looking out and watching her as she walked by?

Lou Jean was not looking out of a window, but hiding behind a trashcan when Anna passed the Sutton's garage. Anna could hear someone softly crying. Curious to see who it was, she pulled back the bushes and peered through the slats of the fence. There were puffs of smoke rising from behind the row of trashcans. "Hello, are you okay? Can I help you?" Anna asked. There was no answer. She asked again, "Are you okay?"

Lou Jean peered over the top of the can with her head barely visible. "Who are you? If you're going to be sneaking around like a cat, you should wear a bell around your neck. Can't a person even take a smoke break without someone spying on them?" she asked.

Anna stepped closer to the fence. "I wasn't spying on you. I was just out walking and I heard you crying. I thought maybe you needed help."

Lou Jean stood up and smoothed her purple cotton dress. "I'm okay now. I burnt my finger on a match." She walked to the fence, holding a cigarette in her hand and stared through the gate at Anna. "Who are you? I ain't seen you around here before."

"My name is Anna Franklin. I live on this street."

Lou Jean howled. "Well hell, no wonder I don't know you. You're one of the rich kids. My mom works for the Suttons. I work here in the summer too, but I hate it."

Anna's neck was beginning to hurt from straining to see around the bushes. "Can I come in?" she asked.

Lou Jean pushed open the gate. They stood face to face. Suddenly shy and not knowing what to say Anna kicked the grass with her bare toe.

"How old are you?" Lou Jean asked.

"Almost fourteen," Anna replied.

Lou Jean grinned, "I'm already fourteen. I had a birthday a couple of weeks ago." She looked around the corner of the garage. "I better go pretty soon. My mom will be mad if I stay away too long. Anyway, she doesn't like me smoking."

Anna did not want her to leave. It had been along time since she had someone to talk to her own age. "What day will you and your mother be back? I can come down and see you again," she said as Lou Jean turned and began walking up the driveway.

"I'll be back on Wednesday around noon. I'll probably be busy most of the day, but you can come by if you want. See ya," she said as she disappeared into the house.

Grace was in the laundry room folding clothes when Anna got home. She sat down on the high stool next to her mother. "Do you need any help?"

Grace pushed a mound of bath towels across the table.

"I met a girl today," Anna said. "Her name is Lou Jean and her mother works for the Suttons." She wanted to see her mother's reaction.

Grace continued to fold. "That's nice dear. Is she your age?" She put another load of clothes on the table. Anna nodded. The clothes pile continued to grow as they smoothed and folded each sheet and towel. "Did I ever tell you that my mother and I were both domestics when I was young? We both worked for the dean at the university where your father went to medical school," Grace said. Anna was surprised. She knew very little about her mother's life.

"You never told me that. I always thought your parents were rich like the Franklins."

Grace smiled. "Heavens no, we were just ordinary working people. You know, Anna, there is nothing wrong with hard work, as long as it's honest."

"Then you won't mind if I get to know Lou Jean even though she doesn't live around here?"

"Not in the least. You need a friend."

YARD SALE

Grace had mentioned to Henry several times that Anna did not have any friends in the neighborhood. Henry said that if he could see his way clear to join Tom Sutton's country club, she would make lots of friends. They would be the right kind of people for Anna to associate with. Perhaps in the fall, they would send her to boarding school. Grace dropped the subject, not wanting either of those things to happen.

On Wednesday Anna was anxious to see Lou Jean. She made cookies and carefully wrapped them in wax paper. She sat on the front porch waiting for twelve o'clock to come. The Sutton's gate was open and she walked slowly up the driveway looking for Lou Jean. Anna was disappointed when she didn't see her and wondered if she should ring the doorbell. She did not want to get Lou Jean into trouble. It wasn't until she turned to leave the porch that she saw her. Lou Jean was on the side of the house, washing window screens. She looked up to see Anna waving at her. "I have some cookies," Anna said, holding up the bag.

"I haven't got time to stop my work. If you want to sit here and talk to me you can, but I got a shit load of these screens to wash." She plopped the soapy sponge into the bucket. Wiping her hands on the same purple dress she had worn the day before, she reached for a cookie. "Thanks. I'm kind of hungry. Are these store-bought or did you make them?"

Anna picked up the sponge and began to wash the screen. "Here let me help you. If we both work, you'll get done much faster."

Lou Jean grabbed the sponge. "Jesus, don't do that. Do you want to get me into trouble? Just sit here and talk to me."

They talked most of the afternoon. Anna told her about Colin and her old neighborhood. She told her that she hated living on Cherry Street and how scared she was going to be when she entered high school.

"You're damn lucky," Lou Jean said. "I would love to go to high school, but I know I won't be able to go. Now that I'm fourteen, my mom will probably just get me a job and I'll end up in a stinky old factory working for some jerk like Mr. Sutton. Besides, even if I could go, I don't have any clothes good enough to wear to high school. I'm going to sneak inside and get us something to drink."

Lou Jean returned with two cold sodas and handed one to Anna.

"Have you always lived in Stockbridge?" Anna asked.

"No, my mom and I moved here from South Carolina about three years ago. She got me out of bed real early one morning and told me to get my stuff together. She said she was fed up and wasn't going to take anymore of my father's crap. After my mom emptied out his wallet, we left my no-good drunken daddy sleeping on the couch. When we got to the bus station, my mom put the money on the counter and told the man to give us two tickets as far away as the money would take us. That's how we got to Stockbridge." Lou Jean paused and peered into the kitchen door to see if her mother was coming. "Since we've been here, we haven't done real well. My mother doesn't make very much money. I'm not complaining. She does the best she can. We have a roof over our heads and food to eat and we don't have to worry about my dad coming home and smacking us around like he usually did when he was drunk." Lou Jean twirled around, holding her purple dress by the bottom hem. " I only have one pair of shoes and they crunch my toes. I sure can't go to school barefooted." Lou Jean could see her mother coming toward the door. "You better go Anna, I have to get back to work."

Lou Jean walked Anna to the gate. "You know what? I think you and me are becoming friends. Next time you come, bring something to drink with those dry old cookies." She giggled as she walked backwards up the path. "I'll see you on Friday, okay?"

Anna nodded and walked home humming to herself.

What was it like having a friend? To Anna, it was everything. She needed someone to share her feelings and her fears with other than her mother. Anna wanted someone to talk to that would not criticize her like her father. That is what she found in Lou Jean. They would talk for hours. At times Anna wondered if she was telling Lou Jean too much. Was she giving away too many family secrets? Yet the words just spilled out of her mouth and she was glad to get rid of them. Anna told her of the intense loathing she had for her father since Renard left the house. She worried about the distance that seemed to be growing each year between her and her mother. It was her father's entire fault.

Lou Jean would share stories about her life with Anna. Ever since she was a small child, she was left alone while her mother worked. Her father would come home drunk and hit her for no reason at all. He called her stupid and worthless. "I wish the bastard had lived long enough to see me grow up. Someday I am going to be important, I just know it but right now I don't even know how I'm going to get into high school."

YARD SALE

In the few hours they spent together each week, they became close friends. Sometimes they talked about boys and wondered what it would be like to have a boyfriend and maybe someone to kiss you. Then, rolling on the grass in fits of laughter, Lou Jean would make kissing noises and hug her own body. It was a good summer.

"I have something to ask you," Anna said to her mother. They were sitting alone at the long dining room table eating dinner. Her father had gone out after Anna heard him arguing with her mother. He seemed to spend less and less time in the house that he supposedly loved so much. Anna didn't care; she wished he would leave and never come back. It was peaceful when he wasn't home.

"What is it, dear?" her mother asked. Grace was tired; she hoped it was a small request.

"It's my friend, Lou Jean. She doesn't have any clothes to wear to high school. I was wondering if I could give her some of mine? I have a whole closet full of stuff and she has nothing. I know some of the things will have to be altered, but you sew so well, it would probably be easy. I have a few extra dollars saved. Maybe we can buy her some shoes."

Grace began clearing the table. Anna followed her into the kitchen carrying her plate. "Why are you so quiet, Mother? Do you think it's a bad idea?"

Grace shook her head. "No, I'm proud of you. I just think it's wonderful of you to want to help your friend, but I don't know what your father will say should he hear that you are giving away your clothes."

"He never pays any attention to me. I doubt if he ever looks at me long enough to know what I am wearing," Anna said.

Grace put her finger to her mouth. "In that case we just won't mention it to him. It will be our little secret." Anna hugged her mother and ran to her room to see what she could find for her friend. Anna had never felt so good about anything in her life. She knew her father would be livid if he even had an idea of what she had done. He was such a stingy man, always making comments to her mother about the amount of money she spent. Her mother had to keep lists to account for every penny he gave her, yet his own spending had increased as he tried to fit into his new lifestyle.

Lou Jean stared at the pile of clothes on the Sutton's porch swing. Picking up a white blouse with blue flowers on it, she held it in front of her. "What's all this about? Are you taking up a collection for charity?"

Suddenly Anna felt uneasy. She didn't want to embarrass her. "No, actually it's some things a friend of my mother's gave to me and they don't fit. I was wondering if you would like to have them? Maybe you could consider going to high school if you took these clothes."

"You don't have to twist my arm. I'll take them, but I still have to convince my mom to let me go to school." A single tear ran down Lou Jean's cheek as she reached out to hug Anna. "By the way, you're not a very good liar. Thank you."

The August heat sent mirages of rippling waves across Cherry Street. Only the whirling sounds of window fans interrupted the first breaths of morning air. It was a lazy time. It was too hot to cook, too hot to clean. The heat sent Anna and Lou Jean to the shade of the back porch or to the air-conditioned theater in town. They spent the last few weeks before school started at afternoon matinees, munching on popcorn in the balcony while they watched their screen idols fall in love. They would stand for hours looking at movie magazines in the corner drugstore, sighing over their latest heartthrob, until the clerk would ask them to put the magazines back on the rack.

They were a mismatched pair. Anna's still childlike body and chestnut hair pulled back neatly in a barrette looked out of place next to the unruly golden curls that danced on Lou Jean's head. Only the small breasts Lou Jean proudly displayed in a tight green sweater broke the straight line of her wiry body. Anna and Lou Jean formed a bond of friendship that summer that would last for the rest of their lives.

Grace picked up the telephone on the third ring, hoping it was Henry calling to say he would be out late. Her head was splitting; she really just wanted to go to bed.

"Mrs. Franklin, this is Miss Bailey, Lou Jean's mother. I just want to make sure that my daughter isn't pestering you. I know she's been spending a lot of time at your house lately." She paused, waiting for an answer.

YARD SALE

Grace rubbed her head, "No, no it's not a problem. I'm glad that Anna has a friend. She had been pretty lonely since we moved here."

"Well, I kinda have been letting up on Lou Jean this summer. Lord knows I could use the help, but I figure she needs some free time. She has done convinced me to let her go to high school. I sure hope I'm making the right decision. You make sure she doesn't get in your way when she is at your house. I mean since we're kind of different from you people."

Grace wasn't sure what she meant. "I really don't consider them very different. Just two young girls with the same hopes and dreams that you and I had when we were young."

"I suppose." Miss Bailey sighed. "I want to thank you for the clothes. I never seen anybody so excited about going to school. She sure is happy."

After Mrs. Bailey hung up, Grace sat holding the phone for a moment, trying to remember when she had those same hopes and dreams. It seemed like a lifetime ago.

Chapter Twenty-Two

Henry stood in front of the full-length mirror in the foyer peering at his own reflection as if he expected it to talk to him, maybe to say "Hello Henry. My, don't you look handsome today." He straightened his collar and smoothed his vest. It was his morning ritual. Grace called it "preening." He would hand her his lint brush and she would slowly move it back and forth across the back of his jacket, deliberately leaving strands of hair. She hated doing this every morning, but he insisted. It was his time to gather his thoughts, to look himself straight in the eye and wonder how he was going to make it through the day. He could see Anna moving about in the hallway getting ready for school. She had become almost invisible to him these days; he had too many other concerns on his mind.

Henry picked up his cup of coffee and went into his study, closing the door behind him. He tapped the pencil on the desk as he studied the paper in front of him. Nothing had turned out as he had expected. They had been in the house over three years; Grace had yet to make any friends and Anna was still hanging around with Lou Jean Bailey. White trash, as he described her. He couldn't believe he moved his family across town and Anna had become friends with the likes of Lou Jean. She probably had Anna running around with boys. He did not want his daughter hanging around with those undesirable children at Stockbridge High School. It irritated Henry that Anna had to attend public high school, but there was not enough money to send her to private school. His expenses were almost twice what he had expected. To make things worse, Tom Sutton had given them a television set for Christmas, which he was reluctant to accept. He was embarrassed since his gift to the Sutton's was a set of carving knives. Grace was thrilled. She thanked Tom over and over again and he just beamed. Henry was livid. He told Grace if he wanted his family to have a television set, he would have bought one for them. There was no need for

YARD SALE

Tom Sutton to put on such airs and embarrass him. The television set became Grace's constant companion.

Henry overheard Anna talking to Grace about college; it was time to put that subject to rest. It wasn't important for girls to have a college education. Anna could find a job after she graduated from high school. He was sure her little pal, Lou Jean, wouldn't be going to college. Henry wadded up the paper he was writing on and threw it at the wastebasket. It fell to the floor next to the others he tossed there the night before. No matter how he figured and refigured, he could not stretch the budget any further. He contemplated giving up his new membership to the country club, but that would be his last resort. Everything was catching up with him. The taxes on the house were past due, he hadn't paid the gardener in over a month, and now the mortgage company was breathing down his neck. There was no way he could ask Tom for more money. Tom was having problems of his own at home. His wife had gone off to Europe and threatened not to come home until he promised to spend more time with her. Tom said she was spending a lot of money and he had to get her to come home.

Tom called Henry into his office. He sat behind his desk, his head in his hands. Henry could sense something was wrong, but he was in no mood for another lecture on company policy. Tom motioned to the chair and Henry sat down facing him. Tom's eyes were rimmed with red. His hands shook as he lit a cigarette.

"Henry, this is a bitch. I got more problems than I know what to do with. My old lady is sending me bills from all over the damn continent and she still won't come home. Before long I'm going to own Italy. Now I got another problem. Seems like someone in this town has been writing prescriptions for some pretty powerful shit and selling it to my employees." Tom slammed his hand down on the desk, causing Henry to jump. "They're coming to work all hopped up and they won't tell me who's giving them the shit. I've never seen so many people who supposedly have backaches. When I ask them who their doctor is, they just clam up and say they don't have to give me that information. Have you got any idea who is doing it?" He leaned forward in an accusing manner.

Henry stood up. "You just wait a damn minute, Tom. If you're accusing me, come right out and say it."

Tom rubbed his head, motioning once again to the chair. "I'm sorry, Henry. I know you've always been on the level, but this has got me crazy. I can't have these men getting killed on the job when they're full of drugs. I guess I could fire their asses, but then I would have to contend with the union."

"Maybe I can find out something," Henry said. This could be an opportunity to get a fat bonus. He knew Tom would be grateful if he could find out who was writing the prescriptions. It shouldn't be too hard. There weren't that many doctors in Stockbridge.

"By the way," Tom said in an apologetic tone, "I'm having a little get together at my house on Saturday night. If you're free, why don't you walk on down to my house? It's just some of the men from the country club and a few friends. We can play some cards, drink a few beers, and who knows, maybe I'll just call one of those escort services. Damn I need some fun in my life."

Henry laughed. "Don't we all. That sounds good to me."

Henry began his investigation that afternoon. He closed off the employees' locker room with the pretense of having it sprayed for roaches. Once inside, he began to search the men's lockers. Inside coat pockets and lunch bags he found several prescription bottles for painkillers from a place called Bullard's Pharmacy. The address on the label was just a few blocks away from the plant.

Henry pulled his car to the curb in front of the pharmacy. A small, faded yellow sign with the word 'Open' hung askew on the front door. Once inside, Henry tried to adjust his eyes to the dimness of the room. Two erratic fluorescent bulbs hung from the ceiling, casting shadows that led to the back of the store. The aisles were cluttered with a disarray of boxes and cans. He could see someone moving behind the partition that separated the counter from the medical supplies. Henry picked up a bottle of aspirin, leaving a ring of dust on the counter. He waited a moment and rang the bell.

A high-pitched voice came from behind the wall. "Be right with you." Howard Bullard came around the corner, wiping his hands on the hem of his soiled white coat. He was a small man, with a few strands of hair combed over the top of his balding head. He smiled, revealing a gold tooth. "What can I do for you?"

YARD SALE

Henry tried to appear calm, handing him the prescription. "I was wondering if you could fill this for me?" The script was made out on one of Henry's own pads.

Howard looked at it quickly and handed it back to Henry. "Uh, no, I'm sorry, no can do. This is a controlled substance and I don't have any here at the moment." He seemed nervous. "Who is this Dr. Franklin? His name doesn't ring a bell."

Henry took the paper and stuck it into his pocket. "Never mind. Thanks anyway." As Henry turned to leave, he noticed three other people waiting in line. He wondered what was really going on here.

Saturday night couldn't come soon enough for Henry. Grace was suffering from headaches again and lay on the couch with a cold cloth on her head, watching television. She left his dinner on the stove. He had no taste for lumpy mashed potatoes and cold dried out beef. He dressed in his favorite brown suit and tan shirt. He put on aftershave and combed a dab of oil into his hair. Henry admired himself in the mirror, turning to check the back of his jacket. Without a word to Grace, he left and made his way down the darkened street to Tom Sutton's house.

Anna called Lou Jean earlier in the day but there was no answer. She was bored. She hated weekends. Her father was usually home and, although he stayed in his study, he would not allow her to leave the house. There was no way to escape Cherry Street. Lou Jean was now working the last few weeks of summer at a variety store in town and they didn't get to spend much time together. When Anna asked her father if she could get a job at the dime store, he yelled at her and told her no daughter of his would work in a junk shop.

Anna heard the phone ringing and jumped from her bed. She ran down the stairs to answer it before her father emerged from his study. She did not know he had already left the house. "Can you come over? I'll meet you at the bus," Anna said breathlessly to Lou Jean.

"I'm already over. I'm at the Sutton's house. My mother has to work tonight because Mr. Sutton is having some kind of party. She hates riding the bus home alone at night. Can you come down here?" Lou Jean asked. "We can watch some TV. If I even get close to the kitchen my mother will put me to work." Anna grabbed her sweater, yelling to her mother that she would be home by nine.

Tom Sutton had invited eight men to his house, but only four showed up. He was disappointed. Maybe he shouldn't have mentioned the escort service, but it was too late now, he had already called for the service to send the women to his house. It was costing him a pretty penny. Those men were probably too scared of their old ladies to risk having a good time. Well, it was their loss. He hoped the women the service was sending would be young and pretty. Henry was the first to arrive.

Anna and Lou Jean lay across the bed in Mrs. Sutton's room, watching television. It was such a luxury, a television set in the bedroom. Lou Jean moved the antenna with her foot, trying to get a better picture. They heard the men laughing downstairs and the sound of women's voices.

"I bet Mrs. Sutton would have a fit if she knew he was having a party here," Lou Jean said. She yawned and stretched her arms over her head. "I'm hungry, let's go get the peanut butter and a couple of spoons." Anna got up from the bed, trying to see the last few minutes of the television program. Sneaking down the back stairs, Lou Jean and Anna made their way across the kitchen with only the small light over the stove illuminating the room. Lou Jean opened the pantry and took out the peanut butter jar. She reached into the silverware drawer and handed Anna two spoons. Lou Jean started back toward the steps. She stopped suddenly when she heard the voices. "Shit, someone's coming. It's probably my Mom. Get over here," Lou Jean whispered as Anna ducked down and crawled across the floor. She sat down behind the kitchen counter next to Lou Jean. They waited a moment in the darkness, hoping that whoever had come into the kitchen would leave. Lou Jean unscrewed the lid on the jar and began spooning peanut butter into her mouth.

"Come on, baby, you know you like me. You've been staring at me for the last hour." It was a man's slurred voice. Anna stiffened. It was her father's voice. She could feel her heart pounding in her chest. She sat as still as a gazelle who had just come face-to-face with a cheetah. The woman laughed. There was the rustle of taffeta and a soft thud. Anna knew her father had lifted the woman up on the kitchen counter just inches from her head. Lou Jean grabbed her arm, turning Anna's face toward her; she put her hand over her mouth. Shaking her head, Lou Jean pleaded with her eyes for Anna to remain silent. There were the sounds of wet kisses and low moans from the woman. Anna wanted to scream. Her face was white hot. Lou Jean took the spoon and with all her strength, hurled it over her head. The spoon hit the side of the stove with a loud clink and landed on the floor behind Henry.

He jumped back. "What the hell was that?" Looking around the room, he did not see the silver spoon shining in the moonlight on the black and white tiled floor. "Come on, let's get out of here," he said. The woman jumped down from the counter and Anna could hear the creaking of the kitchen door as it swung back and forth. She just sat there for a moment, frozen in place.

Lou Jean whispered, "Are you okay? That son of a bitch," she said, as she helped Anna up from the floor. Lou Jean hugged her as tears rushed from Anna's eyes. I'm going to walk you home."

Grace was still lying on the couch when Anna returned home. She lay down next to her mother and put her arms around her.

"I love you, Mother," Anna said.

Grace touched her hair softly, "I love you, too, Anna."

"No! I mean I really love you."

"My goodness, Anna, what is the matter?"

Anna said nothing, but buried her head in her mother's chest, hugging her as tightly as she could. She hated him; she hated her father with every fiber of her body, her mind, and her soul. She began to understand now that he had destroyed her mother and left her just a hollow shell of the person she once was. Anna knew she had to protect her mother from this evil person.

Henry could almost sense a change in the temperament of the house after that Saturday night at Tom's house. Anna began to spend a great deal of time with Grace, helping her in the kitchen, talking to her, and watching television with her in the evenings. Occasionally they would leave the house together and go to the movies or shopping. He wondered what this new closeness was all about. What was it Anna wanted from her mother? At times he could see Anna looking at him with a malevolent stare that made him feel uncomfortable. Was it something Lou Jean had said? He wasn't sure, but whatever it was he was going to put an end to Anna's ugliness. After another silent meal at the long dining room table, Henry cleared his throat and put down his napkin. "It's about time we had a little family talk. I think that there is an outside influence that may be spreading rumors about our family, namely a certain Lou Jean Bailey." He looked directly at Anna. "Well, let me tell you both that what goes on in this house stays in this house and no one needs to know our private business. Is that clear?" Henry waited for a reply, but none came. Anna just looked at him with all the contempt she could muster. Maybe she was making him nervous.

"If I have to, I will pull you out of school and away from your so-called friend and put you in a boarding school. Am I making my point?"

Grace was puzzled by his outburst. He wasn't making any sense. Anna lowered her head and stared at her plate. She had to keep peace in the house to save her mother. Henry threw his napkin on the table. The door to his study slammed and Anna gave a sigh of relief.

Chapter Twenty-Three

Henry sat in his car outside Bullard's Pharmacy until he saw a hand reach up and turn the sign on the door to "Closed." Minutes later a white Mercedes pulled out of the alley into the street. Howard Bullard was at the wheel. Henry waited until he was almost around the corner before he pulled away from the curb. Howard was a slow driver, making it hard for Henry to keep his distance as he followed the car down the narrow streets of downtown Stockbridge.

Howard Bullard pulled up in front of the Two Aces Pool Hall and got out. He lit a cigarette and went inside. Minutes later, Henry stepped inside the smoke filled room. There were six large pool tables and a small bar at the back of the room. Howard stood talking to a group of men holding cue sticks. Henry looked conspicuously out of place in his business suit, getting looks from several men at the tables. He walked to the bar and ordered a beer. He didn't know what he was going to say to Howard, but a week had gone by and Tom Sutton was starting to ask questions again. Howard moved to the bar, nodding to Henry, and ordered a shot of rye whiskey. He downed the shot and pushed the glass across the bar and waited for a refill.

"Hard day at work?" Henry asked.

"What? Oh yeah, it was a bitch," Howard replied downing the second shot. His eyes squinted as he looked at Henry. "You look familiar. Do I know you?"

Henry smiled, "I was in your pharmacy the other day. You're Bullard, aren't you?"

Howard nodded. "Yep, that's me. Been Bullard since the day I was born." He slapped the bar and laughed out loud. Howard pointed his finger at Henry. "I know who you are. You had the prescription I couldn't fill. It was for some narcotic, wasn't it?"

"I have a confession to make," Henry said, "I'm Dr. Franklin. The prescription was for my wife. I'm a company doctor and legally I can't prescribe her medication. It's a little embarrassing for me to admit she has a dependency." Henry looked at Howard to see if he was buying any of his lies. "Anyway, I just thought maybe I could find someone to fill it until I can find her a new doctor."

Holding another glass of whiskey, Howard held out his hand. "Name's Howard. My friends call me Howie, but you can call me Mr. Bullard." He slapped the bar again and laughed.

Henry was not amused, but managed a small smile. "Well now, Mr. Bullard, do you know where I can find a doctor that's not adverse to prescribing what I need for my wife or something stronger if needed?"

"Well, Dr. Franklin, I may be able to help you. Come by the store and we'll talk." He fumbled in his pocket for his keys and staggered to the door. Henry thought what a shame it would be if he wrecked that nice Mercedes.

Henry waited a few days before he went back to the pharmacy. He didn't want to appear anxious and he knew Howard was hiding something. As he entered the shop, he could hear Howard talking loudly. Henry wandered around for a few minutes before Howard saw him. "Be right with you." He continued to argue with the elderly man about the price of the medication until the old man, still shaking his head, took the white paper bag and left.

"Sometimes I just can't get through to these people. They think I can just give this stuff away. Do you have your prescription with you?" Howard took the prescription and held it up to the light. "I can give you about thirty pills, but that's my limit. Let me give you the name of a doctor over in Covington who may be able to help your wife."

Henry wrote the script out and signed it. He had no idea what he was going to do with the medication. Howard disappeared behind the wall, emerging a few moments later with an unlabeled vial.

"Thanks. How much do I owe you?" Henry said as he dropped the bottle into his coat pocket.

Howard grinned. "Just give me two of those signed prescription blanks and we can call it even." He threw his head back and laughed. "Hey, I'm only kidding, Doc. Don't take offense."

Henry stared at him for a moment, wanting to make him as uncomfortable as possible. "You really want to get me in some hot water, don't you? I told you I was a company doctor."

"And I told you I was just kidding. Just give me ten dollars," Howard growled in an irritated voice.

"Look, I'm sorry," Henry said, "I've had a bad week. My wife is nagging me about getting her more drugs and my job isn't going well." Henry tried to look as pathetic as possible. "Besides, I'm running out of money."

"Believe me Doc, I understand. As soon as I get enough dough together I'm out of here. I'd like to go to Hawaii." He moved his arms as if he were doing a hula dance.

"Well I hope you make better money in your pharmacy than I do at my position." Henry sighed, "I would be better off in private practice, but I don't have the cash flow to do anything right now."

Howard leaned on the counter, suddenly interested in the conversation. "There are other ways to make extra money. I have to supplement my income or I'd be working eighty hours a week in this store." Howard lit a cigarette and began turning off the lights in the pharmacy. "You know, there's big money in medication if you know how to work the system, and it is all legal. I helped out a few doctors in Tulsa. Everything was going great, but once they started making a lot of money, they blew me off. So now I'm stuck in this one-horse town starting over again."

"I'd like to hear more about it, but right now I have to get home. How about dinner one night next week?" Henry pulled one of his business cards out of his wallet and handed it to Howard. He didn't want to appear too anxious. "Here's my office number. Call me if you have a free night."

Bullard rolled the card between his fingers. "I might just do that, Doc. See you later."

Henry stopped on the way home and had a few drinks at a neighborhood bar not far from the plant. He drank alone, mulling over the conversation he had with Bullard. He wondered if somehow Bullard could help him out of the rut he was in.

When Henry finally got home the house was dark, except for the light coming from the upstairs bedroom window. Fumbling for his keys, he opened the door and staggered up the stairs to the bedroom. Grace was sitting in bed reading. She gave him that look he hated. Hanging his pants and jacket neatly on a hanger, he didn't see the vial of pills fall from his pocket to the floor. He crawled into bed and began to snore. Grace found the vial in the morning as she was making the bed.

"What are these?" she asked, putting the bottle on the table as he sat reading the morning paper.

Henry looked up for a moment. "Oh, those are some pills I got for you. They will help you sleep and ease your headaches." He sipped his coffee and returned to his paper.

"I don't need anything to help me sleep. I'm just fine," she said.

"Oh really. Is that why I hear you wandering around half the night or staying up until the television stations go off the air? You could at least try them. That's the thanks I get for worrying about you. I just thought they might help."

"Thank you, Henry, but I really don't need them." Grace put the bottle on the table.

"Whatever. It's your choice." He put on his jacket and handed her the lint brush.

Grace cleared the kitchen table after Henry left for his office. She picked the bottle up and carried it upstairs. Sitting on the side of the bed she turned the vial round and round in her hand and finally put it into the drawer of her nightstand.

Howard Bullard called the next day to make arrangements for Henry to meet him at one of the most expensive restaurants in town. Henry wondered if Howard just wanted a good meal or if he really had something to talk to him about. Whatever it was, Henry wasn't planning to pay for Howard's dinner and maybe not even his own. Howard was already sitting at a table having a drink when Henry arrived.

"Glad you could make it, Doc. You're going to love the food in this place. I eat here about once a month." Henry sat down as the waiter filled his glass with wine, which wasn't one of his favorite drinks, but right now anything would taste good.

"Well, let me get right to the point, Doc," Howard said. "I hope this don't piss you off, but I had you checked out real good before I called you to meet me here."

Henry's eyes narrowed. "What do you mean, you checked me out?"

"When you came into my store, I could see you looking around. Sort of checking the place over. I thought maybe you were a narcotics officer. I have to be real careful. I got a friend who owns a detective agency and he did some background on you. You sure do move around a lot."

Henry slammed his hand down on the table, drawing stares from a few other patrons. "I'm not going to sit and listen to this crap. Who in the hell are you to check me out? I think this meeting is over, Bullard." Henry shoved back the chair, almost tipping it over.

"Damn, take it easy. Sit down, Doc. At least give me a chance to explain."

Henry waited for a moment before he sat back down.

"Look, how did I know you weren't sent to investigate me? Those agents are pretty tough. I haven't had any trouble with them up to now. I got to be careful who I let into my inner circle. I sure don't want to spend the rest of my life in jail." Howard filled his mouth with salad. "If you're not up to making a few extra bucks let me know right now, and we can forget the whole thing. I'm not suggesting you do anything to compromise your integrity, but what I am proposing is a way to make a lot of extra money. Who would you be hurting? No one, except the big drug companies and the insurance firms who are always ripping off people anyway." He signaled for the waiter to bring another bottle of wine.

When dinner finally ended, Howard stood outside the restaurant patting his stomach, letting out a loud burp. He waited for the valet to bring his Mercedes. Henry stuck out his hand. "Thanks for dinner. I didn't expect you to pay for the whole meal."

Howard waved him off. "No problem. You can get the next one. Now, how about coming by my house tomorrow night? I'll throw some steaks on the grill and we can talk some more. I don't like to discuss too much of my personal business in public." He handed Henry his business card with his home address on it as he got into his car.

Howard's house was larger than Henry's. It looked like the City Museum with two large concrete lions guarding the front door. The entire first floor was decorated in shades of red with garish gold statues in various poses lining the walls. The sight of Howard in a red satin smoking jacket almost made Henry laugh. He tried to conceal his amusement as he looked around the house. "Nice touch, Howard. Did your wife do the decorating?"

"There is no Mrs. at the moment. I've had a few wives, but right now I'm just coasting. I had a professional decorator help me. It's great, isn't it?" Howard showed Henry into the den and offered him a glass of wine.

"I'm not much on wine. Do you have anything else? Even a beer would be fine." Howard opened the liquor cabinet and told Henry to help himself.

Henry held up an expensive bottle of scotch. "It looks to me you're doing pretty well for someone who is supposed to be struggling."

"Who said I was struggling? I just want a little more padding before I call it quits," Howard replied.

They talked for hours. Henry realized that Howard was just as consumed with making money as he was.

Howard's plan was simple. Henry would create fictional clients and write prescriptions for certain drugs that had a good street value; Howard would fill them. "You know, Henry, some of these pills go for a buck each on the street. You can also write prescriptions with no refills and I'll change them after I give the customer his medicine. Then we sell the extra pills. The deal with the insurance companies is a whole separate issue."

Henry was skeptical. It just seemed too easy. How could they get away with it?

"Look, I'm telling you, it's a piece of cake. My records are as clean as a whistle." Howard leaned back in his chair and blew smoke rings from his cigar. "We just have to take it slow at first. Start with a few prescriptions a month. Go through the old files at the plant. See if you can find employees that have moved out of town or died. You'll be surprised how quickly you can add a thousand dollars to your income."

Henry was hooked. He wanted the money. Howard had a big house, a nice Mercedes and he had never been in trouble with the law. Why couldn't he have a piece of it? He would do it just long enough to clean up some of his bills and maybe buy a few things he had been wanting. They shook hands and ate two large steaks blood rare.

Little by little things began to change at home. At first just a few small objects appeared in the house. Within the next few months there was an explosion of antique furniture, silverware, and rare books arriving almost weekly. Henry told Grace that Tom Sutton had given him an enormous raise and finally things were looking up for him. He caught up his past due bills and he began giving Grace extra money to run the household. Henry's mood improved and he even tried to make conversation with Anna. He mentioned that it would probably be a good idea if Anna went away to college. She wasn't sure what he was up to, but whatever it was she was sure he had an ulterior motive.

Henry wanted to take a vacation. Grace said she would like to go back to Massachusetts and visit Ternberry.

"I said a trip, Grace: like Paris or Switzerland not Massachusetts for Christ's sakes."

Grace decided she would rather not go abroad and told Henry maybe it would be a good idea if he went alone.

Chapter Twenty-Four

Henry was away when Anna went to the prom. He was also away for her graduation and she couldn't have been happier. He had been gone for almost three months. It was a wonderful time for Anna. Lou Jean came to stay at the house and for once there was music and laughter filling the rooms.

"Do I have a tan line yet?" Lou Jean pulled the strap down on her swimsuit.

Anna rose up on one elbow, removing her sunglasses. "I think I see a small difference." They had lathered themselves with baby oil and lay on a blanket in the backyard.

"Damn, I'm hot. I think I've had enough sun for today." Lou Jean rolled over onto her back.

Anna began to laugh. "We've only been out here for twenty minutes." The summer sun felt good on her bare skin. It was a relaxing time. Graduation was out of the way, and with her father out of town for at least another month, she felt free.

Lou Jean stood up. "That's it. I've had enough." She grabbed her towel and headed for the shade of the house.

Anna opened the refrigerator and handed Lou Jean a soda. They sat on the swing on the back porch, the slats making lines on their bare legs.

"I think I might be moving to St. Louis," Lou Jean said.

"What? What do you mean, move to St. Louis? You never mentioned that before." Anna was surprised.

"Yes, I did. I mentioned it a couple of months ago."

"Well, I never thought you were serious. When did all of this come about?" Anna asked.

"I told you I had an aunt who lives there. My uncle died a few months back and she wants my mom and me to come live with her. I've been thinking about it a lot. My mom can't keep cleaning houses forever. Mr. Sutton is getting crazier by the day. Ever since his wife left him, he hasn't been the same."

Anna couldn't believe what she was hearing. How could her best friend move away from her? "You can't leave me here alone. What will I do without you?"

"Well, we're big girls now. We have to get on with our lives. I guess I could stay here and marry Ronnie Butler," Lou Jean said as she rolled her eyes.

"Oh please, that would be even worse than moving to St. Louis," Anna said.

Lou Jean put her arm around Anna. "Please don't be mad at me. I hate like hell to leave you, but this may be my only chance to get away from this place."

"I'm not mad at you. I'm just being selfish. I don't want to lose you. Besides, I wanted you to go to college with me."

"Fat chance of that happening. Where would I get that kind of money?"

"Well, maybe you can take a few college courses in St. Louis. Promise me you'll do that as soon as you can. You're too smart not to go to college."

Lou Jean and Anna never spoke of the night they hid in the Sutton's kitchen. It was a quiet understanding between two friends. Anna could never forget how much comfort Lou Jean had been to her in the days that followed. She would tell Anna stories about her own father, and made up imaginary ways to get rid of Henry. She was a true friend and Anna was going to miss her.

It was their last night together. They sat on the back porch just as they had for so many evenings in the past five years. Anna drank a soda, wiping the cold drops of moisture from the bottle on to her head.

"I'm really going to miss you. I guess you already know that," Anna said.

Lou Jean smiled, "Well, I'm not going to miss you."

Anna poked her in the rib. They were silent for a while, listening to the sound of the August locust singing in the trees, not really wanting the evening to end. Since her father had returned from Europe and Lou Jean was leaving, Anna was sad and depressed.

"Did I tell you my father was giving me his car?" Anna said. "He's getting a new one and he said I could have the Chevy."

"That's great. How come you never told me that earlier today?"

Anna shrugged. "It really doesn't seem too important right now."

Lou Jean stood up and leaned against the rail. "I wonder what your old man's up to? First he said you could go away to college and now giving you his car. Damn, he must really be having a wild time or else he's afraid you know something about him that he doesn't want anyone to find out about. By the way kiddo, when you get to college, find yourself a guy or at least go out on a few dates." Lou Jean took a drink from Anna's soda bottle.

Anna made a face. "Yes, Mother, I'll start dating. I promise."

Lou Jean tried to fix Anna up with dates while they were in high school, but Anna always had some excuse not to go. There were a few boys who were interested in Anna, but she was too shy to talk to them, running in the other direction if she saw them in the halls. Most of the boys thought she was conceited and left her alone. How wrong they were.

Lou Jean looked at her watch. "I have to go, Anna. My mom is waiting for me. The bus pulls out at ten o'clock." She reached for Anna's hand. "I don't want you to come with me to the station. You'll make me cry and ruin my image." She wiped the tears from her face. "I just want you to know you're the best friend a person could have and if I don't hear from you in a few days, I'll send a hit man to do you in." Lou Jean reached into her pocket and pulled out a piece of paper. "Here is my new address and phone number." She ran down the driveway and out the gate never looking back. Anna sat on the porch until the sky grew dark and the fireflies danced above the lawn. She hugged her knees and cried until there were no more tears left inside her. How would she ever make it without Lou Jean?

Anna decided to go to Kansas State University. It was less than two hours away from Stockbridge and she could come home on the weekends to see her mother. Henry was relieved after he realized it was less expensive than the private schools in the area. He had hired a cleaning lady to help Grace and bought himself a new Mercedes. That was all the expense he needed right now. Grace moved into one of the spare bedrooms, saying she slept better when she didn't have to listen to his snoring. He didn't care. He even bought her a second television set for her bedroom. Now she had no way of knowing when he got home at night or how much he had to drink. Grace seldom cooked anymore. Occasionally, she would leave food on the stove for him. Henry found it easier for him to stop at the country club and have dinner. A television set and a vial of pills had replaced him.

Anna fell in love with school almost immediately. She loved the whole atmosphere. Even though she worried about her mother, the relief of being away from her father and Cherry Street made her feel free for the first time in years. She missed Lou Jean, but was quickly making friends with the girls in the dorm. Lou Jean called and said she liked St. Louis. Her aunt's house was nicer than any place she had ever lived. Her mother had taken a job in a dry cleaners and she was working for a law firm as a stock girl and gopher. She liked her job and she was making decent wages. The idea of becoming a lawyer some day seemed appealing to her. Of course Anna reminded her that she needed to start thinking about going to college.

The first year of school went by quickly and Anna was not sure if she could stand being home all summer, but she needed to spend time with her mother. Maybe she could get a job so she wouldn't have to ask her father for money. Grace told her that her father was still spending excessive amounts of money. The house was brimming with more new purchases and there were several gardeners working in the yard. Grace said that when she tried to go into Henry's study to get a book, she found that he had put a lock on the door. Even the housekeeper was not allowed to clean his study. She had no idea what he was hiding; only that a man named Howard called quite often.

Howard let the telephone ring six times before he hung up. He had been trying to reach Henry for over a week. When he called him at work, Henry's assistant always said he was out of the office. Howard decided to try just once more before going to Henry's house. He leafed through the stack of prescriptions on his desk shaking his head and cursing under his breath. He picked up the phone again and dialed the number. Grace answered on the third ring, telling him that Henry wasn't home. He was probably still at the country club. Howard left a message. It was urgent that he talk to Henry as soon as possible. Henry never returned his call.

Henry was surprised when he arrived home the next evening to find Howard's car sitting in his driveway. Howard opened the car door, shielding his eyes from the glare of the car's headlights. "We need to talk. Why have you been avoiding me?"

"Why didn't you just call me? What's on your mind?" Henry asked.

"I've been calling you all week. What's on my mind is that you need to slow down. I have over sixty prescription refills from you already this month. You better give it a rest or we'll be in deep shit." Howard was sweating and wiping his head with his handkerchief. "I told you from the very beginning that you had to take it slow."

Henry lit a cigarette and leaned against the car. "I have a daughter in college now. Things are expensive. I need the money."

"I'm not buying that crap, Henry. You're just getting greedy. You can send in some insurance claims, but don't send anyone else to my store for at least a month. I won't fill their prescriptions. I mean it." He shook his head, as he headed down the driveway forgetting that his car was still there. He turned and walked back up the driveway, still mumbling to himself.

Henry sent in a few false insurance claims and they had been paid with no problem. Tomorrow he would have to research the files of the employees who had left the factory to see what he could do with their records. Maybe just a few back injuries or stomach disorders could tide him over until Howard calmed down.

Anna arrived home from school and could not believe the house. Almost all of the downstairs furniture had been replaced. She walked around looking at all the new furnishings. Velvet, overstuffed chairs and ornate mahogany tables crowded the living room. There were large paintings hanging on almost every wall, along with massive flower arrangements on marble stands. Henry stood in the doorway grinning. "Well, what do you think? Do you like it? It's the best money can buy."

"It's nice, but don't you think you're over doing it? I mean, look at all these things."

Henry threw up his hands. "They're not 'things.' I should have known you would have something critical to say. You're just like your mother. Well, I appreciate having culture and affluence." He turned and left the room and Anna could not keep from laughing to herself.

Anna finally got up enough courage to ask her father what medications her mother was taking. There was an array of unlabeled medicine vials on the table next to her bed. He said they were just things to help her with her headaches and insomnia. Anna knew that was not true. Her mother could barely get out of bed and she was even thinner than the last time she was home. Anna decided she would take some of the pills to the pharmacy and find out what they were. That afternoon when she went to her mother's bedroom to retrieve the bottles, they were nowhere to be found. Her mother said her father had taken them to be refilled.

Chapter Twenty-Five

Anna sat at her desk in her dorm room, writing a letter to Lou Jean. She wanted to tell her all about Parker. They met the first day of her sophomore year. He bumped into her in the student union hall, knocking her books to the floor. He apologized by buying her a cup of coffee. Later that day Parker called and asked her to dinner and now after two weeks they had seen each other every night. She hoped Lou Jean was proud of her now that she had a boyfriend.

Lou Jean called as soon as she received the letter. "What kind of name is Parker? It sounds like some stuffy preppy boy."

Anna giggled. "No. He's not a preppy boy. He's from Wichita and just an ordinary person. We like each other a lot."

"That's great. Tell me more about him."

Anna rambled on and on, hardly taking time to draw a breath. "He is a year ahead of me. His major is political science. He wants to be a politician and he even told me I was pretty. Can you believe that? He actually said I was pretty. I told him he needs glasses."

"Are you two doing it yet?" Lou Jean asked.

"Why does it not surprise me that you're asking me that?" Anna knew Lou Jean had been dying to ask her that question. "He has too much respect for me, and besides I'm not ready."

"Too much respect? Oh please," Lou Jean groaned. "You better get that boy alone."

It was almost time for Thanksgiving and Anna decided to ask her mother if it would be all right to bring Parker home. Grace said it would be nice to have company, especially someone that was special to Anna. Henry wasn't too thrilled but finally agreed, as long as they slept in separate rooms, preferably on separate floors.

The weather had turned very cold and a light snow was falling when they pulled into the driveway on Cherry Street. Parker stared at the house, not really believing that this is where Anna lived. She seemed so unpretentious to be living in this neighborhood. He had only found out recently that her father was a doctor. Henry, greeting them at the door with a glass of bourbon in his hand, was in an unusually friendly mood. He welcomed Parker and kissed Anna on the cheek. The house amazed Parker and Henry was elated. He escorted Parker into each room, pointing out the artwork and antiques. Anna and Grace followed behind like tourists on a museum tour. Anna could not believe that her father had amassed so many more things since her last visit home.

They had dinner in the dining room. Grace looked lovely in a pale blue dress, which Anna had never seen. She wore double strings of pearls around her neck and a sparkling diamond bracelet on her wrist. Anna wanted to ask her mother about them, but she knew better than to bring up the subject in front of her father. Her father decided to have the meal catered and brought in a server to take care of everything. He was afraid that Grace would not be able to cook a full course meal. After dinner, Anna and Parker drank glasses of chilled wine in front of the fireplace. The warmth of the fire made her sleepy. He pulled her close and she curled into the crook of his arm.

Grace had gone to her room and Henry disappeared into his study.

"Your parents are nice. I like them. They're a lot different than I expected. Is your mother always that quiet?" Parker asked.

Anna pulled Parker's arm around her and yawned. "Different in what way? Is my father a little nicer than you expected?"

"Well, you never talk about him much, and when you do, I always get the feeling that you and he don't get along very well. He seems fine to me. He is quite a collector, isn't he?"

"That's my father's latest passion," Anna said. "He wants to see how much stuff he can cram into this house. I wouldn't be surprised to come home someday and find out they had moved to a bigger house just to accommodate all of his possessions."

Parker laughed, "You could put four of my parents' house into this one. I can't imagine buying a bigger house than this one." He kissed her goodnight on the stairs.

Anna could see a stream of light filtering out from under her mother's bedroom door. She knocked lightly. "Mother, are you awake?"

Grace was lying across the bed watching television. "Come in dear, come sit with me." She patted the bed next to her.

"I won't stay long. I'm tired. I just wanted to see if you were okay. You were so quiet at dinner."

"I'm fine, dear. I wish you wouldn't always worry about me."

"What about the pills? Have you stopped taking them?" Anna's eyes scanned the night table, looking for medicine vials.

"Your father started me on a new medication. I only take it when I can't sleep. By the way, I like your young man."

Anna could sense her mother did not want to talk about her medication.

"Where are your pill bottles, Mother?"

"Anna, really, why all the questions? I don't want to talk about this anymore. Your father knows what he is doing and I would never take more than he prescribed. I'm tired. It's time to say goodnight," Grace said as she reached for the lamp and turned off the light.

By early morning the snow had covered the streets and was still falling. Parker decided they should return to school rather than stay until the next day as they had planned. Henry seemed almost sad to see them leave, telling Parker he was welcome anytime.

"I can't see where I'm going, Anna. The windshield wipers aren't clearing the window. The snow is too heavy. We'd better stop somewhere until it lets up," Parker said as he wiped his hand across the steamy glass. They were both relieved when they saw the neon sign of the truck stop restaurant. Parker pulled the car up in front of the building, pushing the snow into a pile in front of the bumper. They ordered hot coffee and warmed their hands on the cups. A trucker sitting at the end of the counter was telling the few customers in the restaurant that the roads ahead were closed. The heavy snow made them impassable. Parker considered turning around, but that didn't seem like a very good idea either.

"There is a motel next door. It's nothing fancy," the waitress said. "I'm sure they have some vacancies. There aren't too many people out driving right now."

Parker looked at Anna, wanting her to make the decision, but she said nothing.

"Well, I think that would be the best thing to do. By morning the roads will be better. I'll get a couple of rooms for us. Hesitating he looked at Anna. "Or should I just get one?"

Anna could feel the flush on her face. She turned on her stool as he opened the door. "Make it just one."

Anna and Parker visited Stockbridge often that year, each time stopping at the same little motel on the way back to school. Her father seemed to trust Parker and said that Parker reminded him of himself when he was young. That was a comment Anna didn't need to hear. Anna knew she was in love with him. She told Lou Jean all about the Thanksgiving weekend. It was embarrassing to talk about and Lou Jean made sure Anna did not leave out any details.

Anna planned a trip to St. Louis to coincide with Lou Jean's completion of her program at the paralegal secretarial school. Anna talked the whole trip, telling Parker about Lou Jean and all the crazy things they did when they were young. He listened, nodding and smiling, not quite feeling the same enthusiasm about the visit. Lou Jean made a reservation for them at a nearby motel and was waiting for them when they arrived. She ran across the parking lot, wearing a tight yellow dress and black high heels. Her arms open wide, she grabbed Anna and they hugged, jumping up and down. "Let me take a good look at you," she said, backing away from Anna. "My, my, love suits you. You look great." Anna could feel her face reddening.

She pulled Parker to her side. "Lou Jean, this is Parker." Parker smiled and extended his hand, which Lou Jean ignored, grabbing him into a tight hug.

Anna and Lou Jean were like two children, talking, laughing, and interrupting each other, while Parker sat on the bed watching television.

"What do you want to do while you're here?" Lou Jean asked. "Sightseeing, shopping, eating out. What? Tell me and we'll do it."

Parker cleared his throat. "What I really want to do is visit the library at the university. I have heard that it is one of the best in the Midwest. I know you girls want to spend some time alone together, so why don't you just drop me off and you two can have a nice visit."

They spent the day together buying silly hats and red tennis shoes. Lou Jean pushed the door open on the small café and dropped her shopping bags down in an empty booth. "My feet are killing me," she said as she kicked off her shoes.

Anna fiddled with the straw holder on the table. "I'm worried about my mother, Lou Jean. I think she's taking too many pills. She doesn't even know what they are. Every time I see her, she looks even thinner. Now that she has a housekeeper, she just lays in bed most of the time and watches television."

"Why don't you take her to a real doctor?" Lou Jean asked.

"I suggested that, but she refused to go, and when I told her I was going to get someone to come to the house to look at her, she told me she wouldn't open her door."

"Seems to me you've done all you can short of taking her to the doctor by force. I guess the rest is up to her."

Lou Jean took Anna to her office where she was greeted warmly, everyone telling her how much Lou Jean talked about her. Afterward they picked Parker up at the library. He looked at his watch, reminding them that they were almost an hour late. At dinner, Anna tried to include him in the conversation.

"Tell Parker about the courses you just completed, Lou Jean," she said.

Parker leaned forward in his chair. "Let me get this straight. Are these college courses or just some kind of night school?"

"It was a paralegal course that I needed to take to get me out of the mail room and into the secretarial pool. I'm trying to decide if I want to go to law school," Lou Jean replied.

"Well, you have to go to college before you can go to law school," he added, as if she wasn't aware of it. "It's a little more in-depth than a six month course in secretarial skills."

Lou Jean didn't answer him and for a moment there was an uncomfortable silence.

Parker had gone to pay the motel bill, leaving Anna and Lou Jean in the room alone. "I thought you had another day off, Lou Jean? I didn't know our visit would be over so soon," Anna said. "It's Parker, isn't it? You don't like him, do you?"

"He's a real cutie. Yeah, he's okay."

"I knew you didn't like him."

"He's a little too pretentious for my taste, but hey, if you love him, that's all that matters," Lou Jean replied. Anna wasn't going to let this go. She wanted to know what Lou Jean meant by her remark. Lou Jean finally admitted that maybe she just took him the wrong way. She felt he was being condescending and looking down on her because she wasn't in college.

"I can't help it, Anna. In some ways he reminds me of your father."

"Don't you ever say that again!" Anna said angrily. "He is nothing at all like my father. Parker is kind and sweet and treats me with respect."

"Hey, I'm sorry. I guess I just didn't have enough time to get to know him. Don't be mad at me," Lou Jean said, reaching out for Anna's hand.

"I'm sorry too. I know he came on a little too strong, but I'm sure he never meant to hurt your feelings. Maybe on our next visit we can spend more time together and you can get to know him like I do," Anna said in an apologetic voice.

Parker returned to the table and they said their goodbyes, both promising to call or write soon. As they drove away, Anna had a strange nagging feeling in her stomach. She was quiet for most of the trip, finally asking Parker what he really thought of Lou Jean.

"She was different than I expected. She's kind of flashy and her English is pretty bad for someone thinking of practicing law. Other than that, she seems okay. You two are an odd pair."

Anna hadn't wanted him to be that truthful. She wasn't prepared to defend her best friend and her boyfriend in the same morning. She hoped in time they would grow to like each other.

Chapter Twenty-Six

Tom Sutton called Henry into his office. "Sit down. We need to talk. I've made a major decision and it involves you."

Henry wasn't sure what Tom was talking about. Since his wife left him, Tom wasn't able to concentrate on his business, and most of time when he talked with Henry he made no sense at all. He always seemed out of sorts. He would walk around the plant yelling at the employees or mumbling to himself. Tom had shut down several production lines and laid off his evening shift. Henry wasn't worried. They had down times before, but business usually picked up. Henry was now relying heavily on Howard Bullard to keep money coming in. Tom walked to the front of the office and stared out the large glass window at the floor below. The machines were humming as usual.

"You know, Henry, I've been at this business for over thirty years now. Day in, day out, coming down here to the plant and busting my butt and what for?" Henry didn't know if it were really a question he was supposed to answer.

"I'll tell you what for. Nothing. My wife is gone. My house is too damn big for me, and I don't even have any kids to inherit this mess." Tom rubbed his head. Opening his desk drawer, he produced a pint of whiskey and two glasses. "Let's have a drink. Let's break company rules and have a swig right here in my office." He poured a shot of whiskey into each glass and handed one to Henry. "The big companies in this state are gobbling up us little guys one at a time. They finally got around to me, and by God they made me an offer I can't refuse. It's my chance to get out alive."

Henry hadn't touched his glass. This wasn't what he had expected. Surely Tom wasn't serious. He couldn't imagine him wanting to sell the factory.

YARD SALE

"You're looking at me like I've lost my mind, Franklin. Well, I'm telling you the truth. I've already signed the papers and as of the first of the month I am no longer the owner of this company." He downed his drink and poured another. "I'm prepared to write you a check for a year's salary and a little extra. I know this is short notice, but I'm sure you're just as glad as I am to be getting out of this place. Looks like you're doing pretty good on your own," he said, pointing to the gold watch on Henry's wrist. "You've been a good friend and an honest employee." He extended his hand. "I wish you well, Henry."

Henry slowly got up from the chair, setting the untouched glass of bourbon on the desk. So that was it. His career at Sutton's Manufacturing Company was over. He had a lot of work to do. On Friday, Henry picked up his check. He returned to his office and began putting a few of his personal effects into a box. When he finished, he locked the door and left only one set of keys with Tom's secretary. Henry stopped by the bank and cashed the check. He put the stack of bills into his safety deposit box. Later that afternoon he went to the country club and ate dinner in the lounge. He stayed and talked with some of the members until after ten o'clock. Once at home, he opened the door to his study and retrieved two large books. As he approached Grace's bedroom door, Henry slammed them to the floor.

"My goodness, Henry, what is going on?" Grace said as she opened her door, pulling her robe around her.

"I'm sorry, I didn't mean to disturb you. I was just getting something to read and I tripped on the rug," Henry said as he picked up the books. "I'll be in my room reading if you need me. Goodnight, Grace."

Henry waited until he was sure Grace was asleep. He silently crept down the stairs and out of the house. Putting the Mercedes in reverse, he let it roll backward to the end of the driveway before he started the motor.

No one really knew how the fire started. The arson squad turned up evidence that pointed to a trash can in the employee lounge. Someone made a fire in the wastebasket using kerosene. Everything in the building, including the upstairs offices, were burned beyond recognition. Tom Sutton and Henry were questioned. Tom was livid at the idea that anyone would think he was stupid enough to burn down his own factory after he had just sold it for a large profit. Henry, of course, told them he was at home. If they had any questions, they could ask his wife. Besides what motive would he have for starting such a fire? After all, he lost all of his equipment, plus the medical records of all of the employees. He tried to explain to the investigators how critical the records were and now they were lost forever. The investigation ended with the report stating that an unknown arsonist or a disgruntled employee caused the fire. Tom was at a loss as to what to do. The insurance company rejected his claim since the building was no longer in his name and the new owners were now filing charges against him as the company no longer existed. To settle the suit, Tom used up all his savings plus the money from the sale of his house. Henry said he was so very sorry. Tom Sutton left town the following week. Henry never heard from him again.

The idea of not having to work made Henry euphoric. He could sleep late in the mornings and spend more time at the club. No more Tom Sutton, no more griping employees. He truly felt rich for the first time in over twenty years. There were so many things he wanted to buy, perhaps even a new car and maybe he would take a trip to Paris. He would have to pace himself, but he was sure with the prescriptions he was writing to Howard's pharmacy and the stash in his safety deposit box, he had enough money to last him for a long time.

Henry had no idea that Howard decided to sever their relationship. Howard had no doubt in his mind that Henry started the fire and he began to feel uncomfortable. Now that Henry was no longer working, all of the prescriptions he wrote were fictitious names, leaving Howard wide open for an investigation. He decided to tell Henry that their business dealings were over.

"I don't think so, Howard. There is no way I can give it up right now," Henry said when Howard approached him. "It's my only opportunity to keep money coming in and I don't plan on quitting now. Don't worry so much. Everything is going to be just fine. It won't be long before both of us have enough money to retire for good."

Howard was nervous. He now knew that he started something he couldn't finish. He had to think of something and quick to keep Henry from ruining everything. "Listen, Henry, how about this: I got one doc on my payroll that works downtown at one of those free clinics. He sends me people all the time. I give them a break on their medicine and I can usually short them at least half on their prescription. Most of them can't even read or write. You could go to work down there one or two days a week and make it all legal again."

"I'll look in to it," Henry said to make Howard feel more at ease.

The bank was almost ready to close when Henry arrived. The teller impatiently looked at her watch and ushered him into the safety deposit vault. He opened his box and dumped the contents on the desk. He couldn't believe it. It had only been four months since Tom had given him his check for a year's salary. There was less than five hundred dollars in the box. He rifled around among the papers looking for more money, but there was none. Henry rubbed his head; he hadn't even paid the mortgage this month. What the hell was he going to do? He stuffed the papers back into the box and put the money in his wallet. He needed a drink, but knew he should avoid the club since he hadn't paid his dues this month.

The Ash Street Clinic was less than a desirable place to work. The building was old and run down with a rusty smell from the pipes that leaked drips of yellow water on the hallway floors. Henry was to work two days a week. The doctor in charge knew he was a friend of Howard's. He gave Henry a knowing look and showed him around the clinic.

Most of Henry's patients were street people and migrant workers from the farms on the outskirts of town. Children with head lice, young pregnant mothers, and old men with sores on their bodies from alcohol abuse were a daily occurrence. Henry washed his hands until they became raw and he finally resorted to wearing rubber gloves. Explaining medication to the patients was difficult. Henry sometimes prescribed a controlled substance even though they did not need it. These medicines made him the most profit. He hated the clinic, yet the money began to again flow into his pockets. It was the only thing that made working there bearable.

Sitting at the scratched wooden desk in the clinic office, Henry fell asleep as he waited for his next patient. He jumped as the phone began to ring. "This is Dr. Franklin," he said.

"Jesus, Henry, we got problems. Big problems," Howard screamed into the phone. "You treated some guy last week who said that he was a migrant worker. His name was Carlos something or other. I remember him because he asked me a lot of questions about the pills I gave him. He was a goddamn narcotics agent. I got a letter today saying that I am under investigation for the sale of controlled substances to illegal aliens. That's a federal offense." Howard was in a panic. His voice cracked, as if he were ready to cry.

"Calm down, will you, Howard? Let's just think about this for a moment. It couldn't be that bad if they just sent you a letter. I think they are just trying to scare you," Henry said in an irritated voice.

"Well, they did a pretty good job of it. I can't fill any more prescriptions until after they have come down here and checked my records. I'm in big trouble and so are you."

Henry sat up in his chair. "What do you mean, I am too? How would they get my name? Don't tell me you kept those scripts I wrote. What kind of idiot are you? Why didn't you destroy them?"

"I have to keep records, Henry. Most of those prescriptions looked legal. I'm down here at the store right now trying to get rid of as much stuff as I can, but I'm scared, real scared. I think I'm going to make a run for it. I can be in Mexico by tomorrow night. I don't plan on spending the next twenty years in prison. If you're smart, you'd start thinking about getting out of the country, too."

"Stay put, Howard. I'll be there in half an hour," Henry said as he hung up the phone.

Henry left the clinic and drove down Ash Street checking out each building until he finally saw the pawnshop sign hanging over a place called Jake's. A large burly man smoking a cigar sat at the counter reading the newspaper. Looking over his glasses he asked Henry if he could help him.

"I'm in the market for a gun. I'm working nights down the street from here, and I would feel safer if I had some protection."

Jake pushed the cigar to one side of his mouth. "I know what you mean," he said patting the bulge under his shirt. "I've been robbed a couple of times." He pulled several guns out of the display case.

Henry finally decided on a 22-caliber pistol. He held it in his hand, feeling the cold steel of the barrel. "Yes, I think this will do."

Jake reached under the counter and slid a box of shells across the glass.

"How much?" Henry asked.

"Fifty bucks and I'll throw in the ammo. I need to do some paperwork on the gun. Let me see some identification."

Henry pulled another fifty dollars out of his wallet and laid it on the counter. "Is this enough identification?"

Jake smiled and picked up the money. He put the gun and shells into a brown paper bag and handed them to Henry. "Be careful now. Don't shoot yourself in the foot."

Henry drove around for a while, stopping once to buy cigarettes and a bottle of bourbon. He loaded the gun in the parking lot of the liquor store and headed toward Bullard's Pharmacy.

The store was dark when he got there. Henry drove past the store and parked his car a half block away. He sat in the car for a few minutes and checked to make sure there was no one around. The pharmacy door was locked and the closed sign hung lopsided on the doorknob. Henry cupped his hands and peered into the window. He could see a stream of light coming from the rear of the store. Howard must have left as soon as he hung up the phone. Damn little weasel, Henry thought to himself. He wanted Howard to still be in the store when someone had apparently come in to rob him. What a shame. Howard was to have been shot during the holdup. Now Henry's plan was ruined. It would have all been so easy. He could have destroyed all of the files and taken care of Howard at the same time.

Henry walked down the narrow alley toward the rear of the store. The bright light startled him and he turned to see a police cruiser shining a flashlight down the corridor. Henry flattened himself against the wall, holding his breath until the car passed. Could they possibly have noticed him? He put the gun in his pocket and ran to his car.

The agents from the Narcotics Bureau arrived early the next morning and impounded Howard's store and all of the records. Henry watched the whole episode on the five o'clock evening news. According to the reporter, Bullard's Pharmacy had been under investigation for some time. Henry's mouth dropped open as the camera panned to the front of the courthouse. There was Howard being escorted into the building in handcuffs with tears running down his face. Apparently he had been caught just as he was leaving his house with his suitcases already in the trunk of his car. Henry began to sweat. What was he going to do? Howard would probably tell the authorities everything they wanted to know. Leaving the country was probably his only option, but he had to have more cash. Henry paced back and forth across his study, finishing off a bottle of bourbon. His mind was filled with ideas. He could sell his car and pawn some of the antiques and Grace's jewelry. He just didn't know how much time he had. Was it hours or days? The thought of prison terrified him. It was all Howard's fault. Everything was going so well until Howard got careless. Now Henry had no choice but to leave. Maybe a change of scenery would be good for him, but what about all of his things? He hated leaving them behind. Henry pulled his suitcases from the hall closet. He would pack and try to gather as much money as he could. He didn't mind leaving his family behind, they could suffer the embarrassment. But where would he go? The bourbon began to make his head hurt, and anger was beginning to boil up inside of him. He slammed the study door and stumbled up the staircase towards Grace's bedroom.

Grace was lying in bed reading when Henry burst into her room. "Do you have any money? Where is it?"

"I have a few dollars in my dresser. What is wrong?" Grace asked as Henry began pulling open the dresser drawers.

"Where is all of your goddamn jewelry?" he snarled as he dumped a small satin box onto the floor, picking up the pearls and two rings.

Grace rose from the bed and began walking toward him. She touched his arm. "What is wrong with you, Henry? You're acting like a mad man."

"Get away from me, dammit. Just get the hell away from me." His eyes were filled with rage.

The car dealership was closed. So was the jewelry store where he bought the pearls. He sat in his car slamming his hand against the steering wheel. He remembered the day he purchased them. They cost over a thousand dollars. Fine, cultured pearls, pure in quality. Grace only nagged him for spending the money. It was always the same. Nothing ever made her happy. She would be sorry. When he was gone, she wouldn't have to worry. There would be no more jewelry or pills from him. His throat was dry. He needed to go somewhere to have a few drinks and settle down.

The knock on the door awoke Anna. A sleepy-eyed girl in pink pajamas said there was an urgent call for her. Anna jumped from her bed and ran to the telephone in the dormitory hallway. She could hear a small voice saying her name. "Mother, is that you? I can barely hear you. What's wrong?"

"Anna, is there anyway you can come home? I need you. I have taken a fall and hurt my head," her mother said.

"I'll be there as soon as I can. Do you want me to call an ambulance?"

"Oh please, no. I'll just stay in bed until you get here."

Anna hung up the telephone. She threw on a pair of jeans and a sweatshirt. Grabbing her purse and car keys, she left school.

The house was dark when she pulled into the driveway. She stumbled across the lawn, tripping on the garden hose, and made her way into the house. Her mother was lying on her side, her head buried in a pillow. Anna touched her shoulder. "Mother, it's me."

Grace rolled over and removed the washcloth from her face. Anna gasped. Her mother's eye was swollen shut and a large gash zigzagged down the side of her cheek, surrounded by purple and red bruises. "Can you walk?" Anna asked. Grace nodded. She dressed her mother and put her small feet into her slippers. Anna carefully lifted her mother from the bed. As Grace stood up, three pill vials clattered to the floor from beneath the covers. Anna retrieved them and stuffed them into her pocket. She put her mother's arm around her own shoulder and helped her down the steps into the car.

Anna waited in the emergency room for over an hour before a young doctor emerged from her mother's room. He motioned for her to join him in the lounge "It appears your mother has a slight concussion and a cracked rib, plus lacerations on her face. Can you tell me what happened?" he asked. Anna related her mother's story to him. She said her mother had told her that she fell in the bathroom hitting her head on the tub. He took notes as she talked. "I don't mean to doubt her story, but it would be hard to get that kind of cut on your face unless you struck a sharp surface. With all that bruising, I was wondering if it would be possible that someone hit her? She also has bruises on her arm."

Anna listened as he continued. "I'm more concerned with her mental state. She seems confused and incoherent. I did not find any evidence of alcohol in her system. Do you have any idea what kind of medication she is taking?"

Anna pulled the three unmarked bottles from her pocket. "I found these in her bedroom."

"Let me see if I can get the pharmacy to analyze these and we can go from there." He patted Anna's hand. "Don't worry. She is going to be fine, but I would like to keep her here overnight for observation. By the way, do you know who your mother's doctor is?"

Without thinking, Anna replied, "My father is her doctor. He is the one that has been giving the medication to her."

"I'll need to talk to him. Please have him call me in the morning."

Anna looked in on her mother before she left the hospital. She was sleeping, her face covered in a white bandage. Anna fought back the tears as she drove home. She parked beside her father's Mercedes, touching the hood as she passed by. It was still warm. The bastard must have just gotten home. Once inside the house, Anna banged on the study door.

Staggering to steady himself, Henry opened the door. "What the hell is going on? What are you doing home from school and where is your mother?"

Anna was shaking. "Did you hit her?"

Henry stepped back, his fist clenching and unclenching. "What the hell do you mean did I hit her? She fell, so I just put her to bed. Where is she?"

"Oh you just put her back into bed with cracked ribs and her face bleeding. Then what did you do, decide to celebrate? She's in the hospital where she belongs. You'd better go see her tomorrow. The doctor wants to talk to you about all the pills you've been giving her. You're probably going to be in big trouble." Anna had forgotten herself. She had never before spoken to her father in such a harsh manner. She backed up, putting some distance between them. Maybe he would hit her too.

Henry began to laugh. "So I'm going to be in big trouble. Well, little girl, you don't know the half of it." His voice was slurred, as he steadied himself on the stair post. "I have more things to worry about than a bunch of pimple faced interns." Reeling around he grabbed for Anna's purse. "How much money do you have?"

Anna opened the front door and sprinted down the steps. He stood on the porch yelling at her. "You come back here, dammit, I need your help. Anna, come back here!"

Anna froze for just a second, remembering that day so long ago when she watched him in the kitchen with Renard. She decided to spend the night in the hospital sitting next to her mother's bed.

YARD SALE

It was dawn when Henry awoke. The leather couch had made deep marks on his face. He looked at his watch. Cursing to himself he began opening the buffet drawers in the dining room. He took out the wooden case of silverware and chose several pieces of crystal. He stacked paintings next to the door and went upstairs to get the rest of Grace's jewelry. Henry jumped when he heard the slamming of the car doors. Looking out of the bedroom window, he could see a brown sedan and a police car in the driveway. He could feel his heart pounding in his chest. Running down the steps, he backed up against the wall and crept through the hallway to the kitchen. He could hear them talking on the porch. Fear swept over him. They were coming to get him and take him away in handcuffs. He had to get away. Howard must have told them everything. Hiding behind the pantry door, he waited. He could hear their muffled voices again. The doorbell rang, once, twice, and then there was silence. He expected to hear the front door being destroyed as he imagined their boots kicking it off its hinges. Several minutes later, the car doors slammed and they were gone. He wondered why they had left. Surely they had a warrant for his arrest. Henry knew they would be back. Walking from room to room, he tried to devise a plan of escape. His mind was racing. He would wait until dark and slip out the back door. He had enough money to book an airline ticket.

Anna called Parker from the hospital to let him know what had happened. He said he was worried about her and she apologized for not calling sooner. She told him about her father and what he had done. Anna cried on the telephone and Parker tried to comfort her.

"Just calm down. I know it's going to be okay. Maybe if you go back to the house and try to talk to him you can get everything straightened out. It could have just been the alcohol that made him so crazy. I love you, Anna. If there is anything I can do, you just let me know."

Maybe Parker was partly right. She would go back to the house and pretend to make peace with her father so that she could get her mother's things out of the house. Who knows what her father would do if she stayed away too long. He might change the locks or forbid her to come back. He was a crazy man and she had no idea what he would do next.

Grace was sitting up in bed with a tray of untouched food on the nightstand.

"You haven't eaten a thing, Mother. Aren't you the least bit hungry?" Anna asked.

Grace shook her head. "No. What I really want to do is go home. All I have is just a little headache. If the doctor would just give me one of my pills, I will be fine."

Anna kissed her cheek. "I'm going home now to talk to Father, but I'll be back in the morning and we'll see what kind of arrangements we can make to get you out of here."

"That would be wonderful," Grace said. "And tell your father I miss him."

Anna wished Lou Jean were here. Lou Jean would barge into that house and give Anna's father a piece of her mind. She wouldn't be frightened at all, but Anna's legs were like rubber by the time she got home. She was hoping he wouldn't be drinking. At least if he were sober, maybe she could reason with him.

The study door was closed as usual. She stopped, raised her hand to knock and changed her mind. Maybe later, but right now she needed a shower and a change of clothes. Henry had seen the car drive in as he stood hiding behind the heavy velour drapes in the study. He watched as the headlights turned into the driveway, giving a sigh of relief when he saw it was his daughter's car. He waited until he heard the shower go off before he went upstairs. She came out of the bathroom, her hair wrapped in a towel. Anna was startled to see him in the hallway. She had never seen him like this. He was unshaven and his clothes were in disarray. He stood watching her for a moment. When had she turned into such a pretty young woman? He never really knew her, and now there was no time.

"Anna, I'm sorry for what I said to you last night. I had too much to drink. Whatever happened between your mother and me was purely an accident. I would never intentionally hurt her. Can you forgive me?" He tried very hard to sound convincing. "How is your mother?"

Anna was frustrated. His voice seemed soft and gentle, but is was too late to show him any sympathy. "She's doing better."

"I have to take a trip tomorrow, but I'll go by the hospital first thing in the morning. Would it be all right if I borrowed your car? Mine seems to be acting up," Henry asked as he followed her down the hall to her room.

She sat down at her dressing table and began brushing her hair. Anna wondered where he was going. He hadn't said anything about a trip. "That's fine. Goodnight." She had nothing else to say to him. She wanted him out of her room, out of the house and out of her life. He stood behind her for a moment, staring at her reflection in the mirror. Finally turning, he left the room. Anna locked her door the minute he stepped into the hallway.

Henry pulled Anna's car into the garage. Hastily loading the trunk with his suitcases, he would leave as soon as she was asleep. He sat at his desk in the dark, wondering how his life had come to this point. Why had so many people turned against him? It was mostly his father's fault, but he couldn't leave the rest of them out: Barrios, Martin, Tom Sutton, that stupid Howard Bullard and even Grace. Why had they all turned their backs on him? They made him what he was now, a broken, frightened man. He hated them all.

Anna laid across her bed, pulling the blanket up to her neck. Her eyelids were heavy. She had only a couple of hours sleep in the past two days. The banging sound startled her. She sat up in bed trying to focus her eyes in the early morning light. She waited a moment until she heard it again. Someone was knocking on the front door. Putting on her robe, she made her way down the stairs.

"Who is it?"

"Mrs. Franklin, I'm sorry to bother you, but we need to talk to your husband."

Anna asked again, "Who are you?"

"We're from the police department and it's important that we talk with your husband. I have identification."

Henry heard the knocking, too. He opened the study door just a crack. Standing in the dark, he listened to the conversation. As Anna unbolted the lock, Henry silently retreated into his study.

"I'm not Mrs. Franklin, I'm her daughter. She is in the hospital. What do you want at this early hour?"

The two men stepped inside the house. She turned on the light, as both men held out their badges. She motioned toward the living room.

"Is your father home?" the older of the two men asked.

"I'll see if he is here," she said.

There was no answer when Anna knocked on door of the study and her car was not in the driveway. "I'm afraid he's not here. He mentioned something about a trip when I came home last night," Anna said, wondering if this had anything to do with her mother. Had the doctor from the hospital reported Henry to the police? "Is my father in trouble? Has he done something wrong?"

The older man held out a picture. No ma'am, this is not really about your father. We just have a few questions for him. Maybe you could help us out. Have you ever seen this person before?" He held a photograph of Howard Bullard, smiling, wearing his white Pharmacy coat.

Anna shook her head, "I don't recognize him. Is he a doctor?"

"No. He owns a drugstore downtown. He has been arrested and we wanted to ask your father a few questions about him. We came by yesterday, but no one was home. We're just curious to know if your father had dealings with him. There were some prescriptions written by your father found at the pharmacy. I'm afraid Mr. Bullard was falsifying the information on them."

Anna shook her head, "It's awfully early. Couldn't these questions wait until later?"

"Mr. Bullard had someone post bail for him and when we tried to contact him, he had already left Stockbridge. If your father has any information that could help us find him before his trail gets cold we would appreciate his calling our office tomorrow." He handed Anna his business card as they turned to leave.

Henry couldn't hear the conversation. He pressed his ear against the door, but the voices were too muffled once they entered the living room. He was waiting for them to come for him. He could hardly breathe from the fear that engulfed him. His mouth was so dry it was difficult to swallow. With his hand shaking, he poured himself a glass of bourbon. What were they doing in there? The voices were in the hallway now. His pulse was racing as he sat down at his desk downing the last of the bourbon. He put his head down and began to sob. He thought to himself that it was all so unfair. He was a good man. He didn't deserve to go to prison.

Anna watched through the window as the men got back in their cars. The house was quiet. She could hear the rhythmic ticking of the mantle clock. She turned on the living room light. It was two o'clock. Anna was wide-awake now. A cup of tea might calm her down. As she stepped into the hallway, she heard a soft click and the study door slowly opened. Frightened, Anna backed up against the wall. Holding her breath, she saw it was her father peering out of the dark room. "Father, you scared me! I thought you were gone. There were some men here looking for you." Before she could say another word, he closed the door. Anna knocked lightly, but he did not answer. Standing close to the door, she said in a loud voice, "Those men are coming back to see you later today. What time are you leaving on your trip?"

"Just go away, Anna. Leave me alone," he replied.

"But don't you want to know why they wanted to talk to you?"

His voice was angry now. "No! Leave me alone I said."

Anna went to the kitchen. She put the teakettle on the stove and sat down to wait for the water to boil. In the morning she would call Parker and see if he could come visit for a few days. She missed him. She did not want to stay in this house alone with her father. Her thoughts were suddenly interrupted by a loud cracking noise. A single blast, like a Fourth of July firecracker or a crash of thunder rumbled through the hallway and ricocheted off the walls. It was a frightening sound that sent a chill down her spine. For a moment she could not move. Her legs shook as she stood up. Anna walked into the hallway and began banging on the door of the study. "Father, are you okay?" She jiggled the doorknob. There was silence. "Please unlock the door!" She screamed louder, but he did not answer her. She reached for the telephone. Confused, she dialed the operator. "I need help. Please, send someone right away. I think there has been an accident."

Anna sat on the steps looking at the door to the study. For a few minutes everything was so still, so quiet, and suddenly there were sirens and flashing lights. Uniformed policemen and ambulance attendants in green scrubs came into the house. She pointed to the door and told them what little she knew; it took only moments to pry open the lock.

The officers backed away as the door swung open. Anna could see her father. He was sitting with his body slumped over the desk. His head was turned sideways. The blood from the single wound in his temple seeped onto the green ink blotter and turned it a dark shade of purple. The gun still dangled from one finger, slightly swaying on his limp arm. Anna never knew she was screaming until one of the officers led her out of the room.

Detective Coury arrived only minutes later after hearing the call on his police radio. He walked around the desk several times, taking a few notes. He picked up the empty bourbon bottle with his handkerchief and set in on the corner of the desk. By the time the coroner arrived, the yard was filled with people. They stood in the driveway in their robes and pajamas, craning their necks to see inside the house. The coroner set his black bag next to the desk and put on a pair of rubber gloves. He took the gun from Henry's hand and placed it in a plastic bag.

"Looks to me like a suicide, plain and simple. The guy just blew a hole clean through his head."

"You know, I think this may have been an accident. Yep, that's what I think," Coury said, leaning against the door.

"You're crazy. How could this be an accident? Do you think he was playing Russian roulette by himself?" Jack Webber had been coroner for over fifteen years. He knew a suicide when he saw one. "Why would you say a fool thing like that?"

Coury flipped open his notebook. Wetting his fingers, he leafed through several pages. "I guess I could a say a stupid thing like 'accidental death' to save myself about a month of paper work. I saw his name on the list of people that were to be questioned about their connection with Howard Bullard. If it's suicide, the district attorney is going to want to know why this guy killed himself. Maybe he knew more than he wanted to tell us." Coury walked around the desk again looking at the body of Henry Franklin. "On the other hand, if it was an accident, it will be that many less pages in the Bullard file. It's not going to change anything. We had Bullard and now that he skipped out of the country, it's a federal case. This is just going to muddy the water. Besides, I got a hysterical daughter in the other room and not another soul in the house. We could wrap this one up real quick. Yes sir, looks to me like he was cleaning his gun and it went off accidentally."

Jack Webber shrugged. The outcome would be the same for him. He had to do an autopsy either way. "Okay, I'll put down accidental, but you owe me one. I wonder what made him do it? By the looks of this house, he was doing okay for himself."

"Who knows, and I'm not going to waste my time trying to find out," Coury said as he steeled himself to face Anna.

She had not moved from the chair in the living room where the officer had placed her. Captain Coury walked into the room. Bending down, he touched Anna's hand.

"Miss Franklin, the coroner is just about to finish up here. We need to take your father down to the police morgue. We always have to do an autopsy in the case of accidental death at home. You can let me know in a day or two what you wish to do with your father's body."

The words began to jar her mind. Her father was now "the body." He was actually dead. She tried to make sense out of Detective Coury's words. "What did you say? You said it was an accident, but I thought," she stopped in mid sentence.

"Yes ma'am, an apparent accident. Seems like he was cleaning his gun and he must not have realized there was a bullet in the chamber. I'm sorry for your loss. Is there anyone I can call to come and stay with you tonight?"

Anna shook her head. "My mother is in the hospital. I have no one else to call."

Flipping open his notebook, Detective Coury said, "I really need to notify your mother about the accident. What hospital is she in?"

"Oh, please, let me tell her. She is in such a state of confusion right now, I don't know if she would really understand what you were telling her."

"Well, it is against protocol, but I guess I can make an exception," Coury said as he closed his notebook and put it in his pocket. "I'm going to leave one of my men with you until morning. It's not a good time to be alone. If you need me, just call the station." Coury touched her hand again. This was the one part of his job he had never gotten used to.

The attendants wheeled Henry's body out of the house covered by a white cloth. The gurney thumped on each step as they made their way to the waiting ambulance. Anna wanted to run after them, lift the cover and make sure it was really her father. She watched through the window until the ambulance was out of sight. The young officer took off his coat and went to the kitchen to make coffee. He tried to make conversation, extending his sympathy and telling her his own father had died just a year ago. It was going to be a long night. Sipping his coffee, he turned on the television and sat down on the couch. Before long, Anna heard his rhythmic snoring.

She sat down in the chair opposite the sleeping officer. She didn't want to be alone tonight. Anna closed her eyes for a moment and the room suddenly seemed to be spinning around, like a ride on the Tilt-A-Whirl. She hadn't thought about that bad memory in a long time.

❧❧❧

It was Colin's seventh birthday, just months before he got sick. Her father begrudgingly agreed to take the family to the fair in the next county. They ate ice cream and cotton candy and rode the merry-go-round. Colin wanted to ride the Tilt-A-Whirl. As he stood in line, her father pushed her beside him. "Here, take Anna with you," he said to Colin. She didn't want to go, but before she could say no, Colin pulled her up the stairs to the ride. She could smell the odor of hot grease as the ride operator put the bar down, locking her into the seat. The music blared as the ride slowly began to move in waves of motion around the circle of lights. As the momentum picked up, Colin screamed with laughter as she was tossed about in the twirling seat. Anna could feel her stomach churning as the ride went faster and faster. Each time she passed the man at the controls, she screamed, "Stop!" When the ride was finally over, Anna slipped beneath the bar and ran for the gate, barely making it to the grass. She began retching and crying at the same time. Her mother knelt besides her, wiping her face. Her dress and shoes were soiled and smelling of sour milk.

"You are such a baby, Anna," her father sneered. "Now see what you've done. We have to leave because of you."

❧❧❧

Sitting in the darkened living room she had that same feeling. She closed her eyes to try to stop the waves of nausea that engulfed her, but the spinning continued. She bolted from the chair and ran to the bathroom. Anna splashed water on her face and brushed her teeth. The early light of morning had begun to cast gray shadows on the ceiling as she returned to the living room and touched his arm. The officer awoke with a start. "Hey,

I'm sorry. I didn't mean to fall asleep. How about you? Did you get any rest?"

"A little," she said. "You can leave now. I have some phone calls to make." She had passed the closed door of the study several times. Once, putting her hand on the knob, she tried to go in, but it just wasn't time yet.

"Parker, it's me. I'm sorry to be calling you so early, but there's been an accident."

He listened intently as she told him about her father's death. "Oh my gosh, Anna, I'm so sorry. I can't believe you had to handle that all by yourself. Are you all right?"

"I'm okay right now, but I really need you. Can you come to Stockbridge today?"

Parker hesitated for a moment. "Didn't you say they wouldn't release your father's body for a few days? I'm sort of in a bind, Anna. I have a final today and one tomorrow. You know it's only two weeks before graduation. I can definitely be there by Friday."

"But I need you now. I have to tell my mother and I'm here alone." There was a silence.

"Anna, I'm sorry. Please, just call Lou Jean and see if she can come. Or maybe you can call a priest. I promise I'll be there as soon as I can. Just be brave. You know I love you."

She stood holding the phone with tears filling her eyes. For the first time since her father's death she was crying. Parker wasn't coming. She needed him and he wasn't coming.

She hung up and dialed again. "Lou Jean, there's been an accident. Can you come?"

"I'll be there this afternoon, darlin'. I'm leaving here as soon as we hang up." She arrived a little after noon, taking the first flight from St. Louis.

Anna fell into her arms. Her body was shaking as she cried uncontrollably. Lou Jean helped her into a chair and listened while Anna told her all that had happened in the past week. "My father has been dead for almost twenty four hours and my mother still doesn't know. I have to get to the hospital and tell her before she finds out some other way."

"First things first. You need to eat something." Lou Jean opened a can of soup and found some crackers in the pantry. She sat Anna down at the table, and handed her a spoon. "I don't know why, but I get the feeling that you're blaming yourself. Did you have any idea that your father had a gun?"

"No, he never mentioned it. Neither did my mother," Anna said.

"I wonder why he decided to clean it tonight of all nights. You did say that the detective said it was an accident?"

Anna sighed. "Lou Jean you sound like a lawyer."

Lou Jean made sure Anna was listening. "We'll go to the hospital this afternoon and tell your mother what happened, then we'll call a funeral home. The best thing would be cremation. It would be short and simple. Afterward, if you're up to it, we can arrange for a small memorial service for your mother's sake."

Anna gave a limp smile. "I knew I could count on you." Lou Jean reached across the table and squeezed her hand. "By the way, where is Parker?"

Anna checked with the doctor when she got to the hospital. Yes, he said, her mother was doing a little better, but she was not ready to be released. "I have called in a psychiatrist to talk to her. His name is Dr. Vargas. Your mother is having problems with withdrawal symptoms from all of the drugs she has been taking, and she has not been very cooperative."

When Anna entered her mother's room, Grace sat up in bed. "Where is your father? Why hasn't he come to see me? I need to talk to him about my medication." Grace's hands were shaking and her eyes were darting around the room. "I'm so tired, but I can't sleep without my pills."

Anna sat by her bed, calmly talking to her mother and rubbing her hands. Lou Jean crept into the room and stood watching as Anna brushed the hair away from her mother's face. Lou Jean's was filled with anger as she looked at the deep cut and bruises. He was such a bastard. She was glad he was dead.

"Mother, I have something to tell you." Anna slowly began telling her mother about the accident. Grace stared at her with blank eyes, and asked why Henry was not there. The nurse gave Grace a sedative and advised Anna and Lou Jean to leave.

"I don't think she understood a word I told her. Do you think she did?" Anna asked Lou Jean as they drove back to the house.

"Maybe you need to talk to that Dr. Vargas and see what's really going on."

They stayed up half the night talking. Anna finally told Lou Jean what Parker had said to her.

"He sure is a piece of work. I expected better of him. I'm sorry, Anna, but I don't think you should count on him coming to help you."

"He promised me he would be here Friday for the memorial service."

Lou Jean put her arm around Anna. "He better come or I'll wring his neck."

Dr. Vargas was waiting for her when she arrived at his office the next day. Anna was surprised by his appearance. A white mustache and beard covered most of his face and small round glasses rested on the bridge of his pudgy nose.

"I know what you're thinking," he said, stroking his beard. "I should shave it off, but it's a good conversation piece." She smiled and he shook her hand. "I'm sorry to hear about your father. How are you doing?" he asked.

"I could be better, but right now I'm worried about my mother. She didn't seem to understand when I told her that he was dead. Is it the drugs?"

"I wish I could say that was the real problem. It would be an easy one to cure, but I'm afraid that's just a small part of it. Tell me, Anna, did you ever get so frightened when you were a child that you couldn't get your breath?"

"Yes, of course. It happens to most everyone, doesn't it?"

"Yes, but then it passes. That is how frightened your mother is right now. She seems to be living in constant dread. She has taken all the painful memories she can't handle and put them away in some corner of her mind. Now they are all surfacing at one time. She wants to believe that Colin is away at school and Joseph and Agnes are still in Ternberry, but most of all that Henry is a loving and kind husband and father. It's these thoughts that are keeping her from hitting bottom. When she took the drugs she didn't have to think about anything. It made the pain of each day bearable."

"Has she said anything about me?" Anna asked. "She knows I love her."

"You have never left any scars on her. She doesn't have to run from you. You're going to have to be strong. I'm afraid you're probably the only person who can help her get through all of the turmoil in her mind." Dr. Vargas stopped and took Anna's hand. "You are the one that needs to help her fight the demons and peel away the layers of bad memories."

Lou Jean made all the arrangements. Henry's body was picked up at the morgue on Thursday and cremated. She rented a small chapel and hired a minister to hold a memorial service on Friday morning. Anna packed a dress for her mother and Lou Jean picked them up from the hospital. When they arrived at the chapel, there was a scattering of people in the pews. There were neighbors and men from the country club. Anna knew very few of them. A single bouquet of flowers adorned the altar. Anna waited in the vestibule, but Parker did not show up. The minister did the best he could with the brief service since he didn't know Henry or the family. Grace sat next to Anna, looking pale, her black dress hanging loosely on her frail body.

She leaned toward Anna. "Where is Henry? Why isn't he here? I thought he would come and bring my pills." Anna was convinced that her mother should go back to the hospital.

Parker called on Sunday morning. He seemed nervous and Anna could tell he was having a difficult time talking to her as he stumbled through his feeble excuse. He spoke in a halted manner, telling her that his parents had advised him to stay at school.

"How could you leave me here alone? I would have never done that to you," Anna said, choking back the tears. "How can I ever trust you to be there for me when I need you?"

"I don't know what else to say, Anna. It's just a difficult time for me. Are you coming back to school? Will you be here for my graduation?"

She paused. She couldn't believe he was asking her that. He hadn't even inquired about her mother or said why he hadn't come to the memorial service. "So this has been difficult for you, Parker. Is it because it wouldn't look good on your resume when and if you go into politics? I'm so sorry that you had to be connected with a family as decadent as mine, with a father who killed himself and a mother strung out on pills.

No, I won't be there for your graduation. I think it's better if you don't call again." She hung up the telephone without saying goodbye. She had loved him for over two years and now it was over. Her life seemed to be ricocheting around her like an out of control lightning storm. She wondered if she would be strong enough to handle everything that was in front of her.

"We need to tackle the study, Anna," Lou Jean said as she cleared the breakfast dishes from the table. I hate to tell you this, but I have to leave in a day or two. My boss is jumping up and down and I have to get back or I may be looking for another job. Somewhere around here there has to be some financial papers and your father's insurance policies. We have to find out how much money he left you and your mother."

Anna knew this moment was coming and she dreaded it. She didn't want Lou Jean to leave. She wasn't ready to be on her own.

"Don't look so sad. As soon as you clean up the mess here I expect to see you in St. Louis. I'm sure by the time you get everything taken care of you'll be ready to get out of this place." Lou Jean put her arm around Anna as they headed toward the study. Anna opened the door. The room was dark, yet she could still see the white sheet that the police had placed over the desk.

"My gosh, this place is like a tomb." Lou Jean pulled back the drapes to let in the morning light. "Are you sure your father wasn't related to Dracula?"

Anna hadn't been in this room in years. Her father had always kept the door locked. It was sparsely furnished. Besides the large oak desk and chair, the only other furniture was a leather couch and a sideboard filled with crystal decanters and glasses. The walls were lined with bookshelves brimming with leather bound volumes. Anna walked around the room, running her fingers over the bindings of the dusty books. "I never saw my father read. I wondered what he did alone every night in this room?"

"Check out the wastebasket. That's one thing he did," Lou Jean said as she pointed to the basket filled with empty bourbon bottles. "Let's just dump all the papers from his desk into a box and take it into the dining room. This place gives me the creeps." Lou Jean shivered.

They spent most of the morning sifting through the two boxes it took to empty out the desk. "Look at this," Anna said, holding up a photograph to Lou Jean. Her father's face was smiling back at her. He was standing with his arm around a pretty young woman. They looked relaxed and happy. The writing on the back of the picture was in French. Who was she, Anna wondered? Was she one of his many lovers, or a mistress he had long forgotten? She took the picture and tore it in half. "I'm going to take a break and make us some coffee."

Lou Jean finally found a file folder filled with pages of jumbled figures and bank statements. There were stacks of unpaid invoices from stores all over the country including a large tax bill that was a year past due. She found a contract for a second mortgage he had taken out on the house. Henry had borrowed heavily against his insurance policy. The policy had been canceled. Lou Jean could not find anything that even looked remotely promising in all of the papers from the desk.

"Now that he is dead, will most of these bills be resolved?" Anna asked Lou Jean.

"It looks like he put your mother's name on most of these loans, which means that all she will inherit is a pile of unpaid debts. Of course, you could try to prove he forged her signature, but that would mean involving her in this mess. Do you think she is strong enough to handle it?"

"Oh, I couldn't possibly do that to her, but I don't want them to come after her. I mean I haven't heard from anyone yet." Anna was bewildered. She had never handled financial matters before.

"Well, kiddo, if they want their money, and I'm sure they do, you will be hearing from them as soon as they find out Henry is dead."

In the next few weeks, Anna was deluged with phone calls and registered letters. Everyone Henry owed money wanted it right away. The worst call came from the bank informing her that if the back taxes were not paid on the house by the end of the month, they would be forced to foreclose on the property. Anna had moved her mother to a convalescent home and they also wanted to know what financial arrangements would be made to take care of the escalating bill. She had been immobile long enough. It was time to stop feeling sorry for herself and try to clean up the mess her father had created for them. The anger inside of her helped make the decisions easier. She would talk to her mother in the morning.

"Well, hello. You seem to be in quite a hurry. I wonder if you have a moment to talk with me?" Dr. Vargas said as Anna passed him in the hallway on her way to her mother's room.

"I'm late. I told her I would be here by noon to have lunch with her. I got caught in traffic." Anna was breathless from her sprint across the parking lot. "Have you been to see her today?" she asked.

"Yes, I have. That's what I wanted to talk to you about. She seems to be doing a bit better. I believe her sense of reality is returning. Let me know how she is after your visit." He smiled and continued down the corridor.

Anna and Grace walked down the path leading to the lake. Anna glanced over at her mother when she was not looking. Her face had healed and the bruises had gone away. The scar from the cut on her cheek was barely visible. Anna wished it would be that easy to get rid of all the wounds that lived inside her mother.

"You're quiet today, Anna. Are you all right?" Grace asked. "I know you're probably tired of coming here to see me. Dr. Vargas said I am making great progress. I should be coming home soon."

"Mother, I was thinking it is time for us to move out of the house. We need a smaller place. I want to sell most of the things and just keep what we need to set up housekeeping somewhere else. Besides, I can't stand being there. I have never really liked that place, but I wanted to know how you felt about my idea before I did anything rash."

"Sell it all Anna, sell it all. I don't want to go back there either." Grace seemed relieved at Anna's decision.

The sun was warm as they sat quietly on a bench. They watched the ducks feeding on the sedge grasses as they darted in and out of the tall pussy willows growing along the shore.

"He's dead isn't he?" Grace said in a quiet voice.

It was a simple question; so simple it hurt to even answer it. "Yes, mother, he's dead."

"Is it all right if I cry now?" Grace asked as Anna took her Mother into her arms.

Chapter Twenty-Seven

Anna paged through the phone book, finally settling on a company called Eleanor's Estate Sale Planners. Eleanor agreed to come to the house and talk to Anna.

"I'm sorry to hear about your father," she said as she stepped into the front door. What is it you want to sell?"

"I need to sell everything in this house as quickly as possible. My father left my mother and me with some very large debts that need to be paid very soon."

Eleanor nodded. "I understand. Let's see what you have in this big house."

Eleanor walked through each room taking notes. Occasionally she would pick up a piece of crystal and hold it up to the light or look under the furniture for markings. After they had completed a tour of the entire house, Anna and Eleanor sat in the kitchen drinking coffee.

"This is a most interesting house," Eleanor said. "I can't decide what exactly your father was collecting. He certainly managed to fill these rooms to capacity. Why in the world did he buy so many things?"

"He just liked buying anything that was expensive. He never seemed to have enough," Anna said. She did not want to tell Eleanor the truth. In her father's warped mind, possessions represented power and affluence. It gave him a sense of accomplishment, something he could never earn on his own merit.

Eleanor opened her notebook and studied it for a few minutes. "Considering your situation, Miss Franklin, I think it may be better if I call in some consigners who would be interested in your furnishings and artwork. We can avoid the problems of having a public auction. I must tell you there will still be a lot of things left. Most of the dealers are not interested in items with little resale value. Some of your father's paintings are very good replicas of the originals. I certainly hope he knew that when he purchased them."

"But what will I do with the rest of the stuff?" Anna asked.

"You have several options. You can give it away, throw it away or try to sell it. I think in your case, you should try to sell as much of it as possible. A yard sale could be pretty profitable."

"I wouldn't have any idea where to begin. Would you be able to help me, Eleanor?" Anna asked.

Eleanor agreed that for her usual twenty percent commission she would furnish the tables and take care of setting up the sale. Anna was nervous, but relieved that soon it would all be over. Maybe then, she and her mother could start a new life together.

For the next few weeks the house was bustling with activity. Eleanor brought different merchants almost every day. Several made long trips to Stockbridge on Eleanor's advice. She assured them that they would not be disappointed with the furnishings and accessories in the Franklin house.

As each day passed, the house took on a new appearance. The faded walls were left barren, except for the outlines of paintings that had been crated and stored in the hallway. The furniture was wrapped in moving pads, and the crystal and china were carefully put into boxes. Each afternoon vans and trucks would arrive and take away the items that had been sold. Anna put a few pieces of furniture that her mother brought from Ternberry in one of the upstairs bedrooms. She packed their clothing and took a box of photographs from the attic. There wasn't anything else she wanted from this house; until her mother reminded Anna not to forget the television set.

After the dealers left each day, Anna would make a quick trip to the hospital to visit with her mother and then armed with the daily newspaper and a map, she would scour the city for suitable lodgings that she could afford to rent. Anna finally settled on a four-room apartment upstairs from Knadel's Bakery, just a few blocks from downtown Stockbridge.

Eleanor worked diligently to make sure that she got the best price for everything that was sold to the dealers. At the end of two weeks she told Anna they needed to arrange for the yard sale, since no one was interested in the rest of the things in the house. The sale was advertised in the newspaper as, "The remaining contents of an opulent home, belonging to the late Dr. Franklin." Eleanor hammered a large sign in front of the gate announcing the sale.

It took three days for Eleanor and Anna to sort and price the remaining items. Anna wished Lou Jean was here to help her through these last few weeks but she was still in London.

There were some things left in the house that Anna had never seen before, yet others jarred her memory and instantly aroused an anxious feeling to surface. There was the garish red lamp that was delivered to the house just days after they moved to Cherry Street. Henry was livid when he discovered that Grace had tipped the deliverymen. In one of the last boxes to be priced, she found the gold handled lint brush and the array of liquor decanters that were retrieved from the study. Anna wanted to pick them up and smash them to the floor. It was Eleanor who came to her rescue, telling Anna to be careful with the decanters. They were worth at least fifteen dollars each. As she passed by Anna, she patted her on the shoulder as if to tell her she understood her frustration.

On Saturday morning Eleanor and two of her workers arrived at the house at five a.m. and began setting up tables in the yard and putting all the sale items on display. "I think you ought to take one more look at this stuff before we start the sale to make sure there isn't anything you want to keep," Eleanor said as she carried a small table across the porch.

Anna walked to the railing and looked out over the rows of overflowing tables that covered most of the yard. "No. There is nothing that I want. I hope we sell it all."

The sale was to begin at nine o'clock on Saturday morning, but by seven a.m. the sidewalk was filled with people waiting for someone to let them in. Cars blocked the street, causing a snarl of traffic that infuriated the neighbors, although they came too. They were curious to see what had been hidden behind the fence of 704 Cherry Street.

"Well, I guess we can open the gate and let the fun begin," Eleanor said as she headed down the driveway.

Earl Holloway got caught in the traffic that was moving slowly down the street toward Anna's house. He had no intention of attending a sale. All he wanted was to get downtown, but the parade of cars blocked the street. He sat in his car until the heat temperature gauge began to rise. Earl parked his car and walked the half block to the house. Anna didn't see

YARD SALE

him in the swarm of people that moved about the yard from table to table, their arms filled with trinkets and dishes. Occasionally the sound of glass breaking or something falling would send Eleanor running.

Earl saw Anna sitting at a table under a large oak tree surrounded by people. She was taking money and putting purchases into paper bags. He wondered if this was her house. He walked around the yard blending into the crowd. There wasn't much he could afford or even cared to buy. On the very last table, Earl found a box of mismatched linens. As he walked toward the tree, it was Eleanor who was now taking the money. He paid the eight-dollar asking price and left. As he walked to the front of the house, he saw Anna again. This time she was sitting on the front porch steps. Perhaps he should talk to her, but what would he say? Earl just smiled at her and continued on his way.

Later that day Earl handed the box to his mother. "I picked these linens up at a sale today. I was stuck in traffic so I decided to kill some time. I thought you might like these since you never buy anything for yourself."

"My, these are very nice. Thank you, Earl," Mamie said as she reached beneath the white paper in the bottom of the box. "Oh look, there is something else in here. It's a lovely handmade tablecloth." She folded the cloth and placed it back into the box. Earl knew she would probably never use the linens. "I'm sure this was put in this box by mistake. Whoever it belonged to is going to wonder where it is."

While Earl was eating his supper at the farm, Anna was watching the last car pull out of the yard of 704 Cherry Street. The gate was finally closed as the sun began to sink beneath the tall oak trees. The sale was over.

Eleanor handed Anna an envelope. "Here you go, kiddo. I hope this helps. We really did quite well. There's just a few things left and I can take them to my shop to sell. My men will deliver the rest of your things to your apartment."

Anna thanked Eleanor and wrote her new address on a scrap of paper.

"What about the house? What are you going to do with it?" Eleanor asked.

"The bank has a buyer. I'm hoping to clear enough to pay the back payments and taxes," Anna replied.

"What a shame, a damn shame," Eleanor muttered as she left.

It was dark in the house and the sound of her footsteps echoing through the empty rooms made Anna move quicker. She walked through the upstairs rooms turning off the lights. In the kitchen she adjusted the thermostat and made sure the back door was locked. On her way through the front hallway, something made her open the door to the study. She stood for a moment looking into the forbidden room. She could still picture her father sitting at the desk with the gun dangling from his hand. She shivered as she flipped off the lights. Anna locked the front door for the last time and put her change of address card in the mailbox. She pulled her car out of the driveway onto Cherry Street, never looking back.

Chapter Twenty-Eight

It had been over three years since her father died. Too often a remembrance of that ruinous time seemed to surface in Anna's mind. She tried to put those bad memories behind her, but staying in Stockbridge didn't seem to help. It would have been so much easier to move away, but Dr. Vargas had become her mother's lifeline. Anna could not bear to take her away from him. He was a compassionate man, helping Grace work through her bouts of depression that sometimes lasted for weeks. Her mother always seemed to rally after her weekly visit to Dr. Vargas.

The adjustment of living in the apartment was a difficult time for Anna and her mother. The smell of fresh baked goods filtered through the hallways, and the hum of the large mixers could be heard all through the night. Anna tried to fill the apartment with things she knew her mother loved, putting fresh cut flowers and green plants on the windowsill. There were new pictures of seascapes purchased at Woolworth's hanging in the living room. Grace was distressed when they could not find her lace tablecloth after unpacking all the boxes. She was convinced that Henry had thrown it away on purpose. Anna knew it must have been sold, but she had no idea who had bought it.

When Anna had finally closed her father's bank account, all of the debts had been paid, but the money from the sale was almost gone. Anna took a job with a small insurance company just a few blocks away from the apartment. Her father's car had been repossessed and she decided to sell her own car to pay the first month's rent. Her college plans had been put on hold indefinitely. There was not enough time or money for her to even think about going to school. Right now it didn't seem important. She needed time to breathe new life into the role that had been thrust upon her. She was now the caretaker for her mother and the sole supporter of the family.

At times when her mother's depression was at bay, Grace would express feelings of guilt, telling Anna that she should find a job. Maybe she could work as a domestic or take in ironing. Anna knew her mother wouldn't be able to handle the pressure very long. Instead, she insisted that she needed her to stay home until she was stronger. Most of Grace's days were spent lying on the couch watching television leaving the breakfast dishes still on the table when Anna came home from work. Lou Jean kept in touch. She had almost completed all of her college courses and applied to law school. She had been dating a lawyer who worked in her office. Even though she didn't want to, Anna sometimes felt pangs of envy wondering what her own life would have been like if she could have stayed in school and maybe even married Parker.

The bus was late as usual. It was the same bus that Anna rode with her mother to see Dr. Vargas every Thursday. Today she was alone. She had questions that needed answers. Questions she wanted to ask him without her mother knowing. Anna laid her head on the cool glass of the window, wondering how much longer she and her mother would be making this trip. Lately her mother's depression seemed better, yet the newest round of bizarre behavior concerned Anna even more. Dr. Vargas had taken Grace under his wing. When Anna questioned her mother about her visits, she would only say that he was helping to heal her soul.

Anna sat in the large wing-backed chair in Dr. Vargas' office. "I think she is better, but sometimes she is miles away in her own world. I worry about her. Two days ago she walked six blocks to the hardware store and bought paint. She painted our bathroom bright orange. She said it reminded her of sunshine. Just before I left to see you, she told me that Mr. Knadel offered her a job in the bakery washing pots and making batter. I just don't know what to think anymore," Anna said, shaking her head.

Dr. Vargas leaned back in his chair. "Sounds to me like she is doing much better. It's been a slow process, but these are very good signs. By the way, I like the color orange."

"But do you think she is well enough to take a job? What if her depression comes back?"

"What is the worst that could happen, Anna? She would have to quit. At least she could give it a try. You're not her keeper. You're her daughter, and a very good one, I might add. I know you are concerned, but you need to ease off a little and let her test the water. You look tired yourself, Anna. How are you holding up?"

She wanted to say she was just fine, but she couldn't. She wanted him to know about the fear that kept the tightness in the pit of her stomach, the unexpected jolts that still woke her at night, perspiration running down her back, thinking she heard a gun going off. She wanted him to know how the image of her father's face after he killed himself would pop into her mind and anger still simmered deep inside her for what he had done to her mother. She took a deep breath, ready to say "I'm fine," but the tears began to flow uncontrollably from her eyes. Dr. Vargas handed her a box of tissues and she continued to cry and blow her nose until there were no more tears left. Her body shuddered as she tried to regain her composure. "I'm so very sorry; I don't know what got in to me. I must be tired. I haven't cried like that in such a long time."

Dr. Vargas sat on the edge of his desk, "Please, Anna, don't apologize. If you feel up to it, I'd be glad to listen to whatever you want to talk about."

She twisted the tissue until shreds fell into her lap. "The whole thing still haunts me. I should have told my mother everything I knew about my father. Maybe she would have left him and he would still be alive." She blew her nose again. "Instead I just kept my mouth shut and when I went away to school, I left her alone with him. Was I any better than he was?" she said.

He waited until she finished, "That's really quite a load to be carrying around for all these years." Dr. Vargas poured a glass of water and handed it to Anna. "You had no control over your father's actions. Besides, I think your mother was well aware of what he was doing. That's why she is having so much trouble dealing with her own guilt. Your father set the stage for his own fate many years before his death. Believe me, Anna, none of these things were your fault."

Anna stood up and walked to the window. She rubbed her swollen eyes, pretending that she was watching the street below. She turned to Dr. Vargas. "I hated him, you know. I hated the way he treated me like I never existed. I hated the way he looked at me and dug his fingers into my arm to keep me from running from him. He killed my brother and my childhood. I detested all of his philandering, all of the holidays he ruined and all the times he made my mother cry. Sometimes he would do something nice for us, something unexpected. It was as if he needed to ease his conscience so that he could make room for more evil. I should feel sad that he is dead, but I don't and I'm not sorry I feel that way."

She was drained and her head was pounding. "I don't have much money, Dr. Vargas, but maybe I could come to see you once in a while. I think right now I need more help than my mother."

He patted her shoulder. "Trust me, Anna, I don't know many people who couldn't use someone to talk to once in awhile. I would love to have you come and see me. Don't worry about the money."

Grace started working evenings in Knadel's Bakery. She would wash the pots and baking dishes while the batter for the next day blended in the large steel bowls. Occasionally Hans Knadel would stay late decorating an elegant wedding cake or preparing desserts for a party. He played German records on his phonograph, his resonate baritone voice filling the room. They would talk about their homelands and tease each other about their accents. Hans decided he would forego the rent for the apartment in exchange for the hours Grace worked in the bakery. It seemed strange to Anna to see her mother leave on her own. Combing her hair and tucking it into a hairnet, she would kiss Anna on the cheek and bound down the steps. Anna was glad to have the time alone. It gave her the opportunity to take long hot baths and read until she fell asleep. Yet, as the weeks passed, she realized she was lonely. She was tired of watching television and tired of reading. She was lonely for her mother's presence.

"Your mother missed her appointment Thursday. I think that was the first one ever. What happened?" Dr. Vargas asked as he met Anna at the door.

"She wanted to help Hans with a special wedding cake. He is teaching her how to decorate cakes. I told her she needed to see you, but she said she would come next week."

"Oh I see, I was superseded by a cake, or was it the cake maker?"

"And just what is that supposed to mean?"

"My goodness Anna, I think I struck a nerve. Are you upset with your mother?"

"Well, it's just that she spends almost all her free time in the bakery. I think Hans may be taking advantage of her."

Dr. Vargas smiled. "In what way?"

"Will you please wipe that grin off your face? You know what I mean. I worry about her. I think she is working too hard and she has stopped taking her medication altogether."

"To be honest with you, Anna, I think I have gone as far as I can with your mother. The rest is up to her. I know she will always have periods of depression, but as long as she understands them, she will be okay. It's time you got on with your own life."

Anna was not sure she wanted to accept what he was saying. How could she get on with her own life? She didn't have one other than her job or her mother. "I'll make sure Mother is here next week and you can tell her yourself."

"That would be fine. Would you like to talk some more about you?"

She rose to leave. "No, I just want to go home. Maybe I'll find a life on the way."

Chapter Twenty-Nine

The insurance company was small and dreary, just two small offices and a reception area. Anna's job was to arrange payments on claims and take care of all the paperwork on new policies. The agents were out of the office most of the time, leaving her alone. It was a boring job and she was tired of it. Anna had finally decided she would look for something else and maybe start taking a few college courses at night. She spread the classifieds out on her desk and began looking through the employment ads. She didn't hear him come in. He closed the door softly and was standing at her desk before she looked up.

"Oh, hello, I'm sorry," she said as she closed the paper and motioned toward the chair in front of her desk.

"My name is Earl Holloway and I have a policy I would like to cash in. My mother passed away a few weeks ago," he said as he handed her the folded pieces of paper.

"I'm sorry to hear about your mother's death, Mr. Holloway. Give me a moment to read through this policy and I can tell you the value." As Anna began to read, she could feel his eyes staring at her. She looked up and smiled; lowering her eyes, she continued to read.

"Excuse me for staring, but your face looks so familiar. I don't get into Stockbridge very often. I was just trying to place you in my mind," Earl said.

"Well I don't get out of Stockbridge much. Maybe we just saw each other in a store or on the street. It's not really that big of a town."

"Maybe so, but you look so familiar."

"Your mother's policy has a cash value of $526.00. I will need a copy of her death certificate and your signature on this form before I can process the claim." Anna handed him a pen and pushed the paper toward him. "And again, I'm so sorry for your loss."

Earl signed the form and stood up. Anna extended her hand. "My name is Anna Franklin, should you need any further assistance."

"That's it," he said. "I remember now. I bought some things at the house on Cherry Street. You were there. The name on the mailbox was Franklin."

Anna felt uncomfortable. She didn't want to talk about the house or the sale. "Yes, that was my house, but it's been a long time ago. Thank you for coming in."

But Earl wasn't finished. He sat back down in the chair and told her the story about buying the linens and finding the tablecloth in the box. His mother would not use it, saying he should try to return it. The next day when he returned to the house, it was empty. He could find no one who knew where the family had moved. His mother kept the cloth in the buffet at his house. What a stroke of luck to finally find her.

Anna was surprised. "As much as I know my mother would like to have it back, it does belong to you since you paid for it. I'll understand if you want to keep it, or maybe your wife would like to have it."

"I'm not married," Earl replied.

"Let me take your telephone number. I know my mother would love to have you bring it back to her." She shook his hand and watched him walk away.

Earl paused as he opened the door, "By the way, you smell like doughnuts."

Grace listened as Anna told her about the tablecloth. At first she was quiet, bobbing her tea bag up and down in her favorite china cup. "Yes, I would love to have it back. I'm so glad Henry didn't destroy it. When you call Mr. Holloway, invite him to dinner. That's the least we can do to thank him."

Earl was coming to dinner on Friday night. Anna closed the office a few minutes early and hurried down Pine Street. She used her lunch hour to buy a new dress and now she needed to stop by the market before going home. She prayed for once the bus would be on time. Anna fumbled for her door keys as she juggled the bag of groceries on her hip; her purse strap clinched between her teeth. As she opened the door, she could smell the aroma of roasted chicken. "Bless you, Mother," she said to herself, dropping the grocery bags onto the couch.

"Anna, is that you?" The booming voice of Hans Knadel resounded from the tiny kitchen. He popped his head around the corner wearing his tall baker's hat. "I have chicken in the oven and I am making a salad. What would you like for dessert?" he said, as he gingerly chopped the tomatoes.

"What are you doing here? Where is mother?" Anna began to empty the bag of groceries onto the counter.

"She was tired. I told her to go lie down and I would start dinner for us so that you would not have to rush."

"Did my mother invite you to eat here tonight?"

Hans nodded, "Yes. I hope that doesn't offend you."

"No. No, that's okay. If mother wants you here, that's fine." She put on an apron and started peeling potatoes.

"You don't like me very much, do you, Anna?" Hans said not looking up from the cutting board. "You know I wouldn't hurt your mother. She's a fine woman and I care for her. We have good times together."

"Does my mother ever talk to you about her past? Has she ever told you about my father or how sick she has been?" Anna asked.

"Yes, she has told me everything. There are days in the bakery when she doesn't talk at all. She is locked away somewhere in her own world. On those days, I leave her alone. Other times she cries and we talk. I tell her about my life in Germany during the war and I cry, too. Lately we laugh together. I'm sorry I did not ask your permission to eat dinner with you. If you wish I can leave now."

"No, you go right ahead and finish this meal. You're doing a great job. I'm going to change my clothes." As she passed him, Anna brushed her hand across his back. He smiled and began chopping the vegetables in time to the song on the radio.

Anna tiptoed past her mother's bed and quietly opened the bathroom door. "I'm not sleeping dear, just resting my eyes," Grace said. "Are you upset with me for inviting Hans to dinner?"

"No, Mother. I guess I was just surprised to find him here. You like him a lot, don't you?" Grace smiled and closed her eyes.

Anna answered the door and led Earl into the living room. He placed the package on the sofa and stood, looking a little uncomfortable, until Hans handed him a glass of beer and told him to have a seat. Anna suddenly wished she hadn't bought the new dress. What in the world was she thinking? He was just returning a tablecloth, nothing else. He wore a plaid shirt and blue jeans. From where she was standing, she could see his thinning hair, neatly combed over the shiny bald spot on the back of his head. Introductions were brief and Hans said he hoped everyone was hungry. Before he set the table, Hans unwrapped the package and placed the tablecloth on the kitchen table, its sides almost touching the floor. Grace smoothed out the wrinkles and stood back to admire the cloth.

Hans was like the great inquisitor, asking Earl one question after another. Earl had been born in the house in which he still lived. It was on a two-hundred-acre farm, twelve miles outside Stockbridge. Seasonal workers helped with the crops, but his real love was for his small repair shop. He loved to tinker with anything electrical and he made repairs for some of the people in town. Hans began to talk about the ovens in the bakery and soon the two men were lost in conversation. Grace looked across the table and made a face, causing Anna to laugh out loud.

Earl stopped in mid sentence. "I guess we're being rude leaving you ladies out of the conversation. I suppose I just don't get out enough."

After dinner, Anna walked with Earl down the stairs and onto the sidewalk. The air of the crisp fall night was heavy with the smell of fresh doughnuts and pastry from Hans' shop.

"I had a good time tonight. I want to thank you for inviting me. Your mother and Hans are nice people." Earl shoved his hands into his pockets. "You look very nice tonight and now I know why you smell like doughnuts," he said. "I have to come back into town next weekend to look at the ovens in the bakery. Do you think maybe we could take in a movie or something?"

"I would like that, and thank you for returning the tablecloth. I know it meant a lot to my mother." Anna watched as he drove away, wondering if he really was going to call her. He seemed like a nice man. The thought of going out with anyone made her nervous. It had been such a very long time since she had a date.

Earl rolled down the window of his pickup and stretched back in the seat. He had eaten too much. Maybe Anna hadn't noticed. It had been a long time since he had a home cooked meal. His mother had been a good cook, preparing dinner for him each night. When she became ill, he tried to take over, almost burning down the house trying to fry chicken. He resorted to bologna sandwiches and soup. He wondered if he thanked Anna for dinner. He couldn't remember. Why hadn't he worn something other than jeans? She had on that pretty dress. And what was he thinking asking her to a movie? My gosh, she couldn't be more than twenty-four. He would be thirty-five in less than three months.

A few more houses on the other side of the railroad tracks heralded the town limits. The farmlands begrudgingly gave up acres to the encroaching suburbs. Earl remembered when this was a dirt road; now his truck rolled smoothly over the paved lanes. It was exactly eleven miles to the graveled side road leading to his house. Seventeen telephone poles and thirty-seven fence posts lined the lane leading to his front gate. He had counted them hundreds of times through the years as he made his way to the house from the fields on hot Kansas afternoons. At night his headlights would at times shine into the eyes of a frightened possum or deer. Tonight there was no counting, just his thoughts going over the evening and seeing the image of Anna's face in his mind. Earl pulled into the shed, the sound of the truck engine disturbing the chickens roosting on the rafters as they cackled in protest for being awakened so late at night. The house was illuminated by the moonlight. As usual, he had forgotten to turn on the porch light when he left. He strode across the yard thinking that the house really needed to be painted. He couldn't even remember the last time it had been done. The white siding was now faded and peeling. His great-grandfather built the original four rooms. Each board had been hewn from trees on the farm and carried by mule teams to the building site. Years later the second story was added on and topped off with a red tin roof. In the summer, rain dripped through rusted nail holes into buckets placed on the attic floor.

Earl put the coffee left from breakfast into a pot and set it on the stove. He waited as the smell of kerosene heated the deep black liquid. He had never noticed before how plain this room really was. His mother always said that she didn't have time for fancy knickknacks. Clutter, she called it, but Anna's apartment seemed so warm and cozy. Earl poured his coffee into a mug and sat down at the wooden table. The same red and white checked oilcloth had been there as long as he could remember. He would buy a new one when he went to town and maybe even purchase some pictures for the walls.

YARD SALE

It was a gentle relationship built slowly on Friday night movies and Sunday dinners in Anna's apartment. Anna and Earl were so polite to each other it was painful for Grace and Hans to watch. They sometimes rolled their eyes at all the times "please" and "thank you" was said at the dinner table. When the weather permitted, they would take a walk after dinner. Earl always told Anna how good the food was and how much he enjoyed coming to her house. She finally had to laugh when he complimented her on a meal of roast beef that was so tough no one could even chew it. "It's okay, Earl. Let's stop by the diner, I'm still hungry."

Two months had gone by and all Anna knew about Earl's family was that they had died and he lived alone. She wanted to ask him more questions, but she knew how difficult it would be to talk about her own past. She wondered if he was ever going to kiss her or even hold her hand. She wasn't bold enough to make the first move.

When Earl finally got up enough courage to ask Anna to come to his house he couldn't believe she had never been on a farm or even owned a pet. She told him her father was definitely not into animals or anything remotely connected with outside work.

Earl spent most of the week cleaning the inside of the house. He scrubbed the tub until it was white again and dusted all the furniture in the living room. He bought fried chicken in town and brought up jars of green beans and tomatoes from the cellar. He was nervous when he arrived at Anna's house to pick her up. He stopped at the bakery to buy an apple pie. Anna bounded down the steps wearing blue jeans and a denim shirt. She climbed into the pickup and handed Earl a box. "Here, I got us an apple pie for dessert."

Earl laughed. "Good. Now there is one for each of us."

The farmhouse was situated between two large oak trees with the barn and the shed that housed Earl's workshop off to one side. It was a stark setting with no flowers or bushes in the yard. Earl helped her out of the truck and gathered up the pies. The house was cool inside with the shades drawn to keep out the heat of the Indian summer. "You can look around if you like. I'll get the rest of the dinner ready," Earl said as he headed down the hall to the kitchen.

Anna peered into the living room. Two chairs and a worn sofa covered with a blue sheet sat facing the television set; its aerial affixed to a coat hanger covered with tin foil. She walked into the kitchen and watched Earl as he tried to balance the bowls of green beans and potatoes on his arm. "Where are you going?" she asked. He pointed toward the door. "Dining room."

Anna took the bowl of potatoes from him. "Let's just eat in the kitchen."

"Would you like to take a walk around the farm? I'll introduce you to my animals," Earl said as they finished drying the dishes.

They ambled through the barn. Anna petted the cow's head and jumped when the cow tried to lick her fingers. A calico cat followed them through the stalls, wrapping herself around Anna's legs. She liked the smell of the hay and the way the sun's rays slanted through the cracks between the boards. They climbed to the top of the loft, looking out over the pond and barren cornfield. "What's up there?" Anna asked pointing to a grassy slope behind the house. She could see outlines of rounded shapes on top of the hill making dark silhouettes against the afternoon sun.

"My family is buried up there," Earl said. He took her hand as they made their way up the hill to the small graveyard. She walked around the graves silently reading the names on the stones. Earl walked behind her, wiping the mossy film off the inscriptions. "Over there are all of my grandparents. Up here in front are my father and mother." He pointed to two small marble slabs, almost buried in the ground and knelt down to pull up a handful of weeds. "This is where my brother is buried."

"But there are two markers," Anna said.

Earl was silent for a moment. He pointed to the first stone. "This is Raymond's grave, but my mother insisted my brother Jessie have a headstone, too. He's not really buried there. It was her way of letting everyone know he wasn't forgotten." Earl took her hand and led her to the small marble bench beneath the oak tree in the cemetery.

"How did your brothers die, Earl? Did they have some kind of illness?"

Earl shook his head. "No. They were both killed on the same day. It happened the day of the county fair. Have you ever been to the fair in Stockbridge?" he asked.

"Only once, when I was very young," Anna answered.

"Well, when you live on a farm, the fair is the most important event of the year. My mother would spend weeks testing recipes for her famous bread and butter pickles. Jessie and Raymond would spend the whole summer raising goats for the livestock show. The blue ribbons meant more than money to them. The fair was great fun for us kids. There was a Ferris wheel and cotton candy and all kinds of games to play."

"I woke up sick on the day of the fair. I made it as far as the bathroom before I began to vomit. My mother put me back to bed with a cold washrag on my head. Jessie and Raymond were both dressed and spending the last few minutes brushing the long hair of the goats. When mom told them I was sick, Jessie let out a roar and said there was no way he would stay home. My dad decided to take them to the fair and come back later for mom and me. I cried until I fell asleep. It was my mother's voice, calling my name that awoke me. I could see the black sky outside my bedroom window. I thought I had slept all day, but it was only ten o'clock in the morning. She told me we had to go immediately to the storm cellar. We were used to summer storms that blew across the Kansas plains turning the oppressing heat into sheets of hail and rain. The lightning would sizzle as it touched the ground, sending sparks into the air. However, this storm was different. It just stayed above the horizon. Boiling charcoal clouds and gusts of wind moved toward us so quickly that we couldn't make it to the storm cellar. As the first bolt of lightning illuminated the room, my mother threw me to the floor. She laid her body on top of me and we could hear glass breaking as the force of the wind pushed against the house. The hail was hitting the roof so hard it sounded like it would break through and land in the living room at any moment. The pressure made our ears pop, as we heard the roar of the twisting black cloud passing by." Earl paused for a moment as if he really didn't want to remember that awful day.

"The tornado lasted only a few minutes and then there was silence. A steady rain began to fall and the temperature plummeted. I began to shiver, my teeth chattering. She lifted me from the floor and placed a blanket around my shoulders. My mother pulled and tugged until she finally was able to open the door. The storm had cut a path across the yard. The roof of the barn had crashed to the ground and the silo lay on its side, rocking back and forth like a giant seesaw. A few dead chickens were visible under the huge tree branch that barely missed falling on the house. There was a tangled weave of metal and wood forming curious sculptures in the yard. My mother made the sign of the cross, thanking the Lord for sparing us. She hurried me inside, and tried the telephone. There was no dial tone and the electricity was off. We waited all afternoon for my father and brothers to come home. We ate cold sandwiches and pickles, and my mom read passages from the Bible as she listened for the sound of the truck. The room grew dark with the afternoon shadows filtering through the shredded window shades. She sat by my bed stroking my hair until I fell asleep. By midnight my mother was half crazy with worry, wondering why they hadn't come home. She was convinced they were delayed by fallen tree limbs and downed electrical lines. She lit candles and sat by the window watching for the headlights coming down the road. It wasn't until morning that two men from the sheriff's department came to our house. They stood on the front porch holding their hats in their hands. My mother screamed and collapsed to the floor. Our pickup truck had been found two miles down the main road. It was turned over onto its back like a turtle, unable to right itself. My father and Raymond were found inside. They were dead. The neighbors and town people searched for Jessie for days. The two goats were grazing in a nearby field, but Jessie was never found. It was after everyone had given up the search for him that my mother decided Jessie needed a headstone, as well as Raymond."

"We boys had been like the three musketeers. Jessie twelve, Raymond eleven and I was ten. I missed them so much I thought I would die. Days became weeks, weeks turned into years and I am still here, but my childhood left that day with the death of my brothers and father. My grandparents came to live with us to help keep the farm running. Neighbors and friends with tools in hand came to help clean up the debris and rebuild the barn. Mother never talked about that day, but in summer when the sky turned dark with the threat of rain, she would walk up this hill. With her head bowed, she would silently pray. Sometimes I think she wanted the storm to carry her off so that she could find Jessie."

Earl let out a sigh as he finished his story. A look of pain and sorrow filled his face. Anna knelt before him and gathered him into her arms.

After that day in the cemetery the bond of sadness connecting them to their pasts and holding them captive was finally unraveling. Anna told Earl about Colin and her father. She told him about Parker and how she never understood why he left her in her time of need. Earl was so easy to talk with. He leaned close to her and listened intently to each detail. At times he took her hand and touched her softly on the cheek. Other times they just sat quietly on the porch swing, the rusted chains creaking with each back and forth movement. They drank the iced tea Earl had finally learned to make under Anna's instruction. He would drive her home and kiss her goodnight at her front door. Sometimes, not wanting to let go, she buried her head in his chest, smelling the soft scent of Old Spice. Anna knew she had a special feeling for him, and Earl knew definitely that he was deeply in love with her.

"Well, well, it's been a long time," Dr. Vargas said as he greeted Anna. "I was surprised to see your name on my appointment book. I thought you had forgotten about the old doc."

Anna sat in her usual spot and pushed a plate of cookies across the desk. "These are from my mother. She said to tell you hello and that she misses your face."

"Tell her thank you and not to be a stranger. It would be nice to see her again before I leave. By the way, you look particularly nice today."

Anna smiled, lowering her eyes to cover her blushing cheeks. "I've met someone special and I just wanted to come and tell you. You've been such a big help to my mother and me. Where are you going? I had no idea you were leaving."

"We'll talk about that later. Tell me who is responsible for that special glow on your face?"

"His name is Earl Holloway and he lives on a farm outside of town," Anna said.

Dr. Vargas reached for a cookie. "I bet if you wanted to, Anna, you could describe him better than that."

She leaned back in the chair, trying to find the right words. "Let's see, Earl is like a favorite security blanket. He's warm and soft and makes me feel safe when I'm around him. He is gentle and kind, and has the patience of a saint, and he listens to me when I talk and…."

Dr. Vargas interrupted her. "My goodness, slow down. I think I get the picture. Am I going to be invited to a wedding any time soon?"

She shook her head. "I just don't know, Dr. Vargas. I haven't dated many men. There were a few boys in high school and Parker. This is the first time in ages that I have felt close to anyone. I'm wondering if maybe I should just take my time. Maybe I'm not ready for a serious relationship."

"Do you have a quota to meet, Anna? Do you want to date other men to see how Earl measures up? He sounds like a pretty nice guy."

She nodded, "You know, he is a nice guy. In fact, he is a great guy." Anna told Dr. Vargas everything she could think of about Earl, like the fact that he was painfully shy and had dated only one woman before her. She told him that it bothered Earl that he didn't have much money and he always seemed to bring up their age difference. Sometimes he felt embarrassed at the condition of the farm, saying he knew no decent woman would ever want to live there."

"None of these things bother me, Dr. Vargas. I don't care how much money he has or that he is a few years older than me. I always tell him that, but I'm not sure he believes me. Do you think he wants to stop seeing me?"

"Why don't you ask him?" Dr. Vargas said as he munched on another cookie. "Maybe he cares for you more than you realize. You've got to reach down inside yourself, Anna, and find out what you want for yourself. If what you want is Earl, you'd better let him know."

"I guess I haven't allowed myself to have dreams of my own in such a long time." Anna's face broke into a smile. "You're right, I'm going to tell him exactly how I feel. I'm going to tell him that I love him." She jumped up and hugged him.

"I've been thinking of retiring for quite a while," Dr. Vargas said. "Now that most of my cases are settled, it seems like a good time. I want to sit on the bank of Lake Michigan and catch some of the big fish my friends tell me about. The sun is beginning to set on this old white hair. I need to take time for myself before the lights go out." He winked at her as she rose to leave.

"My mother and I will truly miss you, Dr. Vargas. I don't know how we would have made it through these last past years without you. Please take care of yourself and send us some postcards."

He kissed her forehead and walked her to the door. "Now go. I think you have someone more important than me waiting for you."

Earl looked out the door of the workshop when he heard the car pull into the yard. "Anna, what in the world are you doing here in the middle of the afternoon? Is something wrong?"

"Nothing is wrong, Earl. I just came to tell you something. I came to tell you, I love you."

YARD SALE

A grin spread across his face as he picked her up off the ground and swung her around. "Anna Franklin, I love you so very much. Will you marry me?"

When Lou Jean got the news that Anna was getting married, she insisted on coming right away to help with the plans. They decided to be married before Christmas so they could spend it together at the farm. It would be a simple ceremony in the church rectory with just Grace, Hans and Lou Jean. Earl was so happy he hadn't stop grinning since Anna had said yes. Anna begged Lou Jean to take it easy on Earl, since he was shy and had very tender feelings. Lou Jean, of course, said she would show him no mercy.

The airport in Kansas was crowded with passengers trying to make their way home in time for the holidays. Lou Jean decided it was a perfect time for her to take the week off to prepare for what she called, "a miraculous event."

Earl and Anna stood to the side of the gate as the passengers exited the plane. She had tried to prepare Earl for Lou Jean, telling him that she was loud and boisterous with a heart of gold, and was her very best friend, next to him, of course. It was hard to realize that Lou Jean was now practicing law and was quite successful. Yet when she heard her coming down the tarmac talking to someone in her high-pitched drawl, Anna was not sure if she had prepared him enough. Letting out a scream, Lou Jean tottered across the floor in a tight green dress, her usual three-inch heels only allowing her to take baby steps. She hugged Anna, peering over her shoulder at Earl. "Well, hot damn, you must be Earl. Come here, darling, let me take a look at you." He just stood there with his hands by his sides, not knowing what to expect. Putting her arms around him, she kissed him, leaving a bright red imprint of her lips on his cheek.

Earl grinned. "I think you and I are going to get along just fine." Anna was relieved.

"Well, how is your mother taking all of this?" Lou Jean asked, as she stretched out in the back seat of the car.

"I think she is okay," Anna replied. "She seems to be happy for me. I guess I get a little paranoid once in a while. I'm always worried that her depression might return. It's been a while since she had a setback. I have been trying to prepare her for the move. I keep telling her about the farm. I told her she could have a garden and a big country home to live in. I also promised her I would bring her into the bakery every day. By the way, how is your boyfriend?"

Lou Jean laughed. "Which one? I've been through number two and number three since January. I can't seem to find that special person. Not like this sweetie." She leaned forward and pinched Earl on the cheek. Anna rolled her eyes; it was going to be a long week.

They stopped by the hotel to drop off LouJean's luggage before going to the apartment. Hans was making dinner and wanted them at the apartment by six. Lou Jean loved Hans immediately. She made jokes about his meal and he laughed at her ribald sense of humor. She teased Grace about having a boyfriend. Grace blushed, telling her that was nonsense. The evening was filled with good food and laughter.

Lou Jean and Anna spent the next afternoon shopping for dresses before going to the hotel for an "all night gab session." Lou Jean screwed up her nose when Anna picked out a cream colored suit. "You get buried in a suit, not married in a suit," Lou Jean said, holding up lime green chiffon. "Hey, I think I might wear this." They shopped until their feet could take it no longer, stopping at a malt shop to eat huge bowls of ice cream.

"I want to check on my mother before we go to the hotel," Anna said on the way home. "I'm a little worried. This is the first time I have ever left her alone all night."

Groaning, Lou Jean said she was too full to move and would wait in the car. Anna ran up the stairs to the apartment. She could see light coming from the kitchen as she opened the door. It wasn't her mother, but Hans who greeted her. Holding a bowl of grapes in his hand, he stood behind the open refrigerator. Anna could see his hairy legs and bare feet sticking out below the door, wondering if he was completely naked. To her relief, as he stepped from behind the door, he was wearing her mother's flowered bathrobe. The silky material wrapped around his rotund body, barely meeting in the front.

"Oh, Anna, you surprised me. I was just getting us a snack. Your mother told me you wouldn't be home till morning."

"Please don't mention to her that I came by. I don't want to embarrass her."

Hans pulled the robe closer to him, smiling sheepishly, "Would you like a grape?"

"Hey, what's wrong with you?" Lou Jean asked as Anna got into the car, slamming the door with all her might.

"I just can't believe this. Hans is up there with my mother. He's wearing her robe." She threw the car in gear and began to back up. "So much for her being lonely."

Lou Jean let out a whoop. "I'll be damned. I swear I think you're jealous. Your mother is getting some and you're not."

"Very funny," Anna said. "Very funny."

"We need to talk," Grace said as she watched Anna packing dishes into a box. "I don't want to disappoint you, but I'm not coming with you to the farm."

Anna put the cups back on the counter. "What do you mean? You can't stay here by yourself."

"Hans has asked me to go with him. He is closing up the bakery and buying a motor home. I think they call them RVs. He wants to do some traveling and maybe settle down somewhere in Florida."

Anna sat at the kitchen table wondering why her mother waited until two days before the wedding to tell her. "Are you getting married, Mother? Is that your plan?"

Grace shook her head. "No. Not right now. We may sometime in the future, but right now we just want things to stay like they are. We enjoy each other's company, and he is good to me. You have your own life to live; you don't need me tagging along."

"Oh, Mother, you would never be in the way. I feel like I'm deserting you."

Grace put her arms around Anna. "Listen to me, don't you ever feel that way. You have taken care of me for all these many years and I don't know what I would have done without you. Now it's time for us both to move on. I was afraid to tell you, but actually I'm quite excited about the trip. Just keep my room ready at the farm."

Hans and Grace left for Florida just hours after the wedding. Hans said he wanted to get on the road before he changed his mind and reopened the store. They said their good-byes on the apartment house steps, the brown and white motor home taking up three parking spaces at the curb.

Grace promised to call at least once a week to let Anna know her whereabouts. The sign on Knadel's Bakery read simply, "closed until further notice."

Anna cried as they drove away. Honking and waving, Hans maneuvered the trailer around the corner. As she stood with her arm around her new husband, she prayed that her mother knew what she was doing. Earl kissed her fingers, putting his hand over the gold band he had placed there just hours before. He said if her mother and Hans were half as happy as he was, there was nothing to worry about.

They decided to spend their first night together at the farm, making plans to have a real honeymoon later. Anna wished Lou Jean were still in Stockbridge. She had to leave just minutes after the wedding to get to the airport. Giggling as she got into the taxi, she teased Anna by remarking that her mother was now living in sin.

If Anna had any trepidation about living on a farm, her fears quickly vanished. Even though she missed her mother, Earl filled her life with more love and attention than she knew was possible. He marveled every day at the fact that she was his wife, saying he was the luckiest man alive. He wanted her to quit her job, but she assured him the extra money would come in handy. She didn't want to hurt his feelings, but there was definitely a need for a few improvements to the house.

Anna began to learn the ways of farm life, not without a few scratches and bruises. She found that it was not a good idea to take eggs out of a nest while the hen was still sitting in it and never turn your back on the goats. Earl taught her to make a fire in the wood stove without smoking up the whole kitchen and to keep the water running in the bathroom to prevent the pipes from freezing. Each day was like a new experience and she loved it. They would sit by the fire in the evening talking or reading. She sometimes looked up from her book to see Earl staring at her. Smiling, she would pull him close. At night, in the darkness of the bedroom, Anna could hear the field mice skittering across the attic floor. Earl teasingly told her that if she didn't keep her toes tucked under the covers the mice would come and chew on them. She would snuggle close to him and squeal. Anna began wearing socks to bed each night.

YARD SALE

The tractor was in the yard when Anna woke up. "Here, eat this, then we're gonna go get a Christmas tree," Earl said, smearing a biscuit with butter.

Anna yawned. "Can't we go into town a little later? I'm still half asleep."

"What town?" Earl grinned. "We're going to cut one ourselves. The biggest, fattest one we can find."

They bundled themselves in heavy coats and boots. Crunching through the snow, Earl helped Anna onto the tractor and headed up the hill past the cemetery and into the grove of pine trees lining the woods. She was excited. She and her mother had used the same aluminum tree for the past three years. The snow fell from the branches as they passed under the tall evergreens that stood guard over the pasture. The moment they saw the majestic white pine they knew it was the one. Anna laughed, saying it was probably too big to fit into the house.

Earl brought yellowed dusty boxes down from the attic filled with shiny ornaments and garland. Anna strung popcorn on a red string as Earl tested the lights. It was a beautiful tree, leaning slightly to the left; they tilted their heads to look at it. She crossed her fingers as he plugged the tangled web of cords into the socket. When Anna turned off the lights, the room took on a soft glow. "Our first Christmas tree," she said. "It is the best tree I have ever had in my life. I wish Mother were here to see it."

"I know you miss her Anna. I guess if you wanted me to I could invite some of my relatives over for a visit, maybe on Christmas Eve," Earl said.

Anna was surprised, "Relatives? You never talked about relatives. You mean to tell me we have family?"

"I didn't want to bring it up. I really haven't had much to do with them in the past ten years and they might not even consider me part of the family anymore. Oh, I see some of them around town once in awhile. We nod to each other when I pass them on the road, but that's about it," Earl said.

"What happened? How could you lose touch with your family?" Anna asked.

Earl took her hand and led her to the couch. "Sit down. I'll get us some coffee and tell you another long story."

"When my Mother came to the United States from Germany she was sponsored by my grandparents. In those days farm families would provide them room and board in exchange for help on the farm. When my mother, her name was Mamie, arrived in Kansas she was young and scared and spoke very little English. Grandma Holloway treated her like a servant, making her work from morning till night. My dad, James, liked her and knew his mother was treating her unfairly. She and my father would take walks in the evening and little by little their friendship grew into something more. They knew they were in love. My grandmother was furious when she found out and forbid him to be with her. Unfortunately, mother was already pregnant with Jessie. My grandmother called my mother all sorts of names, telling her she wished she had never come to this country. After my parents were married, grandmother still treated her like she was a hired hand."

"Mother had three children in three years and by the time I was born my mother and my grandmother couldn't even stand being in the same room with each other. Our house was filled with relatives and friends every Sunday for dinner and most of the holidays. After my mother cooked the meal, she would stay in her room, feeling ill at ease around them. She knew they must think less of her since she had to get married and was still living with her in-laws; however, it was really my father who refused to move. Little did she know that Grandmother Holloway told all of the relatives that my mother did not like them. She also convinced them that Mamie tricked my father into marriage so that she could stay in this country. Since mother was never around to defend herself, the relatives believed my grandmother. Mother had to ask permission for everything she wanted to do in the house. Grandmother was constantly telling her that she was not doing a good job raising us boys. Mother begged my father to move away, but he said he couldn't. Since all of his brothers had their own homes, he had a good chance of inheriting the house and farmland. My dad only had a sixth grade education. Farming was the only thing he knew."

"Grandpa Holloway finally decided that there was too much tension in the house. He was getting old and becoming more and more crippled with arthritis. He said it would be better if he let my father take over the farm. He and my grandmother would move into a small house in town. My grandma didn't go peacefully. She screamed and cried, telling him that he was breaking her heart. After my father and brothers were killed, my grandparents moved back in with us. She just loaded up the truck and moved in the day after the funeral. My mother was so numbed by the deaths she didn't try to stop her. Grandmother was once again in charge. She rearranged the furniture and started inviting the relatives over every Sunday for dinner while Grandpa sat in his wheelchair, not having the energy to fight with her."

"The year I was fourteen my grandfather passed away and just months later, my grandmother came down with pneumonia and died. It was at my grandmother's funeral that my mother stood up and announced to the family that they were no longer welcome in her house. The relatives had no idea how she felt all those years or what they had done to offend her. My mother refused to accept their apologies. I guess they thought we would move away, but mother kept the farm going. She hired migrants each spring and fall to harvest the crops, and although we had a meager existence, we made it."

"I would see my cousins at school, but I wasn't allowed to bring them home. I know some of my uncles came by to see my mother, but she refused their help. When my mother died last year some of my relatives came to the funeral. They were polite and courteous and told me to let them know if I needed anything, but I was too embarrassed to even ask for their help."

Earl got up from the couch and gathered up the coffee cups. "So that's why I never see my relatives."

Anna pondered over Earl's story for days and finally convinced him that they should at least try to make contact with his family. She would send each family member an invitation to a Christmas Eve gathering. She spent the day roasting a turkey and making cookies. Christmas songs played on the radio as she spread her mother's lace tablecloth on the dining room table. Earl brought in stacks of wood and pine boughs to burn in the fireplace. By five she had showered and changed into her wine colored dress. She was nervous, arranging and rearranging the decorations on the table as she listened for the sound of cars. The snow began to fall again and the frosted windowpanes gave off a soft reflection of the Christmas tree. It was only when she heard Earl say, "Oh my gosh," that she went to the front door. A stream of yellow car lights formed a parade on the snow-covered road. Passing through the gate, the cars filled the yard, parking in rows in front of the barn.

"How many are there, Earl? Look at all those cars. I don't have near enough food."

They filed into the house. Aunts, uncles, cousins, second cousins, cousins twice removed and a few distant relatives who needed a few minutes to figure out how they fit into the family. They carried presents wrapped not in Christmas paper, but in white wedding paper with silver and blue bows. There were casserole dishes and trays of food placed on the dining table next to her tray of deviled eggs and cheese ball. She was hugged and kissed, her cheeks red from scratchy beards, as each one greeted her and welcomed her into the Holloway family. The men gathered around Earl shaking his hand and patting his back. He grinned and hugged the older men. Some of the women cried, saying they were sorry about his mother. They wished they hadn't listened to Grandmother Holloway. The women asked Anna questions. She tried to answer as many as she could. No, she had never quilted; yes, she would love to learn to make jelly. They complimented her on the house, and told her how glad they were to be invited. As the room filled, so did Anna's heart. She looked around at the women with babies in their arms and children playing on the staircase and finally felt like she was a part of something that could not be taken away from her ever again.

Earl closed the door on the frigid winter air as the last car pulled out of the yard. "Look at all these presents," he said, sitting down on the couch in front of the Christmas tree, still wearing the Santa Claus hat someone had placed on his head.

"I know. It's amazing, she replied, dipping her fingers into a bowl of chocolate pudding. They seemed so glad to see you. I can't believe they were so generous."

Earl gently pulled her onto his lap. "You got chocolate on your nose." He kissed her face. "And what do you want for Christmas, little girl?"

Anna put her arms around his neck. "Just one thing, one tiny little thing. A baby."

Angela Marie Holloway was born the following September.

Chapter Thirty

The seed corn has been stored in the barn over the winter. There were huge piles of yellow kernels just waiting to be planted in the newly plowed fields. The spring rains had come and gone and Earl arranged for the workers to begin planting, over the insistence of his uncles that they would be glad to help. He felt he couldn't cancel out on the migrant workers who depended on him each spring for their wages. He just prayed for a bumper crop.

Anna's pregnancy made her prey to the Holloway women, each one telling of her experience in childbirth. Anna decided she wanted her baby born in the hospital and with as little pain as possible. She called her mother as soon as she knew for sure that she was expecting. Her mother was excited, but could not say if she and Hans would be in Kansas when Anna gave birth. Anna was not satisfied with her mother's answers. Calling early one morning, she was able to talk with Hans.

"What's going on with Mother?" she asked. "Is she okay?"

Hans sighed. "I don't know, Anna. One day she is singing and laughing, the next day, it's all tears and boohooing. I feel like I'm following a bouncing ball. She is on me constantly about taking her to Ternberry. Maybe if I take her there she'll be happy and we can stop by to see you on the way back."

"Do you think she can stay until the baby is born?" Anna asked. "I would really love to have her here with me."

"That's up to her, but I promise we'll be there in a month or so. You take care of yourself," Hans said and blew kisses into the telephone.

Earl helped Anna clean the house and prepare dinner before the afternoon heat took over the kitchen. She kept looking out the upstairs window as she changed the linens on the bed. When Anna saw the cloud of brown dust swirl up from the road, she knew it was the RV.

Breathless from the weight of her unborn child, she hurried down the stairs. Hans maneuvered the motor home under the shade of the oak tree and moments later pushed open the door. The sight of his huge tanned body in Bermuda shorts and a flowered shirt made Earl cover his face with his hand to keep from laughing. Anna ran to her mother. Grace hugged her daughter, kissing her cheeks as they both began to cry. Hans just looked at Earl and shrugged his shoulders.

"Oh, Sweetheart, you look wonderful. I must say pregnancy agrees with you. Stand back and let me look at you," Grace said as she held Anna at arm's length.

"I don't know about the rest of you, but if I don't get out of this heat, my head is going to boil," Hans said, wiping the sweat from his forehead. "Let's get inside where it is cool. I need to soak up some air-conditioning."

"Sorry," Earl said. "We don't have air-conditioning."

"Damn, at least tell me you have a lot of fans in that house."

Earl shook his head, "Sorry, we don't have electricity either."

"Well crap, how do you watch television? I can see a big aerial up on the roof."

"Bottled gas," Earl replied.

Hans waited a moment before he saw the grin spread over Earl's face. "Ach, you had me going for a minute. I almost bought that story. Can I have a beer, a cold beer?" Hans said as he headed toward the house.

They ate dinner in the dining room, the hum of the fans spreading the tepid air around the room. Anna told Grace about her life on the farm. She wanted her mother to share in her happiness. Grace said she was tired from the long ride. All she wanted was a cool bath and a place to rest. Anna took her to the upstairs bedroom, the afternoon heat still present in the room.

"It will get cool up here as soon the sun clears that line of trees," she said, pointing to the hill behind the house. That should be pretty soon."

Grace nodded. "Don't worry, I will be fine. I'm too tired to worry about the heat."

Anna was disappointed. She wanted to show her mother her handiwork, the furniture she had painted for the baby's room and the jars of strawberry preserves she had made and stored in the cellar. Most of all, she wanted her mother to see how happy she was being married to Earl.

Anna was anxious to talk to Hans and find out what was really going on. She opened a bottle of beer and poured it into a frosted mug. "Here, I thought you might be thirsty," she said, handing the mug to Hans. "Do you feel like talking?"

He nodded and patted the seat of the wicker chair next to him. "When we first got to Florida, everything seemed fine. We found a nice RV park and spent most of our days sightseeing or walking on the beach. Grace seemed happy to be back at the ocean. Sometimes she would spend hours just sitting in her lawn chair and staring out into the surf or picking up shells. Her bouts of depression started a couple of weeks later." Hans picked up a piece of newspaper and began fanning himself. "I kept asking her if she wanted to go back to Kansas. She said no, then the next minute she was telling me how much she missed you. It got real confusing. I got tired of sitting in the motor home, so I started playing cards with some of the men and I tried to get her to make friends, but she said she would rather be alone. Everyday I would ask her what she wanted to do. There were plenty of good restaurants where we could eat for only a few dollars, but she insisted on cooking every meal."

Anna looked into the front door to make sure her mother had not come downstairs. "I'm sorry, Hans. Go on with your story."

"Well she started talking non-stop about Ternberry until I got sick of hearing its very name. That's when I decided it was time to pack everything and started driving up the coast toward Massachusetts. Once we got there, we spent the whole day looking for the right road. We stayed at a motel and started looking again the next day. No one seemed to know where it was. It was almost as if it had vanished. Grace was distraught, but after three days of searching, I told her I had enough and we headed here. She was quiet and withdrawn the rest of the trip." Hans shook his head. "I love your mother, Anna, but I am beginning to believe she just wants to see how far she can push me. I would never leave her, but she can sure irritate the hell out of me sometimes. I've been thinking about selling the bakery in Stockbridge and buying a little business on the beach. Maybe that will make her happy."

Anna put her arm around his shoulder. "I want to thank you for taking care of her. I know it hasn't been easy. She cares for you, Hans. I'm sure of that."

Anna and Grace planned to spend the day shopping. Grace wanted to buy some things for her grandbaby. As they drove to Stockbridge, Anna pointed out all the new buildings. Grace was amazed at how much the town had grown.

"Mother, please stop, you've bought enough," Anna said as Grace picked up a white nightgown off the counter. "This baby can only wear so many clothes. Thank you so much. Now let's go eat lunch. I'm starving."

The restaurant was cool and dark, causing Anna to shiver as she slid into the booth across from her mother. "Ah, wonderful air-conditioning. Someday we hope to have it at the farm. Let's eat something light. I've invited some of the relatives over for a barbecue tonight and they always bring plenty of food."

"Oh, you didn't tell me that, dear. I would have bought a cake or something when we passed the bakery. I wish I had known," Grace said in an annoyed tone.

"Is there a problem, Mother? They really want to meet you. They hear me talking about you all the time."

Grace nodded as she looked at the menu. "No, there's no problem. I just thought we would have more time to ourselves."

"We'll have plenty of time. I plan on this being a very long visit."

Earl had already started the fire in the barbecue pit by the time Anna and Grace got home. Hans was helping him set up tables under the shade trees. His face was red with beads of sweat rolling down his forehead as he sang a German song.

"Looks like you had a good shopping spree," Earl said as Anna held up the bags. "Uncle Louis is already on his way. You ladies had better get ready. The others will be here soon." Grace disappeared into the house.

Earl carried the large platter of barbecue to the outdoor table that was already filled with bowls and casseroles. As he passed Anna, he touched her arm. "Where is your mother? Everyone is asking about her. I haven't seen her since you got home. Maybe you better check on her."

Anna quietly opened the bedroom door. The curtains were drawn and moved slightly as the afternoon breeze began to make its way through the room. "Mother are you all right?"

Grace rolled over, a dampened washcloth covering her head. "I have a terrible headache. I think it may be a migraine. I just need to lie here for a few moments until the aspirins begin to ease the pain," she said, wiping her face with the cloth.

"But all of these people are here to see you. Do you think you could at least come down and sit in a chair?"

"No, dear, I don't think so. Not right now. Give me a few more minutes."

"Please try, Mother. This is so disappointing," Anna said as she left the room, closing the door behind her.

Grace waited a few moments after Anna left before she tiptoed to the window. Pulling back the curtains, she watched as her daughter moved about the yard, talking and laughing with her new family. She watched as they ate and afterwards cleared the tables. The empty casserole dishes were packed away into their baskets. Grace watched as they kissed Anna goodbye. Her daughter was very lucky.

It was her mother's voice that woke Anna in the early light of morning. "Anna, I'm sorry to wake you but we are getting ready to leave and I want to say goodbye."

Anna sat up in bed, "You're what? Leaving now? What time is it?"

"It's early, dear. Hans decided last night that he wants to go back to Florida. His gout is starting to act up and he wants to get on the road before it gets too hot."

"But why now, Mother? I thought you would be here for at least a couple of weeks. What about the baby? Will you be here in September when the baby is born?"

"Well, of course. You don't think I would miss that, do you? Now you just go back to bed. Hans told me to tell you goodbye."

Anna got up from bed, "I want to tell him goodbye myself, Mother. Let me get dressed and I'll be right down."

By the time she made it to the front door, she could see the RV pulling out of the yard. She never even had a chance to kiss her mother goodbye.

"Earl, get the truck," Anna screamed as she hurried across the yard. "I'm going after her."

"What do you want me to do, Anna?" he asked.

"Follow the RV. She is not going to leave me without giving me an explanation."

Anna climbed into the passenger seat. Looking confused, Earl took off after the trail of dust leading to the main road. Anna leaned over and began honking the horn. It took a few minutes for Hans to realize that it was Earl and not some local country boy wanting to pass. He guided the RV into a small clearing as Earl pulled in next to him.

"Hey, what's going on? Did we forget something?" Hans said as he opened the door.

"I want to see my mother. I need to talk to her." Anna was almost out of breath as she climbed into the motor home.

"I think I'll go sit with Earl. This is between you two." Hans threw up his hands and ambled over to the truck.

Grace was sitting in the back of the RV. She looked surprised when Anna made her way down the narrow aisle.

"I want to know what's wrong, Mother? Why did you leave so suddenly and why didn't you come downstairs last night?"

"I was going to call you and explain. I'm sorry for the way I acted."

"Sorry is not good enough. I'm not going to accept that. I want you to tell me right now why you want to run away and I know it has nothing to do with Hans' gout." Anna had never spoken to her mother in sharp tones and Grace could sense her daughter's hurt and anger.

"I should never have asked Hans to take me to Ternberry. That was a mistake. It really upset me that we could not find it, but when I saw you I thought everything was going to be okay." Grace slid over on the seat, giving Anna room to sit down. "You have a home now, plus a loving husband and a family. I have always wanted you to be happy, but forgive me for being envious. I felt like such an outsider. Since I am no longer a burden to you, you really don't need me around anymore. I have taken up enough of your life."

"You've got to let all that go Mother and enjoy what we have now. Do you remember what Dr.Vargas told you on your last visit? He said you should have a happy life and never look back. There are so many people who love you and pretty soon you'll have a new grandbaby. We're a team, you and I. I want you here with me because I love you and you are one of the most important parts of my life. Please don't run away from me."

Hans stuck his head into the RV. "Excuse me, I know this is a private conversation, but it's hotter than hell out here. Can I come in?"

"Sure you can," Grace said, "but before you get comfortable, do you think you could help me get my things together? I'm going to be staying with Anna and Earl for a while longer. You're welcome to stay too, Hans."

"I would like that, Grace, but I have some business to take care of in Florida and when you return, you're going to be in for a big surprise," he said as he pulled her suitcases out from under the seat. "Have a nice visit. I'll send you a plane ticket when you're ready to come home. Turn your head," he said to Anna as he took Grace into his arms and kissed her goodbye. "Come back to me soon. You know I love you."

Grace settled into the spare bedroom, helping Anna with the cooking and cleaning. She joined the Tuesday afternoon quilting sessions with Earl's aunts. They slowly pieced together the colorful quilt for the newest baby in the Holloway family. Grace made pies from the apples on the tree by the back door and sewed curtains for the nursery. In the evening they sat on the porch. Anna would sit in the rocking chair Earl had made, resting her swollen feet on a pillow. Grace watched as her daughter gently stroked her bulging stomach, telling Anna she was now in the "nesting" stage of her pregnancy. It was Grace who held Anna's hand during the fifteen-mile drive to the hospital. Angela came into the world kicking and screaming. The doctor called her a real live wire. Earl couldn't stop grinning as he stood by the nursery window watching his new baby daughter. On the day Grace was to leave, Anna watched her mother as she gently rocked Angela. "She looks like you, Mother," Anna said. "I like her red hair."

Grace nodded, "Yes, she does. I hope that's all she inherits from me."

Chapter Thirty-One

It was the changing of seasons that Anna loved the most. She marveled at the vibrant fall colors of the trees as they dressed themselves in red and orange brilliance. Anna couldn't believe how long the snow stayed sparkling white, never touched by shovels or passing cars. Only the soft indentions of animal tracks marked the icy expanse. Spring was by far her favorite season. The earth opened up, pushing the crocuses and hyacinths into the morning sun. The fields were filled with new sprouts of corn sending their shoots into the fresh rain washed air. It was in the spring that Colleen Leigh was born. Earl and Anna had hoped for a brother for three-year-old Angela who insisted that a new baby was not necessary. Anna and Earl were grateful for another healthy baby.

When summer arrived, the mood in the house changed. It was those summer months that determined how much money the family would have to live on for the rest of the year. Would there not be enough rain or too much rain? Would beetles and grasshoppers descend on the crops before they had time to be harvested? The heated winds that blew across the open Kansas plains held a daily threat of storms. Torrential storms could spawn in minutes, covering the sky with ashen gray clouds and sending the thunder and lightning to rattle the windows and flicker the lights.

It was Earl who hated the summer most. He would listen to the weather reports daily while reading the paper, commenting to Anna about tornados that had touched down in other counties. Each year he restocked the storm cellar, putting in fresh jugs of drinking water and stocking up on batteries for the radio. When the storms descended on the farm, he would come in from the field to be with his family. He stood like a sentry at the front door, making sure they were all safe. Anna would go to him and put her arms around his waist. "Maybe we should move somewhere else, some place where there is no threat of tornados."

"Where would we go?" Earl asked. "This is our home. I just have to learn to deal with the storms a little better." Anna knew each bolt of lightning and gust of wind reminded him of that fateful day so many years ago.

Today was one of those sultry summer days. The fans in the house helped little with the sweltering heat. Anna spent the early hours of the morning cleaning the kitchen and frying chicken for supper. Lou Jean was coming to visit and Anna wanted everything to be perfect. "You've got to let me dress you, Angela. Auntie Lou Jean will be here real soon and I still have things to do," Anna said as she tried to pull Angela's pajama pants off. "Please stop kicking me."

Angela squirmed until she was able to duck under her mother's arm, running down the hallway laughing. Anna sighed, wondering when her daughter was going to get used to the idea of wearing clothes. She still spent most of her time running around the house naked, leaving a trail of clothes behind her.

"Come back here and let me comb your hair." Anna picked Colleen off the floor and searched the upstairs rooms until she heard a soft giggle coming out of her bedroom. She could see the tangled mass of auburn curls bobbing up and down from behind the bedpost. Anna grabbed Angela's arm and began to pull the comb through her hair.

"Ouch! You're hurting me. I don't need my hair combed." Angela tried to pull away from her mother.

"I want you to be good for me while Auntie Lou Jean is here. She is my best friend and I haven't seen her for a very long time and please keep your clothes on!" she said as Angela took off running.

It had been almost three years since she had seen Lou Jean. Angela was just a baby the last time she was home for a visit. Lou Jean had taken a position with a law firm in London. She begged Anna to come visit her but it was almost impossible. Earl agreed to watch the children, but Anna knew they were too much for one person to handle.

Lou Jean arrived in a flurry as usual. Bags and boxes spilled out of the back of the trunk as Earl unloaded her luggage and carried it into the house.

"Come here and give your old friend a hug," Lou Jean said when Anna appeared in the doorway holding Colleen. Lou Jean hugged Anna, gathering the baby into her arms, as Angela peered from behind her mother's skirt. "You come here too, squirt. I have lots of presents for you."

Lou Jean's life had taken numerous twists and turns in the past few years. She had switched from criminal law to corporate law at the advice of most of the judges in the district courts in St. Louis. It seemed that most of the time she was in contempt for her actions during the trials. Corporate law had been good to her. Her ability to argue and wear her opposition down made her life much more profitable. She now spent most of her time in London, working for an overseas corporation.

"Are you happy?" Anna asked as they sat in the swing, sipping iced tea and trying to keep cool in the warm afternoon sun.

"I think I am or let's say I should be," Lou Jean replied as she rested her bare feet on the porch railing. "I make more money than I ever imagined, but I guess I still have that feeling every once in a while that I would like to meet someone special and settle down. Especially when I see you and Earl, but I don't know if I would be that lucky. I like living in England and my practice is going great, even though most of those Brits don't know what language I'm speaking." Lou Jean stretched and walked to the edge of the porch. "I may come back some day and settle down. Maybe I'll buy a farm. It's nice to have enough money to help my mom, especially since she found a new religion in the church bingo halls."

Angela came screaming through the door in her underwear with Earl right behind her. Lou Jean laughed. "Angela sure is a little ball of fire."

Anna nodded. "That's putting it mildly. It's like trying to catch the wind in a bottle. She is never still for one minute. Thank goodness Colleen is just the opposite. I couldn't handle two like Angela. A few months ago she crawled under the front porch looking for one of the kittens and disturbed a mother skunk. It took me weeks to get the smell out of her hair, much less the house. Then last week she put a rock up her nose. We had to go to the emergency room to have it removed. I just don't know where she comes up with all her ideas. Mother says it's because she feels so safe and loved that she doesn't have any fear."

Lou Jean smiled, "Are you sure she's not my kid? By the way, how is your mother doing?"

"Pretty good. Hans rented a building on the pier. With the money from the sale of the RV and his bakery in Stockbridge, he bought enough equipment to open a doughnut shop and is now officially known by the locals as 'Hans the Doughnut Man.' They both work in the shop and have a furnished apartment upstairs. It's right on the beach and mother can see the ocean from every window. They seem happy, although my mother said that Hans now weighs over three hundred pounds and has trouble making it up the steps to the apartment."

"Sounds like he enjoys his own baking," Lou Jean said. "Is your mother still having problems with depression or has Hans cured that too?"

"She seems fine, except a few months ago Hans called me in a panic. He had found a bottle of unmarked pills under the mattress when he was changing the sheets. He was so upset. I told him to take them to the pharmacy and see what they were. I waited all day for him to call me back."

Lou Jean shook her head. "Oh, God, please don't tell me she is back on that stuff."

"No, they were hormones. Seems like she was having hot flashes. Hans was so embarrassed, he bought her a new television set. Needless to say, she had no idea what was going on."

Lou Jean let out a howl. "Damn. I guess she's trying to stay young. Who can blame her?"

Earl poked his head out of the front door. "Supper is just about ready. Are you two hungry?"

"Supper? What are you talking about? I didn't see the pizza man pull in," Lou Jean said as she followed Anna inside.

"I fried chicken this morning and he's fixing the rest of the meal. Earl is getting to be a pretty good cook," Anna said with a grin.

"Oh Lord, you better hold on to this one."

Lou Jean pushed her plate aside and rested her head in her hands. "That was great. What are we having for breakfast?" She yawned. "I've got to get some sleep, kiddo. Jet lag is catching up with me." She kissed Anna on the cheek and went to bed, sleeping for the next fifteen hours. She awoke to find Angela sitting on the foot of her bed naked.

"Hi, Auntie Lou Jean. Are you ready to come outside and see my chickens?"

By the end of the week Angela and Lou Jean had become best friends. They played in the creek, tracking muddy footprints across the kitchen floor. Angela taught Lou Jean how to gather eggs and slide on the hay bales in the barn. The games of hide and go seek in the house became loud and rowdy with Anna stepping in to calm them both down. On the last day of her visit, Angela took Lou Jean's hand as they headed up the hill to pick blackberries.

"Are you sure there are no snakes up here?" Lou Jean asked as they waded through the purple clover covering the slope.

"Maybe, but they run away real fast when they see you coming," Angela said as she swung her bucket back and forth.

"What's that over there?" Lou Jean asked as they passed the small enclosure of gravestones surrounded by rows of yellow flowers.

"That's the place where my daddy's family is buried. They're all dead, you know, but you don't have to be sad. My momma says that they have angels that watch over them to keep them from being lonely. Do you like angels?" Lou Jean nodded and squeezed her hand.

The visit passed too quickly for them all, especially Angela who insisted that Lou Jean come live with them. Earl and Anna waved goodbye as Angela, completely naked, ran after the car.

In the days that followed Lou Jean's visit, Angela was restless. She missed having someone to play with. "I want to go outside," she said in a whining voice.

"I have told you we will go outside as soon as your sister wakes up. Please let me read." Anna picked up her book and reread the same sentence for the third time.

"Can I go out in the workshop with daddy? I promise I won't bother any of his stuff."

"If he is busy you come right back," Anna sighed as she watched Angela scamper across the yard toward the workshop. She sat down and continued to read.

The back door closed with its usual creak. "Looks like it's getting ready to rain," Earl said as he began to wash his hands in the kitchen sink.

"Did she bother you?" Anna asked looking up from her book.

"Who? I was out there by myself."

"But Angela went out there to be with you. I watched her go across the yard." Anna rose from her chair and walked to the back door.

"I bet she's in the barn trying to find those new kittens. I'll go get her," Earl said as he opened the door. He strode across the yard feeling the cool air that signaled rain. He shivered as he opened the barn door and called her name. "Angela, if you're in here you had better answer me.

Come on now, kiddo, it's going to rain." He called again. The only sound he heard was the quiet rustling of the cows as they moved about in the stalls, flicking their tails to rid themselves of the ever-present flies. Earl opened the barn door and yelled her name into the yard as loud as he could.

"I didn't find her, Anna. I looked all over the barn and in the workshop. She's not there." The rain clouds were moving in a band across the northern sky and the first flashes of lightning could be seen in the distance.

"She's not in the house. I checked every room. Oh my God, Earl, where is she?" Tears began to well in Anna's eyes.

"Go back inside. I'll find her. She has to be around here somewhere," Earl said calmly, trying not to appear alarmed. Anna stood at the door watching as he went back into the barn. She ran across the yard to look in the chicken coop. Earl climbed the ladder to the loft, making his way across the bales of hay and calling her name. He began to feel uneasy. She had never done this before. He remembered the stories of children who had disappeared from the farms. There were children who had been swallowed up by the overflowing creeks or had walked into the maze of cornfields and were never found. He tried to put those thoughts out of his mind. As he heard the first clap of thunder, his heart began to race. Earl pushed open the wooden loading door in the loft and looked out over the yard and hillside. The wind caught the door, almost pushing him to the ground. It was only as he fought to keep his balance that he saw the glimpse of something white on top of the hill. He shimmied down the ladder, his feet slipping. He could feel the splinters of wood catching in his fingers. The boiling clouds had turned the sky dark and the first few drops of rain began to fall. As he raced up the hill his footing gave way under the slippery grass, but he couldn't move fast enough. "Please, God, let her be okay, please, let her be okay."

She was lying by the tree, her eyes closed, just a few feet away from the cemetery gate. The wind whipped her auburn hair across her face. Earl dropped to his knees and gathered her into his arms. "Angela! Answer me! Are you hurt?"

Angela opened her eyes. A small grin played across her lips, "I'm okay Daddy."

"Oh, baby, you scared me. I thought something bad happened to you. What are you doing up here?" Earl continued to hold her close to him, rocking back and forth as the rain streaked down his face mixing with the tears flowing from his eyes.

"I came up here to talk to the angels. If you be real quiet maybe we can hear them." Angela took Earl's face into her small hands. "Don't be scared, daddy. The angels won't let the storm hurt you."

Chapter Thirty-Two

As each year passed, more and more memories were pressed into the photo albums lining the living room shelves. Pictures of the big yellow school bus picking Angela up for her first day of school, the girls sitting under the Christmas tree, and one of Colleen smiling a toothless grin. There were souvenirs of their vacations to see Grandma Grace and Hans. This time Anna would be going to Florida alone. There would be no photographs on this trip, nothing to put in the memory book.

"Do you have everything?" Earl asked as he closed Anna's suitcase.

"I think so. I really don't need to take much," she said putting her white gloves into her purse.

Angela stood leaning against the doorframe, her arms folded over her chest. "I still don't see why I can't go with you. After all, I'm ten. I think I'm old enough to go to a funeral."

"I know you are, sweetheart, but this is a memorial service. Hans has already been cremated and Grandma Grace is going to spread his ashes over the ocean. She wants me to be there with her. Besides you have to help daddy with Colleen and I don't want you to miss any more school."

"That's gross, throwing a dead person into the water," Angela said, sticking out her lip, still protesting.

"I will only be gone for three days and when we come back I will take you to church and you can light a special candle for Hans." Anna kissed Angela on the cheek as she passed through the door.

Earl picked up the luggage and followed Anna down the stairs. "Maybe I should come, too. Are you sure you're going to be okay?"

"Mother understands it's harvest time and you have the workers coming tomorrow. There is no way you can cancel on them at this late notice. She knows that you cared a lot for Hans."

"Do you think she will agree to come back to Kansas to live with us?" Earl asked.

"I don't know, darling. I just don't know."

It was a heartfelt reunion. Grace looked small and frail, her auburn hair now streaked with gray, her eyes rimmed with red and her hands slightly shaking she waited by the gate for Anna.

"Oh, Mother, I'm so sorry."

"I'm so glad that you were able to come. I miss him, Anna, I miss him so much."

Anna made tea in the small kitchen and carried the tray into the living room of the apartment. She poured her mother a cup and settled back into the massive lounge chair.

"That was Hans' chair. It was just about the only place he could get comfortable these past few months. He was so very heavy, and his gout made it almost impossible for him to walk. I had to have the bed reinforced just to hold him. The doctor kept telling him to lose weight, but he would just laugh and continue to eat whatever he wanted. He was having so much trouble breathing that he had to sit up to sleep. Hans just went to bed three nights ago and never woke up." Grace sipped her tea. She was quiet for a moment. "I couldn't find a coffin big enough, Anna. I think that's why he wanted to be cremated."

Anna went to her mother. She rocked her in her arms just as she did her children when they were sad or hurt.

The pier was lined with the friends and neighbors Hans and Grace had made over the years. They bowed their heads in silence as the small boat propelled its way out of the cove. They threw wreaths of flowers into the water as soft, mournful music played in the background. The captain was kind, anchoring the boat a mile off shore; he went below to give them time alone. Anna knelt beside her mother as Grace said her prayers and final goodbye to Hans. "The last thing he said to me was that he loved me. I shall always remember those words," Grace said as she slowly opened the urn and watched the foamy sea carry his ashes away.

As they left the pier Anna took her mother's hand. "You can't stay here in Florida by yourself. I want you to come back to Kansas with me. We can pack some of your clothing and have the rest of your things delivered. When we get back to the apartment I need to call Earl."

"I know I can't stay here alone, but I hate the idea of having to once again count on you to take care of me. I'll just come for a little while, until I can find a place of my own," Grace said sadly.

"That was your mother who just called," Earl said to Angela and Colleen as he returned to the dinner table. Grandma Grace is coming to live with us and I want both of you to make her feel very welcome. They will be home tomorrow afternoon."

Colleen smiled. "I like Grandma Grace. I'm glad she's coming here."

Angela shrugged. "Just so I get to keep my room, I guess it will be okay."

Grace was tired from the trip when they arrived at the farm. She decided to skip dinner and go to bed. "Am I staying in the guest room?" she asked as she started up the stairs.

"It's not the guest room anymore, Mother. It's your room. Once your things get here, you can arrange it anyway you want. Have a good rest." Anna hoped it wouldn't be too difficult for her mother to adjust to her new life.

"It's so good to be home. Did the girls behave themselves?" Anna asked Earl as she hung her dresses in the closet.

"They were fine. How is your mother doing? Is she going to be okay?"

"She's very sad right now and she is worried about her money situation. Mother has never handled finances. They had to use up most of their savings when Hans was sick. By the time we paid for the funeral expenses and arranged to have her things shipped here, the account was almost depleted. I didn't have the heart to tell her about that yet. She loved him and money was never an issue. I don't think my mother ever considered what would happen to her if Hans died. I'm glad she had those happy years with him."

The delivery van arrived a week later from Florida. Grace stared at the pile of boxes in the middle of the bedroom floor. There was not much to show for sixty years of living: a television set, a few pieces of furniture and the rest of her clothing.

Taking her robe off of the hook behind the door, she walked down the hall to the bathroom. Leaning over the railing, she made her announcement. "I'm going to take a bath now. Does anyone have to use the bathroom?" Grace filled the claw foot tub and settled into the warm water. She rested her head against the smooth porcelain and closed her eyes. The adjustment of living on the farm was not easy. She still felt like a guest in her daughter's home. Each change seemed to bring on a major discussion, leaving Grace always apologizing for her presence. She was now aware of her money situation, knowing that in just a few short months, she would be completely out of funds. Once again Anna came to her rescue. Just as she had when Henry died. What was the use of her staying here and becoming an extra burden to Anna? She should just sink down in the tub and let the water cover her. Then she would no longer be a bother to anyone.

There was a light tapping at the door. "Grandma Grace, I was wondering if you would braid my hair? Would you like to read my new book with me? Grandma Grace, are you okay?"

"I'm fine, sweetheart. I'll be out in a minute." Maybe there was someone who needed her. Sweet, gentle Colleen.

Chapter Thirty-Three

"Damn, can you believe it? You're going to be forty. The big Four-O. It's time for a face-lift and a boob job. What do you think about this fateful day?" Lou Jean asked, laughing.

"What do I think? I think it's three-thirty in the morning. Where are you?" Anna said as she reached across the bed and turned on the lamp.

"Damn, I always forget about the time difference. I'm in Paris, but I couldn't let this day go by with out wishing you a happy birthday."

"Technically, my birthday isn't until tomorrow. So I have one more day to be thirty-nine. By the way, you're two weeks older than me. You tell me how it feels to be forty."

"I wouldn't know. If anybody asks, I'm only thirty-six. I might as well tell you. I'm thinking about getting married."

Anna sat up in bed. "You sure know how to surprise me. When did all of this happen?"

Actually we have been talking about it for about a month, but yesterday he officially proposed. His name is Aubert and he lives here in Paris."

"You never mentioned him. How long have you known him?"

"Whoa, slow down," Lou Jean said. "I've known him for about six months. I met him while I was representing his company in a corporate litigation. At first we didn't get along at all. We argued all the time but then it all seemed to come full circle and we started seeing each other. He's sexy, suave, sophisticated, and rich. I don't know what he wants with me. I want you to come to Paris and stand by my side when I get married, and before you start giving me a hundred excuses, I have it all worked out."

"But I can't. My goodness, I can't come to Paris." Anna patted Earl on the back. "Lou Jean is getting married. She wants me to come to Paris."

"Okay, here's the deal," Lou Jean said. "Aubert has an apartment in Paris. You can stay there. I bought you a non-refundable airline ticket, so you can't say no."

Anna smiled to herself. "Paris, I can't believe it. You really want me to come?"

"I said so, didn't I? Can you be here by Friday?"

Anna patted Earl on the back again. "She's serious, but I just can't."

Earl pulled the cover up over his head. "Anna, go to Paris!"

The limousine driver held up the sign with Anna's name on it as she came through the gate. Embarrassed, she walked up to him "I'm Anna Holloway."

He tipped his hat, taking her small valise. "I am here to retrieve you. Miss Lou Jean said to tell you she was sorry she couldn't meet you, but will be home as soon as possible. Let me collect your other luggage and we will be on our way."

Anna settled into the back of the automobile, sinking into the plush red seat. She was too excited to think about how tired she was after the long flight. It was all so different. There were long boulevards with cars moving in all directions and lining the sidewalks were small cafes with bright green awnings. The evening was alive with the ever-twinkling lights of the city. She caught a glimpse of the Eiffel Tower, pointing it out to the driver. He nodded and she could see him smiling in the rear view mirror.

Aubert's apartment was on the Boulevard du' Montparnasse over looking the Seine River. It was a tall white building with ivy covering the walls and railings. She was met at the door by a valet who spoke very little English. He led her up the stairs to a bedroom. Opening the door onto a small balcony, the white sheer curtains wafting in the evening breeze, he placed her suitcases on the bed. He said something in French and left. Anna walked around the room. There were fresh flowers on the nightstand and a stack of soft cream-colored bath towels on a velvet bench. A clear blue bottle rested in an ice bucket with a crystal glass turned upside down on the tray. Anna picked up the note resting on the bed pillow. It was from Lou Jean.

Anna: Make yourself at home. Sorry I couldn't meet you. Had to work late. Will be there as soon as I can. Love, Lou Jean.

YARD SALE

Minutes later Anna heard the door open and her friend's familiar voice. "Hey, girl, you better be awake," Lou Jean said as she rushed up the steps.

"I'm not asleep. I'm too excited," Anna said as she came in from the balcony. "My gosh, you look different. What did you do to your hair?"

Lou Jean was dressed in a black business suit. Her once unruly blonde hair was now cut short and dyed a deep chestnut brown. "Do you like it?" she asked, twirling around. "This is my new image. Aubert said I needed a more sophisticated look."

"When do I get to meet this mystery man of yours? I can't wait to see who this person is that had enough strength to capture your heart."

"Oh, please," Lou Jean said, placing her hand on her forehead. "First tell me about your family then I'll give you the whole scoop."

"Well, let's see. Earl is fine. He's working too hard as usual and of course I worry about him. Angela is fourteen. She drives me crazy with her attitude and every time I pick her up from school, she is with a group of boys. My sweet little Colleen has become my mother's best friend. Colleen helped Mother plant a little garden and now they are writing stories. And me, I cannot believe I am really in Paris."

Lou Jean poured Anna a glass of wine from the blue bottle and pulled off her panty hose. "God, I hate these things. Aubert won't be in town till tomorrow evening, so I thought tomorrow we would do the touristy thing and shop for something to wear to dinner. How does that sound?"

"Wonderful." Anna smiled. "Now show me the rest of this house. I have been dying to see it."

She awoke to the sound of cars passing outside the window and for a moment Anna forgot where she was. It didn't take long. Lou Jean opened the door and jumped on the bed. "Get up you lazy bones. It's almost noon. I know you're tired from the trip, but it's time to hit the streets of Paris."

Anna walked down the steps of Aubert's apartment and felt like she was in a movie set. Lou Jean grabbed her arm. "Come on. The stores of Paris are waiting for our money."

Hours later, Anna sat on the edge of the bed and kicked off her shoes. "My feet hurt, I don't think I've ever shopped that much in one day."

"Try on your dress. I want to see how you look in it. I'm going to go take a shower," Lou Jean said as she left the room.

Anna walked down the hall to the bathroom. "Lou Jean, I need help. I can't wear this thing. Look at it." She tugged on the front of the red silk dress.

"What's wrong with it? You look like dynamite. Stop pulling, you're going to rip it."

"I'm hanging out. I can't pull it up any further. I didn't notice this in the store."

"You look great. I wish Earl were here to see you. Now let's try putting your hair up. Lou Jean stood behind Anna looking into the bathroom mirror. "Hey, we're not too bad looking for forty-year-old women."

A waiter in a black tuxedo escorted them to the table. He pulled out Anna's chair and she tried to sit down without bending forward, feeling terribly self-conscious in her new dress. The restaurant was elegant. Each table held a vase of red roses surrounded by gleaming silver candles that sparkled beneath the crystal chandeliers. Lou Jean ordered wine in French and held out her cigarette as the waiter produced a gold lighter.

"So now you speak French. How impressive," Anna said.

"I call it pigeon French, but somehow I can get my point across. Aubert is trying to make me into a lady. Would you believe I have even been to the ballet? A real yawner. He wants me to be a connoisseur of the arts." She grabbed for the ashtray and stubbed out the cigarette. "Crap, hand me my purse. I need a breath mint. Here comes Aubert."

Before Anna could turn her head, he was at the table, bending down to kiss Lou Jean on the cheek. "And this must be Anna. Lou Jean didn't tell me how lovely you were."

"She cleans up real nice once she gets the hay out of her hair," Lou Jean cackled, watching as Anna's face turned red.

"Never mind her. You know how she loves to tease," Aubert said as he looked at Anna. She could swear he was staring straight at her chest with his dark blue eyes. Lifting the white napkin, he raised his eyebrow. "Smoking again? Did you enjoy your cigarette? I thought we had decided to quit."

Lou Jean didn't answer him, pretending to puff on an imaginary cigarette.

YARD SALE

Aubert ordered dinner and more wine. Anna was flushed. He was so attentive, always looking directly into her eyes when he talked to her. He asked her questions about Kansas. He said he couldn't believe she had a teenage daughter. The meal arrived with course after course of unrecognizable food that was delicious, followed by more wine. The orchestra began playing in the lounge and Aubert led Anna and Lou Jean to a table next to the open door of the balcony. Anna stood breathing in the fresh air, hoping to clear her head. He took her hand. "Come and dance with me. It will make you feel better to move around."

Before she could protest, he had guided her through the maze of tables and on to the dance floor. Anna could feel his face slightly touching her hair as he pulled her close to him. Too many glasses of wine made her dizzy as his body moved her to the rhythm of the music. Slowly giving in, she relaxed into his arms. When they returned to the table, Lou Jean was talking to a group of people.

"It seems that Lou Jean has run into some of her business acquaintances. You may not know this, but your friend is a very respected lawyer." Aubert smiled at Lou Jean as she turned around and waved to him. "I was lucky to have her come to Paris to represent my company. Lou Jean is very well known and has a waiting list of people wanting her legal services. That is why I am keeping her here," he said, patting Anna on her knee. "You understand, I am only kidding."

Once back at the apartment, Anna begged off from Aubert's invitation to have another glass of wine. A nice hot shower and a bed was all she needed to end this perfect night.

Anna didn't hear him come in. As she walked into the bedroom brushing her hair, he was leaning against the door with an open bottle of brandy and two glasses in his hand.

"Lou Jean went to bed. I thought you might change your mind. I hate to drink alone," Aubert said as he sat down on the bed. She wondered how long he had been standing there. Had he watched her while she dried her body or was she already in her robe?

Anna pulled the robe closer around her. "No, I don't think so, Aubert. I'm really tired." She was beginning to feel uncomfortable. Maybe she appeared too friendly at dinner or when they were dancing. Surely he didn't think she was flirting.

Aubert set the glasses on the nightstand and moved towards her. "Perhaps you would like some help getting ready for bed." His hand tugged on the sash of the robe as he moved closer to her. He kissed her on the neck before she could protest. "You have a beautiful body."

Anna moved back and tried to push him away. "Please don't do this. I'm sorry if I have given you the wrong impression."

"On the contrary, Anna," he said, pulling her toward the bed.

Anna stomped down on his foot as hard as she could and ran toward the bathroom. Her heart was pounding as she turned the lock on the door. Aubert knocked lightly. "You can come out now, Anna. I'm leaving."

Her knees gave way as she slid to the floor. She sat in the darkness with her legs cramping until the first light of dawn filtered into the bathroom skylight. She then crawled across the bedroom floor and wedged a chair under the doorknob.

In the morning Lou Jean tried to open the door. "Anna, are you okay? I can't get the door open."

Anna jumped out of bed. Her head pounding, she pulled the chair away. "It must have been stuck. I'm sorry I slept so late. What time is it?"

"I was getting lonely downstairs. Aubert is gone for the day. He had some business across town. You and I have a lot to do today. We need to pick out flowers and a cake and look at invitations."

Anna didn't know what to say. She wanted desperately to tell Lou Jean what had happened, but the words would not come. Was it right to tell her now that she seemed so happy? How could she ever face Aubert again? She needed to talk to her mother. Why was it so hard to tell her best friend the truth?

After another day of shopping, Anna helped Lou Jean carry all the packages into the apartment. "Would you mind if I go upstairs and lie down for awhile?" Anna asked rubbing her head.

"No, go ahead. I'll call you when Aubert gets home. I thought we'd just have a nice quiet dinner here tonight."

Anna dialed the number and waited for the overseas operator to connect her, "Hello. Colleen, is that you sweetie? It's Mother."

"Hi, Mom. How are you? Are you having a good time? When are you coming home?"

"Everything here is fine. Can I speak to Grandma?"

Colleen hesitated. "Okay, let me get her. I love you, Mom."

Grace was surprised to hear from her daughter. "Anna, is everything okay?"

"Oh, Mother, I have a real mess on my hands. I need your advice."

Anna told her mother exactly what had happened. "Do you think I should tell Lou Jean? It may have just been that we both had too much to drink."

"Anna, you have to tell Lou Jean. If you want my opinion, I think he knew exactly what he was doing. You have to give Lou Jean the chance to make her own decisions. Do you want your best friend to spend her life like I did, living each day with a cheat and a liar? Aubert was taking advantage of you. He probably never thought that you would tell Lou Jean."

"I was never sure if you knew about the other women in father's life," Anna said softly.

"I knew, Anna, and I was a fool to put up with him. I have lived to regret it. Do Lou Jean a favor and tell her."

Lou Jean sent a tray to Anna's room with a note saying that Aubert was not home yet. She had a headache and would see her in the morning. Anna was relieved. By then maybe she would have enough courage to tell Lou Jean what happened.

"Pack your things, Anna. You and I are going to my apartment in London. I want to introduce you to Big Ben," Lou Jean said as Anna came downstairs the next morning. "I've changed my mind about getting married. Aubert and I had a long talk last night. I have decided I don't want to get married after all. I need to get back to London and take care of my office. I'm sorry I brought you all the way over here and now, no wedding, but it's been great. You're not mad, are you?"

Anna sat down on the bottom step. "You know something, don't you?"

Lou Jean hesitated for a moment and sat down next to her. "I just happened to pick up the downstairs phone last night. I was going to make a call and I heard you talking to your mother. I didn't mean to eavesdrop, but I heard part of the conversation and I just couldn't hang up. I'm sorry for what Aubert did to you."

"I should be the one saying I'm sorry for ruining your wedding," Anna said as she put her arm around her friend.

"I guess that's why I was hesitant when he asked me to marry him. I've seen the signs before. I was never comfortable with the attention he paid to other women. When I questioned him about it, he would just laugh and tell me I was being silly. When I heard you talking to your mother, I got a cold chill. All I could think about was that time in the Sutton's kitchen when your father was there with that woman. I could picture Aubert doing the same thing and I was almost sick to my stomach. I waited up for him last night and told him it was over. I can't believe I was that foolish."

"He's a fool, Lou Jean, for giving you up. He doesn't deserve you."

Lou Jean began to laugh, "You are so right. As soon as we get to London I'm going to get a bottle of hair dye and a carton of cigarettes. But he sure is good looking, isn't he?"

"He sure is. Too bad he's such a shithead," Anna said. "What about all that stuff we bought yesterday for the wedding?"

"Don't worry, Anna. It's all on Aubert's credit card. By the way, now I know how Aubert got the broken toe. Too bad you didn't kick him somewhere else."

Three days in London and Anna was ready to go home. She was terribly homesick and missed her family yet it was hard to leave her friend, knowing it would be a long time before she saw her again. "You're going to be okay, aren't you? I hope you won't be too lonely."

Lou Jean assured her it wouldn't be for long. "I may be alone, Anna, but I won't be lonely. I'm thinking of going to Italy. They say that Italian men are real romantics."

Earl met Anna in Kansas City and grabbed her up in his arms. She talked all the way home, telling him all about Paris and London. Anna was relieved when Earl didn't ask too many questions why Lou Jean called off her wedding. He was just glad she was home. Colleen and Angela had made a welcome home sign and posted it at the end of the road and Grace had a wonderful home-cooked dinner waiting on the table. This would be her last trip alone without her beloved family.

Chapter Thirty-Four

Earl sat at the kitchen table with his ledgers and papers spread out in front of him. He watched as Anna finished drying the last cup and placed it in the cabinet. She turned and smiled at him. He loved her so much. How did he ever get so lucky to have a woman like her?

He walked to the window rubbing his eyes. He could still feel the grit from the dust storm that had passed through two days ago, leaving everything in its path a muddy brown color. Anna and Grace had rushed to close the windows. They put towels and newspaper on the sills, but the dust still seeped through the cracks. The weatherman called the dust storms a phenomenon of nature. They rolled across the plains picking up the earth and turning it into a whirling mass of destruction. To Earl, a dust storm was worse than the plague. It burned your eyes and left a dry bitter taste in your mouth for days. Most of all, it covered the corn that was struggling to grow in the dry, parched ground. The dust was so thick it choked the last bit of life from the once green stalks.

"What's wrong, Earl, do you have a headache?" Anna asked as she watched her husband run his hand back and forth across his brow.

"No, I was just thinking it's time to call a family meeting, Anna. I'm going to telephone Uncle Louis and have him get everyone together this evening."

They heard the familiar slam of the kitchen door. "What about a meeting? What are you having a meeting about?" Angela asked.

"Nothing you need to know right now. It's family business." Earl was used to her constant questions. Lately Angela had developed selective hearing. Although she would ignore Anna's request to help with the dishes or clean her room, she could hear a private conversation when she was a block away.

"Oh, well pardon me. I had no idea that I wasn't a part of this family. Come on, Colleen, we might as well go to the creek." The door slammed again.

"One of these days I'm going to be standing next to her when she makes one of her smart remarks and I just may not be able to help myself from popping her in the mouth," Earl said as he watched Angela stroll across the yard with Colleen following behind her.

"It's just her age, Earl. She isn't quite an adult, and goodness knows she is not a child anymore," Anna said, trying to keep peace in the house.

The creek was a small haven on the farm. The crystal clear water tumbled over the rocks and formed a pool just perfect for swimming. Earl had carved a path through the tall shade trees leading to the water's edge. In the early months of summer the water was cold and deep, but by late August the pool grew smaller and was suitable only for tadpoles waiting to grow legs.

Colleen and Angela sat in the cold water, covering themselves with mud from the bottom of the creek. "We'd better go," Angela said as she stood up and began to wash the mud off of her swimsuit. It's getting late and the mosquitoes are starting to eat me alive. Besides, Dad is having some kind of meeting at our house tonight and I want to find out what it's all about."

Angela swatted at her legs as they made their way down the hill toward the house. "Damn, I'm hot already. If we had air-conditioning, we wouldn't have to sit in that stupid creek all day just to keep cool."

"I like the water. It's fun," Colleen said.

"You would. You're such a child." Angela ducked as she passed under the window and sat on the floor of the porch.

Colleen watched her sister edge closer to the open window. "What are you doing?"

"Shhh! I'm trying to listen. How am I ever going to know what's going on around here?" It was Uncle Louis who was speaking. "I know what you mean, Earl. I'm in the same boat. I don't know how much longer I can hold on to the farm. Vanetta and I are about ready to call it quits. I haven't made a cent in three years."

Earl cleared his throat. "I still owe the bank for last year's expenses and now it looks like there won't be much of a profit this year. I have some acreage behind the woods that's not good for farming and I've had several developers interested in it. They're willing to pay me top dollar. I sure don't want a subdivision in my back yard, but I just don't know what else to do. I have one daughter in high school and another about ready to start and not one thin dime saved for college." There was a low murmur in the room. "I know it's always been the Holloway family farm, but the truth is I just can't make it anymore. The interest rates are getting higher every year and so are my labor costs," Earl said in an exasperated voice.

"You do what you have to, Earl. We are all behind you. It's a damn shame, but I think it's called progress," Louis said. He shook Earl's hand as Grace called them to supper.

Colleen primed the pump handle as Angela stood waiting to clean her muddy feet. Angela splashed the cold water on her legs. "Well, Daddy doesn't have to worry about saving money for me to go to college because I'm not planning on spending four years in some dumb school. I'm going to London to live with Aunt Lou Jean, or maybe I'll go to New York."

"Well, I am," Colleen said. "Grandma Grace said I should be a writer."

"You just do that, little sister. You go to college, but just count me out."

Three days after Earl signed the papers to sell the property, he awoke to the sound of trucks coming down the gravel road, making their way to the backfield. The roar of the heavy digging equipment tearing into the virgin earth, pulling up rocks and tree roots would last for months. Each crash sent the deer and rabbits further into the woods. He could see the cranes looming above the tree line from the upstairs bedroom window. Earl watched as the yellow monsters devoured the trees and vegetation. He still had the feeling that all of this equipment was trespassing on his property. The bank note had been paid and he was relieved that the girls' college funds were now secure. It was time to move on and just be thankful that he still had most of the farm left. He pulled down the bedroom shade.

Earl put his coffee cup into the sink as the rest of the family sat around the breakfast table. "I have an announcement to make. I've finished with the budget and it appears to me that we will have money left over. Today we are going to Stockbridge to do some shopping. We all need clothes and it's time to replace that wringer washer with a new electric one. The old refrigerator and stove have seen better days too. It's time to replace them."

Grace let out a whoop. "Thank goodness, no more burned biscuits."

"Are you sure, Earl? This is just wonderful, but can we afford it?" Anna asked in a worried tone.

"I'm sure. Now everybody get ready. We can eat lunch in town and maybe supper too."

Colleen and Angela ran up the stairs. Earl could hear them giggling as they tried to push each other out of the way.

"Angela, are you ready? Grandma and Colleen are already in the car. Come on you're holding up the parade," Earl yelled in the front door.

Angela bounded down the steps wearing an orange tee shirt and frayed denim shorts. "Whoa. You wait just a minute, girl. You're not going to town wearing those clothes."

"Why not? What's wrong with what I'm wearing?"

"Well to begin with, that must be your sister's shirt, and your fanny is hanging out of those shorts. Go back inside and put on some jeans and a different top."

"It's too hot to wear jeans and besides there is nothing wrong with what I have on. All the girls at school dress like this. If I can't wear what I have on, I'll just stay home." She stomped her foot and opened the screen door.

"Well, that's your choice. I hate to see you miss out but we have to leave. Are you coming with us?"

Angela whirled and went back into the house. "I guess not," she screamed.

Anna looked at Earl. His face was red. She knew he was trying to hold his temper and not go back into the house after her.

"Maybe we should let her go with us. She was really looking forward to this trip."

"Look, Anna, I know it's tough to be fifteen, but if she's doing this now, what's going to happen when she's sixteen? She thinks wearing those clothes will get her some attention. She'll get her attention all right, the wrong kind. I was a teenage boy one time and believe me I know what I'm talking about. She has got to learn some respect for us and for herself. Now let's go before Colleen and Grandma burn up waiting for us."

YARD SALE

"How did you get so smart, Earl Holloway?" Anna said as they walked across the yard.

Earl put his arm around her. "It must be from being married to you."

Earl circled the car around the yard. As he headed toward the gate, he looked into his rear view mirror. He could see Angela running down the driveway waving her shirt and jeans over her head. He hesitated for a moment before he pulled on to the road.

Angela pouted for a week, refusing to eat dinner with the family or come out of her room. Anna had bought her a few things, but she would not even look into the bags. After a few days, Anna took the bags and handed them to Colleen. "You might as well take these. Someone around here should get some use out of these things." As soon as her mother left the room, Angela grabbed the bags away from Colleen.

"Give me those. I'll look at them later." It was only the beginning of the battle that she and her parents fought for the next few years.

Chapter Thirty-Five

"I'm coming to visit. Get a bed ready for me," Lou Jean said. "I should be at your house Friday afternoon."

"You must be desperate to be coming to Kansas in July. You know we still don't have air-conditioning," Anna said.

"I don't care. I need to be around some real people. I am exhausted. I'll see you soon."

Anna heard the car pull into the yard as the guinea hens let out their familiar warble. She sat up from the couch where she had fallen asleep. Rubbing her eyes, she looked at her watch. It was one o'clock in the morning. Lou Jean was only six hours late.

In the morning Grace made breakfast and sat down at the table with Anna and Lou Jean.

"So, what is going on with you? You look so tired," Grace asked as she handed Lou Jean a second cup of coffee.

"It's been a hell of a year. I lost two cases back-to-back and even had my life threatened by an idiot from one of the companies. I want to take a couple of weeks off and just do nothing. I better go upstairs and see my girls before they come looking for me."

Lou Jean lay across the bed, snuggling close to Colleen as she watched Angela put curlers in her hair. "Well how's school, kiddo? Any good looking boys in your class?"

Angela made a face. "Not very many. Did Mom tell you that I'm finally allowed to go out with boys? Dad made me wait until I was sixteen. I think I was the last girl in my class to date. They are so strict."

Lou Jean smiled. "Well, it doesn't look like it has hurt you to wait. Your mother said there has been a steady stream of boys in and out of this house for the past year and your dad is not getting much sleep. What are you doing, going down the alphabet?"

"It's hard, Aunt Lou Jean. I've known all of these kids since kindergarten. They're more like friends. I want a real boyfriend."

"Well, you have plenty of time. Next year you'll be a senior and that's a pretty fun year. By the way, have you talked to your parents about coming to London after graduation?"

"I want to go to London so badly I could just die, but they said if I don't go to college I can't go anywhere. All they talk about is my education. I'm sick of hearing it." Angela began to lather cold cream on her face. "I have a job already at Save-Way Market. It's only part time, but already I've been moved to the fastest lane. I'm the best checker in the store."

"Oh well, that's a distinction you can't live without," Lou Jean said. "You could at least give college a try for one semester."

Angela sat on the bed. "Well, obviously it wasn't important enough for my mother to finish, so why do I have to go?"

Lou Jean rose from the bed. "Let me tell you something about your mother that you probably don't know. Did she ever tell you that she was the one that gave me clothes to wear so that I could go to high school? Every day she brought extra food in her lunch bag for me. When I finally started college and whined that I couldn't do the work, she was the one who kept encouraging me. It broke her heart when she had to quit school with only one year to go. Don't ever tell me that it wasn't important to your mother."

Angela rolled her eyes. "Well, excuse me. I'm sorry, but that was her life and this is mine and I still don't want to go to college."

Lou Jean sighed. "Whatever."

Anna put the pitcher of lemonade and glasses on the table and settled in the swing next to Lou Jean. They sat quietly for a few minutes listening to the wind rustling the branches of the big oak tree, signaling a summer storm that was quickly approaching. "I love this porch. It seems like just the place to settle your problems," Lou Jean said.

Anna nodded. "Right now my only problem is how to deal with Angela. She drives poor Earl crazy, but I think he has done a good job with her. I'm too much of a softie. I just pray that all that fire in her eyes will be put to good use some day. I cannot even imagine what would have happened to me if I would have talked to my father the way she talks to Earl."

Lou Jean smiled. "I know what you mean. I must be losing my touch, too. I think I actually lost an argument to Angela today."

Flashes of lightning lit up the afternoon sky as gusts of wind began to move the tall corn stalks back and forth in expectation of the coming rain. "I'm not much of a corn expert. Do you have a good crop this year?" Lou Jean asked as she leaned against the porch railing.

"Not really. The last few years have been terrible. When we sold the acreage, we hoped things would improve, but we are still ending up in the hole each year. Every year we pray the next will be better."

Lou Jean lit a cigarette. "Anna, will you please tell me what Earl is doing out there in the field? I have been watching him run up and down the rows for about ten minutes. Is he doing some kind of rain dance?"

"He's trying to hook up some kind of gadget to keep the crows out of the corn. They come down every afternoon and just strip the stalks," Anna said as she walked to the edge of the porch.

Lou Jean squinted her eyes, watching Earl's head pop up and down between the tall green stalks. "Damn, why doesn't he just put up a scare crow? Better yet, he can put up a scarecrow with his picture on it. Those crows would stop stealing your corn and they'd probably bring back everything they have taken."

Anna began to laugh. "You tell him when he comes in. I'm afraid he would take me serious." The next clap of thunder sent Earl running toward the porch.

Lou Jean stayed for almost two weeks; her longest visit ever. With the hi-fi blaring in the upstairs bedroom, Lou Jean taught Colleen how to do the Stroll and the Mashed Potatoes and gave Angela her entire make-up kit.

"A girl can never have too many clothes or shoes," she said as she watched Earl raise his eyebrow at the array of boxes and bags lying on the living room couch after their shopping trip.

"You are spoiling my children," he said.

"That's what I plan on doing. What else do I have to spend my money on? By the way, look what I bought for you." Lou Jean pulled a pair of red Bermuda shorts out of one of the bags.

Lou Jean dropped Angela off in front of the grocery store. "I'm going to try and come back around Christmas. You take care of yourself and quit giving your parents so much grief." Angela laughed and waved goodbye.

YARD SALE

Angela hated working Saturdays at Save-Way. The never-ending line of customers circled around the aisle and into the produce section. Today she wished she had worn her tennis shoes instead of sandals. Pulling her foot out of her shoe, she stood on one leg. She picked up her microphone and once again called for someone to bag groceries.

"Well finally, what took you so long?" she said without looking up.

"Sorry. I just finished in the stock room," he replied.

She could feel his eyes on her. "What are you staring at?"

"You don't have to bite my head off. I thought I was staring at a pretty girl."

Angela turned and looked at him. He was kind of cute. She wondered who he was.

"It's time for my break. Do you want to get a soda or something?" She asked as she flipped the 'closed' sign on her register. He followed her outside and sat down on the window ledge. Angela put two quarters into the soda machine.

"Thanks, I owe you one," he said, wiping the cold droplets of water off the bottle.

"What's your name?" she asked

"Jared Braden. What's yours?"

"Angela Holloway. Are you new in town? I haven't seen you around here before."

"I've only been here about a week. I'm staying at Louis Holloway's house. I came here to look at his place. I'm thinking of buying it."

"Louis is my uncle," Angela said, surprised that no one had told her about Jared. "You look awful young to be buying property. How old are you?"

"I'll be nineteen in two months," he answered with a proud smile. "Well my break is up, I better get back to work. Thanks for the soda. Do you think I could call you sometime? I don't know many people in town. Maybe you could show me around or we could go to the movie."

She smiled. "Sure. We better go to the movie. A tour of this town would last about ten minutes. Let me give you my number."

Angela invited Jared to dinner the following Sunday. Since he was staying with Uncle Louis, she knew her parents would not object. She prepared him for the inquisition that would face him during the meal.

"So, why did you decide to come to Stockbridge, Jared?" Earl asked as he handed him the bowl of mashed potatoes.

"I saw an ad for the property in the Farm Journal. When I came here and looked at it, I knew it was just what I was looking for. I've been working since I was thirteen and I've saved every penny I could. I always planned to buy a place of my own but all of the property I looked at so far was way out of my price range," he said as he handed the bowl to Anna.

"What kind of farming are you planning on doing? I guess you know we have all been suffering the last couple of years," Earl said. "That's why Louis has decided to sell."

Jared seemed excited to talk about his plans. "I'm not going to farm, Mr. Holloway. I plan on raising dairy cows. This is just about the best grazing land I have ever seen. My dad said he would co-sign a loan, and I think I've got enough to buy a few head of Holstein to get started."

"How old are you?" Earl asked.

"Nineteen, sir." He looked over at Angela. "Well, almost nineteen."

Earl shook his head. "That's a mighty big idea for someone your age. Have you thought at all about college?" Angela rolled her eyes. She had been waiting for the subject of education to come up.

"No sir. I just finished a year's apprenticeship on a big dairy farm in Omaha and I'm raring to get started with a place of my own."

"Did Angela tell you we expect her to go to college?" Earl said, watching the expression on Angela's face. He waited for her to speak up, but she sat quietly pushing her food around her plate.

"No sir, she didn't, but I think that's great," Jared replied.

Anna watched out the back door as Angela and Jared walked hand in hand across the yard. "I'm worried about this one, Earl. He actually has plans past Saturday night. Angela seems different since she met Jared. She is not as sassy and she has been nicer to her sister."

"Don't worry, Anna. Angela wants London and Paris and air-conditioning. I don't think she'll settle for a barn full of cow manure," Earl said putting his arm around his wife.

Anna sighed. "London's a long way off when you're in love."

Jared became a fixture at the Holloway house. He helped Earl fix the engine on the truck and repaired the holes in the front room screens. He teased Colleen about boys, sending her into fits of embarrassment and giggles. Grace too was fond of Jared. She made sure there were fresh fruit pies when he came to dinner and blushed when he told her she was the best cook in the county. It was Anna who held back. She was pleasant to him, but decided it wasn't time yet to accept him completely. She could tell by the way they looked at each other that they were in love.

It was only three months until graduation and Angela still had not made a decision to go to college. When the letter came from the high school informing Anna that Angela's grades had to improve in order for her to graduate, Anna decided it was time to put a stop to the relationship that would take away her daughter's future. She had been dreading the confrontation. After showing Earl the letter from school, Anna convinced him it was time to come to a decision.

"You can't be serious," Angela screamed as she jumped up from the couch. You called me in here to tell me that. Well you just can't be serious."

"We are serious. You have got to stop seeing Jared until your grades improve. You also need to fill out those college admission papers that are gathering dust on the desk," Anna said as Angela stomped around the room.

"I'm not going to college and I'm not going to stop seeing Jared. I love him. We want to get married and besides, I'm pregnant."

Everything seemed to move in slow motion as Anna heard the stinging words echo in her ears. She could see the color draining from Earl's face as he clenched his hands into a fist. "I'll be right back. Don't you dare leave this room," he said as he threw open the front door and bounded down the front stairs.

"Daddy, come back, I need to talk to you!" Angela cried. She tried to catch him, but it was too late. Earl was already in the truck and heading out the gate.

Earl took the steps two at a time and pounded on the door. It was Louis who answered. "Damn, Earl, do you have to break my door down?"

"I need to see Jared. Is he here?"

"Yeah, I think he's still sleeping."

"Well, wake him up. We have some talking to do."

Jared came to the door barefooted, tucking his shirt into his pants. "What's wrong? Is something wrong with Angela?"

"You better believe something is wrong. Get your shoes and get in the truck," Earl said as he turned to leave. Jared picked up his shoes and followed Earl into the yard.

"I'm not getting in the truck until you tell me what's wrong," Jared said, bracing himself against the truck door.

"Angela told me she's pregnant. I thought you were a pretty decent kid. You sure fooled me," Earl said angrily.

Jared looked stunned, dropping his shoes to the ground. "Whoa, wait a minute. No sir! We never did that. If she is pregnant it sure isn't mine. We talked about getting married but that is as far as it went." He leaned against the pickup as if the wind had just been knocked from his body.

"Well, maybe you had better come with me so we can both get to the bottom of this."

Jared climbed into the front seat and they rode to the farm in silence.

"Where is she?" Earl asked as he walked into the living room with Jared right behind him.

"She's upstairs in her room." Anna was still sitting in the same chair.

"Angela, get down here, and I mean right now!" Earl yelled. As she slowly came down, the stairs, she passed Jared giving him a limp smile.

"Now what's going on with you? Are you pregnant or not?"

She slowly shook her head. "No, I'm not. I made that up."

"Why in the world would you tell your parents something like that?" Jared stammered. "You could have got me shot. You know I love you, but dang, Angela, that was bad."

Angela put her hands over her face and sobbed. "It's because I needed to get their attention. I've tried and tried, but they really never listen to what I have been trying to tell them." She whirled around, facing her parents. "Look at me. Listen to me for once. Please let me live my own life. Even if Jared hates me now and walks out that door, I still don't want to go to college."

"I'm not going to leave you, Angela, I love you," Jared said softly.

Earl drew in a breath and took Anna's hand. "Well, I guess we have done all we can. I have a proposition for you, that is, if your mother agrees.

If you two can keep your hands off each other long enough for Angela to finish high school, we'll give you a proper wedding." He turned to Anna. "Is that okay with you?" Anna slowly nodded her head.

"Oh Daddy, I love you both so much." Angela hugged her father and ran to kiss Jared. Colleen and Grace rose from the top step of the stairs, where they had been silently watching. They grinned at each other and went back to bed.

Two months after Angela graduated, Anna sat with Grace in the first pew of the church. She watched as Colleen walked down the aisle in her blue taffeta bridesmaid dress. She smiled as she passed her mother and took her place at the altar. The organ music filled the church and the first strains of the wedding march began to play. Anna could feel a chill running down her spine. She promised herself she wouldn't cry. Earl stepped into the vestibule, looking handsome in his gray tuxedo, holding tightly to his daughter's arm. Anna could see Angela smiling beneath her sheer veil. She looked radiant in the satin gown Grace had made for her as the sunlight danced through the stained glass windows. She looked so much like a woman, yet she was still so very young. As Earl lifted the veil to kiss his daughter, Angela looked over at her mother and mouthed the words "I love you." Grace handed Anna her handkerchief as the tears began to flow down her cheeks.

"If she is half as lucky as you were, she'll be fine," Grace whispered. Anna listened as her first-born child said her vows and became Mrs. Jared Braden. After the ceremony, the newlyweds left the church in a flurry of rice and good wishes.

"Oh my gosh," Jared said as they reached the bottom of the steps. Tied to the back of his truck were two large black and white cows. They wore red bows around their necks with a note attached to the "Just Married" sign. It simply said, "Have a good life! Love, Lou Jean."

Angela began to giggle. "I guess that beats some old shoes tied to the back of the truck."

Three years later when Colleen graduated from high school Angela had already given birth to Aaron and was expecting again. Anna hoped they would wait a couple of years before having children. The money they had saved for Angela's college was used as a down payment on the dairy farm. Earl said it would make their life a little easier since Jared still had to work evenings at Save-Way to earn enough money to keep the farm going.

Chapter Thirty-Six

"He calls me Gamma. It is so cute," Anna said. "But every time I get close to him he kicks me. I don't know why he does that, but Angela thinks it's funny." She propped the telephone on her shoulder and opened the oven to check on her roast.

"So, when is she going to pop out the new one; anytime soon?" Lou Jean asked.

"In about two months," Anna sighed. "I sure don't know why she got pregnant so soon. After all, Aaron is still a baby. Lord knows she doesn't need another one right now. I went to see her yesterday and Aaron was eating green beans for breakfast. It was ten o'clock and she didn't even have her beds made. I swear, it's just like those two are playing house."

"Anna Holloway, listen to yourself. When did you get so critical? What's wrong with green beans? They're good for kids and I sure wish I could find someone to play house with. Sounds like a hell of a lot of fun," Lou Jean said.

"I guess you're right, but I still worry about them. They only had four calves this spring. It's going to take them forever to build a herd."

"Well, maybe I need to send them a bull. Where can I get one?"

"Don't you dare. You've done enough already," Anna said, not wanting to tell Lou Jean that the two Holsteins she had given them for a wedding present were both bulls.

Angela sat on the edge of the bed watching Colleen put her sweaters into her suitcase.

"I can't believe you're leaving. It's going to seem so strange with you gone. I know Aaron will miss you and so will I."

"I can't believe I'm going either. It's all so scary. I've never been away from home for more than a week," Colleen said as she pulled another suitcase out of the closet. "I'm going to miss this room. I remember when you got married how happy I was to have it all to myself, and the first week after you were gone I slept downstairs on the couch."

"You'll do great at college. At least one of us will make the family proud. But why do you have to go all the way to Missouri to go to school?"

Colleen sat down next to her sister. "Because that's where I got the best scholarship to study journalism. You know mom and dad are proud of you, too. Just take care of them for me and please take care of Grandma Grace. She is having a hard time accepting the fact that I am leaving."

Angela kissed her sister on the cheek. "I hear Aaron screaming. I'd better go before he kicks mom again. I'll see you Christmas. Jared's ready to take you to the station."

Colleen walked around her room making sure she hadn't forgotten anything. She stared at the snapshots of her friends stuck on the mirror of her dresser and her high school banner on the wall. She pulled down the window shade and closed the door. Colleen stepped over the floorboard in the hallway that always made a creaking noise. Putting her bags by the door, she looked into the living room. "What are you doing, Mother? I thought you were outside with the kids."

"I was just glancing through this old photo album. I haven't looked at it in such a long time."

Colleen sat on the arm of the chair, looking over her mother's shoulder. "Oh, there's me and Angela sitting in the creek."

Anna turned to a picture of Colleen in her prom dress and one of her in her uniform from the Tastee Freeze. Colleen made a face. "Oh please, turn the page."

"It all seems to have happened in a blink of an eye. I closed my eyes one day and you were grown," Anna said as she closed the book.

A black and white photograph slipped from the pages and drifted to the floor. Colleen reached to pick it up. "Who is this mom?" Colleen asked pointing to a picture of a smiling young woman holding a baby. Behind them was a large white house.

"That's Grandma Grace and Colin. It was taken at Ternberry. She was very pretty, wasn't she?"

"Yes, she was, and she looks so happy. Would you mind if I took this picture?"

"Of course not, you take it. Have you said goodbye to your father?"

Colleen nodded. "We talked earlier. I know he's happy for me, but right now he seems pretty sad. We have talked about this day forever and now it's here. I am really going to miss all of you, Mom." Colleen put her arms around her mother.

"Not half as much as I'll miss you. Now go before I start crying."

Grace knelt in her garden and pulled weeds from between the flowers. "I'm leaving now, Grandma, can I have a hug?" Colleen said as she bent down next to her.

"You can have more than a hug, sweetheart, you can have all my love to take with you."

"You are the one person I am going to miss more than anyone," Colleen pushed the wisps of hair back from her grandmother's face.

"Why, because you think I won't be around when you get back?"

"Don't you dare say that. You had better start writing down all those things we talked about these past years. You know I'm going to write a book about you someday."

Grace reached across to her favorite white rose bush. She carefully snipped off a perfect rose and handed it to Colleen. "Press this between the pages of your journal when you get to school. Whenever you see it, think of me."

Colleen ran to the truck and climbed in next to Jared. "Let's go. I'm ready."

Chapter Thirty-Seven

Earl sat across from Robert Lewis and watched as he read through the papers. He stared out the bank window, hoping that the figures he had scrutinized were wrong. As he laid his glasses on the desk, Robert cleared his throat. "The bottom line is that you have very little money left. You have been drawing on the account for the past three years and when you withdrew the money to dig a new well, it almost depleted the account. Your last three deposits were just enough to keep you current."

Earl rubbed his forehead and leaned forward in the chair. "I was afraid you were going to give me bad news. It doesn't look like this year is going to be much better and my tractor is starting to act up."

"I know the land developers would be more than happy to have your land if you decide to sell another parcel," Robert said, closing the folder.

"I just can't do that right now. My gosh, there are new homes being built right and left on my road. Pretty soon Jared's place and mine will be the only farms there."

Robert stood up and extended his hand. "Well, Earl, I have known you since you were a kid and you always told me you would never sell. If you want to hold on to your land, that's fine, but you had better keep an eye on things. The interest rates are going up again and farm loans will be hard to come by."

Earl thanked him and left. It took two attempts to start the truck. Groaning, it finally shifted into gear. "That's another thing; I need a new truck," Earl said to himself. He dreaded breaking the news to Anna.

Anna peered around the kitchen door, wiping her hands on her apron as Earl slowly removed his cap and placed it on the hanger. "What's wrong?" she asked.

"Nothing, nothing's wrong. I had to stop by the bank and check on some things. Is there any coffee left?"

YARD SALE

She poured the coffee and sat down at the table. "You're not telling me everything. I can see it on your face. Now what's the matter?"

"Our money is running out again. I thought we were going to be okay for a long time. I never planned on putting in a new well. I'm sorry, Anna. I wanted to give you a better life than this."

Anna reached across the table and grabbed his hands. "Earl Holloway, I don't ever want to hear you say that again. I love our life together. I have an idea that I've been mulling over in my mind and before you say no, I want you to hear me out. I have been thinking about this for quite a while. I know how you like to tinker around in your workshop and how you're always fixing things for everyone. My goodness, you've probably repaired everything in this house at one time or another. I think it would be a really good idea if you gave up farming for a while and opened a repair shop. I know everyone would be happy to have someone in this area to repair appliances. I hate to see you working so hard every year."

Earl sat for a minute, sipping his coffee. "How could I open a shop? I don't have the right equipment to open a shop. What would I do with the fields? I can't let them go barren?"

"Jared needs more pasture space for his cows. He would be willing to pay you to use our land. I have decided we could have a big yard sale and possibly make enough money to get you started. Mother and I have talked about it and I know there are enough things in this house to have a great sale. There are antiques in the attic and the rafters of the barn are filled with boxes of stuff we never use. We could also sell some of the farm equipment that you won't be needing anymore." Anna was on her feet now, walking around the room. She was too excited to sit still.

"My gosh, I can't believe all this. How in the world did you ever come up with this idea?" Earl asked.

"Please, don't tell me you've forgotten about the last sale I had. That one saved my mother and me from the poor house. I hear you getting up in the middle of the night, and I watch you stand by the window staring out at the tops of those houses and I know you're worried about our future. We could at least try. Please say yes," Anna pleaded.

Earl grinned. "Well, I guess we could give it a shot. It would be kind of nice having my own business. Now tell me about this sale."

Anna decided they would start with the attic and work their way down through the house. Earl and Jared carried the heavy pieces to the first floor as Grace and Anna unpacked boxes covered with layers of dust.

"What a shame," Grace said as she held up the yellowed linens that had dry rotted in the heat of the attic. "Some of this stuff is ready for the trash bin."

As each day passed, the house became a maze of old furniture, pictures and boxes with pathways leading to each room. Jared passed out fliers at the Save-Way Market and Angela made signs announcing the sale and nailed them to the posts along the road to town.

It wasn't until the flatbeds were pulled into the yard that Earl began to feel uneasy. He remembered years long ago when his grandfather would take him to farm sales. The auction company would set up flatbeds in the yard and all of the occupant's belongings were brought outside. When the bank foreclosed on their farms they had no choice, and everything they owned would be auctioned off. It was a sad time for many families as they watched from the sidelines as their life's possessions were sold to pay their debts. Many of the families walked away with only the clothes on their backs. Earl would never let that happen to his family. He would keep them safe even if he had to sell every acre of land he owned. He watched as Anna and Grace carried the last of the dishes from the house and placed them on the tables. Anna had faith in him. He couldn't let her down. This sale would be a new beginning for the Holloway family.

Angela drove into the yard and lifted baby Adam out of the car seat. "My gosh, look at all this stuff. Is there anything left in the house?"

Anna bent down and hugged Aaron as he struggled to get away from her. "Of course, these are things that were tucked away in the attic and upstairs closets. Most of it belonged to Earl's family. I never had the heart to ask him to get rid of it before, but now it has a purpose. We better get ready. Look at all those cars lined up on the road," Anna said as she steeled herself for what promised to be a long day and hopefully a profitable one.

Holding on to the small metal cash box, Jared positioned himself at the card table by the gate. He had deemed himself head cashier. Most of the men gathered around the barn asking Earl questions about the farm equipment, while the ladies ran to the tables trying to elbow their way into first picks.

"This is crazy. Everyone is grabbing stuff," Angela said as Anna approached the tables. "I can't keep track of anything and I think I hear Aaron yelling. He is probably giving Grandma Grace trouble."

YARD SALE

"I don't want to stay on the porch!" Aaron struggled as he tried to free himself from his great-grandmother's arms.

"I'm sorry he's being such a pain. If you just watch the baby, I'll let Aaron help me." Angela took him into the house. "There are some things on the dining room table that you can help me bring out into the yard, okay?"

"Sure, Momma, I'm going to help." Aaron scampered across the hallway. He carried out the dresser scarves and linens and placed them on the tables.

Anna moved through the crowd answering questions. Each buyer wanted to make sure he was getting a real bargain. She smiled, remembering that every sale brought them closer to "Earl's Appliance Repair Shop."

It wasn't until Angela was almost across the yard with the soda for Jared, that she saw the red-haired lady handing him money. Jared was putting her purchases into a paper bag as he juggled Aaron on his lap. Angela ran across the yard. "Excuse me, ma'am, excuse me. Did you just buy a tablecloth?"

The woman stopped, looking at Angela as if it were none of her business. "Yes, I did. I paid five dollars for it."

"My little boy must have brought it out here my mistake. It belongs to my grandmother and it really wasn't meant to be in the sale. Could I please have it back?" Angela bent down in front of Aaron. "Where did you get the things you brought out of the house?"

"Out of the drawers in the dining room, Momma. Did I do a good job?"

Angela tousled his hair and stood up. She took a five-dollar bill out of the cash box and handed it to the red-haired lady. "Here, I'm sorry about the mix-up." Angela reached for the bag.

The red-haired lady clutched the bag to her chest as if she expected Angela to snatch it out of her hand. "Well, it's really just what I have been looking for. I'm going to cut it up and make pillows."

Angela drew a breath and dug into the pocket of her jeans. "Here is five dollars more. Now, can I please buy it back from you?"

The red-haired lady took the bill from Angela and reluctantly handed her the bag. Putting the money in her purse she walked back towards the sale.

Angela stuffed the tablecloth further down into the bag. "I got to get this back in the house without Grandma seeing it. Damn, that was close."

"Ooh, Momma, you said a bad word," Aaron said, spilling soda into his father's lap.

By the end of the day, Jared was so tired he lay on the porch. Earl groaned as he sat down on the swing. "Whew, that was some day. There isn't much left. I don't think I could move another thing."

Anna appeared in the doorway. "I have some sandwiches and soup made. Come eat. We need to discuss the new shop." Earl lifted his tired body off the swing and put his arms around his wife.

Chapter Thirty-Eight

Colleen pulled the zipper up on her jacket and adjusted her backpack. Spring was late this year and the lingering cold wind curled around the buildings on the campus. Walking as fast as she could, she headed for the coffee shop. Waving to a few of her friends, she ordered hot chocolate and went to the pay phone. "Hi, Mom, it's me."

"Hi, sweetheart. It's good to hear your voice. How is everything at school?"

"Just fine. I'll be home on Saturday for spring break. I can only stay a week; so don't make any big plans. I just want to see everybody and get some good sleep in my old bed."

"Why aren't you sleeping? What's wrong?" Anna asked.

Colleen laughed. "Now, Mother, don't worry. It's just that sometimes it's noisy in the dorm and unless I'm really tired, it's hard to fall asleep." Colleen knew better than to tell her mother anything except positive things about school. The first year of school had taught her that lesson. She was lonely in the beginning and sometimes called home a couple of times a week. Her mother could sense her moods and immediately begin to worry. "I'd better get going. Tell everyone I love them. I'll see you soon." Colleen hung up before her mother had time to ask any more questions. She dreaded telling her mother that she decided to take summer classes again this year.

"I just can't understand why you have to go to school this summer, too. This is the second year in a row you won't be home," Anna said as Colleen helped her set the dinner table. "You know how we miss having you here with the family."

"I thought Dad explained that to you. It's just that it helps me so much. I can concentrate much better when I only have a few classes and the dorm is almost empty. I'd like to be able to graduate in four years. I thought that is what you wanted me to do." Colleen softened her tone.

"Of course I do, but I miss you and so does Grandma Grace and I worry that you're not getting enough sleep and good food on campus."

"Let's just have a nice visit, Mom. Besides you have a lot to keep you busy with Dad's business and the boys. Does Angela come over every day or is it just because I'm home?"

Anna sighed. "Yes, almost every day. It seems so funny because she couldn't wait to get away from here. I think she gets lonely at home. Jared works out in the pastures and barns until almost dark. It's difficult when she is here because the boys want to stay out in the workshop with their grandfather. Angela forgets that this is our livelihood now and he has to get his work finished. Maybe you can have a talk with her. By the way, she's pregnant again."

The next morning after breakfast, Colleen helped Grandma Grace into the car and walked around to the driver's door.

Grace settled into the seat and patted Colleen on the hand. "This is nice. It's fun, just you and me going off by ourselves. It's been a long time since we spent time alone. So what is this big secret mission we're on?"

Colleen pulled onto the main road. "Well, let me see, we can have lunch at Zephyrs. I know you like that place. I thought we might go by the nursery and see if they have any plants in yet. I also want to go to the bookstore to buy you a journal. You have been telling me for years that you were going to write down everything you could remember about your life."

"I'm seventy-five now, Colleen. That's an awful lot of writing, and besides there's some of it I'd rather forget."

"You promised me, Grandma. All I can say is you had better get busy. How can I become a famous author if you don't give me some material for my first book?"

Grace fell asleep on the ride back to the farm after their day in town, her arms wrapped around the bag that held the blue and gold journal.

The week passed quickly. Her mother doted on her, cooking her favorite meals and making sure the boys were quiet in the morning so that she could sleep. Colleen helped Grandma Grace plant new flowers in front of the porch and for the first time in years, she spent hours talking to her father while she sat with him in his repair shop.

YARD SALE

Colleen packed her things in her car and headed back into the house to say goodbye to everyone. She could see the worried look on her mother's face.

"I just hate the idea of you driving all that way by yourself. You be sure and call the minute you get to school," Anna said.

"I will, Mom. I'm a big girl now."

Chapter Thirty-Nine

Professor Given handed Colleen the book, his finger pointing to the third paragraph. "Now read it again slowly and see if it makes sense to you."

After a few moments, she looked up from the page. "It still doesn't make any sense. I still am not getting the author's point."

"Because there is no point. The author of this book had no idea what he was talking about. The man is a babbling idiot." Professor Givens walked to the front of the room and began erasing the black board. "You have a keen eye, Colleen. Not too many students would make that observation."

Colleen smiled and stretched her feet out in front of her in the empty lecture hall. She watched as he began putting papers into his briefcase. She loved his class. He was so animated, always walking around the room waving his hands as he read one of his favorite passages. He made literature come alive. She also liked the way he smiled. Looking over the top of his wire rimmed glasses he would carelessly brush his black hair away from his face. "I think that's about all we need to cover today," he said. "I need a cup of coffee. You want to join me?"

"Yes, I would like that," she said, wondering if she had sounded too anxious. He held the door open for her as she hurried to put her binders into her book bag. They walked across campus in silence. Colleen could feel her heart thumping in her chest. What would they talk about? Was he just being kind or did he really want to have coffee with her?

He sat the tray down on the table and hung his jacket on the back of the chair. "Is that okay? I wasn't sure what you wanted in it," he said handing her the cup.

Colleen took a sip of the bitter coffee. "It's just fine." There was an awkward silence. Colleen stared into her cup, trying to think of something clever to say.

YARD SALE

"How old are you, Colleen?" he asked.

"I'm twenty. How old are you, Professor Givens?" Why did she ask him his age?

A broad grin covered his face. "I'm twenty-eight and my name is Richard, but that is for after class. Now let me get you something else to drink before you gag on that stuff."

She watched him walk across the room. Leaning against the counter, he turned around and smiled at her. She hurriedly dropped her eyes.

He ordered her hot chocolate. "Here, this should be better. So what are your plans after the summer session ends? Are you going home?"

Colleen blew into the steamy cup. "I was just home for spring break. I'm going to stick around campus. I have a lot of reading to catch up on."

He picked up his jacket and coffee. "If you get bored, let me know. Maybe we can go into town and eat in a real restaurant. See you later. I have another class."

A week had gone by since the summer session ended. She waited anxiously for the mail to come every day. The day the letter finally arrived at her dorm, Colleen tore open the envelope and began looking over the paper for her grades. She received an A in American Literature, which was Richard's class. She breathed a sigh of relief and decided to go across campus to thank him personally.

Colleen knocked lightly on the door to his office. He was sitting with his feet propped on the desk, reading. "Hi, I hope I'm not interrupting. I just wanted to thank you for the grade."

"I don't know why you're thanking me, Colleen. You earned it. What is that old saying, brains and beauty are a dangerous combination," he said, smiling.

Colleen knew she was blushing and suddenly felt uncomfortable in his presence. "Well, thanks again."

"Are you in a hurry? I was just going to get some lunch. It would be nice to have company. I would love it if you would join me."

Colleen called Lou Jean's office three times, leaving messages for her to return her calls. She decided she would try once more then make her own decision.

"Lou Jean Bailey, can I help you?" she said just as Colleen was about to hang up.

"Aunt Lou Jean, it's me, Colleen. Do you have a minute to talk?"

"Why sure, darling. I got your messages, but I have been up to my eyeballs in alligators. So what is this urgent matter you need to discuss with me?"

Colleen had heard her mother say many times that if you had a problem, Lou Jean was the one to talk to. She could solve anything. Colleen knew there was no way she could ask her mother or even Angela about Richard. "I've been seeing this guy on campus, and now he has asked me to go away for a couple of days with him and I don't know what to do. Sometimes I think we're just friends then he'll say something that makes me think he wants it to be more. I just can't make up my mind if I should go with him."

"Why, is he married?" Lou Jean asked.

"No, it's nothing like that." Colleen wavered for a minute, knowing she really didn't want to tell Lou Jean the whole story. "He is an associate professor and I'm taking one of his classes. It wasn't anything we planned. I just really liked him right away and there is some kind of strange chemistry that keeps pulling us together."

"Hello! Have you read your college rulebook lately? You keep mucking around with one of the professors and you get booted out of school and he loses his job. You already knew that. What do you want me to say, sure, sweetie, go screw your teacher and have a good time!"

"It's not like that at all. We just enjoy each other's company." Colleen was angry at Lou Jean's remarks.

"You just go right ahead and get pissed off at me. You were the one who called me. Did you ask him what student's company he enjoyed last year? I'm telling you right now, he doesn't want you to go away with him to talk about Shakespeare. Your parents will be devastated if you lose your scholarship over some weekend fling."

Colleen's voice softened. "I guess I'm getting defensive because I know you're right. I just had to hear it from someone else. Thanks for the pep talk. I'll let you know what happens."

Colleen slipped into the car next to Richard, brushing the rain from her hair. "Whew, it's really coming down. I didn't think you would be here," he said as he pulled away from the curb. "Let's just go to my place rather than go downtown in this mess." He opened the door to his apartment and she stepped inside. Before he turned the light on, he pulled her close into his arms and kissed her.

Several hours later, Colleen sat on the edge of the bed with the bed sheet wrapped around her naked body and watched the rain streak down the window.

"What's wrong?" he asked, running his hand down her back. "You're so quiet tonight. Are you thinking about our trip?"

She turned to him, laying her head on his chest. "I can't go with you, Richard. As much as I want to, I know it's not a good idea. In fact, we both know what we've been doing for the last few months is not a good idea."

In the shadowed light of the bedroom, he could see the tears glistening on her face. "I know, Colleen, I know. I've had a few close calls myself, like the night in your dormitory. Maybe we better stop seeing each other for a little while, at least until the session ends. God, I'm going to miss this," he said as he pulled her back into the bed.

The sun was coming up as Colleen slipped into her jeans. Putting on her shirt, she watched as he slept. She couldn't help hearing his words over and over in her head. Why did he say he was going to miss "this" instead of "I'm going to miss you?" She wanted to wake him and ask him. Maybe Lou Jean was right. She had just read too much into the relationship. She closed the door quietly behind her and walked the seven blocks to the dormitory in the rain. A week passed before she spoke to him again. He was leaving the campus to take a position in an Eastern college. They said goodbye and he told her he would think of her often. She knew that wasn't true. She decided it was time to go home for the summer.

Chapter Forty

Colleen brushed the crumbs off the kitchen chair and sat down. Angela began folding the mounds of clothes on the table. "How many weeks of laundry is that?" Colleen asked.

"Not even one. I wash almost every day," she said as she stuffed the sheets into the basket. Angela picked up Andy off the floor and wiped his face on the corner of her shirt. "I need to put him down for a nap. I'll be right back."

Colleen wandered around the kitchen, picking up the toys on the floor. She cleared a space on the kitchen counter for the dish rack.

"What are you doing? I'll get to them later. Let's sit down and talk," Angela said, as she returned to the kitchen.

"You talk and I'll wash," Colleen replied, filling the sink with soapy water.

"So, what made you decide to come home this summer? I thought with only one year of school left you would probably stay on campus again." Angela picked up the towel and began to dry.

"Well, for one thing I felt like I really needed to spend some time with my family, and secondly, I need to get a summer job. I can't expect Mom and Dad to keep paying for everything. My senior year is going to be pretty expensive."

Aaron ran into the kitchen from the back yard. Adam followed screaming and holding his knee. His pants were torn and small droplets of blood ran down his leg.

"Oh my gosh, what happened?" Angela lifted him up and sat him on the sink.

"I fell. Aaron made me fall. He tripped me."

Angela pulled up his pant leg and wiped the wound with a paper towel. "You know what, mister, I think you're going to live." She tenderly wiped the tears from his eyes and kissed him on the head. "You boys need to stop fighting and making so much noise. Andy is sleeping. Now please go upstairs and play quietly for a while. Can you stay for dinner, Colleen?"

"Sure, who is doing the cooking?"

Angela flicked a handful of soapsuds at her sister. "Smart ass."

Colleen watched as Angela moved around her kitchen. Who was this person that had taken over her sister's body? What happened to smart mouth Angela, that sassy person who never had time for anyone but herself?

"What are you staring at? I know I'm showing already. I guess by the fourth pregnancy your stomach muscles are just shot," Angela said.

"I think you look fine. It's just us. We're actually having a normal conversation, and when I see you with the kids I'm just amazed. Where did all this motherly instinct come from?"

"I think it was just inside of me waiting for the right time to come out. I love Jared to death and I love my kids. The hardest part has been learning to watch my language around them and not be so bitchy all the time. I get bored with Jared always talking about cows and the price of milk, but in a lot of ways he reminds me of Dad. I think that's so funny because all Dad and I ever did was butt heads." Angela walked to the bottom of the stairs, listening for the baby. "Jared and I have spent every night for the last six years together. He even slept on the floor of my hospital room when I had the kids but sometimes I wish things were like they were when we first got married. We had so much fun all the time."

"That's because you were young and carefree and still in lust," Colleen said. "It makes everything so much better."

"So tell me, sis, what do you know about lust?" Angela asked smiling. Colleen refused to answer her.

They made fried chicken and mashed potatoes for dinner, talking to each other more than they had for years. Colleen rambled on about dormitory life and her classes, deliberately leaving out the part about Richard. "This year I'm not seeing anyone special. I've had a few dates, but honestly I just don't have much time. By the way, did I tell you Aunt Lou Jean wants me to come to London when I graduate?"

Angela made a face. "That's my trip, or it would have been if I hadn't gotten married. I guess I'll never get to London. Hell, I probably won't ever get out of Kansas."

Colleen could hear voices through the open kitchen window as the two men came across the yard. "Who is that with Jared? He doesn't look familiar."

"Oh, that's Dr. Dave. He's our vet. He comes out here about once a week to take care of the cows and other animals. I forgot he was still here," Angela replied as she rose to greet her husband.

Jared hugged Colleen. "It's good to see you again. Let me introduce you to my friend. This is Dr. David McFarland."

Colleen stuck out her hand, but he just smiled. "I don't think you want to shake this hand, I've been checking cows. It's good to meet you. Now I better go wash up before we eat."

Colleen turned to her sister. "So you forgot he was here. You invited him for dinner, didn't you?"

"Sure did. Now let's have some supper conversation that doesn't involve cow intestines or manure."

David pushed his chair back, holding up his hands as Angela insisted he have another piece of pie. "I can't. I'm about ready to burst. All I need is a cup of coffee."

She handed him the cup. "You two go out on the porch; Jared and I will clean up the dishes." Colleen made a face at Angela as she walked toward the door. David leaned back in the chair, resting it against the wall. A mother cat and three kittens came out from under the porch, while a couple of beagle hounds lay sleeping under the hay wagon. Two pygmy goats nibbled at someone's shirt that had been left hanging on the porch railing. "Looks like the beginnings of a menagerie, doesn't it?" he said, as Colleen tried to shoo a chicken off the porch.

"Angela always loved animals. The boys must take after her. I guess you love animals, too. I mean being a veterinarian," Colleen stopped. "I don't know what I'm saying. I'm just rambling."

David laughed. "Yes I do love animals, but I almost gave up practicing last year. When I got out of vet school I joined a practice in Topeka. I got burnt out real quick just taking care of cats and dogs. Anyway I really wanted to be a large animal practitioner. I love the smell of the barns and the people here are great. Most of all I like being my own boss. I'm working twice as hard and making half the money." He stood up and moved toward the steps. "Which reminds me, I had better check on that pregnant cow one more time before I leave. It's been real nice meeting you." He was almost to his truck, when he hesitated for a moment and walked back to the porch. "Did I hear you tell Jared at supper that you were looking for a job? I've been thinking about hiring someone to get my office organized. I'm really bad about keeping my records straight and I'm hardly ever there to take my phone calls. Think about it. If you're interested, drop by the office." He retrieved his medical bag from the front seat of the truck and headed toward the barn.

Colleen took the cups back into the kitchen. Grabbing Angela by the waist, she tickled her. "Now do you want to tell me what that was all about?"

"I just thought you two might hit it off. He's a really nice guy and kind of cute, don't you think?"

"Please, Angela, don't play matchmaker. I really need a job more than a boyfriend."

Colleen searched the classified ads for over a week looking for a summer job. She refused to go back to Taste-Freeze and declined Jared's offer to work at Save-Way. When she called David, he said his offer was still open.

McFarland Animal Clinic was situated on the last street in town. It occupied a small brick building in a row of bungalows that once housed the families that had made their exodus to the suburbs. Colleen tried the door. Finding it locked, she stepped back and rang the bell. There was no answer. She waited a minute than pushed the button again, hearing the bell echo inside the house. As she stepped off the porch with her car keys in her hand, someone called from the side of the house. "Whoever it is, I'm around back. I'll be right with you." Colleen circled around the row of hedges that blocked the view of the backyard. David was inside a large chain link cage with seven or eight dogs.

David waved to her as the dogs jumped up all around him. "Well hi, how are you? I have to feed these critters before they eat my arm off." He poured food from a large bag into the metal bowls lining the pen.

"Whom do these belong to?" she asked.

"Me, I guess. They're strays. Some of them have been hit by cars and left on the side of the road. Others just wandered off and never found their way home and no one has ever claimed them."

The dogs began gulping down the food as David poured water into the long trough attached to the fence. "I try to find homes for them. Every once in a while I get lucky, but right now I'm almost to my limit. Let me finish up here and we'll go inside."

He held the kitchen door open for her and went to the sink to wash his hands. "This is my kitchen and my lab." As he lathered his hands, he motioned with his head to the side door. "That's my living quarters. The other bedroom is my surgery room, and I use the living room for my office and waiting room."

The telephone was ringing as they made their way to the front of the house. David followed the cord until he reached under a stack of papers on his desk. Pulling the phone out, he covered the mouthpiece. "You go look around. I'll be with you in a minute."

Colleen walked around the room looking at the certificates on the wall and pictures of David with various animals. "I guess you can tell by now that this place is a real mess. I only see clients in this office once a week. The rest of the time I'm out in the field. It would be great to have someone here to answer the phone and make appointments. I never realized how complicated all this office work is. Now do you have any questions? I sure would love to have you come and work for me."

Colleen shook her head in amazement. "Any questions? Yes, of course. I have about a hundred, starting with this desk."

David picked up the black bag sitting by the door. "Sorry, I'd love to answer them, but that call I got was sort of an emergency. If you decide to stay, I'll try to be back around four and we can talk. Here's my pager number in case you need me."

He left before she could say anything else. Colleen sat down in the office chair. She put her head in her hands and tried to decide if she should just write him a note and leave. What had she gotten herself into?

The phone rang only once all morning. The man calling refused to talk to anyone but Dr. Dave. She straightened the papers on the desk and dusted the chairs in the waiting area. Not sure what else to do, Colleen decided to find a broom and sweep away the hairballs rolling out from under the desk. Pushing open the surgery room door, she heard a soft whining. Listening again, she peeked inside the room. Lying on the floor on a checkered blanket was a large redbone hound. He struggled to stand up. His feet were entirely wrapped in bandages. He was covered with a maze of stitches across every part of his body. "Oh my gosh, you poor thing," she said as he let out a low growl. His lip curled up over his mouth as he stared at her with liquid brown eyes. Colleen shut the door and went back to the desk. It was almost noon and she was hungry. She managed to find a jar of peanut butter and some bread in the kitchen cupboard. Opening the refrigerator door, she came face-to-face with a raccoon head sitting in a plastic bag. Colleen slammed the door shut, quickly losing her appetite.

Around one o'clock, Dave called. "I'm glad you've decided to stay. Is there anything going on at the office that I should know about?"

"Other than the fact that you have a growling dog in the surgery room and a raccoon head in the fridge, everything is just dandy," she said, half hoping he would tell her to just lock the door and leave.

"He's just a pup. He got caught in a hay bailer. He's got a pretty nasty disposition right now, but I can't really blame him. I put over seven hundred stitches in him. His owner wanted him put down. He used to chain him to a tree and that dog had some pretty bad scars even before the bailer got him. I think he'll pull through, but the raccoon, well I'm afraid he is a lost cause. I need to have the head tested for rabies. You can box it up for me if you want."

Colleen gasped, "No thanks. Give me something else to do. What is the dog's name?"

"You know, Colleen, I don't think he has one. Why don't you pick one out for him?"

Tuesday was not much better than Monday. David never came to the office at all. There were two hang up calls and a lady wanting to talk about spaying her cat, getting very upset when Colleen told her she knew nothing at all about the surgery. She tried to make her way through some of the papers, rearranging them into several stacks and rearranging them again.

By the end of the week, Colleen began to catch on to a few of the routines of the clinic. She forced David to sit with her and sort through the papers. "I found all these on your desk," she said, holding up a stack of ledgers.

"Those are my client's statements. I need to send them out, but I know some of these people can't pay," David said, leafing through the papers.

"I think you should at least try. After all, you're not in this business for charity. You need to get paid for your services. Here, give them to me," she said as she picked up her purse. "I'll be the bad guy. I'm going to the post office to get some stamps."

Colleen named the hound Merlin, telling David he must have a little magic in him to survive a hay bailer. As his wounds began to heal, he was able to hobble into the waiting room and prop himself against the wall. He would growl every time she passed him. It wasn't until she offered him part of her lunch that he crawled across the floor and proclaimed a spot under her desk for his own.

David walked into the office and danced around the desk, holding up three checks. "Hallelujah, three of my clients paid their bills, thanks to you."

Colleen laughed. "Well surprise. It's about time." She hesitated for a moment. "I wonder if I could ask you something? This is a little embarrassing, but I've been here three weeks and I haven't gotten a paycheck."

"Oh good Lord, Colleen, I'm sorry. I told you I wasn't a good businessman. I meant to tell you to pay yourself." He picked up the checkbook from the desk and signed a check.

"But wait a minute, the amount is not filled in," she said as she took the check from him.

David grinned. "I know. You're worth a heck of a lot more than I can pay you. I have no idea how much money is in my account. You fill it in."

Colleen opened the door to the clinic and flipped on the light. Turning the sign on the door to "open," she could hear Merlin scratching at the surgery room door. He greeted her with his familiar howls and a wagging tail. The answering machine was blinking with messages. She grabbed her pen and began to write down the names and numbers. She was on the phone when David came in. Smiling, she waved to him and continued to write. He set a cup of coffee and a doughnut on her desk and headed to the back door with Merlin close behind. It was a morning routine that she had followed every day for the past three months. David came back into the office and sat on the corner of her desk.

"Now I want you to promise me that you will hire someone as soon as possible. You should have done that a week ago, but hopefully you can find someone who can catch on to the routine before I leave. I've got all this month's statements ready to mail out and the drug order ready to be placed," Colleen said as she watered the two new plants she had hung in the front window.

"Yes, ma'am. Anything else, ma'am?" David replied as he saluted her.

Colleen grinned. "I'm sorry for being so bossy. It's just that I don't want all of our hard work to go to waste."

"You mean your hard work. I can't tell you how grateful I am and I can't believe it's already time for you to leave. It seems like just yesterday that you started working here."

"I know. This summer sure has gone by fast, but my classes start next Monday and I have to get ready to go back to school."

"Well, is there time for us to at least have a farewell dinner before you go off and leave me?"

"I have a great idea," Colleen said. "Why don't I pack a lunch basket and we can go up to the pond on Sunday and go swimming?"

"Sounds good to me. Do you want to invite your family to come along?" he said, hoping the answer would be no.

"Actually, I've had quite enough of family stuff. Between all the relatives and my mom, it's been a pretty busy summer. Hopefully we can sneak up there without the boys seeing us. Now go away, I have to get to work." She shoved him off the desk and picked up the ringing phone.

He stood by the surgery door, watching her and wishing they had more time together.

After parking his car in a small grove of trees, David started up the hill. Colleen was already waiting for him. Sitting on the small bench by the graveyard fence, she waved to him as he walked toward her. "Follow me, we just have a little further to go." Colleen picked up the picnic basket and blanket, leading the way down the path her father had carved into the woods many years ago.

"Wow, this is really nice," David said as they reached the clearing just beneath the canopy of trees that provided shade along the edge of the pond. He took the basket from her and spread the blanket on the ground. David peered over the bank as he watched the small silver minnows dart in and out of the rocks. "The water is so clear."

"Wait until you get in. You won't believe how cold it is." Colleen pulled off her shirt. "Come on, I'm burning up."

He watched her as she slipped into the water, her black suit hugging every curve of her body. Taking off his shoes and shirt, he gingerly made his way to the bank and waded toward her. "It's freezing," he said, as his teeth began to chatter.

Colleen swam further out into the pond. "See that tree over there? When we were kids and the water was as deep as it is now, Angela used to jump off of that big branch hanging over the water. I never had the nerve. She would call me chicken and dare me, but I was scared to death to jump. I think I'm going to do it today before I lose my nerve." David treaded water and watched as Colleen swam effortlessly across the pond. She stood for a moment looking up at the tree and began to climb up the slanted trunk.

He swam toward the tree. "Wait for me. We'll jump together."

They held hands as they stood on top of the swaying tree branch. Colleen sucked in her breath as he counted to three. She could feel the rush of air beneath her seconds before she hit the water. Their heads popped to the surface, Colleen still holding her nose. "I wish Angela could have been here. She won't believe I finally did that, but you're my witness."

Scrambling up the mossy bank they collapsed on to the blanket laughing. David rolled over, shaking the water from his hair. She could feel his eyes on her, as he softly touched her back. Without a word, Colleen sat up and pulled her towel around her body. "I guess we had better eat this food, before it gets too warm." They ate in silence, Colleen pretending to watch the mallards that had taken over the pond.

David sat behind her, picking apart his sandwich and throwing the bread to the ducks. He didn't want her to turn around. If she did, he could never tell her what he had been thinking about for the last couple of weeks. "I just want to let you know I'm going to miss you. I love coming into the office and seeing you there each day. I love the way you laugh and how you make me feel when I'm around you. I only wish that on the first day I met you I would have asked you out instead of giving you a job."

She was silent for a moment. "David, please."

He held up his hand, "I know, I promised myself I wasn't going to say anything. You've made it clear from the beginning what your plans were and I tried not to let my feelings get in the way. I would never ask you to change your plans for me, but do you think you'll ever come back to Stockbridge?" David stammered.

Colleen rose from the blanket and began putting the plates into the basket. "I can't answer that question right now. I haven't a clue where I'll be a year from now. If I were finished with school, I might have a better idea, but right now that is my first priority. I hope you understand." Colleen gathered up the paper plates and cups. "I think we should go now. I really don't feel like swimming anymore."

They walked to the end of the path as the laughter of the afternoon faded away. She looked sad now, her head down, not saying a word. Why had he been so stupid? He should have never told her how he felt. He hesitated for a moment, kicking the soft dirt with his toe, his hands shoved into his pockets. "I sure ruined our last day together, didn't I?"

"No, it's okay, David, but I think for right now it's better if we don't say anything else."

"Will you at least come by the office tomorrow before you leave? I have something for you. It's a going away present." Colleen quickly kissed him on the cheek and started down the hill. He watched as she passed the cemetery and finally disappeared behind the barn.

The note was on his desk in the morning when he arrived at the office. She had come by earlier and left her key. She wished him luck and told him she would always remember this summer. She said that he was special to her and at a different time, she might have been able to return his feelings, but it was just too difficult of a decision to make at this point in her life. Colleen thanked him for everything and asked if he would please keep Merlin with him. Maybe someday she could send for him. He folded the rose colored paper and put it in this desk drawer along with the small velvet box containing the silver charm of a hound dog. He didn't want to spend the day in the office. David turned the sign on the door to "closed." He whistled for Merlin. Together they drove down the two-lane road past Colleen's house. He slowed for just a moment, wondering if she had left already.

Chapter Forty-One

Graduation was two weeks away and Colleen had made arrangements for her parents and Grandma Grace to stay in the student hall. Her mother said the trip would probably be too hard on Angela, since she was due to have a baby any day. Colleen invited Lou Jean, but her office said she was on a business trip in London. She vacillated about inviting David, but decided against it, since Angela said he moped around for months after she left, but had finally started dating a girl from the next town. Colleen wondered who she was and what she looked like. It had been hard for her to stop thinking about him. She felt ashamed that she had been too much of a coward to face him on the day she left. She never wanted to take the chance that he might have been able to change her mind about leaving Stockbridge. It was not going to be easy to tell her mother that she accepted a job with a company in St. Louis and was due to start the week after graduation.

The auditorium was filled with blue hats and tassels as the graduating class tossed their caps into the air. Colleen held up her diploma as she made her way down the stairs of the stage to her family. Earl caught her in his arms and kissed her. "Congratulations, baby girl," he said as Anna wiped the tears from her eyes. Grandma Grace hugged her, handing her a box wrapped in white paper.

"You can open it later when you have more time. Now let's go eat, I'm hungry."

Her mother sat quietly in the restaurant listening as Colleen told them about her new job. She would be working for a publishing company, probably doing menial jobs at first; hopefully she could work her way into the editing department. She felt honored to have been chosen for this position, since half of her class had also applied to Edison Publishing Company. Earl listened intently, nodding his head in approval. "I'm proud of you darlin, that's what you've worked for. I can come with you and help you find a place to live."

"That's the great part. When I told Lou Jean about my job, she offered to let me stay in her aunt's old house. It's been empty for quite a few years. She wouldn't take no for an answer," Colleen said, glancing at her mother for some kind of reaction.

Grandma Grace looked at Anna who was staring into her plate. "What's wrong with you? Surely you didn't think she was coming back to Stockbridge. What in the world would she do there?"

"You know I'll worry about her being all alone in a strange city. I just thought she would find something a little bit closer to home."

Earl reached across the table and took Anna's hand. "Well, honey, you just go ahead and worry. It wouldn't be the same if you didn't."

The following week, Colleen moved all her few possessions into the house on Autumn Street. It was one of the small frame houses built in the nineteen-fifties that were referred to as "track houses." At that time it was the beginning of a new concept called subdivisions; street after street of houses that were all built the same. It had been a proud time for all those young couples that were able to purchase their first home with no money down. It was the kind of neighborhood where kids played in the street until dark and the neighbors got together for cookouts and Fourth of July picnics. Now after all these many years, the trees had grown tall; their roots crawled across the front lawns and lifted up the sidewalks. Garages and rooms had been added to a few of the houses and new children played in the street.

The house was cramped when Lou Jean and her mother came to stay with her aunt, but to Colleen it seemed like a mansion after living in the dorm for four years. After her aunt died and her mother went into a nursing home, Lou Jean had all the old furniture carted away and closed the house, using a leasing company to care for the lawn and the utilities. Lou Jean was glad that someone could finally find some use for it. It had been difficult for her to part with it, since it had been the only real home she ever lived in.

Colleen opened the door with her very own key. Walking around the house, she opened closets and cabinets, elated with all the space. She smiled at the avocado green refrigerator still humming away in the kitchen and the orange shag carpet that covered the living room floor. That, she said to herself, would have to go. Colleen was startled when the doorbell rang.

"Surprise!" Lou Jean shouted as Colleen opened the front door.

"Aunt Lou Jean! What are you doing here?"

"I felt really bad about not making it to your graduation, so I thought I'd better get back here as fast as I could and make sure you got settled and that everything in the house was still working. Gees, this place still looks the same." She walked down the hall, pointing to a small bedroom on the left. "This was my room. Do you have any idea how great it was to have my own room? See that window over there? I crawled out of it many times when my mom and aunt were asleep. Living here was the first time in my life that I wasn't ashamed to bring my friends home. I know that sounds awful. My mom did the best she could, but boy did we live in some dumps."

They sat on the kitchen floor drinking Cokes and emptying out the boxes as Colleen told her all about graduation and her new job. Her mother insisted on sending her some furniture and Jared was on his way from Kansas to deliver it to her. "I don't know what she is sending me. You know Mom. It's probably everything in her house."

"Sounds like your mom hasn't changed very much. I sure do miss her. I have to get to Kansas real soon."

"I know she really would love to see you." Colleen reached into one of the cartons. "Oh, my gosh, look at this!" she said, holding up the package wrapped in white paper. "It's the present Grandma Grace gave me graduation day. I packed it away right after I got back to the dorm."

Untying the blue ribbon, she opened the box. "It's my grandma's tablecloth. I wonder why she gave it to me? She loves this old cloth," Colleen said, rubbing the soft material against her cheek.

Lou Jean held up the yards of white material. "She must love you more, but this thing is full of holes."

The doorbell rang again and Colleen could see Jared's truck sitting in the driveway. "Did you have trouble finding this place?"

Jared took off his baseball cap and stepped inside. "I sure did. I drove around for about an hour. I have never seen so many houses in such a small place. Are you sure you are going to like it here?"

"She certainly is," Lou Jean said as she came around the corner. "Hi, farmer boy. How are you doing? I hear your wife is pregnant again. What are you trying to do, start your own baseball team?"

Jared fumbled with his hat, looking down at the floor. "No. We just like kids."

"Well, you better," Lou Jean replied. " Now let's get some of this stuff in the house so we can at least have a place to sit." By the time the truck was empty, the house was almost full of furniture.

Jared wiped the sweat off his face and sat down on the floor. "I'm hungry. Is there anything here to eat?"

"Food is on the way. I just ordered a pizza," Lou Jean yelled from the living room.

They sat around the chrome kitchen table, eating off the green dinnerware her mother had sent to her; the dishes that had been left over from the yard sale and had been carefully packed and returned to the attic. Lou Jean was full of stories about her time in Washington. She lit a cigarette and leaned back in her chair. "So, how are Angela and all those kiddos doing? You sure haven't said much about them," she said, turning to Jared.

He reached for another slice of pizza. "Well you haven't given me time to say much of anything. The kids are fine, growing like weeds, but Angela, I don't know, she's changed a lot.

We hardly talk to each other and she spends a lot of time at her mother's house. Our house looks like a pigpen most of the time and she doesn't even take care of herself anymore. She wears jeans and my tee shirts every day. Once in a while I get a hot meal, but not very often."

Lou Jean's eyes narrowed. "Well, let's see. As I recall, in less than eight years, you took a vivacious, shit kicking, eighteen-year-old and turned her into a mother of three and another one popping out real soon. What do you expect? Should she meet you at the front door in her June Cleaver apron? I bet you smell real good when you come in from being with the cows all day."

Jared pushed the chair in and leaned against the sink, as if he needed to put distance between himself and Lou Jean. "I help her when I can. I take the boys with me every chance I get and I give them baths at night."

"Well, pardon the hell out of me. How big of you to help take care of your children. When do you take care of Angela? When was the last time the two of you went out someplace nice to have dinner without the kids tagging along? I bet she would enjoy a meal that's still hot without getting something spilled in her lap. Do you have any idea when she has been able to sleep one entire night without one of the kids waking up? I hear your dairy farm is doing real well. You could probably afford to hire someone to come in twice a month and help her clean up the 'pig-sty.' Maybe Angela is not feeling real good about herself right now." Lou Jean rose from the table, pointing her finger in Jared's face. "Let me tell you something, little boy. I see those fancy divorce lawyers representing women who have a hell of a lot less to complain about than Angela. You'd better watch it, or she and her sagging boobs might just end up in London."

"Dang, I don't know why you're getting so mad at me. Maybe I don't always show it, but you know I love Angela. I've got to get going. I can't stay away too long, with the baby coming real soon," Jared said as he nervously reached across the counter for his hat and keys. Colleen tried to soften the conversation, telling him not to pay too much attention to Lou Jean. He could at least spend the night before making the long drive home. Jared couldn't leave the house fast enough, telling Colleen he would see her later. Pulling his truck onto the street, his headlights disappeared around the corner before she closed the door.

"Lou Jean, I swear, you are really bad. I think you scared the hell out of my poor brother-in-law," Colleen said as she collapsed on the floor laughing. "He's probably at the city limits already. What's going on with you? You must have really had some rough times with men lately."

"Honey, you don't know the half of it. I can't stand whiny-ass men. Now I got a lot of pent up energy left. What do you say that you and I tear that shitty orange carpet off the living room floor?"

Angela called early the next morning. "Oh, Colleen, I think Jared must have met someone while he was in St. Louis. Where did he go after he left your house? He came home with roses and wants to take me to dinner on Friday night. He's even talking about taking a vacation without the kids. Do you think he is feeling guilty about something?"

Colleen smiled, "No, I just think he has remembered how lucky he really is. Do me a favor, if you go out to eat, Angela, wear a dress."

It was Colleen's metamorphosis, this new experience of living alone. She awoke each morning to an empty house. She got ready for work with only the sound of the radio to keep her company. She ate dinner alone at night while she read or watched television. Colleen loved her little house on Autumn Street. It became her cocoon, interrupted only by an occasional door-to-door salesperson or some neighborhood child wanting to know if there was anyone living there who could come out to play. Colleen painted and repapered every room and covered her yard sale couch with white muslin. She kept fresh flowers on the coffee table she had assembled. She bought a used lawn mower and canceled the yard service. When the first snow of winter came, Colleen dressed herself in warm clothes and boots. Armed with her king size snow shovel, she was disappointed to find that one of the neighbors had already shoveled her driveway. It was only after one of her talks with her mother that her peaceful existence was ruined by the already nagging guilt feeling that she should be at home in Kansas.

Colleen propped the telephone on her shoulder while she reached for her coffee. "I can't help it, Lou Jean, mom has already called me four times this week. I didn't feel guilty while I was away at school. Now that I made my choice to stay here, I have to steel myself every time she calls just to keep from giving in and telling her I'll come home."

"It's your rite of passage, sweetie. You need to get out on your own and make your own screw ups. Your mom really misses you, but I think most of your guilt trip is of your own doing. Find some new friends and start dating. I think you have spent enough time alone. I'll call you next week to see how you're doing."

Colleen tried dating a few times without much success. There was a man from her office who had asked her out several times before she accepted. They had a pleasant enough evening, but his unusual interest in the fact that she lived alone made Colleen uncomfortable. As she opened her front door his wet kiss landed on her eye with the suggestion that they could continue the evening inside. Her adamant "no!" ended the evening and the relationship. The fellow from the hardware store who had helped her while she was working on the house asked her to lunch. She found herself looking at her watch halfway through the meal, as he talked about the price of flanges and pipefittings.

"I've tried, Lou Jean, but I'm just not the kind of person who likes to go to bars and I don't know too many people here in St.Louis."

"You're waiting for the fireworks aren't you?" Lou Jean asked. "Well, keep your matches handy. You never know when there will be someone out there that needs a little fire lit under him. Just don't give up. Lord knows, I haven't."

Her talks with her mother always ended with the same question. "When are you coming home to visit?" She told her mother several times that she only had one week of vacation and was saving it for Christmas. In a weakened moment she said to her mother, "Why don't you and daddy come here and visit me? I have plenty of room."

They came the following weekend. Anna brought boxes of homemade preserves and pickles. "Your place is very nice, honey. You did a great job on the house," Anna said as she walked from room to room. Before the day had ended Anna sent Earl to the hardware store to buy a new lock for Colleen's front door and safety latches for the basement windows. "You know you can't be too careful living alone."

Colleen showed them around the city the best she could, trying to avoid any place that would give her mother more to worry about. When the police car sped by with his siren blaring, her mother craned her neck, watching from the car window.

"I think it's time we should go home," Earl said on the third morning. "If we stay much longer, your mother is going to kidnap you and take you back with us. She is just not used to the city. All of the sights and sounds are making her a nervous wreck. We'll see you at Christmas."

Taking her first week of vacation time, Colleen put the presents she bought for her family in the backseat of the car. Her mother had called three times to remind her to be careful driving home.

The snow had already begun to fall when Colleen pulled into the long gravel road to the farmhouse. She could see the lights from the tall Christmas tree shining through the window in the evening light. Angela's children played in the yard, trying to scrape enough snow together to make a snowman. It was like every Christmas she could remember since she was a child. The smell of good food wafting from the kitchen and presents now piled even higher under the tree with the advent of four grandchildren. It was good to see Grandma Grace, who seemed to be getting smaller each year. Grace pulled Colleen into the kitchen and wanted to know all about her life in St. Louis. "Are you happy living alone?" she asked. Although her fingers were now twisted with arthritis, she delicately peeled the apples for the pies.

"I still miss being with all of you and the family, but for the most part, I love it."

Colleen sat near the Christmas tree gathering up her presents and putting them in her open suitcase. Angela sat in the rocker holding baby Addie.

"I thought maybe David would be here sometime this week. I wanted to see Merlin. He does know I am home, doesn't he?" Colleen asked.

"No he probably had no idea you're home. He was going to Kansas City to spend Christmas with his parents. He left Merlin at my house."

"How is he?" Colleen asked, "I mean David. Is he okay?"

Angela shrugged. "I guess so. I don't see him very often, but when I do, he always asks about you. I wish he was in town, he would be over here in a flash."

"I tried calling him several times, Angela, but there was no answer." Colleen said, as she closed the suitcase. "I'll stop by today and see Merlin."

"I was thinking maybe you should take Merlin home with you, Colleen. He seems pretty miserable at my house. He hates the other dogs and the kids just make him nervous," Angela said. "I know David wouldn't mind."

Colleen was surprised. "I can't do that. You know how much I love that dog. I'm afraid to even go over to your house and see him. I don't want to upset him. Merlin would be alone all day when I'm at work. That wouldn't be fair to him."

"All he wants to do is sleep all day anyway. He would probably love being in a house by himself instead of having kids climb on him all day. Besides, David said he has seemed a little depressed ever since you left."

Anna packed a basket for Colleen and made her take an extra blanket in the car. Colleen said her goodbyes and drove down the road to Angela's house. As she stepped from the car, Merlin came bounding across the yard and around the car, his large ears flapping as he howled in his typical hound dog voice. He jumped up on Colleen. His front paws landed on her shoulders and he began licking her face. Before she left Angela's house, Merlin was sleeping comfortably on the back seat of her car. Colleen turned to him as she started the car. "This could be a mistake, a real big mistake."

Chapter Forty-Two

They were known as the "cube heads." They were the employees who worked behind the frosted glass panels on the second floor of Edison Publishing. Colleen's promotion from the sorting and filing department landed her a position in one of the three by five cubicles. Each morning she would slide into her chair and turn on her computer, spending the rest of the day editing the text that rolled across the screen. There was constant clicking and humming from the thirty or so other computers. She kept reminding herself that this was only a temporary step to the next level. Maybe she would even get an office with a window. After only ten months with the company, Colleen was glad to be a "cube head."

It was almost a daily occurrence. The computer screens would go blank, and for a brief moment, heads would pop up over the glass walls and the sound of actual voices could be heard. Today was no different; the small cracking noise left her with a blank screen. Colleen stood up and stretched. Turning around she came face-to-face with a red headed woman leaning over her cubicle.

"Hi, I'm Rosalie. I just wanted to see who was on the other side of the fence. I just got moved to this side of the office."

Colleen introduced herself and they chatted for a few minutes until the ever-present hum started again. "Do you ever eat in the cafeteria?" Rosalie asked loudly as she sat back down at her desk.

"Sometimes, but mostly I bring my lunch," Colleen replied and started reading the words on her screen.

Rosalie rolled her chair back and peeked around Colleen's cubicle. "Don't bring anything tomorrow. Meet me in the cafeteria at noon. I'll treat you to lunch."

Rosalie had been with Edison for almost three years and still hadn't made it past the second floor. "I guess my skills aren't good enough. I know you have to be in the top ten percent on your evaluation to even be considered for the editing department upstairs," she said as she poured dressing on to her salad. "I'd like to find a job somewhere else but the pay here is too good for me to give it up right now. My husband and I just bought a house a year ago and we have a lot of expense. Are you married?"

"No," Colleen answered.

"Well, maybe we can get together sometime and take in a show or something. My husband, his name is Rick, works nights and I get lonely. I'd better get back to work. I was a few minutes late this morning," Rosalie said as she rose to leave. "By the way, I'm having a cookout this weekend, nothing special, just some burgers and hot dogs. I invited some of the people from work and a few friends. Why don't you come?" Rosalie wrote her address on a napkin.

Colleen awoke early on Saturday morning. After making coffee, she opened the newspaper, contemplating going to a few yard sales. Instead she decided to clean the house, but by noon she was already bored. She showered and put on a clean pair of white shorts and a navy blue tee shirt. Taking the napkin with Rosalie's address off the refrigerator door, she left the house. Colleen wondered if she should take something. She stopped at the supermarket and bought an apple pie.

"Hi, I'm glad you could make it," Rosalie said as she took the pie from Colleen. "If I can find my husband, I'll introduce you to him but right now I have to go inside and make the burgers. Fix yourself something to drink," she said, pointing to a table filled with bottles and cups. Colleen poured herself a paper cup of wine from an already opened bottle. She recognized a few people from the office. They smiled; she smiled back and began to wander around the yard. This was a mistake, coming here, she thought to herself. She was never really very good in strange crowds. She was always too shy to jump into a conversation and introduce herself. Colleen sat down next to a blonde-haired woman holding a baby. "Your baby is cute. How old is he?" she asked after a few uncomfortable moments of silence.

The girl shrugged. "He's not mine. It was either hold him or go inside and make potato salad. I really need a cigarette. Here you want to hold him?" She sat the baby in Colleen's lap and made her way across the yard. The baby looked at Colleen. His lower lip puckered out and he began to cry. She held him close and rocked him back and forth, trying to soothe him as he cried even louder.

It was a man's voice that came to the rescue. "I think you need some help. Here, let me take him."

"Thanks. I don't think he likes me very much," Colleen said. "Is he yours?"

"No. His mother is in the house. Don't move. I'll be right back."

She watched him walk away. He turned and smiled at her. She decided to stay and wait for him to return. The next time she saw him he was standing by the barbecue pit, wearing a tall chef's hat and a red apron.

"Oh, Colleen, I'm so sorry. I still haven't had time to introduce you to anyone," Rosalie said as she juggled a large platter of hot dog buns. "My husband always does this to me. He says, 'let's have a cookout' then I have to do all the work. I hope you're having a good time."

Colleen nodded. "I'm fine. Who is that guy with the chef's hat on?"

"Oh, that's Jeff. He works with my husband. He came with Julia," she said, pointing to the blonde-haired girl that had been holding the baby. Colleen waited until Rosalie was across the yard before she slipped out the gate and into her car. She was sure she wouldn't be missed.

Colleen could hear Merlin's familiar howl as she stepped from the car. "Okay, okay, I'm coming." Opening the door, she threw her purse onto the couch and grabbed Merlin's leash off the kitchen table. He danced around her as she buckled his collar. It had become an every evening routine for him. He pulled her out the door and onto the sidewalk, taking the same familiar route. Merlin sniffed at the ground, tugging on his leash as Colleen tried to keep up with him. It gave her time to think on their long walks together. Tonight was no different, but instead of thinking about what she would have for dinner or wear to work the next day, she was still thinking about Jeff. Why had he told her to stay put and never come back to talk to her? Why would he even pay any attention to her, since he was with someone else? She tried to put him out of her mind, but something about his smile and the way he looked at her made her curious to know more about him. Merlin stopped for a moment and looked up at her. She realized she had turned down the wrong street. She patted his head as they headed for home.

After her shower, Colleen made herself a cup of tea. Merlin had already settled for the night, curling up on the end of her bed. She could see the answering machine blinking two messages. Brushing her hair, she sat down on the bed, and pushed the button. "Message one. Hi Colleen, it's Rosalie. Sorry I didn't catch you before you left today. I'll see you on Monday. By the way, I gave Jeff your telephone number. I hope you don't mind." "Message two. Hello, this is Jeff. I hope you remember me. I was at Rosalie's barbecue. I looked for you after I got finished with the cooking but you were gone. I was wondering if you would like to go out for coffee? I'll be home all day tomorrow. Call me if you get this message. The number here is eight one…" there was a click. The tape had run out. Colleen turned the machine on again and listened to the same message over. His message had been too long. She thought about calling Rosalie to get his number, but decided it would just be better to let it go. She still couldn't understand why he would be calling her on the same day that he had a date with the blonde-haired girl.

Jeff called Sunday morning apologizing for the early hour, but he just couldn't wait any longer to see if she had gotten his message. They talked for almost an hour before he asked her out to dinner. He never mentioned Julia.

She changed her clothes three times before deciding on a simple white dress. Jeff arrived right on time. She smiled and invited him in, pushing Merlin away from the door.

"Wow, that's some dog. I bet he doesn't let too many people in this house uninvited," he said as he backed up against the wall. "You look really nice, Colleen."

Colleen picked up her purse. "Thanks. Merlin won't hurt you if I tell him it's okay. He's just real cautious around strangers."

They ate in a small restaurant on the riverfront with a view of the Gateway Arch in front of them. The shining ribbon of steel illuminated by the almost full moon loomed into the evening sky. "It's really quite awesome, isn't it?" she asked. "I wish I had the courage to go up to the top."

"I would love to be your tour guide. Why don't we give it a try next weekend?" That meant he was planning to ask her out again.

"I can't believe you're really a farm girl," Jeff said, pouring more wine into her glass. "Me, I've always been a city boy. I've never been on a farm in my life."

It was easy conversation, as they drifted from one subject to another. Jeff told her about his job at the advertising agency. He said he had been a job hopper since he got out of college. "I love working with the public. I just haven't found my niche. The job I have now is the closest I've come so far."

She was relieved when he finally got around to talking about Julia. They had been friends since college, dating occasionally, usually when Julia was between boyfriends. He assured Colleen that his relationship with Julia was strictly platonic.

"How about you?" he asked. "I can't believe there is no one special in your life."

"There hasn't been in a long time. I dated a few boys in high school and college but I'm just not very good at casual dating."

Jeff leaned on his elbows. "I was married once. It seems like a lifetime ago. We were both freshmen in college and we thought the world would end if we didn't get married. Her parents were furious. I guess they had a right to be since we were so young. When it only lasted six months, they were even more irate."

"What happened?" Colleen was surprised at what he had told her.

He shrugged. "You know, young love, no money, no plans. There really wasn't any foundation to keep us together. She went home for the summer to visit her parents and I got the divorce papers in the mail. I hear that she's married now and has a couple of kids." They lingered over the last bit of wine. The waiter looked at them impatiently after he brought the check. "I guess we had better leave before they throw us out," Jeff reached for the check.

She was nervous as they pulled into her driveway, not really sure how she wanted this evening to end. Colleen fumbled in her purse, looking for her keys. "I had a really nice time tonight." Merlin began to bark and scratch on the door. "Sorry to rush you, but I have to walk my dog. He's probably standing there with his legs crossed," she said laughingly and wished she hadn't said such a stupid thing.

Jeff took the keys and opened the door. "Mind if I tag along? I could use the exercise."

They walked in silence for a few moments; Merlin turned around occasionally to see who this stranger was that had invaded his nightly routine. Jeff took her hand as Merlin stopped to relieve himself on a tree. He didn't even try to kiss her goodnight. He just gave her a hug saying he would call her tomorrow. Lou Jean was right. She did need fireworks. It felt like the Fourth of July.

It had been almost four months since Colleen and Jeff started dating. At first they would date only on the weekends, but slowly, as time passed, they began to see each other almost every night. Colleen knew she was falling in love with him. If only she had enough nerve to say the words, but each time she even came close, Jeff seemed to pull away.

Jeff lay with his head against the couch, his arm around Colleen. "I am so tired. I don't know if I can drive home. We should have started watching this movie earlier." He stretched and stood up. "You know if you really cared about me, you wouldn't send me out in the cold dark night."

Colleen hesitated for a moment, wondering if he was really serious.

"Well, are you going to let me stay or not?" Jeff asked, playfully grabbing her feet. By the following week, Jeff's toothbrush and razor were in the medicine cabinet in Colleen's bathroom.

Colleen reached for the phone, picking it up on the first ring. She glanced over at Jeff, but he was still sleeping. Ducking under the cover, she said hello in a soft whisper.

"Hi, it's me, your mother. Why are you whispering? Are you sick?"

"No. I'm fine, Mom. What time is it?"

"After nine. I'm sorry if I woke you. I didn't realize you slept this late."

Jeff lifted his head, his sleepy eyes half open. "Who is it?"

Colleen put her hand over the mouthpiece, "Shhh, it's my mother."

"Colleen, are you there? I thought I heard you talking to someone," her mother said in a questioning voice. "I have some good news. Lou Jean is coming to Stockbridge for Thanksgiving and I want to make sure you're still planning to come home."

"When did I decide that? I don't remember that conversation," Colleen said, yawning and pushing Jeff's hand away as he tugged on the strap of her nightgown.

Anna was still talking. Colleen caught the last sentence. "Please say you'll come. It will be so good to have everyone here."

YARD SALE

She covered the phone again. "Would you like to go to Kansas for Thanksgiving?"

"If that's where you'll be, I guess I'll be there too," Jeff said.

"Mom, I was wondering if it would be all right if I brought someone with me?"

"Of course, Dear. You bring whomever you want, as long as you come home. I'll see you in two weeks, and do be careful. You know how I worry."

She was nervous taking Jeff to Stockbridge with her. Not so much for her family, but for him and especially since Lou Jean was going to be there. She tried to prepare him for his visit, giving him a rundown of each family member. He needed to talk loud around Grandma Grace and he shouldn't bring up anything remotely scary or dangerous around her mom. Angela would ask him a ton of questions, but he could talk to her dad and Jared about almost anything. Most of all she told him to be careful around Lou Jean. She has ears like radar and would pick up the slightest hint of anything they didn't want her to know; like the fact that Jeff stayed at her house exclusively for the last two months and only went to his apartment to get clean clothes and pick up his mail. He had to remember that they could not sleep in the same bedroom, and if anyone asked, they were just really in the beginning stages of their relationship. Jeff told her to relax and remember that dealing with people was his forte and that everything would be fine. She smiled. "You haven't met my Aunt Lou Jean."

"God damn what is that smell? Roll down the window, quick!" Jeff said as he fanned the air with his hand.

"Oh, that's just Merlin. He always gets gas when we travel." She was laughing, watching Jeff stick his head out the window and make gagging noises.

"Jesus, that's more than gas. It smells like he died. Can't you give him some Rolaids or something? Damn we still have a couple of hundred miles to go."

Colleen reached into the back seat and patted Merlin on the head. "He'll be fine. It just takes him a little while to settle down." Jeff groaned and held his nose.

The weather was mild for November. Glimpses of autumn leaves still clung to some of the trees as they drove through the sloping hills of the Ozarks and into the flat plains of Kansas. As they entered the main street of Stockbridge, they passed a new super hardware store and Colleen pointed to the now boarded up Save-Way Market. It too had been replaced by another recent addition called The Mega Food Mart. There was a subdivision just a few miles from the gravel road that signaled the beginning of the Holloway property. Peaked roofs and paved streets had devoured the once open fields where corn had grown just a few short years before. Colleen pointed to the road and Jeff turned the car into the second to last gravel driveway on Pike Road.

"I thought you said you lived in the country. You're almost living in suburbia," Jeff said as he parked his car next to her father's workshop. Merlin jumped from the car and bounded up the steps to greet Aaron and Adam who had emerged from the house when they heard the car.

"Mother, Dad, this is Jeff Fisher, my friend from St. Louis." It sounded so stilted, but she couldn't say, "this is Jeff, the man I adore, the man I sleep with almost every night, the man I think I want to spend the rest of my life with."

"Oh my," Anna said, wiping her hands on her apron. "When you said a friend, I just assumed...never mind. Please come in. We're glad you could join us for Thanksgiving."

Colleen knew she should have told her mother that it wasn't a girl friend, but then there would have been so many questions. This was so much easier.

Jeff met all of the family in less than half an hour. He was polite, he smiled, he complimented. He was the perfect gentleman. Colleen could see her mother smiling, and for the first time in two days she relaxed. It was an easy afternoon so far. "When is Lou Jean coming?" Colleen asked her mother.

"She is late as usual. Dinner is almost ready. We'll wait just a few more minutes."

They had just sat down to eat. Her father was standing at the head of the table with his favorite carving knife in hand when they heard the car horn. Everyone knew that Lou Jean had arrived. Anna ran to the door followed by the children. "Sorry I'm late. I just couldn't make a decent flight connection. Hope you've got lots of food. I'm starving." Lou Jean took off her coat and sat down. "And who is this?" she asked looking across the table at Jeff.

Colleen introduced her to Jeff. He stood up, reaching across the table to shake her hand. "I'm pleased to meet you. I've heard a lot about you," he said smiling.

"Well that's strange, I haven't heard a damn thing about you. Colleen and I will have to have a little talk."

Colleen swallowed nervously. She was in for the inquisition, lawyer style.

Anna and Colleen washed and dried the dishes. Colleen was trying to steer clear of Lou Jean as long as possible. She peeked around the kitchen door to make sure Lou Jean hadn't cornered Jeff. She was relieved that he had gone to the workshop with her father.

"I gotta have a smoke. Take a walk with me," Lou Jean said as Colleen stood on the porch watching Jared play touch football with the boys.

Colleen pulled her jacket collar up as they started up the hill toward the cemetery. "Gosh, I haven't been up here in years. Look, you can see all the new houses."

"Okay tell your Auntie Lou Jean what's going on. Who is the stud boy you brought with you?"

"He's not a stud boy. He's a sweet, kind, considerate guy and I am in love with him," Colleen said, shoving her hands into her jacket pocket.

"How long have you known him? Are you two living together?"

"I've known him for about four months and we are not officially living together, but that may all change pretty soon. Please don't tell mom, not yet anyway."

"What, do you think I'm nuts?" Lou Jean said. "I love your mother too much to give her that much to worry about. Just be careful. Make sure you know enough about him and that you're doing it for the right reasons."

"Is that it? Is that all the lecture I'm going to get?"

Lou Jean stubbed her cigarette out under her foot, "Yeah, for right now. You look too damn happy, but listen if you want me to run a check on him, I'll be glad to do that for you."

Colleen began to laugh, "No, thanks, I'm sure you wouldn't be able to come up with anything I don't already know. Let's go back to the house, I'm freezing."

By the end of the three days, Jeff had enamored the whole family. Earl told Colleen that he thought Jeff had a "good head on his shoulders."

Grandma Grace and Anna were both flustered by his compliments on their food and how he knew where Colleen had gotten her good looks. From them, of course. He couldn't believe how good Angela looked after having four children. Jared, who was usually quiet, spent hours talking to Jeff about football and of course cows. It was only Lou Jean who seemed distant. Watching and listening to him talk, she made little or no comment.

Jeff put the suitcases in the car while Colleen stood on the porch once again saying goodbye to her family. Grandma Grace kissed her on the cheek and slipped the notebook out from beneath her sweater. "I did the best I could, Colleen. I wrote down everything I could remember. The rest is up to you. Just make sure if you write my story, you make me young and beautiful."

"I don't have to make you beautiful, Grandma. You already are." Colleen began to flip through the pages as Jeff turned on to the highway.

"What's that you're reading?" Jeff asked.

"It's my grandmother's journal. I can't believe she really did this for me."

"Are you going to read all the way home or do I have to talk to Merlin to stay awake?"

Colleen closed the book. "We'll talk. How do you like my family?"

"They're great. I had a good time."

"What about your family? You never talk about them, Jeff. Where are they?"

"There's really not much to tell. My parents have been divorced for years. I don't have a clue where my father is and the last time I talked to my mom, she was living somewhere in Florida. I haven't seen her in years." He didn't seem to want to talk anymore.

Chapter Forty-Three

Colleen swiveled in her chair, facing the tinted glass window of her fourth floor office. She watched as the pigeons walked the ledge like circus performers on a tight rope, occasionally stopping to brace themselves against the cold March wind. She looked at her watch, wondering why Frank had asked her to stay late. There had already been three staff meetings that day. Surely it wasn't bad news. He had nothing but compliments for her since her promotion to the editing department just after Christmas. She was the youngest member in the department and she was finally feeling comfortable in her new position. The intercom made a buzzing noise and Frank's voice came over the speaker. Colleen walked down the hall to the beveled glass doors that opened into Frank's private office. He was a friendly man and yet when it came to Edison Publishing Company, he was all business. He had been in charge of this department for over twenty years and was well known in the literary world as one tough editor.

"Hi, glad you could make it," he said. "I'm sorry I asked you to stay late, but I wanted to make sure I had a chance to talk to you before I leave on my vacation. I'm impressed with most of those articles you have been writing on your own time. I sent a few to our publishing division in New York and a fellow named Bob Unger asked that you come and see him. He publishes several monthly magazines and is interested in talking to you."

Colleen hesitated for a moment, trying to take it all in. "I never knew you liked the articles. I can't believe you sent them to our New York publishers. I was just hoping you would give me your personal opinion."

Frank grinned. "I'm a sly devil, but I know talent when I see it and I think you have a shot at becoming a decent writer. So take this," he said, handing her a business card. "Here is his name and address, but remember, if he tries to get you to stay in New York, just tell him you love working for me." He smiled and walked her to the door.

Jeff's car was already in the driveway when she got home. "You'll never guess what happened to me today," she said, throwing her purse on the couch, barely missing Merlin.

"Well, I hope it's better than what happened to me. What's your news?"

"Frank wants me to go to New York and talk to the publishing department about the articles I have been writing." She was breathless. "Can you believe it? New York! I really want you to come along. Do you think you could get a few days off from work? I have so much to do. I have to find someone to watch Merlin and oh..."

Jeff grabbed her hand. "Slow down, sweetheart, we can work all of those details out."

"Can you come with me? Please, say yes?" she asked in a pleading voice.

"Sure, no problem, but there is one more thing we should do in New York."

"What's that?"

"Get married."

Colleen threw her arms around Jeff's neck. "If this is a proposal, the answer is yes."

Jeff laughed and kissed her. "It sure is, babe. I'm sorry I don't have a ring, but I'll get one as soon as we get to New York."

"By the way, what happened to you today?" Colleen asked.

"Nothing as important as your news. Now lets makes some plans."

Colleen and Jeff were married at the courthouse in New York. They splurged on lobster and champagne in an expensive downtown hotel that evening. The next few days were a whirlwind of meetings and sightseeing. Bob Unger agreed that Colleen's articles were good enough to be included in one of the company's monthly issues. Before she left New York, he gave her a contract to look over.

Colleen leaned back, adjusting the buckle on her seat belt. "I'm sorry we couldn't stay in New York any longer. I just have to get back to work. The trip seemed to go by so quickly."

Jeff reached over and kissed her. "That's okay, babe. It was fun while it lasted."

YARD SALE

Colleen looked at the double row of diamonds sparkling on her finger. She pulled the contracts out of her briefcase and began to read over them again. Jeff stared out the plane window for a moment watching the runway drop away below them.

"Can I see that?" he asked.

"Oh sure, I was just reading through some of the fine print. I still need to have Frank look it over before I sign it," she said, handing him the papers.

"It seems like they are willing to pay you a decent amount of money. Looks like a good deal to me."

She smiled. "I know. I can easily double my salary if I just submit four articles a month. I could have probably held out for more but I was just too shocked with this offer."

"I was thinking that maybe once you get going with your new projects we should look for a new place to live," Jeff said. "Maybe something a little bigger, more room for Merlin."

"I don't know, I really like my...I mean our house. It's cozy. Maybe next year." She yawned and settled in for the trip home.

Frank looked over the papers and told Colleen to sign them quickly before they changed their minds. She called Jeff's office to tell him that Frank agreed with her decision to accept their offer. The receptionist was curt, telling Colleen that Jeff no longer worked there. She grabbed her purse and told her secretary she would be gone the rest of the day. He was watching television when she got home. "So why didn't you tell me you quit your job?" she asked.

"I tried to, but you were so excited about the trip, I just thought I'd wait. I didn't want to spoil your mood. Don't worry, babe, I already have three interviews set up for tomorrow."

"But you only worked there six months. You told me when you took that job that it was exactly what you wanted," Colleen said in an irritated voice.

"I thought it was, but you know me. I'm a people person. I'll have a new job by the end of the week and I bet it will be better than that crappy place. Now let's eat. I have a special dinner all ready for you," Jeff said, leading Colleen into the kitchen.

Chapter Forty-Four

Earl opened his paper and finished the last of his coffee. "Are you two just about done with your jelly making?" he asked, watching Anna and Grace fill the mason jars with the bubbling strawberry liquid. "You know I think you could probably buy it cheaper at the supermarket."

Grace shook her finger at him. "You know that stuff is full of preservatives and our jelly tastes much better. Besides, it's tradition."

Earl poured himself another cup of coffee, getting that look from Anna that said he had enough caffeine for the day. He needed to change the subject before she started talking about his health again. "Have you heard from Colleen lately?"

Anna shook her head. "She called me last week. She's still worried that we're mad at her for getting married in New York. I tried to convince her that we weren't. She knows I was disappointed, but it's better than having them continue to live together and me pretending I didn't know."

Grace removed her apron and threw it on the counter. "Is that for my benefit? You know that Hans and I could have gotten married if we wanted to. He asked me all the time. I was the one that kept saying no. So I guess we were a real embarrassment to you."

"Mother, please, this has nothing to do with you. All we wanted was to give Colleen a nice wedding," Anna said as she rolled her eyes, watching Earl grin behind his paper. "I was thinking maybe we could send her some of the money we had put aside for her wedding as a present. Maybe there's something they need, or they may want to take a real honeymoon. What do you think?" Anna asked Earl as she sat down at the table.

"Sounds good to me. Figure out how much you want to send and I'll get a cashier's check. Maybe we could save a little for ourselves and go on our own second honeymoon," he winked at Anna, making her blush.

YARD SALE

Colleen kicked off her shoes as soon as she got inside the door. She should have known better than to wear a new pair of shoes to the office. She rubbed her foot on her leg, trying to steady herself as Merlin jumped about in front of her. "Just a minute, let me look at the mail and change my clothes. You can hold it that long." Leafing through the advertisements she found another brochure from the real estate company. Jeff had circled a picture of an enormous house, putting an arrow next to it and a smiley face. She threw the mail on the desk and pulled off her blouse on the way to the bedroom. Once in her comfortable sweats, she picked up Merlin's leash and pushed the button on the answering machine. "Colleen, it's me," Angela said. "You've got to come home. Grandma Grace is in the hospital."

She quickly dialed Angela's number. "What's wrong with Grandma?"

"We don't know yet. She collapsed in the kitchen this morning and Dad called an ambulance. They think she might have had a stroke or maybe a heart attack. They're really not sure yet."

"I'll be there as soon as I can." Colleen hurriedly dialed Jeff's office. "Jeff, my grandmother is in the hospital. We have to go home as soon as possible."

"I'm sorry to hear that babe but maybe I could wait and come after you find out all the details. It's kind of a tough time for me to be taking off, but if you really want me to go with you, I'll leave right now."

"You're right," Colleen said. "I'll let you know how she is in the morning."

"Do you think you'll be home by Friday; that's our one month anniversary?"

Colleen wasn't really worried about the anniversary right now. All she wanted was to get home to see her grandmother. "I'll let you know, okay?"

She called his office from the airport and left a message for Jeff on his answering machine. "I'm sorry I was so sharp with you. You know I love you a lot. I'll call you in the morning."

Her footsteps echoed on the tiled hospital hallway as she made her way down the third floor corridor to the intensive care waiting room. Anna met her at the door. Angela was asleep on a small green sofa while her father sprawled out in a stiff corner chair. "Hi, Mom, how is grandma?" Colleen asked as she hugged her mother.

"The doctor said he didn't think it was a heart attack or a stroke. At this point they really don't know what happened but they're going to run some tests in the morning."

The nurse escorted Colleen into the dimly lit room. She could hear the slight whooshing sound of the breathing machine as it pumped air into her grandmother's frail body. She looked so small lying in the white bed, her hands folded across her stomach.

"She's asleep right now," the nurse said, adjusting the drip from the I.V. fluids.

Colleen sat down next to her bed and held her grandmother's small hand. It was warm and soft, just like she always remembered. She rubbed her grandmother's cheek, trying not to cry or even think about the possibility of losing her. Grace opened her eyes slightly; she smiled and squeezed Colleen's hand. "You're going to be all right Grandma. I'll be back to see you a little later," she said, leaving the room as the tears rolled down her face.

They had breakfast in the hospital coffee shop. Earl was tired from a sleepless night. He rubbed the back of his neck. "You would think they would make it just a little more comfortable for the families. Every bone in my body hurts."

"I'm stiff too, Dad. I think they do it on purpose. They would rather we went home, but that's too bad, I'm not leaving," Colleen remarked as she put her hands on her aching back.

Anna looked at her watch. "We can't stay down here too long. I don't want to miss the doctor. He said he would let us know something by nine o'clock." She put her napkin on the table. "I think I'll go back upstairs."

Earl patted her arm. "Look it's only eight-thirty. You stay here and talk to Colleen. Angela and I will see if the doctor is here and, for goodness sakes, stop thinking the worst. It's going to be okay." Earl took the check off the table and left before she could say another word.

"He is such a good man. I just don't know what I would ever do without him," Anna said. "I don't know how he has put up with me and Grandma Grace for all these years."

Colleen touched her mother's arm. "That's because he loves you, Mom. He would do anything in the world for you."

"Speaking of love. How is everything going with you and Jeff?"

"Fine, except I wish I could just get him to stop buying things for me. He is always bringing me presents and stuff for the house and sometimes I'm not sure where the money is coming from."

Anna's back stiffened in the chair. "You've mentioned this to me before, Colleen. It is beginning to concern me. What kind of things is he buying?"

"I didn't mean to get you upset, Mom. He's just a very generous person."

"You just make sure you know what he is doing with the money and that he doesn't buy more than you can afford. Married people shouldn't keep secrets."

"Where is all of this coming from? You act like Jeff is doing something wrong," Colleen said, puzzled by her mother's reaction.

"Have you read Grandma Grace's journal yet?" Anna asked.

"What does that have to do with me?"

Before Anna could answer, Angela came through the door, waving to them. They were needed upstairs. The doctor wanted to talk to all of them. They rode in silence in the elevator, watching the floor numbers over the door.

The doctor was writing something down inside the metal chart, not looking up, although they stood just inches from him. He closed the folder, putting his glasses in the pocket of his white jacket. "We have run all the necessary tests and it is my conclusion that your mother just had some sort of fainting spell. As far as I can tell she is fine. I hope I am in as good health as her when I am eighty. I think she needs to begin taking it a little easy. She needs some mild exercise every day and a little more rest. You are all going to have to be patient with her. She is a headstrong little lady."

Anna began to cry, leaning on Earl's shoulder. She wiped her face and thanked the doctor over and over. He smiled as he tried to escape down the hall.

Grace was standing at the door of her room barefooted, holding the back of her hospital gown closed. "Is someone going to find me something to wear home before I catch pneumonia with my backside hanging out?"

Chapter Forty-Five

"I have a surprise for you. A big anniversary surprise, so close your eyes," Jeff said as he led Colleen through the front door. Colleen opened her eyes and looked around the room, not believing this was really her house. A white velvet sofa curved around the living room with two zebra print chairs facing each other. The middle of the room was swallowed by a black lacquered cocktail table. There were new drapes, new pillows and in the corner of the room, a large ceramic vase in the shape of a tree trunk, with monkeys climbing on the vines.

"What in the world...where did all of this come from?" she asked almost breathless.

"Isn't it great? I decided to redecorate while you were in Kansas. I got most of it at Caulfield's, but a few of the pieces came from an antique shop downtown."

Colleen sat down on the edge of the couch. "Where are our old things, our couch and chair, my table?"

"Some of the stuff is in the garage, and as far as that old coffee table, well I put it out for the trash along with some of your other yard sale finds."

"But where did the money come from to buy all of this? It really looks expensive."

"We received a sizeable check from your parents as a wedding present. I was sure you wouldn't mind if I cashed it. You know we really needed new furniture."

"Are there any more surprises in the other rooms?" she asked.

"Just a few things. We have some new linens and dishes. Tell me what you think of the new furniture?"

"I guess I would have liked to have helped pick it out. We hadn't even talked about buying new furniture. Besides, that money was a gift for both of us. Did you spend all of it? And could you please tell me what is that monkey thing in the corner?"

"That 'monkey thing' is a very expensive antique umbrella stand," he said rolling his eyes. "I should have known I couldn't do anything nice for you without you being concerned about the money. Well, you needn't worry. I can send it all back in the morning," he said angrily. "I thought you would like the change since you don't want to move."

"Please don't get mad, Jeff. I'm really tired right now. Maybe I just need a few days to get used to it." She looked around the room. "Where is Merlin?"

"I took him to the kennel. He was in the way when they were bringing in the furniture. I forgot to pick him up. I can get him tomorrow. Besides, I don't want him on the new couch."

"No, I'll go get him now. He must be miserable," she said, picking up her keys. "Put some sheets on the furniture."

By the time she got home with Merlin, Jeff was already in bed. She noticed a new lamp on the nightstand and cream-colored satin sheets on the bed. How much money had he spent? It would be awkward to ask her mother the amount of the check, especially after her mother's speech at the hospital. She was probably just being silly. With Jeff's new job and her increased salary, they could afford a few new things.

"Are you awake? We need to talk," she said, turning on the new lamp.

He rolled over, his head resting on his arm. "What? It's late. I'm tired."

"I just want you to understand why I reacted the way I did. It's not the furniture. Ever since I was a child I would always see my mom and dad sit down together and discuss their finances. I never once saw them make a major purchase without checking with each other. I've always had to be pretty frugal with my money. This kind of spending is all new to me."

"Christ, you act like I took our last dime and blew it. I wouldn't have done this if I knew it would have upset you. I just wanted to see you smile for a change," Jeff said.

"It does make me happy. I'm sorry I got upset. Let's get some sleep." She kissed his cheek and he turned over, his back facing her. Merlin put his head on the side of the bed, his sad eyes looking at her, wondering why he was no longer welcome next to her. She patted his head and wiped the tears from her face. This had been their first real argument.

They made up in the morning. Jeff agreed to return the white couch for something more practical. She agreed to compromise and keep the zebra chairs. He really loved the umbrella stand, but gave up the two crystal vases that teetered on the mantel each time the front door was closed. Colleen kept finding new things around the house almost every day. She had to bite her tongue to keep from asking what each thing cost. When they returned from New York, Jeff had said with all her new responsibilities at work, he could at least take care of the banking. She hadn't seen a bank statement since they were married, but she trusted him.

Colleen made herself a sandwich and a glass of tea. She tucked Grandma Grace's journal under her arm. Balancing the plate on her knee, she tried to get comfortable in the zebra chair. Finally giving up, she carried the brown lounge chair in from the garage and pulled it down the hall into the small bedroom she now used for an office. Colleen loved this old yard sale chair. Curling her feet under her, she turned on the floor lamp and began to read her grandmother's words.

I was born in Monmouth, Wales in January, nineteen hundred, and eleven and moved to the United States when I was ten.

Her grandmother told her about her life in Wales many times. It wasn't until Colleen began to read the journal that she understood why her grandmother never went any further with her stories than when she first came to America. Grace started her story into the past with the death of her father. She wrote about how lonely and frightened she was after her mother decided to return to Wales and it was only after she met Henry that she felt safe. When he left her the first time, she spent the next two years trying to get over the sting of rejection. It was only after Henry asked her to marry him that she felt redeemed. He promised to take care of her and she believed him. After their marriage he turned into someone she hardly knew at all. His fits of temper and long hours away from home convinced her she had made a mistake. It was after Colin's birth that she thought about leaving him, but she was a good Catholic. How could she face being a divorced woman, alone with a small child? When they moved to Ternberry with Agnes and Joseph all of her unhappiness seemed to fade for a time. She loved it there. The jagged edges of her life seemed to be smooth and calm for a while. She wrote of her sadness when Joseph and Agnes died and when Henry made her leave Ternberry. It was the beginning of the slow erosion of her marriage. Grace admitted that Anna was put aside after Colin's death and all of her emotions turned inward to grieve for her son and the guilt she felt. It was only after they moved to the house on Cherry Street that Grace finally just gave up and let the world slip by her. Each cutting remark from Henry, each bout of his rage and each time he came home drunk smelling of someone else's cologne pushed her deeper into her depression. It was the prescription drugs provided by her own husband that seemed to temporarily ease her pain.

There were pages written on Henry's philandering ways with other women, his constant lying and incessant spending habits. He was always buying things they couldn't afford and turned their home into a museum. He was obsessed with his desires to have possessions that were better than his father's. It was difficult for her to write about the argument they had the night before he died. He came to her wanting money, and when she said she had none to give him, he screamed at her that she was nothing but a stupid, worthless woman. He said he had never loved her and only married her so that he could finish school. She lashed out at him and he hit her, sending her crashing into the corner of the dresser. She blamed herself for letting Henry take her life away without her permission.

Anna's life was miserable, too, but Grace did little to help her. Anna refused to give up on her mother, helping her to overcome her addiction to the drugs and with her bouts of depression. Grace felt she had shamed her daughter by going off and living in sin with Hans. What she wanted more than anything was to find a way to pay tribute to Anna, some way to thank her for all she had done and for giving her a new start in life. Perhaps Colleen could put her story into better words. Words that would let Anna know how much she loved her. Colleen closed the book. Rubbing her eyes, she realized she had been reading for over three hours. She picked up the phone and called her mother.

"Mom, I read the journal. Why is it you never told me about your childhood? I had no idea."

"Why would I want to put all those bad memories in your mind? I made peace with them years ago."

"I want to write Grandma's story. Is that all right with you?"

"When you gave the journal to your Grandmother I thought she would just put it away somewhere, but I would see her sitting on the porch writing. Whenever I came around, she would close the book. I'm ashamed to admit that one night after she was asleep, I went into her room and read it. I think it would honor your grandmother if you would write the story. It will be considered fiction, won't it?" Anna asked.

On Monday morning Colleen talked to Frank about the possibility of presenting a fictional novel to the publishers in New York. "Write a couple of chapters and send it to them. If they like it, they'll let you know. Since you know most of them, you may be able to get past the red tape. You have my blessings," Frank said. "I'll be honest with you, it's not easy being a new author these days."

Writing the manuscript became Colleen's full time obsession. She began to think about the characters in the story as if they had come to life and were acting parts in a play. She named and renamed them, trying to find just the right combination of syllables to echo in her ears. She found herself vacillating over every small detail as she tried to get the first few chapters on paper. Her portable typewriter became a third appendage, as she spent her lunch hour and every spare moment at home writing. Jeff seemed almost as excited as she was, constantly asking her questions and wanting to read what she had written. She covered the paper with her hand. "No, you have to let me finish these first few chapters first."

He grinned. "You are really into this, aren't you? What do the publishers do? Send you an advance if they like the story?"

"Hardly," she answered. "I'll be lucky if they even accept the first draft."

The first three chapters were finished and sealed in an envelope. Colleen handed the package to the courier and watched him carry her manuscript out of the office and on its way to New York. It would be four weeks before she received a telephone call from one of the publishers she dealt with on a regular basis; a stern sounding gentleman who was more often than not critical of her work. He often returned her magazine articles to her with red pencil marks on them as if he were grading a paper. She sat listening to him as he ambled on, telling her that the story wasn't something he personally wanted to publish but he had passed it on to several of his colleagues. One woman in particular seemed interested. Her name was Ann Hardin. He would have her call Colleen. Another three weeks passed before she called. She would read the rest of the manuscript when it was finished, telling Colleen that if the quality was the same as what she had already read she would consider publishing the manuscript.

They danced around the room, laughing and hugging. Jeff poured champagne into tall crystal glasses and they drank to what they both hoped would be a successful outcome.

Colleen decided she needed to go to Kansas and get more information from her grandmother. Jeff begged off, saying it would be cheaper for her to fly home for the weekend. She kissed him goodbye at the airport gate, telling him Merlin had better be there when she returned and no more new furniture. He grinned, crossing his heart. "I promise. Nothing new for the house."

Grandma Grace sat with Colleen on the porch beaming as Colleen asked her questions and wrote her answers down in her own notebook. At times Grace would hesitate as if she was embarrassed to say the words out loud to her granddaughter. Colleen tried not to push her. They talked about the house on Cherry Street. She had never been back there since that day so many years ago when she went into the hospital. It was a bad memory and she had no desire to ever see it again. To her, it was a sad and miserable place. They talked until Grace said she was tired and needed to go to bed. Colleen kissed her cheek and helped her up the steps.

Colleen borrowed her father's car and drove into Stockbridge. She maneuvered the car down the tree-lined streets in the section of town that years ago had been considered the most desirable place to live. She parked at the curb in front of 704 Cherry Street. The moonlight cast a yellow glow on the rusted iron gate that guarded the once elegant house. The façade of the house was now overgrown with tangled vines and weeds that hid the boarded up windows. A faded "for sale" sign lay on its side in the front yard. Its previous owner, finally giving up the cumbersome burden of keeping up the property, had moved to the suburbs leaving the house to deteriorate with each passing year. It seemed like a fitting end to a house that had caused her mother and grandmother so much pain. She walked back to the car; turning to look up at the second story, wondering which room had been her mother's.

"I know you're on a tight schedule, Colleen, but before you leave I would like to invite Angela and her family over for lunch," Anna said.

Colleen looked up from the typewriter. "Sure, Mom, that's fine."

Angela served the children at the small kitchen table and settled into her chair.

"What's wrong?" Colleen asked, as she looked around the table. You're all staring at me like I'm giving away some family secrets. My book is going to be a fictional novel based loosely on some real facts. Don't get all nervous."

"There's nothing in the book that's going to embarrass my kids, is there?" Angela asked. "You know, s-e-x," she said, cupping her hands around her mouth.

Colleen smiled. "You'll just have to wait and read the book."

"Well at least tell me, am I in it?"

"No, it's Grandma Grace's story. You're not in it and neither am I."

"I think Angela was looking forward to being a celebrity," Jared said as an olive flew across the table.

Colleen paid the taxi driver and started up the driveway. She noticed the sleek silver car sitting in her driveway, wondering who could be visiting at this late hour. Turning on the living room light she took a quick glance around the living room. Breathing a sigh of relief, she opened the bathroom door and heard the water running in the shower. "Hi, I'm home. Whose car is that in our driveway?"

Jeff stuck his head around the shower curtain. "It's mine, but don't get excited. It's only on lease."

Chapter Forty-Six

"Hi, I need a good lawyer. I was wondering if you knew one?" Colleen said when she finally got through to Lou Jean.

"That's very funny. As a matter of fact, I knew a damn good one but he's dead now. Why do you need a lawyer? What's going on?"

"I have the contracts on my manuscript and I need someone to look them over before I sign my life away," Colleen said.

"I'll be in Washington sometime this week. I can catch a plane and be down to see you on Friday. I can't believe there are no lawyers in your firm that can help you with your contracts."

Colleen flipped through the stack of files on her desk. "None that I trust as much as you."

"Anybody home?" Lou Jean yelled as she opened the front door. The taxi driver put her briefcase and two suitcases on the porch.

"Here, let me help you," Colleen said, wiping her hands on her jeans. "I wish you would have called me from the airport. I could have come and picked you up."

"Good Lord where did all this stuff come from?" she asked, turning to see the new furniture in the living room.

"Jeff bought it. What do you think?"

"Do you really want my honest opinion?" Lou Jean said, making a gagging noise.

"I heard that," Jeff peered around the kitchen door.

"Can I smoke in here?" Lou Jean asked, pulling a pack of cigarettes out of her pocket. "What are you doing home, Jeff. Don't you ever work?"

Jeff laughed. "Right now I'm in between jobs. My company downsized and I was the first one to go."

Lou Jean lit her cigarette. "Is that a fancy way of saying you got fired? Well if you would stick with one job maybe you would build some seniority. What's that, four jobs in the last year?"

"Man, you are tough. My wife is going to be the breadwinner for a little while. I've got a couple of interviews that look promising, but right now I'm the house boy."

"Okay, house boy, get me a beer. Can I sit on this thing?" Lou Jean said, pointing to one of the zebra chairs. "It won't bite me in the ass, will it?" She sat down, patting the chair as a signal to Merlin that he was welcome to join her. Jeff frowned as Merlin climbed onto Lou Jean, his long legs dangling from her lap.

While they ate dinner, Lou Jean continued to throw barbs at Jeff, asking him why it was so difficult for him to keep a job and wasn't he even a little bit embarrassed living off of his wife. Jeff continued to be jovial, but Colleen could see that he was not enjoying Lou Jean's cutting remarks. Jeff carried the plates to the kitchen, returning with the coffee pot.

"I think I'll go for a walk while you two look over the contracts. I need some fresh air."

"Take Merlin with you," Colleen said.

Jeff frowned and grabbed Merlin's leash off the hook. Merlin disappeared into the bedroom. "He doesn't want to go with me. You'll have to take him later."

"So what's the story on him?" Lou Jean asked, pouring herself a cup of coffee. "Don't you mind that he doesn't work?"

"He works most of the time. Why are you being so tough on him?"

"Well, I can tell you sure aren't tough on him. It seems to me he has mighty expensive taste for someone who doesn't have a steady job. What if you decided to have kids? Are you going to keep working and let him stay home and play nanny?"

"Sometimes Jeff's spending habits cause a small problem, but he is getting better. I've talked to him about letting me take over the finances and he agreed it might be a good idea."

"It might be a good idea? It's a damn good idea," Lou Jean said. "I think you had better get a handle on the situation before he puts you in the poor house. The thought of that man walking around with a checkbook and credit cards scares me. I'm looking around at all this crystal and crap and I know it's not cheap. What's that ugly monkey thing in the corner?" Lou Jean put on her glasses. Once she began to read the contracts, she shifted into a business mode that Colleen was not accustomed to; a professional demeanor usually reserved for her clients.

"I can't find anything wrong with this deal at all," she said after she had read the last page. Looks to me like they have covered all the bases. If your manuscript turns out to be a best seller you could make yourself a few bucks, plus it would put you in much greater demand for your articles and future books. Don't get too excited though. It depends on how much influence your publisher has in the literary world and how much time she wants to put into promoting your book. The ball is really in her corner." Her voice softened. "I can't tell you how proud I am of you. I think it's great that you're writing this story. Now, what's the name of my character?"

Lou Jean left before Jeff returned from his walk, telling Colleen that he would probably be happier if he didn't have to answer any more of her questions. She refused Colleen's offer to stay at the house or drive her to the hotel.

"I'll be fine," she said, as Colleen walked her down the driveway to the waiting taxicab. Lou Jean hugged her goodbye, looking over Colleen's shoulder at the cars in the driveway. "Please tell me the Jaguar is yours and the sedan is Jeff's." Colleen smiled a limp smile. Lou Jean knew the answer to her question.

Several weeks went by before Colleen heard anymore about her manuscript. She received a short note from Ann Hardin saying that Colleen should call her to discuss the book. Colleen left several messages, but Ann was either out of town or in a business meeting.

"I have to go to New York again. Frank thinks it will help move things along quicker if I get to know Ann personally. He's going to set up a meeting," Colleen said as Jeff lay on the couch watching television.

"Sounds like a good idea to me. When will you be back?"

She leaned over the couch and kissed him on the neck. "Probably in a couple of days. I have all evening to get ready. Want to help me take a shower?"

"You go ahead. I'm kind of tired tonight."

When Colleen got out of the shower, the house was dark and Jeff was already in bed. She put on her sweats and tennis shoes and took Merlin for a long walk.

Ann Hardin agreed to meet Colleen in a trendy downtown restaurant. Colleen took a taxi to the hotel. Looking at her watch, she threw her luggage on the bed and hurriedly changed her clothes. She hailed another taxi and the meter ticked away as they sat in traffic for over half an hour. Out of breath, she ran the last few blocks to the restaurant hoping Ann had not given up on her. "I'm so sorry I'm late, Miss Hardin, there was so much traffic," Colleen said, looking at the attractive dark haired woman sitting alone at the table. She held out her hand. "I'm Colleen Fisher."

Ann smiled and shook her hand. "This is New York. Everyone is always late."

They talked about the manuscript over wine and dinner. Ann asked her where she had come up with the idea for the book. She was impressed with Colleen's style of writing and told her if the rest of the manuscript was as promising, she would honor the contract. "Look at the time. I really must be going. I'll be waiting for more pages."

She breezed out of the room, stopping several times to talk to different people in the dining room. Colleen waited for a moment before the waiter brought the check enclosed in a leather folder. She tried not to look surprised when she saw the amount of the bill. She smiled, handing him her credit card.

He returned to the table a few minutes later. "I'm sorry, madam, but there seems to be a problem with this card."

"There must be some mistake," she said. "Please try running it through again."

The waiter looked annoyed. "I have tried twice already, madam. Do you have another card or perhaps cash?"

Colleen frantically riffled through her purse pulling a hundred dollar bill out of her wallet. It was all of the cash she had with her. She laid it inside the folder and he disappeared into the kitchen. She was too embarrassed to wait for her meager change. Taking her jacket, she hurriedly left the restaurant.

She heard the familiar click of the answering machine. "Jeff, I need to talk to you right now. Please pick up the phone," Colleen said in an anxious voice.

"Hi, where are you? I was asleep," he replied.

"I'm still in New York. I have a big problem. I tried to use my credit card at the restaurant tonight and I was told it's over the limit. My God, Jeff, that's a ten thousand dollar card. How could you have possibly spent that much money?"

"There you go again, Colleen. Why do you automatically assume that I spent all the money? Something is probably screwed up at the credit card company. Let me do some checking. Give me your number and I'll get it straightened out. Please don't get so upset. Get a good night's sleep and I'll call you back first thing in the morning."

Upset really wasn't the word for how she felt. They had argued several times about money in the past weeks. Jeff was still insisting that they buy a new house now that her manuscript was in the works. She was tired of realtors calling her about houses that they could not afford. Jeff's new job was based on commission and he was bringing home very little money.

By late morning she tried to reach him since he had not called her back. There was no answer. She left messages on the machine. By noon she was furious. It was time to check out of the hotel. Colleen went to the ATM in the lobby. Putting in her personal identification number, the screen simply read, "Account Invalid." She called her bank in St. Louis.

"I'm sorry, Mrs. Fisher, but that account has been closed," the teller said. "All of the funds were withdrawn a few days ago."

Her mouth was dry and her hand shook as she dialed Lou Jean's telephone number in London.

"Lou Jean, I have a problem, can you wire me some money?"

The living room was dark as she fumbled for her keys. Stepping inside the door, it was Jeff's suitcase she tripped over. It was sitting next to the door along with his overnight bag and briefcase. As he came down the hallway he was startled to see her.

"I didn't hear you come in. How did you get home?"

"It doesn't matter. I have been trying to get in touch with you since yesterday. I waited at the hotel as long as I could. Why didn't you call me back? We really need to talk."

"There's nothing to talk about, Colleen. I'm leaving," he said, putting on his jacket.

She was stunned. "Leaving for where? Where are you going?"

"Probably to a motel until I get the mess at the bank straightened out. What gave you the right to have your damn lawyer friend freeze my bank account? And I'm sick of you always nagging about money." She had never seen him this angry.

"I have no idea what you're talking about," she said, still standing in the doorway.

He pushed her aside, picking up his luggage. "I have nothing to say to you, Colleen. This marriage has been one big mistake. I'll be back later for the rest of my stuff, and by the way, I hate your Goddamn dog!" The door slammed, sending Merlin rushing to the kitchen.

She didn't know exactly how long she sat in the darkened living room. Her mind raced through the last few days. She should be the one that was angry, not him. Surely he would calm down and be back. Colleen lay across the bed fully clothed. Hearing a soft thud, she could see Merlin as he circled twice, making himself comfortable on Jeff's side of the bed.

Colleen called Frank the next morning and told him she was not feeling well and needed a few days off. He never asked what was wrong, although he could sense in her voice that she was on the verge of tears. "Okay, you call me when you're feeling better. Take care of yourself," he said as he hung up the phone.

Existing on tea and toast, she did not leave the house for three days. She sat by the phone, listening to the messages pile up until the tape was completely full. Jeff did not call and each night Colleen went to bed waiting to hear his key in the door. It was the insistent ringing of the doorbell that woke her from a restless sleep. Rubbing her red-rimmed eyes, she looked at the clock. That must be Jeff at the door, she thought to herself as she leaped from the bed. Her head aching, she ran to let him in.

"Wow, you look rough," Lou Jean said, looking around the room for signs of Jeff.

Colleen's wrinkled robe hung loosely on her body. Her voice was strained. "He left me. I thought you were him. I don't know where he is."

Colleen sat down on the couch, putting her head in her hands she began to slowly rock back and forth. "I just don't know what to do. It's like my insides have been ripped out of me."

"I hate to say this, Colleen, but you need to get a grip on yourself. You're falling apart and that is not going to help this situation one bit. I bet he was surprised when you got home before he had a chance to get out of the house. I'm sure he wanted to be as far away as possible before you hit the door." Lou Jean was livid. She paced around the living room. "I was the one who had his account frozen. My name was on the court order. The little bastard drew all your money out of the bank and put it in his own account. I'll bet that really pissed him off when he went to the bank and couldn't even get a penny of it. He wasn't even smart enough to go to another bank."

"What are you talking about? You are not making any sense," Colleen said, trying to decipher Lou Jean's confused ranting.

Lou Jean knelt down in front of Colleen, taking her hand. "Honey, you know you're like family to me. After you called me from New York, I made a few phone calls. I got more information than I really needed. Right now I want you to jump in the shower and put on some clean clothes. I'll make you something to eat and tell you everything I know."

Colleen tried to eat the sandwich Lou Jean had made for her. "I feel better now. The shower felt good, but I'm not really hungry," she said nibbling on the corner of the bread.

"Well, how about a beer? It's loaded with calories." Lou Jean popped open the can and poured it into a tall glass.

Colleen took a small sip. "I'm ready to hear what you found out, but please, take it slow. My brain is pretty mushy right now."

"I will, babe. After you called me from New York I knew Jeff must be up to something. I called a private detective and had him run a check on him. Lou Jean reached into her brief case and pulled out an envelope. "Hold on to your hat, Colleen, this may be a little painful."

Almost everything Jeff had told Colleen about his life was lies. He had never finished college. He had been married three times before he met Colleen. Once when he was in college, again four years later to a wealthy woman in Florida and just recently to a girl named Julia. All of his marriages ended in less than a year. Jeff was heavily in debt. He had been moving from state to state to escape his creditors. Once he had filed bankruptcy, leaving a trail of unpaid accounts. He hadn't really had a steady job in over three years, and before moving in with Colleen he had been living with Julia.

"Julia was the blonde girl I met at the barbecue the day I met Jeff. Was he married to her then?" Colleen asked in a strained voice.

"No, they were divorced, but he was still staying at her house. According to her, she couldn't get him to leave. What did he tell you about his parents?"

"Not much, only that they were divorced. He said he hadn't seen his dad in years and his mother lived in Florida."

"Not true, just another cover story. They are alive and well and living in Ohio. I'm sure he was afraid if you met them they would give you an earful," Lou Jean said as she finished reading the file.

Colleen sat with her hands cupped around her glass, staring at the table. "I feel like such a fool. How could I have been so taken in by him, and why do I feel like I still want him to come back?"

"Because right now you're feeling sorry for yourself and you haven't gotten pissed off yet. Believe me I know. I've been there a few times myself." Lou Jean poured the rest of the beer into her glass. "You were in love, remember. There were flowers and music and sex. He only told you what he wanted you to know and you believed him. At least you found out after eight months. How would you have like to have been Grandma Grace and live through this nightmare for over twenty-five years?" Lou Jean put her arm around Colleen.

"That's what makes it even worse. When I read those pages in the journal about my grandfather I have a hard time believing my grandmother could have been so gullible to be taken in by him and here I am, doing the same thing. But why, Lou Jean? He must have loved me a little when we got married."

"I'm sure he did, honey," Lou Jean said. "He probably loved you as much as he was capable of loving anyone other than himself. He knew you had potential and determination. Something he lacked completely. Jeff was a needy person. And here you come along, a pretty girl living on her own in a new city. Then he finds out you even have a good job. Being a cheat and a liar came so easy to him. I can see how he fooled you. Now I want you to pull yourself together. I'm going to stay here a couple of days. We can tie up loose ends and then you can go to London with me."

One of the difficult parts of the breakup was telling her parents. Colleen called her mother as Lou Jean sat next to her holding her hand. Anna cried, saying how surprised and sorry she was. She wanted to know what had happened, but Colleen was too upset to go in to detail. Lou Jean took the phone and talked to Anna while Colleen went back into the bedroom to fall apart again. Right now Colleen wanted to go home to Kansas. She wanted to sit on the porch with her dad and talk about the weather and watch Angela's children play in the yard. Most of all, she wanted to fall into her mother's arms and let her make everything better, yet

YARD SALE

something inside of her told her she needed to take care of this on her own. She would talk to her father about her plans to go to London. He could break the news to her mother gently so that she would not worry.

Chapter Forty-Seven

Colleen called the classified department of the daily paper. "I want to put an ad in the paper for a yard sale. Yes, that's right, yard sale. Just put that it will start on Saturday at eight o'clock. Entire contents of home for sale. Owner moving, everything must go." She spent the afternoon making signs and posting them around the neighborhood.

"What's this about a yard sale? Why don't you just chuck this stuff and we can close up the house?" Lou Jean said as she overheard Colleen on the telephone.

"No. I want to drag it all outside and sell it for pennies on the dollar. I want total strangers to come and buy it. I want to see each thing carried away by someone who doesn't have the slightest notion how much pain this crap has caused me. I want to see the happy looks on their faces when they get an incredible bargain. It's a cathartic experience, and besides, I can use the money," Colleen said as she carried the zebra chairs into the garage. Pushing and shoving, she began to move everything into the kitchen while Lou Jean talked on the phone for hours trying to clear up her business matters in Washington. Waving her hand, she signaled Colleen to be quiet as she banged and slammed the boxes on the kitchen floor. In the past few days Lou Jean had made it almost impossible for Colleen to feel sorry for herself. She talked until Colleen would tell her to stop, putting her hand over Lou Jean's mouth.

"So it didn't work out. It's not the end of the world, you know. You have a bright future in front of you," she said, sitting on the edge of Colleen's bed. "I'm twice as old as you and have made twice as many mistakes. I'm living proof that life goes on and sometimes good things come out of really bad situations." She talked on for hours about anything she could think of, at times making Colleen laugh.

"Please let me get some sleep, I don't want to hear any more right now." Colleen pulled the cover over her head. "My ears are tired from

YARD SALE

listening to you. I have to get up early in the morning." Yet lying there alone, she thought about all the nights she and Jeff slept in this bed and the many times they made love, falling asleep in each other's arms. How could he just walk away? The rejection was almost too much to bear. The anger was building in her.

Lou Jean locked the front door and turned off the living room light. She checked on Colleen to make sure she was still sleeping. She undressed in the bathroom and turned on the shower. Closing her eyes, the warm water ran down her face. Today was like a repeat of that time so many years ago when Anna had called, asking her to come home. She remembered consoling her dear friend as Anna blamed herself for her father's death. Now Colleen needed her help to deal with all the pain and hurt someone else had thrust upon her. Lou Jean wondered why she could always be so strong for other people. Was that her sole purpose in life? In all of those many relationships she had over the past years, why did she always run at the first inkling of commitment? It was easier for her to end a relationship than to be the one who was left behind to deal with the anguish and heartbreak. It was her armor, her protection against being hurt. She was supposed to be the strong one, but as she stood with her head against the cool tiles of the shower stall, she wondered if there would ever be anyone who would love her enough to hold her so tight she couldn't run away. Looking at her reflection in the mirror she said out loud, "Get a grip and stop feeling sorry for yourself."

Saturday morning. Colleen padded through the dark kitchen. After making the coffee, she opened the back door to check the weather. It was barely dawn and the pink sky of morning was still visible. The morning dew settled on the tables she had set up in the yard. Colleen grabbed a dishtowel and headed outside.

"My God, what time is it?" Lou Jean asked, stretching her arms over her head. "It's still dark outside. Who gets up this early to go to a yard sale?"

Colleen smiled. "You just don't know. The people will start coming around seven. Now I need some help getting this stuff outside.

Those boxes in the living room are the things I want to keep. I'm going to put them in a storage unit. All the rest of this stuff is going."

Lou Jean groaned. "Did I ever tell you I had a bad back?"

Colleen began to unpack the boxes and bags after checking her cash box to make sure she had enough change. Picking up a pair of leather gloves she had never seen before, she thought to herself that Jeff must have spent all of his time shopping instead of working. Lou Jean had convinced her that he probably planned to take most of it with him, but she caught him off guard. Hadn't he said he would be back for the rest of his stuff? He was going to be in for a big surprise. When he moved in with Colleen all of his possessions fit into two cardboard boxes. The clothes he bought since they were married now filled three closets. Those same clothes were now hanging on a clothesline between two trees in the front yard. Jeff's forty-dollar shirts were blowing in the breeze, priced to sell at two dollars each.

Lou Jean stood on the front porch sipping coffee and smoking a cigarette. She watched as Colleen arranged the linens and china on the tables. She could see the sadness in her eyes as she placed the silver champagne bucket and two glasses next to the set of satin sheets. The yard was a blur of colors and textures as each empty space was filled with Jeff's extravagance. A bowl of red glass apples, unopened video cassettes, and a purple cashmere scarf still encased in plastic were placed on the table next to three sets of silver salad utensils. What in the world was he thinking? He must have been the Shopping Network's favorite customer.

While they were dating, Jeff marveled at her yard sale finds. After they married, he said he really didn't enjoy her bringing someone else's stuff into their house. She found it to be great fun, looking for bargains or finding some unexpected treasure that cost only a few dollars. Today she would be the one haggling with the early morning risers that were trying to get the best merchandise for the least amount of money.

"I'm ready, let the madness begin," Colleen said as the first car pulled into the driveway.

The two ladies coming up the driveway seemed to be yard sale professionals. Each going in a different direction, they gathered up as much stuff as their arms would hold. Stashing it under the table, they went back a second time to make sure they hadn't missed anything. Colleen totaled up their purchases. "I must say you have lovely things for sale. Why, most of it looks practically brand new. Will you take five dollars for these sheets?" one of the ladies asked as Colleen put everything into two shopping bags. Colleen smiled to herself. A set of two hundred dollar satin sheets for five bucks. That sounds reasonable. She never liked them anyway.

By ten o'clock, Colleen needed a break. She sent Lou Jean into the yard to handle the sale. Lou Jean lasted all of ten minutes. Sticking her head in the kitchen door she yelled for Colleen. "Hey, come out here. I need help."

Colleen poured her coffee into a thermal mug and grabbed a doughnut off the table.

"That guy over there wants to buy the ugly monkey thing. You don't have a price on it," Lou Jean said pointing to the man in blue jeans and a plaid shirt standing by the tree with his arms wrapped around the heavy piece of ceramic.

"Hi, how much do you want for this?" he asked as he turned toward her.

Colleen broke into a smile. "Oh my gosh, David. What are you doing here? It's so good to see you."

"Angela called me and said you were thinking about going to London, but you were worried about Merlin. I thought maybe it would help you out if I took him home with me for a while." His eyes shifted downward as he juggled the vase in his arms. "I'm really sorry to hear about your marriage. I can't imagine anyone leaving you."

Colleen's face flushed. "I should have known better than to mention my problems to Angela." She wanted to change the subject. "Now about this monkey thing. What in the world do you want with it?"

David laughed. "Don't you think it would look great in my waiting room? You know how many of those dogs hike their legs on the desk. Maybe if I put this in the corner, it will take on an all new dimension."

"It's perfect," Colleen said. "Merlin's in the house. I better take care of my customers. Why don't you go see him and have Lou Jean find something to wrap that thing in? We wouldn't want it to get broken before it has even been christened."

David stood on the porch for a moment watching Colleen until his thoughts were interrupted by the familiar howl coming from the kitchen. He set the vase on the floor, kneeling down to greet Merlin, who jumped and twisted with delight. "Well, hi there. You sure have put on some weight," he said, rubbing Merlin's ears.

"Excuse me, that's a hell of a way to greet a lady," Lou Jean said as she came around the kitchen counter.

"Oh, I'm sorry. I didn't see you standing there. I was talking to the dog," he said as his face reddened. He held out his hand. "I'm David McFarland."

"So you're Dr. Dave. I've heard Colleen talk about you but she never told me you were so cute. Would you like a cup of coffee?"

David shook his head. "No thanks, I've had five cups already this morning. How is Colleen doing?"

"I think she is going to be okay. It's going to take a little time, but she'll be fine."

Lou Jean leaned across the counter, watching David play with Merlin. "You married?"

"Nope, never got around to it. I've found the right girl, but things just haven't worked out for me." They talked for a while. David told her all about his growing practice and asked questions about Colleen's book. He never mentioned Jeff. Lou Jean knew that David had more than a casual interest in Colleen.

"I guess I better get going. I've got a long drive home. Do you have anything I can wrap this in?" he asked.

"Ah, the ugly monkey vase. Sure let me find something. Wait! I've got an idea. Don't move." She returned seconds later, carrying a tattered tablecloth. She laid the umbrella stand on its side, rolling it into the cloth. "Now look, here's the deal. Don't let Colleen see you put this in your truck and what ever you do, don't throw this tablecloth away. When you get home, put it somewhere safe. I don't have time to tell you the whole story. All I can tell you is that this old cloth means something special to Colleen. You'll know when it's time to give it back to her." He looked confused as she gently pushed him toward the door. "Now go talk to Colleen."

"So, is the sale over?" David asked as they sat on the porch steps watching as the last two people left the yard.

"Pretty much. There may be a few stragglers, but I'm ready to close it down." Colleen looked at her watch. "It's almost noon." She struggled for something to say.

"Is there anything I can do for you, Colleen? I can stay if you need help."

"Thanks, but right now I have to get myself back into a better frame of mind. I'm committed to finishing my book. I think going to London may help. I just want to get away for a while and clear my head. She reached across and touched his arm. "I can't tell you how much it means to me that you would come all this way to get Merlin."

"I came to see you too, Colleen."

Lou Jean opened the door, handing David two sodas and a bag of potato chips. "Here, I thought maybe you guys were hungry. Lighten up! You're both standing there with long faces." David began to laugh and for a little while the tension was lifted.

They heard the rattle of the truck before it came into view. It was an ancient pick-up truck, its wooden sides bulging with yard sale finds. Furniture and bicycles had been tied to the back and packed into the passenger's side of the front seat. The old man carefully opened the door trying not to disturb the items stacked against the back window. He walked slowly around the yard looking at what was left of the sale. "I'll give you fifty dollars for the rest of this stuff," he said pulling a worn brown wallet from his back pocket.

Colleen did not hesitate. "Sold, it's all yours. Take it away."

David helped him carry the remaining boxes and few pieces of furniture to the driveway.

"Well, that's a stroke of luck," Colleen said as she began to fold up the tables and take down the clothesline. I am so glad it's all gone. I wish I could ask you to stay, David, but Lou Jean and I are leaving tonight."

"That's okay. I have to get back to Stockbridge. It was good seeing you again." David whistled for Merlin. "Come on, boy, we're going to take a long ride." Merlin bounded down the steps and into the waiting truck. Colleen reached inside the window and hugged his neck, the tears running down her face. "I didn't realize that saying goodbye would be this difficult." She nuzzled Merlin's face. "You be a good boy. I'm going to miss you so much."

David kissed Colleen on the forehead. "I'll take good care of him for you. Come back soon." As he started the engine, David wondered if there would ever be a time when Colleen would miss him that much. Merlin's head popped out of the open window. His soulful eyes looked at Colleen as he waited for her to climb in next to him. She watched until the truck turned the corner, half expecting Merlin to come running back to her.

YARD SALE

By five o'clock the house was empty. Colleen swept the kitchen floor and set the rest of her luggage by the back door. She had phoned the post office to stop her mail and finally made the dreaded call to tell Frank goodbye.

"What are you looking for?" Lou Jean asked as she jangled the door keys in her hand.

"I had my grandmother's tablecloth in a white box. Now I can't find it. I was going to send it home to my mother for safekeeping." Colleen began to open her suitcase. "I may have put it in here by mistake."

"We don't have time for that right now. It's probably in one of those boxes we took over to the storage unit. I'll have the manager check into it for you," Lou Jean said, hoping to distract Colleen from looking any further.

"Just let me look one more time."

The taxi driver began to honk his horn. Lou Jean grabbed Colleen by the hand. "Come on, we have to go."

Chapter Forty-Eight

Colleen wiped the steam off the window with the sleeve of her sweater. She sat down on the window seat with her hot cup of tea. She watched the afternoon Christmas shoppers hurrying from shop to shop in the frigid rain. Their umbrellas reminded her of an ocean of black mushrooms. After four months she was used to the daily pattern of the crowded streets outside her door. What she hadn't gotten used to was the cold biting rain and gray skies that were almost a daily occurrence in London. She missed the sunshine and the blue skies of the Midwest with its warm autumn air and the beautiful fall colors of the trees. Yet nothing could compare with the sight of Westminster Abbey, or the rolling hills and castles of England. Colleen pulled her sweater closer to her body. Shivering, she padded across the thick wool carpet, checking the thermostat before she sat back down at her computer. She loved Lou Jean's apartment instantly. It was an expensive piece of real estate that Lou Jean had claimed for herself. Removing the walls between two small loft apartments she had turned the apartment into one of the largest in the area. Colleen had expected a carnival of colors and shapes, only to find that Lou Jean had tastefully decorated all the rooms. There were large paintings and over stuffed velvet furniture. When Colleen expressed her surprise, Lou Jean laughed.

"Yes, it's a pretty great place. It's not as homey as the farm, but it serves my needs. Even the weather sometimes lends itself to my moods. I love the rainy days when I can just stay indoors, light a fire and lay around and read." It was a side of Lou Jean that Colleen had never seen.

Lou Jean took Colleen around the neighborhood. She introduced her to the doorman, Jack, and her neighbor, Deirdre. A few days after arriving in London, Lou Jean had repacked to leave on another business trip. Picking up her raincoat and briefcase, she showed Colleen the list on the refrigerator. "I've written down some information you'll be needing.

Here's the number for the grocer, the cleaners, and the pharmacy. Deirdre will help you out with everything else. I want you to enjoy your stay and get some work done. Take my bankcard. You can use it if you need money," she said, tossing the card onto the desk.

Colleen picked the card up and held it out to Lou Jean. "I just can't take any more money from you. I still have some money left from the sale."

"Look, kiddo, I expect every penny back after you publish your manuscript. I have it all written down in my little black book. You can go home any time you want, but I think it would be a good idea to stay at least for a little while."

"When will you be back?" Colleen asked.

"Who knows? I have to go to Greece for a while, then some place in Germany. I'll let you know as soon as I find out something. Take care of yourself." Lou Jean hugged Colleen and picked up her suitcase. "By the way, I mailed your divorce papers today."

She had not expected to be left alone in London so soon after her arrival. After a month she was bored and tired of working on her manuscript day and night. Deirdre helped her find a job in small bookstore just blocks away from the apartment. She worked part time selling cups of steaming tea and newspapers to the patrons who came daily to sit at the small tables and talk. Occasionally, she would sell a book, but mostly they came to browse and stand in the narrow aisles reading the new arrivals. Some day she hoped it would be her book they would be reading. Colleen began to fall into a routine that was calming and left her little time to feel sorry for herself. Her goal now was to finish her book and be home in time for Christmas. Working at the store seemed to give her new energy and enthusiasm. Rising early each morning she would make herself a pot of coffee and two slices of toast. She would then go immediately to the computer, writing until late afternoon. At times the words seemed to flow from her mind   Other times, she would find herself struggling for hours with a word or a sentence trying to capture the right mood or feeling. Just thinking about Jeff for a moment or two would give her enough emotion to fill a page. She had to remember that this was Grandma Grace's story, not hers, but she was sure the pain and hurt were the same for both of them. Her nights were spent editing and making corrections on what she had written that day. When her eyes grew so tired that the pages blurred, she would shower and climb under the soft quilts of Lou Jean's high bed. She had grown used to her solitude and the comfort of the apartment.

"When are you coming home? It's only five days until Christmas." Anna interrupted the conversation between Angela and Colleen as she listened on the extension. "You sound hoarse. Are you all right?"

"I'm okay. I have to mail my manuscript to Ann Hardin tomorrow. I've already booked a flight. My throat has been a little scratchy since yesterday. I think I'm just coming down with a cold." Colleen rubbed her aching head.

"You take care of yourself. We are all so anxious to see you. It's beginning to snow. I think it's going to be a white Christmas," Anna said.

The manuscript was finally finished. Colleen sighed as she edited the last few pages. Leaning back in her chair, she felt a mixture of sadness and relief that the characters that had lived in her head for the past year were now put to rest inside the pages of her book. She would never forget them. She popped another cough lozenge into her mouth and sealed the large manila envelope that would carry the manuscript to Ann Hardin's office. Putting on her coat and gloves, she walked the three blocks to the post office. The temperature had dropped sharply. By the time she returned home, her feet were stinging from the icy water that had seeped through her shoes and her head was throbbing with pain. She needed to pack, but she was just too tired.

In the morning, Colleen called Deirdre's apartment, hoping to catch her home, but there was no answer. She made herself a cup of tea and went back to bed. Her throat was so sore she could hardly swallow, wincing with each gulp of tea. She sank down into the blankets, but her body would not stop shaking. Falling back to sleep, she awoke later that afternoon bathed in dampness with fever raging in her body. Reaching for the telephone she tried Deirdre's number again. She answered on the second ring. "Deirdre, I'm sick. Can you come over?" she whispered into the phone.

Deirdre opened the door to the bedroom and softly called Colleen's name. "I'm here now," she said. "My goodness it's freezing in here and you're burning up. You need a doctor, and quick. How long have you been like this?" Deirdre asked carrying a cold cloth from the bathroom.

It took hours before a stodgy old man carrying a worn black bag came to the apartment. He was one of the few doctors who still made house calls. He sat on the edge of the bed taking her pulse while the thermometer dangled from her lower lip. He looked over his glasses. "Put it in your mouth." A few minutes passed before he made the simple statement. "You need to go to the hospital. Your fever is dangerously high and you are dehydrated." Looking at Deirdre he asked, "Can you drive her or shall I call someone?"

Colleen turned to Deirdre. Hardly able to speak, she asked, "Will you call my mom?"

Anna was frantic after talking to Deirdre. She wanted to catch the first plane out of Kansas. "I'm her mother. I should be there with her," she said to Angela on the phone. "I haven't been able to get much information from the hospital. Only that Colleen has some kind of virus and is in stable condition."

"Hold on, Mom. I have someone here who wants to talk to you," Angela said.

"Mrs. Holloway, it's David. I know you are worried and upset, but why don't you let me go to London to check on Colleen. It's almost Christmas. You have grandchildren and family to look after. I promise I will call you the minute I get there."

"Thank you, David. I don't know if I could sit still long enough on that plane to make it to London. I am so worried about her. We'll be waiting for your call," Anna said in a relieved voice.

Two days passed before Colleen finally felt well enough to sit up in her hospital bed. The nurse fluffed her pillow and pulled the sheet tightly over her body. "You look a little better today. Your temperature has finally returned to normal. I have instructions to remove your I.V." She gently pulled out the needle, putting a small piece of tape on Colleen's hand.

Colleen opened her eyes, the single overhead light shone in her face. "What time is it? Better still, what day is it?"

The nurse smiled. "It's Tuesday, Christmas Eve, and you have a visitor. He's been here all night. So let's get you sitting up."

Colleen touched her hair, feeling the tangles stick in her fingers. Her mouth was dry. She needed a drink of water and a toothbrush.

"Hi, sleepy head how are you?" David said, standing at the end of the bed with a bouquet of red roses in his hand.

Deirdre drove them home from the hospital. Colleen still could not believe that David had come all this way to check on her. He helped

Colleen into the apartment and lifted her into the high bed. "Can I get you something to eat or drink?" he asked.

"There is probably nothing here. I haven't shopped in days." She lay back against the pillow and closed her eyes. "I'm really tired. I'd like to sleep for a little while." It was evening when she awoke. Turning over, she could smell something wonderful coming from the kitchen. She must be getting better. She was hungry.

He carried the tray into the bedroom and set it carefully on the nightstand. "I found a little store a couple of blocks down the street. They were already closed but took pity on me and opened their door, since it was Christmas Eve. I have eggs and bacon and a chicken I can cook tomorrow for Christmas dinner."

Colleen showered and put on clean pajamas. Curling up in front of the fire, David covered her with a blanket and handed her a steaming mug of hot chocolate. He sat down on the floor in front of the couch. "This is nice. Lou Jean has a great apartment. By the way, does she know you have been sick?"

Colleen shook her head, "No. She has come to my rescue so many times I just couldn't bother her again." She touched the back of his head, letting her hand rest on his shoulder. "I can't thank you enough for coming all this way to help me, especially on Christmas Eve."

"I have something for you." Rising from the floor, he rifled through his duffle bag and pulled out a package wrapped in bright red and gold paper. "Open it," he said, smiling in anticipation.

Colleen untied the ribbon and lifted out a framed photograph of Merlin in a Santa hat. "Oh, this is so cute. How in the world did you ever get him to sit still?"

"Bribery. I gave him a ham bone after I took the picture. There's something else in the box."

She pulled back the gold tissue paper and opened the small velvet box. She held the charm up to the lamp, watching the light dance off of the little dog dangling from a silver chain. "Thank you. It's lovely," she said as she put the chain around her neck. Lifting her hair, David secured the clasp.

"Listen," Colleen said. "Do you hear the bells? Midnight mass is starting at St. Paul's Cathedral. Merry Christmas, David."

They spent Christmas day watching old movies on television. David reminisced about the summer she worked for him and she finally told him all about Jeff. It was difficult for her to talk about him, especially to David. "It really doesn't make too much sense. I haven't sorted everything out yet. He turned out to be completely different from what I thought he was. He was a liar and a fraud, and it's still tough to think I was so gullible."

David shook his head. "I'm so sorry he hurt you, Colleen. You look tired, maybe you should go back to bed."

She stayed in bed while David baked the chicken and boiled the last two potatoes. Deirdre gave him a box of instant pudding that he prepared and decorated with peppermint candies. They ate in front of the fire. The mantle had been decorated with the red and gold paper from Colleen's present. She sat quietly studying his face as he spooned the pudding into his mouth.

"Why are you really here, David?" she blurted out.

The question caught him off guard. He rose from the floor and began gathering the dishes. "I came because you were sick and I hoped my being here would make you see how much I really care for you."

"I can't make you any promises right now, David. I need a little more time to heal, but I am so very glad you came." She stood up. Putting her arms around him, she kissed his cheek.

"I know that you still need time, Colleen, but I'm willing to wait."

The next day Colleen was feeling better and it was time for David to leave. "Are you sure you have everything?" Colleen looked around the room. "Be sure and tell my mother that I am fine and I will be home as soon as I can."

"Now remember what the doctor said. Stay in bed at least three more days and you should be good as new."

"Yes sir. Is there anything else, sir?" she said laughing.

"Only this." David pulled her into his arms and kissed her, a soft, lingering kiss that kept her in his arms until he reached for his duffel bag and opened the door. Colleen watched as he headed for the elevator, wishing that he wasn't leaving so soon.

Colleen sat at her typewriter staring at a blank piece of paper. She had tried for days to start her second manuscript, but the words seemed to escape her. The ringing of the telephone interrupted her thoughts.

"Get down here quick. The Literary Guild is running a program on the telly today and Ann Hardin is one of the guests. She's going to talk about the new books coming out this year. Everyone is here waiting for you," Deirdre said all excited.

The store was crowded with all of the regulars and a few curious people interested in what was causing such a stir. They sat at the tables and on the low leather couches, their eyes riveted to the television set mounted on the wall.

Colleen stood behind the counter, tapping her fingers nervously as she watched the host introduce Ann Hardin. Ann breezed onto the stage in her usual manner, taking a seat next to the host. She talked for a moment about herself and then began her critique of the new books coming out in the spring. Ann was telling the host about an exciting new author who would surely make her mark in the literary scene with the advent of her first novel in fiction. Colleen screamed when her name was mentioned. A cheer went up in the bookstore. The owner asked for a signed copy to put in his window as soon as possible. The realization that her novel was actually going to be published suddenly made her queasy. "Well, Grandma, I hope you like it," she said to herself. "You're the one who made it all possible."

"I think this is what you have been waiting for, Miss Colleen," Jack said as he carried the box into the apartment. He pried open the lid and Colleen gently removed the packing material. Picking up one of the books, she ran her hand across the smooth cover and the raised letters that said, "Return to Ternberry" written by Colleen Holloway.

The call she was waiting for finally came. "Colleen, it's Ann Hardin. I have arranged a book signing tour for you. When can you leave London?"

Several days later Colleen looked around the apartment to make sure she had left everything in order. Leaving two copies of her novel on the desk, she wrote a short note to Lou Jean.

"Thank you so much for everything. You have been a Godsend to me. Please take a copy of my book to the bookstore and please...take time to read the other one yourself. Love, Colleen."

Colleen stepped into the waiting taxi that would take her to the airport. She looked back at Lou Jean's apartment and wondered if she would ever return to London. It had been a long emotional journey since she arrived here, but she had resolved her inner conflicts and the memories of Jeff no longer haunted her.

"Where are you?" Lou Jean asked. "This connection is really crappy."

"I'm somewhere in Minnesota. St. Paul, I think," Colleen answered. "It's hard to keep track. I've been in ten cities in ten days."

"I started reading your book the day I got home. I couldn't put the damn thing down. Seriously, it's very good. It made me cry, and that's hard to do. I want to know about this place in the book called Ternberry. Is that a real place?" Lou Jean asked.

"Yes it is. I did some research before I started the book. Colleen tried to talk over the static on the telephone. "It's a point of land just outside of Port Arthur, Massachusetts. My great grandparents named it. I was told it has been turned into a bed and breakfast. Grandma Grace and Hans tried to find it one time. She was really disappointed when they couldn't locate it."

"It sounds like someplace I'd like to visit," Lou Jean said. "Maybe I'll look into it."

Chapter Forty-Nine

Colleen ended the book tour after three months of traveling. Ann Hardin said it was very successful. With a sigh of relief, Colleen caught the first plane to Kansas.

"I can't believe how your children have grown," she said to Angela as they greeted her at the airport. "Aaron is as tall as you."

"I'm almost twelve, Aunt Colleen," he replied with a smile, revealing the silver braces on his teeth.

"Mom has been fussing around all day. You would think the Queen is coming to visit instead of her own daughter. You look good, Colleen, I like your suit." Angela looked down at her own faded jeans, feeling a little bit out of place.

The family sat down for dinner at the long dining room table. There were so many questions. Adam wanted to know if she was famous. Jared was curious about living in London and Grandma Grace asked three times for someone to please pass the mashed potatoes. "I would really like to see David and Merlin, too." Colleen said. "I miss him." She looked up shyly to see her father grinning. "I mean Merlin of course."

Angela handed her grandmother the potatoes. "David is not here right now. He has gone backpacking out west for a few weeks. He took Merlin with him. If you took the time to keep in touch with him you would have known that. This is the second time you came home and didn't bother to let him know that you were coming." Anna changed the subject sensing a tension between Colleen and Angela.

Colleen stood on the front porch drinking her coffee while her father sat next to her on the railing. He put his arm around her shoulder. "I'm proud of you for writing that book. I sure felt sorry for the lady that was supposed to be your grandmother. I can't believe she took so much guff off of that husband of hers. She should have kicked him out long before he died."

"Thanks, Dad. I'm glad you read it," Colleen said, leaning against her father. "I was more worried about my family liking the book than any old dumb literary critic. Why do I feel so uncomfortable being here? It seems like everyone is walking on eggshells around me. I know Mom wants to ask me about Jeff, but it's like she is afraid to and somehow I get the feeling that Angela is mad at me."

"Well, a lot has happened to you. You've been away a long time and our life just kept moving on at the same pace as always. You just need to get back in the old groove. It's time to have some fun. Go shopping with your Mom, feed the chickens. Maybe you should spend some time with your sister and get to know her kids."

After two weeks on the farm, Colleen began to write the beginning of her second novel. She had slept as much as she wanted and eaten far too much. Her mother told her that Grandma Grace was becoming increasingly forgetful, sometimes confusing the children's names and constantly losing things. She still loved to cook but was always leaving out half of the ingredients. "I guess at eighty-three she is entitled to be a little forgetful," Anna said. "By the way, Lou Jean should be here soon. She is plotting something, but I don't know what it is. She talked to your father on the phone the other night for about twenty minutes."

The answer to Lou Jean's surprise came early the next morning as they all slept. Colleen was the first one out of bed after hearing the loud honking of a horn. She looked out the window to see the morning sunlight bouncing off the roof of the shiny RV parked in the yard. Earl went to the front door, still putting on his shirt. "Good Lord, what are you trying to do, wake the dead? Why can't you just knock on the door like a normal person?"

"Because I'm not normal, that's why," Lou Jean said as she bounced down the steps of the RV. "Where is everybody? We're going on a road trip," Lou Jean yelled as Anna appeared on the porch followed by Grandma Grace still wrapped in her robe.

"Lou Jean Bailey, have you lost your senses? Do you have any idea what time it is, and what in the world are you talking about, a road trip?" Anna said as she came across the yard, her arms open to give Lou Jean a hug.

"I got the idea from Colleen. I read about this place in her book. I did some searching and I found it. I thought it would be a great idea if we took Grandma Grace and went to Massachusetts for a couple of days." Lou Jean waved to Grace. "Hey, Grandma, you want to go to Ternberry?"

Anna turned to Earl. "You knew about this, didn't you? That's why you wouldn't tell me what you and Lou Jean were discussing."

Earl threw up his hands. "What can I say? She threatened me."

Colleen stood at the open window smiling, wondering how Lou Jean would ever convince her mother and grandmother to go to Massachusetts in an RV. If anyone could do it, she could.

Lou Jean spread the map out on the kitchen table. "Here it is, right here," she said, pointing to a small red circle in the corner of the map. "At first I was going to send you all airline tickets but I was afraid you wouldn't use them. I decided I had better come get you myself. It took me three days to learn how to park that damn RV without running over the sidewalk. Now I've already talked to Angela and she wants to go with us. All you need to do is pack and we can leave this afternoon. I figure it should take us about a day and a half to get there."

Colleen listened as Lou Jean made every effort to convince Anna to make the trip. When everything else failed, she tried to make Anna feel guilty that she was denying her mother the privilege of seeing Ternberry one more time.

"Mother, do you really want to go to Ternberry? You know it's a very long ride," Anna said turning to Grace.

"I would love to go, Anna," Grace replied. "I'll go upstairs and start packing."

Luggage was strewn across the front porch as Earl padded back and forth storing what he could in the side compartment. Colleen and Angela waited on the porch as Anna fretted over the list she had prepared. "Now, do you have any questions about what I have written down?" she said to Earl as she pointed to the plants by the porch that needed to be watered. "I just can't believe we're doing this. I wish I would have had more notice."

"Why? So you could worry some more? Let's just go and have a good time," Lou Jean said as she picked up the cooler.

"Is that all you think I do is worry? Well frankly, I'm getting a little tired of you arranging my life. You've done this to me ever since we were kids. It's 'Anna do this' and 'Anna do that.' Maybe I don't want to go to Massachusetts. Did everyone know about this trip except me?" Anna folded her arms across her chest as Colleen and Earl looked on, not saying a word.

Lou Jean put the cooler down and lit a cigarette. "Fine, don't go. I should have known better than to think you would do anything spontaneous. I'm sorry I pissed you off. If I recall when we were young, you were the one that organized my life. All I wanted to do was go to high school and you kept nagging me about college and how many times have I had to put up with you correcting my English and bugging me about smoking?" Lou Jean threw her bag down beside the RV. "Besides you do worry about everything."

"Well, somebody has to. I'm sure you don't," Anna said, shaking her finger at Lou Jean.

"Don't you think I would have liked to go to college? I had to stay behind while you went off and became a big shot lawyer running all over the world. Then you take Colleen off to London and leave her there alone. She should have been at home."

"Wait a minute, Mom, that's not fair," Colleen said. "It wasn't Lou Jean's fault. You knew when I went away to college that I probably wouldn't come back here to live. What in the world would I have done in Stockbridge?"

Angela interrupted. "What's wrong with Stockbridge? Are we too much of a hick town for you? All I hear is Colleen this and Colleen that. I guess your life is too important to stay here. Let me tell you something, little sister, mom was pretty upset when you just bopped off to New York to marry Jeff. You didn't even ask them to come to the wedding. None of us know why you got divorced and what about David? He's still mooning around asking about you all the time."

Colleen stood her ground. "My private life is none of your business, and while we're on the subject, who do you think took a back seat while you were pulling all your stupid stunts when you were young? And who do you think sat with Mom while she cried for hours when you got married at eighteen instead of going to college? It was me," Colleen said angrily. "Besides, you have treated me like crap ever since I came home." She stomped across the porch and sat down on the swing. "I don't even know why you're taking this trip if you dislike me so much."

Angela followed Colleen on to the porch. "Did I ever say I didn't like you? That must be your imagination. It's just that you could come home once in a while and help out. Mom never gets a break. Instead you come home and get your name in the local paper and people stop you on the street wanting you to sign their book. Big deal. Try raising four kids."

"Hey that was your choice," Colleen said, her face just inches away from her sister.

"Well this is just great. Now see what you've done?" Anna said, turning to Lou Jean.

"Me! What the hell did I do? All I did was show up, but now I guess it's time for me to make an exit. I just want to tell you one thing, Anna Holloway. You are more important to me than any damn trip. I would gladly trade everything I own in a heartbeat for what you have with Earl and your family. It was a stupid idea." She put her head down to hide the tears that had welled up in her eyes.

Anna ran down the stairs throwing her arms around Lou Jean. "I'm sorry too. I guess I was jealous that you showed up here like you haven't a care in the world, but you're right, I wouldn't give up one day of my life with my family. Now let's get the rest of this stuff in the RV. You will promise me you won't smoke on the trip?"

Lou Jean rolled her eyes. "Yes, Mother."

Earl let out a sigh. Watching the four women go at it, he decided a few minutes more and he would get out the hose.

"Are you finished arguing?" Grandma Grace asked as she stood at the door of the RV, her purse across her arm. "Are we going to take this trip or not? If we wait much longer I'll have to go to the bathroom again."

Earl scooped Grace up in his arms and sat her inside the door. "Have a good trip."

Lou Jean drove as Anna sat next to her in the front seat. Colleen could hear the low murmur of their conversation, with occasional outbursts of laughter as the two friends connected once more. Colleen leaned over to check on Grandma Grace, who had fallen asleep on the small couch. She looked over at Angela who sat staring out the window. "Can I sit here?" she asked, pointing to the captain's chair next to Angela.

She shrugged, "If you want."

"Angela, I have an idea. I'm going to be home for a while so maybe I can watch Grandma while Mom and Dad take a vacation. I can watch the boys if you and Jared want to go away."

Angela snickered. "I can just see you watching those four Indians. The only one who can handle them is Jared. He has the patience of a saint."

"You're lucky to have him," Colleen said, watching the light and dark shadows fall across the window.

"I'm thinking about taking some college courses this fall at the junior college," Angela said, her voice softened. "I'd like to get a teaching degree and when all the kids are in school I could get a job."

Colleen nodded, "I think you would do very well in college. You were always smarter than me." She reached across the seat and took her sister's hand. "I'd like to tell you what's been going on in my life. That is, if you want to listen."

When they stopped for lunch the next day, Lou Jean once more brought out the map. "We're almost there. Now, I don't want to step on any one's toes, but I rented three rooms at the inn. It's their slow season, so it shouldn't be too crowded. Is that okay with everybody?"

Anna smiled. "Okay. I get the point. It's fine. What else do you have planned for us?"

Lou Jean positioned Grace in the front seat of the RV as they approached the long winding road leading to the point. "Do you remember any of this, Grandma Grace?"

It had been over fifty years since Grace traveled this road, but the first sight of the ocean breaking through the trees suddenly caused her to sit up straight. There were a few houses along the road now and a billboard advertising cottages for rent, but the tall pines still reminded her of that time so long ago when she first came to Ternberry. As the afternoon sun slipped behind the clouds, Lou Jean turned the RV into the gate that announced that they were now at the Seaside Bed & Breakfast.

Anna sucked in her breath as she saw the large white house with the blue shutters sitting on top of the gentle slope. Below the dunes the tranquil surface of the sea reflected the golden hue of the sun against the sandy beach. "Oh, Mom, it's beautiful. It's just like you described it to Colleen."

"Can I get out here?" Grace asked as Lou Jean maneuvered the RV around the circular drive leading to the front door. "I just want to take a little walk."

YARD SALE

Lou Jean opened the door and Grace stepped out, letting the soft salty air gently caress her face. She walked carefully between the clumps of sea oats and made her way to the edge of the bluff. They sat in the RV watching her as she stood with her back to them, looking down at the beach.

"Do you think she is all right?" Colleen asked Anna.

"She'll be fine. It's been a long time. I think she is trying to remember everything she can about this place."

Grace peered over the edge of the bluff and looked down at the large brown rock where she had sat with Colin while he played in the pools of water. She remembered listening to his laughter as the large waves crashed against the rock, washing across his tiny feet. Grace slowly bent down and picked up a seashell. It was just like one of the rainbow colored shells that she and Colin collected and took back to the house to show Agnes and Joseph. Martin always worried that he would put them in his mouth, but Colin would hold them tightly in his chubby fingers and throw them across the room. It was only when Henry was home that she had to leave the bucket on the front porch. She put the shell in her pocket and slowly walked up the path to the house. She hoped Henry wasn't home yet. She wanted to take a nap in the big white bed all by herself.

The house had remained much the same as Grace remembered it, except for a few new pieces of furniture and the expanded dining room. The owners were pleasant and told them to make themselves at home. Grace settled into the room she once shared with Henry. She opened the curtains and stood looking out to the sea. She wondered when Joseph and Agnes would be home. Martin must have taken them to Boston. She hadn't seen them in quite a while.

Colleen stood on the edge of the water watching the waves creep up the shore to meet her. Every once in a while an errant spray would cause her to jump backward.

"What are you doing out here all alone, sweetie? Are you unpacked already?" her mother asked.

"Yes. I was just taking in this awesome sight. What is it about the ocean that's so fascinating?"

"I guess partly because at times it's so calm and mysterious. No one really knows what is going on beneath the surface. It is as unforgiving as it is beautiful. Kind of like life."

"My goodness, Mom, you're getting pretty profound," Colleen said. "Let's take a walk."

Anna pulled off her shoes and stepped into the water. They walked along the beach until Ternberry was completely out of sight. It took that long for Colleen to tell Anna all about Jeff.

"We'd better start back. It's getting dark," Anna took her daughter's hand.

The next three days passed quickly. Grandma Grace slept late and stayed in her room during the warm daylight hours, while Angela and Colleen managed to get sunburned laying on the beach. Lou Jean and Anna sat on the porch and talked for hours. It was a peaceful time filled with laughter and a renewal of friendships.

"Where did Angela disappear to after dinner?" Lou Jean asked, lighting a cigarette and settling down in the porch swing next to Anna.

"She went upstairs to call Jared. She said she wants to make sure everything is okay at home. I think she is missing him and the kids," Anna said, waving the smoke away from her face.

"What should we do to celebrate our last night here?" Lou Jean asked. "How about I make a jug of margaritas and we can go sit on the beach."

Anna laughed. "Sounds good to me."

Lou Jean spread the blanket on the sand, picking up the small rocks that caused turtle like bumps in the material. She sat down and poured the green liquid into her glass. "A toast to my best friend who I love like a sister. Actually, better than a sister."

"Thanks, I love you too," Anna said raising her glass.

"You know, Anna, I could get real used to this life." Lou Jean lay back on the blanket with her glass balanced on her stomach. "I'm thinking of buying this place."

"You're what! Why in the world would you want to do such a thing? I'm sure I won't get an answer that makes any sense at all," Anna said, shaking her head in amazement.

"I actually like it here. You'll go home tomorrow and your life will be the same as if it never missed a heartbeat. I need a safe place. A real honest to goodness home." Lou Jean sat up and took a long drink from her margarita. "I have learned a lot about slowing since we've been here. I'm proud of all my accomplishments, but I'm tired of hotel rooms and flying off to London. If I make the owners a good enough offer, maybe they will sell it to me. They already told me that they hate the cold winters here. You and Earl could come here to live for a while. He could tinker all he wants on this old house and he wouldn't have to worry himself sick about tornados."

"You're serious, aren't you? I can see that look in your eye. You know Earl would never leave Kansas, and I could never leave my grandchildren. What are you going to do about your law practice?"

Lou Jean wriggled around on the blanket trying to get comfortable. "I can change to personal injury law and make more money than I'm making now with half the effort."

"As much as I want to say that this is just another of your wild schemes, I think it may be good for you," Anna said. "Who knows, maybe with all the calm and solitude you may even give up smoking."

They lay on the blanket looking up at the cloudless sky, which was occasionally interrupted by the bright colors of a three-cornered parasail. Lou Jean pointed to a man tethered to the boat by a long rope. His legs dangled in the air from the small seat of the kite. "I have always wanted to try that," Lou Jean said. Anna closed her eyes and smiled.

Colleen and Angela ran across the warm sand with their shoes in their hands. "Move over," Angela said as she settled herself next to Lou Jean. "Hand me that jug."

"Did anyone check on Grandma?" Anna asked.

Colleen poured herself a margarita. "She's sound asleep. I was going to wake her and ask her to join us but she looked too comfortable."

Lou Jean sat up, leaning on one elbow, and watched a jogger running down the beach. "I wonder if he lives around here? He's not too shabby looking."

"No, he isn't considering he's about half your age," Anna said, laughing.

"So what. That is what makes it interesting."

Angela took a sip of her drink, "How many men have you been with, Aunt Lou Jean?"

"What is this, true confessions? To be honest, I'd have to sit down and count. What about you?"

Anna sat up. "Now, I don't need to hear this sort of conversation about my children."

"You know Jared is my one and only. We used to make love in Colleen's room when Mom and Dad were in town," Angela said, giggling.

"My room, how come?" Colleen asked. "I sure hope you changed the sheets."

"Because you had the front bedroom and we could see when the truck was coming down the road." She giggled again. "Come on, baby sister, time for you to fess up. What happened when David came to London and you two were all alone?"

"Nothing at all. But one time in college my roommate came home early and this guy named Richard had to sleep under my bed half the night."

"That's it. I don't want to hear another word about sex from any of you," Anna said.

"Did I ever tell you girls about your mother's red dress?" Lou Jean looked over at Anna.

Anna rolled over on top of Lou Jean, putting her hand over her mouth. "Lou Jean Bailey, you say one more word and I am going to dump this drink right on your head." Lou Jean roared with laugher, as Anna stood up. "Not another word out of any of you. I'm going to bed." Anna grabbed her shoes and headed toward the house.

"I hope Mom wasn't shocked. I have no idea why I said that. She probably thinks we're terrible," Colleen said helping Lou Jean fold up the blanket.

"You must be kidding. Do you think your mother didn't know about Richard? She said every time you called home, you mentioned his name. She knew something was going on. And she knew about you, too, Angela. She was worried you would get pregnant before you got married." Lou Jean lit a cigarette and looked up at the shower of stars that had suddenly burst into the evening sky. She put her arms around Colleen and Angela and kissed them both.

As they walked up the path, Angela shook her head. "God, I can't believe I am going to have to go through all of this with my kids. I'm going to go crazy."

YARD SALE

Lou Jean turned to see the jogger moving back down the beach. "Maybe I better go back and make sure we didn't forget anything. I'll see you girls in the morning."

In the early morning hours during those few minutes before she was fully awake, Grace dreamed she was still living in the apartment above the bakery. She could hear Hans singing his German lullabies and smell the aroma of bakery goods. He waved to her. "Good morning, Grace dear. Come, I have made fresh bread." Grace shook her head. "I can't come Hans. I am too tired." She could see his smiling face as his image faded off into the distance.

Colleen sat on the edge of the bed, listening to her grandmother's rhythmic breathing. Grace turned, coughing slightly. She opened her eyes. "Is it morning already? It seems like I just went to sleep. I was having a good dream."

"I'm sorry if I woke you, Grandma, but we have to be leaving soon."

Grace sighed. "You know what I wish Colleen? I wish we could stay here for a while longer. I still have some old memories I need to visit."

Colleen helped her grandmother out of bed. "Maybe we'll come back some day when we can stay longer."

"I want to thank you for writing this," Grace said, as she pulled Colleen's book out from under her pillow. You know, Colleen, I don't think too much about the hard times anymore. I have a lot of wonderful memories. I used to have plenty of regrets, but now they are just moments in my life strung together with all the good times." Grace walked to the window and opened the white shutters. She watched the surf send sprays of water over the big brown rock. "I remember years ago, Dr. Vargas told me that each experience in life is like a precious bead on a fragile thread. Sometimes we make bad choices and the thread breaks. Throughout our lives we lose a couple of beads but we still have a beautiful necklace. He said sometimes we have to buy a stronger string. I never knew quite what he meant. He was always talking in metaphors. Much later in my life it made sense to me. When I met Hans, the bad memories seemed to find their place in the back of my mind like the broken beads that rolled under the couch. I've added a lot of bright shiny beads to my life, and your book is like the clasp that holds it all together. Grace took Colleen's hand and held it tightly. "Fill your necklace with priceless pearls. Find someone to love you and make you happy. I want to hear you laugh again."

Colleen put her arms around her grandmother. "I love you so much, Grandma."

Colleen helped Grandma Grace pack her suitcase and held her arms as they went down the steps into the waiting RV. Grace turned and looked up at the house. Her eyes traveled to the catwalk. She thought she could see someone holding a baby waving to her. She smiled to herself. "Goodbye Ternberry."

At the end of the driveway, Lou Jean stopped the RV and got out. Using her lipstick, she wrote on the Seaside Bed and Breakfast sign. "Future home of L.J. Bailey."

Anna stretched and yawned. She was anxious to get home. The rain had slowed them down but now they were on the last stretch of long highway before turning into the road leading to Stockbridge. She wondered if Earl had watered her plants and if he had fixed himself proper meals while she was gone. She missed him, but pretended to Lou Jean that she was glad to get away for a while. Somehow she knew she hadn't fooled her friend.

"Drop me off first, okay?" Angela said. "Thanks for taking me along. I had a good time." She kissed Colleen on the cheek. "Bye, baby sister. See you soon." She was already standing by the door of the RV.

"Let me at least stop this thing before you jump out," Lou Jean said, turning the trailer into the yard.

"Hi guys, I'm home!" Angela yelled as she gathered Addie up into her arms. "Well, baby girl, you have two different shoes on." Jared hugged her as the boys danced around asking what she brought them.

Colleen sat in the RV watching her sister. The trip had been good for them. She felt closer to Angela than she had in a long time and maybe even a little envious.

As they made the turn into the last gravel road, Anna counted the seventeen poles leading to her home and her waiting husband.

"Well, I better get going. I have to get this thing back to the dealership before the salesman thinks I really want to buy it. I'll see you all real soon." Lou Jean waved to Earl as she pulled out of the driveway.

"I have a surprise for you," Earl said, putting his arms around Anna and Grace as they walked into the house.

"Oh my gosh, air-conditioning! Colleen, come quick, we have air-conditioning!" Anna screamed.

Two weeks after their trip to Ternberry Anna received a call from Lou Jean telling her that she had indeed purchased the property. She was on her way to London to close out her apartment, and then it was back to Massachusetts to settle into her new life. Earl laughed when Anna told him what Lou Jean had done. "Well, I guess I know where we will be spending our summers."

Chapter Fifty

Earl always went to bed before Anna. He called her a night owl. She liked the stillness of the house, interrupted only by the rhythmic ticking of the grandfather clock in the hallway. She would sit alone reading until her eyes grew tired. Anna would then turn off all the downstairs lights and walk to the front door. Pulling back the curtain, she would look out into the yard. Tonight a full moon illuminated the farm. She had stood at this door many times when the girls were young, waiting to hear the sound of tires on the gravel road and see the headlights turning into the gate. Knowing they were home safe, she would hurry upstairs so that they would not see her. They always knew she was there, hearing her footsteps as she tried to quietly tiptoe across the squeaking floor. As she walked up the stairs on this evening, she straightened a picture in her gallery of loving faces lining the wall. Anna passed her mother's room. A small stream of light filtered out from under the door. Knocking softly, she turned the knob.

"What's the matter, Mom? Are you having trouble sleeping?"

"I just needed to say my rosary. I haven't done this in quite a while and I have so much to be thankful for. Every now and then you have to let God know you're still thinking about him," Grace said in her melodic voice. "I love you, Anna. Now go to bed."

"I love you, too. Sleep well. I'll see you in the morning," Anna whispered as she blew her mother a kiss.

She climbed into bed and laid her head on Earl's back. The warmth of his body made her feel safe. She could hear his snoring that had kept her awake many nights. Tonight it seemed to lull her to sleep.

Anna poured his coffee as they sat at the breakfast table talking just like they had every morning for the past thirty years. The red-checkered tablecloth had been replaced many times. She always managed to find a new one just like the original that was on the table the first time she came to the farm. They would talk about the weather or the grandchildren or about something Earl had read in the paper. It was their time together. Earl would pour a second cup of coffee into his thermal mug, kiss her on the cheek and go out to the tool shop to start his day. Anna would then go upstairs and make sure her mother was up. Grace hated to sleep late. They would have biscuits and jelly together at the same little table and plan out their day.

Today Grace would not wake up. She lay on her side, her pink curlers tucked under her hair net. When Anna touched her arm, she knew that sometime in the night her mother had died. Anna pulled Grace's small body into her arms and rocked her gently.

Later that morning Anna made a phone call. "Lou Jean, can you come to Stockbridge? I need you."

Lou Jean was waiting on the porch when Earl and Anna returned from the funeral home after making the arrangements for Grace's burial. Anna decided to keep it simple. She knew that is what her mother would want. Grace's only request was that she be buried in the little cemetery on the hill. Anna hadn't cried all day, but the sight of Lou Jean made the tears well up in her eyes.

"Oh, Anna, I'm so sorry," Lou Jean said as she gave her a hug.

"I was worried you weren't going to make it here in time for the funeral," Anna said.

"You know better than that. Now don't worry about anything here at the house. I have everything under control."

Colleen sat on the couch watching the room fill with relatives and friends who came to pay their respects to the family. "I can't believe she is gone," she said to Angela, wiping away her tears. "We just talked last night. She told me she was really tired and needed a long sleep. Do you think she knew something?"

Angela sighed. "I don't know. I loved her too, but she was really old. I guess it was just her time," she said as she walked to the door. "There's someone here to see you, Colleen."

Merlin stood on the porch. His sorrowful face pressed against the screen. Colleen dropped to her knees and hugged his neck. She looked up to see David leaning against his truck. Merlin jumped around her as she tried to walk down the stairs.

"He's getting you all muddy." David tried to calm Merlin, who continued to howl and jump on Colleen. "I'm so sorry to hear about your grandmother."

"Thank you," she said putting her arms around him.

Lou Jean motioned to Anna. "Come on out on the porch with me. I need a smoke." Lou Jean rested on the porch railing. "I have a few things to discuss with you. I had a will made out last week and when I die, your family will inherit Ternberry. Now that I'm a property owner, I thought I'd better get all my affairs in order."

"I swear, Lou Jean, why are you talking about dying? You're going to live forever," Anna said, trying to humor her friend.

"Well, I would like to believe that, but just in case, I want to make sure it stays in the family. I want it always to be a place where your children and grandchildren can go whether they're happy or sad. I want it to be a safe haven, like this farm. This place has always felt like home to me."

Anna wiped her eyes with a tissue. "Lou Jean Bailey, I think you're going soft on me. Don't make me cry again."

Lou Jean reached over and took her hand. "If you tell anyone I'm going soft, I'll deny it."

The sky was overcast as Grandma Grace was laid to rest in the little cemetery on the hill. Anna stood with her two daughters watching as the mahogany casket was lowered into the ground. As the procession of mourners began to walk down the path, Anna knelt and placed a single white rose in the grave. "Goodbye, Mother. I will love you forever."

"If you don't mind I'd like to stay here for a little while," Colleen said. Anna bent and kissed her daughter on the head.

Merlin waited until everyone left before he slowly walked from behind the fence and settled in front of Colleen. She patted his head as she looked out at the sea of black and white cows that covered the pastures, hearing an occasional bawl from a calf that had strayed from its mother. There were unfamiliar sounds of traffic on the newly paved roads leading to the houses just beyond the tree line. These last two farms on Pike Road had become a tranquil oasis for her family. She could imagine by now her father had changed his clothes and was tinkering in the workshop. Angela and her mother were preparing food for the relatives as the grandchildren raced through the house. The door to the first bedroom at the top of the stairs was closed. Fresh linens had been put on the bed and Grandma Grace's robe with the slight smell of Chantilly still lingering on the collar, hung on the hook behind the door. She picked up one of the roses that had fallen to the ground and placed it between the pages of her Bible. The creak of the iron gate interrupted her thoughts.

"Are you okay, Colleen? Your mother sent me to check on you."

Colleen slid over on the little bench and David sat down.

"I'm fine. Except for the terrible sadness I feel for my grandmother's death, I am better than I have been in a long time."

"What are you going to do now?" he asked.

"I'm going to stay in Stockbridge for awhile. I have a real need to be close to my family. I'll probably rent an apartment in town so that I can work on my manuscript, but first I have to go to Ternberry. Lou Jean wants me to help her have a yard sale. She told me she is run over with stuff. I thought I would buy some furniture from her."

"So you're going to leave me again," David said, putting his arm around her.

"Actually, I was hoping you would come with me and help bring the furniture back."

His face broke into a grin. "Sure, that would be great. You can tell me all about Ternberry on the way."

Colleen shivered. "We'd better go. I think it's going to rain."

David took her hand as they started down the hill with Merlin following close behind. "By the way, Colleen, I think I have something that belongs to you."

Questions, Comments, Book Reviews are always welcomed!

E-mail Marlene direct at mitchellm3504@bellsouth.net
or go to
www.bearheadpublishing.com to contact the publisher.

Thank you for reading Yard Sale!

Printed in the United States
107003LV00001B/234/A